THE
WARDEN

THE
WARDEN

DANIEL M. FORD

TOR

TOR PUBLISHING GROUP
NEW YORK

This is a work of fiction. All of the characters, organizations, and events portrayed in this novel are either products of the author's imagination or are used fictitiously.

THE WARDEN

Copyright © 2023 by Daniel M. Ford

All rights reserved.

Map by Jennifer Hanover

A Tor Book
Published by Tom Doherty Associates / Tor Publishing Group
120 Broadway
New York, NY 10271

www.tor-forge.com

Tor® is a registered trademark of Macmillan Publishing Group, LLC.

Library of Congress Cataloging-in-Publication Data

Names: Ford, Daniel M., 1978– author.
Title: The warden / Daniel M. Ford.
Description: First edition. | New York : Tor, Tor Publishing Group, 2023. |
Identifiers: LCCN 2022056793 (print) | LCCN 2022056794 (ebook) |
ISBN 9781250815651 (hardcover) | ISBN 9781250815668 (ebook)
Classification: LCC PS3606.O728 W37 2023 (print) |
LCC PS3606.O728 (ebook) | DDC 813'.6—dc23/eng/20221202
LC record available at https://lccn.loc.gov/2022056793
LC ebook record available at https://lccn.loc.gov/2022056794

Our books may be purchased in bulk for promotional, educational, or business use.
Please contact your local bookseller or the Macmillan Corporate and Premium
Sales Department at 1-800-221-7945, extension 5442, or by email at
MacmillanSpecialMarkets@macmillan.com.

First Edition: 2023

Printed in the United States of America

0 9 8 7 6 5 4 3 2 1

To Elizabeth and Abby,
I know you will both be as smart, as fearless, and as strong as Aelis.
Maybe cuss less.

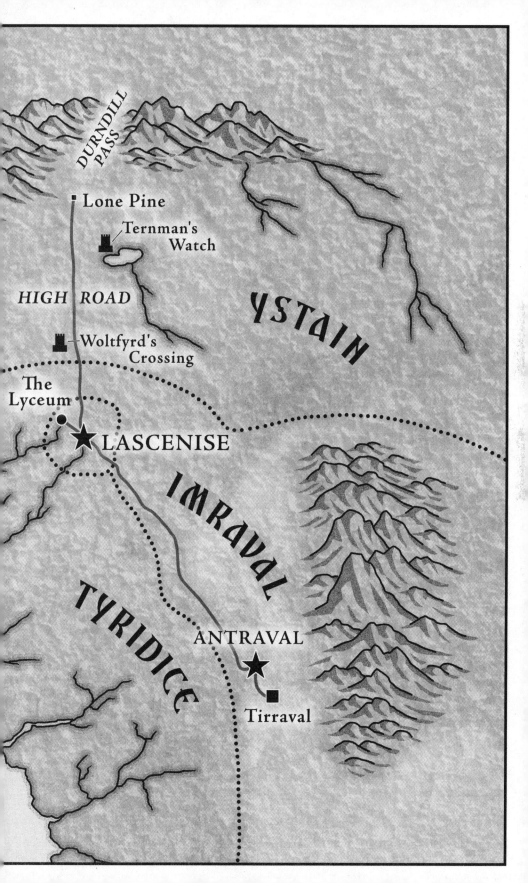

THE
WARDEN

1

THE TOWER

Now, standing in front of the tower, it was far too real.

"It's in ruins," Aelis said, trying desperately to grab at authority by turning her dark eyes on the village boy who'd led her to the place.

"The walls are sound," the boy protested, feebly. "It just needs a roof, is all." He was already backing away from her, and once he was a couple of yards away, he turned and ran, his feet pounding dust and rocks into the air.

Aelis turned back to the squat tower. She could see cracks and holes snaking up the gray stone structure, crumbling mortar, and rugged ivy climbing up the rounded wall. After two weeks on increasingly bad roads in a mail carriage, she had hoped there would at least be a comfortable bed waiting for her. *Might drown inside that tower in a storm.*

Crows hopped about, squawking, eyeing her as she jerked on the lead of the borrowed packhorse to get it started up the track that wound toward the rotting doors. The tower was a good mile or more from the village's center, situated on a hill that overlooked the path that led to the cluster of homes that surrounded the green of Lone Pine.

"Enough for privacy. Close enough I can be fetched quickly in a crisis." Aelis took a deep breath. "Far enough away that they can pretend I'm not here." *If only I wasn't.* Aelis had a brief vision of the cobbled avenues of Antraval, wide enough for carriages to pass one another without troubling the foot traffic, and she thought briefly about knocking down the tower and using it for paving stones just to have the feel of them beneath her feet.

"At least it's far enough away not to smell the sheep shit."

She gave the packhorse another tug and was delighted to find an intact hitching ring bolted to the front wall. The tower was perhaps twenty-five feet tall, with the door—that had once been strong, solid oak bound in iron but was now rotting boards bound in rust—six feet of that.

She looped the packhorse's lead through the ring and gave it a light hitch. She tested the ring itself and was rewarded with a shower of dust and stone chips as she pulled it out.

Carefully, shielding the horse from it, she tucked the ring back into the now gapingly empty spot in the stone and bit her bottom lip as she considered the problem.

Raising her hand and flexing her fingers, she spoke the single word, the simplest expression of the abjurer's art; a ward. It wasn't much—a conjurer could've fixed it rather more permanently—but it should stop the ring from pulling out easily. She tugged again, found it snug.

"Well. Won't last forever, but at least I can get unpacked without chasing this horse."

She decided to leave the silver- and brass-bound chest atop its back for later and instead gathered her saddlebags, bulging with books, and slung them over one shoulder. Then she untied a wooden writing case and tucked it under her free arm.

Aelis thumped the door with her bootheel, and humphed as it swung open without so much as a proper ominous groan, though it did tilt badly.

"Hardly appropriate for a wizard's tower." The interior was a mixture of light and dark, mounds of furniture hidden beneath dust-covered sheets. A sudden shadow darted in the murk.

Aelis threw down her burdens, whipped her leaf-bladed sword clear of its sheath, and was halfway into a personal all-purpose ward when a small goat pranced up to her, yelled at her for disturbing it, and went clattering out the front door.

Not before treading on her bag of books and leaving a fragrant trail of piss right down the front steps, though.

Carefully, very carefully, Aelis lowered her sword till it touched the ground before her, and spoke a two-word dispelling—just enough to make sure the spell she'd gathered discharged harmlessly.

The goat, standing a few feet outside the open door, turned back to stare at her.

"I'm going to have you for dinner," Aelis said, pointing the tip of her sword at it before sheathing it with care. "And I'm going to wear your hide when it gets cold."

The goat yelled again, an ugly and grating sound, and trotted off, unconcerned with her threats.

"As if I'd ever wear goatskin," Aelis murmured as she bent to pick up the dropped books and case.

◆   ◆   ◆

It took her till near nightfall, and many a curse and a fervent wish that she could whip up an undead servitor or two—just one would've gone a long way—but Aelis got her gear unpacked, or at least stowed carefully, and one of the two rooms in the bottom floor of the tower swept and washed. She was leery of the rotting ladder leading up to the second floor, not to mention the suspicious-looking buckles in the boards that she could see a foot or so above her head. There had been nothing usable in the tower save the niches built into the walls, where she'd assembled her library, reasoning that unpacking books would make a new place feel more like home.

It wasn't a large collection, no more than two dozen volumes. Aelis wished she'd had room for more, but the post carriage had strict limits, and more space simply could not be had at any price.

She did take some satisfaction in how well lit the place was, as she'd set out candlesticks in silver holders carved with her family arms, three lamps with carefully trimmed wicks, and her alchemy lamp, set to a soft white. A nagging voice suggested to her that replacing any of these valuable supplies would be difficult, but Aelis convinced herself that for one night it was necessary.

She certainly wasn't frightened of the dark gathering outside her tower, though night was coming on faster this far north than it would have at midsummer at home.

Aelis's mind flashed with images at the thought of the word *home*. People in light summer silk and linen. Entire townhouses lit by alchemy lamps, each room a different brilliant color. Iced wine, squid and prawns pulled fresh from the sea and barely tossed in a pan, then salted and doused with citron juice.

Aelis sat up from the folding chair she'd assembled and realized that her stomach was growling. She surveyed what she'd unpacked, as if food would turn up.

"If it's going to," she said to no one in particular, "I'd prefer something light. Perhaps a selection of cheeses—one blue, one crème, one hard and ripe—and some pickled fish."

Nothing replied to her request, and Aelis sighed and stood. She picked up her swordbelt from its place at her chair, buckled it back on, and started for the door.

"I thought it was always cold up here. Nobody told me I'd sweat. I'll have to send for lighter clothing," she muttered, before sighing. "Send *where? How?* I've no birds, no mirror, and if I sent a letter ordering one, by the time any new robe reached me it would be fall." She considered the wardrobe she'd brought; mostly black, accented with blue and green. All but her most formal robes were divided for riding and cut carefully for her to make use of her sword, dagger, or wand as necessary. She'd sent home gowns and formal dresses as well as anything that had too much thread of gold and silver and gemstones worked into it.

Aelis sighed and slumped back into her chair. Her hunger hadn't abated, but something about the thought of trudging all the way back to the village on foot, with dark upon her, made hunger more appealing than searching for supper.

"Wait." She laid a finger over her lips. "They're supposed to provide me with food. That's in the basic agreement . . ."

She stood up, seized the nearest candlestick, and walked briskly to the door. It hung slack on its hinges and didn't properly close but Aelis had bound it in place the same way she'd plugged a hole in the roof against the weather; by a simple ward.

She released the ward with a flick of her fingers and a single spoken syllable and pulled it open, wondering what might lie beyond it, warm and fragrant, in a handmade basket.

"It might not be prawns and squid, but surely they've fresh bread, butter, cheese, sausages." For a moment she was taken with the idea of a fat goat sausage she could lay across a fire and eat with bread.

When the door finally opened, she looked down. No basket on the stoop; nothing. But no matter. She stepped outside, down the three short stairs, and looked to the left. Then to the right. Then she walked all the way to the end of the path, carefully lowering her candlestick to the ground.

Conscious that she might look ridiculous waving a candlestick over the grass and the stones, were anyone there to watch, Aelis straightened and walked with her head high and her back stiff until she was through the door to her tower.

"Well," she sniffed. "Surely a simple oversight. No doubt they'll correct it in the morning. They had better," she added. "I'm not about to go down among them and *ask* for supper now. Besides . . . surely many of them are after their sleep now. Rise with the sun and go to sleep with the moons, aye?"

It was only then that Aelis realized she'd forgotten to unpack her orrery, but her walk outside had shown her only scudding clouds and a brief glimpse of Elisima's green moon waning to a thin slice. That task could wait for the next day.

Instead, she set down her lamp by her chair and looked over the bookshelves, quickly selecting Aldayim's *Advanced Necromancy*. Deftly, her fingers found the long black silk ribbon sewn into the book and flipped it open, laying the heavy wooden covers on her lap.

> *Correct identification of specimens is the foremost task of the would-be Necrobane. Herein one finds all the necessary and telltale marks that distinguish what force has animated a corpse, an amalgam, a gestalt, or a spirit and to what end . . .*

"Nothing like Aldayim and undead identification to put off the appetite," Aelis murmured, hunching over her book and soon forgetting about the tower, the heat, her empty stomach. About everything, in short.

◆ ◆ ◆

Six weeks to the day before, and eight hundred miles or so to the south, Aelis had burst into her adviser's office, trembling with shock and anger.

"Lone Pine? Where in all the seventy-seven hells is Lone Pine? *What* is Lone Pine?"

"Good morning, Miss de Lenti," Urizen said. Aelis hadn't sent word ahead or asked for an appointment, and so she found the wizened little gnome standing on his desk, papers arranged on a stand in front of him. His hands were folded behind his back, and a pen floated in the air over the exams, occasionally dipping to the page to make one mark or another. "To what do I owe the pleasure?"

"Lone Pine. I'm posted there. *Why?*"

"Those decisions are made far beyond me, Miss de Lenti."

"How many graduates this year?"

"Nearly three hundred. A truly impressive class."

"How many passed tests in three Colleges?"

"What does that have to do with anything?"

"Urizen, I know you know the answer to that much, at least. How many passed tests in three Colleges?"

The pen floating in the air gently settled onto the desk. The gnome pulled his spectacles free from where they perched on his long, thin nose, breathed on them, pulled a silk square from his pocket, and began polishing them.

"You're stalling. You could clean those with a simple wave of your hand and the lightest bit of Conjuring."

"What you know about Conjuring would fall through the holes of a sieve," Urizen shot back. "And . . . eleven."

"Eleven graduates tested successfully in three Colleges," Aelis repeated. "And they are sending one of them to the frontier."

"The frontier is a dangerous place."

Aelis held out an arm to show the green and blue silk stripes against the black of her robe. "Do I have a red stripe here?"

"Oh come off it, Miss de Lenti."

She only just stopped herself from correcting him with *Lady* de Lenti. Urizen finished polishing the spectacles and turned his gray eyes to her, the white whiskers at the sides of his face bristling. "Invokers are hardly the only Wardens prepared to face the dangers of the frontier—"

"There has to be a reason for this, Magister," Aelis interrupted, her voice too like whining for her taste.

"Well, yes. Obviously, the Committee thought your talents matched a need there."

"Ressus," Aelis snarled. "That son of a bitch still believes women shouldn't practice necromancy, and he could never stand that I was the best student among the class. I'll—"

"Do nothing," Urizen said quickly. "Because you do not know that for sure and because I am treading perilously close to violating professorial ethics, not to mention confidentiality standards. I remind you that the identities of the assigning committee members are strictly anonymous, even to one another."

"It has to be him. I know it. I feel it in my bones," Aelis said, not quite ready to slink away in defeat.

"Let me remind you that his full name is Archmagister Ressus Duvhalin, Chancellor of the College of Necromancy. Yours is considerably smaller."

"Could you at least tell me," Aelis said, "where the remaining ten graduates who passed in three Colleges are posted?" Then, unable to stop herself, she added, "If any of them have been sent to the forest primeval like I have, I'll eat my hat."

She saw the gnome only just suppress his laugh. "You're not wearing a hat."

"I'll buy the most expensive gods-damned hat I can find and pay a chef to prepare it for me, then."

Urizen sighed. "I am not going to get through this stack of first-year Magical Theory exams unless I help you sort this out, am I?"

"Afraid not."

"Some days, Miss de Lenti, I curse the moment I was assigned to advise you."

Aelis smiled. "You don't mean that, Magister Urizen."

"Oh no, Aelis. I do. It just so happens that those days don't *quite* outnumber the moments when I've thought otherwise. I've seen you overcome too many challenges to go to pieces over a temporary assignment."

"Two years is a broad definition of *temporary*, Urizen. And no one even tells us what factors into whether we are reassigned, or where . . ."

"Aelis." Urizen stepped down off his desk with slow dignity and walked up to her. For all that the gnome's head barely reached her navel, he had an unnerving way of forcing her to look down and meet him eye to eye, a presence that put him in command of their exchanges. "It may well be that this is your assignment and nothing can be done about it, in which case I will expect you to pack your equipment, go north, and do the best job you can possibly do, no matter how dirty your hands have to get while you are there."

"And do what, trap myself into another posting in some even more forsaken place? Get attached to some pioneers?" Her voice drifted into a sigh.

"Tomorrow, Lady de Lenti un Tirraval, you will have to take an oath that binds you in service to the Magisters' Lyceum and to the Estates House and the Crowns. If you do not wish to take that oath . . ."

"And let the last five years of hard work go for nothing? Why would you—"

"If you do not wish to take that oath," Urizen's voice cracked like a whip, and Aelis quieted instantly, "no one will force you to do so. Should you decide to take it, you will be bound by your honor and your power to carry out the tasks assigned to you whether you like them or not."

Stunned by the force of her mentor's tone, Aelis merely whispered, "I am no hedge wizard."

"Then prepare to accept your assignment with a modicum of dignity and professionalism. Maybe even grace, if you can find any in the wine fugue you currently occupy."

Aelis's back straightened with the precise caution of the drunk who believes no one else can tell they're drunk.

"I apologize, Magister," she began, slowly and formally.

"Oh," the gnome sighed, waving a hand vaguely in the air. "I remember my own graduation week." Urizen smiled then, his face wrinkling, showing his age. "At least, that is, I remember the stories other people *told* about my graduation. Go," he said, waving a hand. "Get a decent meal and some rest and sober up a bit, and I'll send a bird with news. If I learn any."

"I will. And thank you, Magister," Aelis said, giving him a short formal bow before turning for the door. She stopped just outside in the long, dusty hall, poked her head back in, and added, "Actually, Magister, I lied to you just now."

Urizen was already clambering back up to look down at the papers on his desk. "About what?"

"I'm not going to sober up."

◆　◆　◆

She awoke in the chair she'd been reading in, with Aldayim open on her lap. Reflexively, after wiping at her eyes with the back of her sleeve, she looked back into the book.

> . . . *depending on whether the particular specimen is animated by its own will or by that of a Necromancer determines how the necrobane proceeds* . . .

"With a Lower Order Banishment of the animating will or a selection of Suppressing and Severing," Aelis murmured as she gently pulled the silk ribbon into place, closed the book, and placed it back into its empty spot on the shelf. "If the former, a Lower Order should be all that is required, given that a spirit still clinging to its corporeal remains is not likely to be sentient enough to be aware of the power available to it," she went on, as she stood and stretched, cracking her back and shoulders.

"These chapters of Aldayim were always a surefire soporific," she added as she massaged her lower back. "No more sleeping in chairs," she chided. "Can't have the people see me hobbling about and deciding I'm some kind of horrid crone."

She thought back to her passage through the village green. As soon as the people had seen her black robes, they'd scattered, children grasped and pulled away by their parents. The way the crowd melted made the remarks she'd so carefully labored over on the ride up turn to ashes in her mouth. The only people who'd stuck around were the two innkeepers, Rus and Martin, and then only to quietly help her load up their packhorse.

"Oh fuck," she suddenly spat. "Their horse. I ought to have brought it back . . ."

She paused only to grab her swordbelt and buckle it on as she headed for the door. She dispelled the much-weakened ward holding it closed with a flick of her hand, threw it open, and looked to where she'd left the horse.

Her ward was good enough to hold the horse's lead to the ring, but not, apparently, the ring to the wall of the tower, for the horse had ripped it free and then dragged lead and ring down along the path, where it was happily grazing.

In a rush, she swept forward and patted its neck. The horse ignored her and kept grazing. It seemed none the worse for wear, so she gathered up the reins, twisting them in her fist, and, with some urging, led the animal away from its grazing and on to the walk back to Lone Pine proper.

The village seemed deserted. She glanced up at a mostly cloudless sky, with the sun bright and one half of Anaerion's red moon hanging low in the sky. Not too late in the day, then.

The inn, with its central location by the village's crossroads, didn't appear to be busy, possibly not yet open for the day. But as she led the horse on, she heard a throat clear and then a voice call out to her.

"Finally remembered to bring our Pansy back, eh?" She turned to find Rus—a compact man of middle years, bald and sharp-eyed—carrying a large basket over one shoulder. "She would've come in handy this morning."

"I am abjectly sorry," Aelis said, drawing herself up to her full height, which was still an inch or two shy of Rus. "In the rush of everything last night, I simply forgot."

"It's alright," he said as he walked up to the horse, set the basket on her back, and began securing it to the pack frame. Aelis caught a glimpse of its contents; rabbits, gutted and ready to be skinned. "She's none the worse for wear, and a smart enough beast. She'd've come home in her own time. Probably got at the verge around your tower, I expect."

"She did," Aelis agreed. "Pulled the hitching ring right out of the mortar."

Rus ran his hand along the horse's brown neck. Pansy lowered her head to nuzzle at his hand, and then at his pockets, before turning back to the grass. "It'd help you to learn, and to remember—folk here treasure their beasts only just below their kin. You'll do nothing to improve on the impression you made on these people if you let them think you're careless around animals."

Aelis stifled the first thoughts that came to her about the opinions of the people who'd written to the Lyceum for a Warden and then run away as soon as she'd arrived, and forced a smile to her face. "I'll do well to remember that, goodman Rus."

"Just Rus, please," he said. "How did you settle in? Is the tower in decent repair?"

"In point of fact," Aelis said, "it's a crumbling heap. The door is out of frame, I haven't tried to go to the upper floor, the roof lets in daylight, the weather, and likely enough any number of birds, and I've not bothered to examine most of the furniture."

"Well," Rus said with a shrug, "you'll want to fix most of that before winter. Snows come early out here."

Aelis stood and stared at him for a moment. "How do I . . . fix it?"

"Folk here'll give you the loan of tools, I'm sure."

I have passed the Tests of three Colleges of the Magisters' Lyceum. I am an Abjurer, a Necromancer, and an Enchanter and have few equals of my own age within those disciplines, but I am not a gods-damned carpenter, mason, thatcher, or hod carrier, Aelis wanted to scream.

"I believe," she said instead, carefully, "that the finer details of the agreement to post a Warden here indicate that the residence is to be well maintained."

"With all due respect, Warden, you'll find perhaps three people here, not counting Martin and me, who know how to read the contract made on their behalf. Further, their lives are about to become far too busy to go providing a good deal of free labor on the tower of a wizard they're all terrified of."

"What do you mean, their lives are about to become too busy?"

"With the turn of the season coming on, some of the folk who raise the real long-haired sheep you may've seen around are going to have to do their second shearing. Some folks'll be culling their herds, everyone'll be harvesting, there'll be markets to drive animals to. And before all that's done, pioneers and explorers and salvagers will be coming down out of the frontier and the lost territories, looking for lodging and splashing gold about as they pass through. It's a busy time."

And that all sounds just fucking delightful. Not for the last time, Aelis bit her tongue to drive away thoughts of bright plazas and glittering parties. "I see." By now, Rus had finished securing his basket and took up the horse's lead, but manners seemed to dictate he wait till she finished and let him go.

She didn't. "This is a more delicate question," Aelis said. "But, ah, the tower is not equipped with a kitchen, or food storage. There are things I can do to deal with the weather or a stuck door," she added, "but I can't conjure food out of the air."

"I know you can't," Rus said with a grin. "No brown stripes on your sleeves."

Aelis laughed, but rather humorlessly, as even the word *food* had seemed like an aggressive lure to her stomach, which began reminding her, rather powerfully, that it had been more than half a day since she last ate. "True. And even if I had passed a Conjurer's test—"

"I've eaten conjured food a time or two," Rus said, a smile creasing his blunt features. "And I'm sure we've got something you could break your fast with. Though it'll be nothing like what a lady of your stature is used to."

"I give you my word upon my family and my power," Aelis said, "that I will offer no complaint to any food I can eat within the next hour."

"Well, if you'd be so kind," Rus said, "back up at the top of the hill behind the inn there—" he pointed to where he'd come from—"there are some more baskets like this one. I sure could use some help bringing them down, and I'd like to get Pansy here rubbed down and into her stall as quick as I can."

"Of course. Won't take but a moment," Aelis said. Squaring her shoulders, she set aside the pangs in her stomach and trotted up the hill. *Urizen did say I'd probably have to get my hands dirty,* she thought to herself.

2

THE ORRERY

What must be done at first included hauling heavy baskets full of small game animals and birds down the hill from where Rus had pointed out. Then, steeling herself for whatever gustatory horror lay before her, she walked into the crossroads inn to find Martin setting a laden tray down at the table nearest the door, where a window's shutters had been pulled back to let in a shaft of midmorning sunlight.

Martin was a taller, lankier man than Rus. He moved with a slight stoop in his right shoulder, but the tray was steady and the contents far more tantalizing than she'd imagined. Instead of the platter of fish heads, rock-hard black bread, and cup of thickened buttermilk she'd been half expecting, there was brown bread, fresh and crusted with salt and seeds, small bowls of butter and soft cheese, two soft-boiled eggs, a pitcher of water and one, she was guessing, of small beer.

"Rus didn't give me much warning," Martin said in a soft, slightly fussy voice that was at odds with his sharp features, quick eyes, and the white dot of a scar on his cheek. "This was all I could muster."

"Believe me, goodman," Aelis said as she sat, trying to maintain manners and not tear into all of it at once, "it will more than suffice."

"With a half-hour warning I could've had fresh griddle cakes, with apples and nuts . . ." Martin sighed and dusted off his hands on the flour-covered apron he wore, which seemed to only stir up the flour and further dirty his hands. "I've work to do to be ready for midday bite and then supper," he said, his tone slightly mournful. "If you'd be so kind as to join us for another meal today, I promise you won't be as disappointed."

Aelis was trying to find the space to tell him that she wasn't disappointed at all before politely tucking in when the door opened and Rus strode in, went directly to Martin's side, and slipped an arm about his waist.

"The girl is starving, Mart. Let her eat. Offer unnecessary apologies and doom and gloom later," Rus said.

With a sniff, Martin slipped away from Rus's embrace and stomped back into the kitchen, where Aelis heard a few quiet but pointed smacks as a tool or a pot hit a wooden counter harder than they needed to. Rus offered her a brief smile, and being finally able to eat something made her forget all about being called "the girl" instead of "the Warden."

The bread was perhaps a bit tougher on the jaw than the bread she was accustomed to, and at the Lyceum all the finest things in the world could be had for ready coin. But she found no fault in its flavor, and once she took up a knife and spread butter on it, she had to set it down or she'd devour the entire half loaf in one go.

Rus, meanwhile, had taken a seat across the table from her. "I'm sure it doesn't compare to the food you've had in the grand halls and palaces in Tirraval and Antraval, but Mart does his best."

"They say hunger is the best sauce," Aelis said, "but only because they likely haven't had Tirravalan cognac and cream over green pepper–crusted beef. However," she added quickly, "I have had no better at more famous tables."

Rus smiled, a cautious glint in his knowing gray eyes. "I'll try to give Mart your compliment," he said, "but he won't listen. He'll only drive himself to spectacle for the next meal he makes you."

After swallowing a mouthful of egg that she sprinkled with salt, Aelis cleared her throat and looked up at Rus, his words finally landing at the forefront of her mind. "Why would you imagine I've eaten in palaces in Antraval?"

"Your name is de Lenti un Tirraval, isn't it?" the innkeeper countered.

"It is," Aelis admitted. "Though while I serve as Warden it is . . . somewhat reduced to simply 'de Lenti.'"

"Well, we're not accustomed to being visited by the daughter of a count."

"I'm not visiting," Aelis pointed out. "I'm here to stay."

"Don't misunderstand me, now," Rus said. "The folk are glad to have a Warden near. Some of them remember Montross with fondness, though I never knew him. They like what it represents, that the world is reaching out to them, they just . . ." He paused, and gestured pointlessly with his hands.

"Expected a man, with a staff, and possibly a beard. I know," Aelis said as she spread some of the soft white goat cheese onto the heel of the bread. *And I expected a comfortable hotel in Antraval with Humphrey or Miralla nearby.* "Montross was your last Warden?"

Rus nodded. "We didn't settle here till a couple years after the war. He'd been assigned just after it ended."

"What became of him?"

"They say he just wandered off into the wilderness. Told no one what he was about, took no guide. Just said he'd an errand and . . . vanished."

"And I'll bet he had a beard and a staff."

"Possibly even a pointed hat," Rus said, just before she took a bite of bread and cheese, and Aelis had to laugh.

Reluctantly, Aelis set the last of her bread on the wooden plate before her. "You and Martin seem like the only locals who aren't terrified to step in my shadow."

"We've both seen the work of Lyceum training in our days," Rus said, "including that of your primary school. Most of the village folk haven't."

"Necromancy, Rus. You can say it."

"Listen, Warden, I have work to do. Always work to do here. And if I may, let me make this the last advice I'll give you; find some of it yourself. If you can show practical skills to the people right away they'll come around, fast." He stood up, quickly, pulling a length of rag from the pocket of his apron and quickly wiping at a spot on the table.

"I'm here to help," Aelis said, noting how quickly and deftly Rus had avoided further conversation. "I am. But I'm no farmer, nor a laborer. I would only get in the way of people who were. Although," she added, as the innkeeper stood up and pushed his chair back to the table, "I will have a look around later, and see what there is I might do without impeding the effort of someone better qualified."

"Good," Rus said. "And if no one delivers any food, come back here for supper. We'll make sure you stay fed. Just leave the tray; we'll get it."

Aelis waited till Rus had walked past her to swipe a finger through the remnants of the butter, and another through the soft goat cheese, then sucked them both clean at the same time. She began the walk back to her tower wondering if she really should hope for a sudden outbreak of animated skeletons.

A small one, she thought as she walked. *Nothing that'd require more than a First Order Severing or Banishment. Perhaps a Second Order if I wanted to show off a bit.*

Of course, that was nonsense. Even a manageable outbreak would present more danger to the people here than she'd like.

"I doubt any of them will need any serious wards laid," she murmured. She was struck with the sudden inspiration of making and handing out wardstones with simple abjurations on them to keep doors held fast against the wind and roofs secure against the weather.

"Except I haven't got enough silver to engrave them with, and I'd need to put one in every home, every hole in a roof, every window," she said aloud. "So that's out."

She'd come up with no great plans by the time she reached her tower, so she bent to the work of unpacking and cleaning. She pulled the dustcloths off the furniture and hauled them outside, tossing them over the wall of the rising walk and getting dirt all over her clothes and hair in the process.

What she found beneath them was largely serviceable: two battered but sturdy tables, assorted stools and chairs, and a creaky-doored wardrobe. She dutifully stored her clothes in it, after carefully inspecting it for moths, webs, eggs, and other signs of unwanted intruders. She set her case of instruments, of soft calf hide with brass fittings and her crest tooled into the side, on one of the tables, along with a few other implements she took care unpacking: a mortar and pestle of hard, pebbled stone, an alembic, a number of racks and glass flasks.

Whatever steps she took, Aelis understood that she was merely delaying what was perhaps her most important—and most mind-numbingly difficult—task.

Setting up her orrery.

It traveled in its own case, and on the long series of carriage rides up through the middle of the continent into Ystain and then to its borders, she had fussed with it like a mother might with a child.

She flipped open her case of instruments and pulled out the heavy chisel she'd use to pry open the top of the orrery's packing crate, which had been carefully nailed shut under her own supervision.

It seemed to take an age to dislodge each nail just enough to pry the wooden slats loose, to be set delicately aside in order to work on the next one. Removing the top layer of the wooden crate was only the first step. Inside, packed tightly with straw till it just barely fit in the crate, was a hard leather case. Dropping quite a bit of straw on the floor in the process, Aelis drew it out and set it on the table.

The leather itself was soft, wrapped deftly around a hard wooden frame, with solid bronze clasps. She undid them, slid back the top, and carefully reached in to pull her metal-and-crystal contraption free and set it next to its case, its silver arms jangling slightly.

The base was of solid dark mahogany, with six silver arms attached in concentric rings to a central silver post, atop which sat a faceted blue crystal—the earth. Aelis leaned in close to eye the painstaking detail worked upon it, representing the larger continents and island chains in paint and in the minutest facets. She thought of the hundreds of miles between where she stood now, in northern, barely civilized Ystain, and her home in Tirraval and the grand cities of the south. She'd never before been farther north than the Lyceum, and even that was no more than a day's ride on good roads from Lascenise, the last outpost of what she considered true civilization.

"I'd need one of the tightest lenses in the Lyceum to find Lone Pine here," she muttered, peering at the crystal earth, then set about inspecting the six moons for dust. All six—represented by smooth spheres of polished blown glass in black, blue, red, green, yellow, and white—were clean. Black was the farthest out, the Unseen Moon—or the moon most folk didn't want to see, didn't want to acknowledge, Aelis thought.

Aelis was rather more familiar with Onoma's moon than most.

With a sigh, she looked up through the broken wooden slats of the second story's floor above her, trying to get a glimpse of the sun. "Can't be noon yet," she muttered. Of course, a village like Lone Pine was unlikely to have any clocks.

"Going to have to do this the hard way, then," Aelis said, and went back to the case. Buried deep within it was a small leather-bound book. Its pages were set with incredibly close script and illustrations so tiny she wished for a glass to study them.

"Now then," she murmured, hunching down, elbows on the table, to read. "I know that Anaerion's moon is half full and showing in the morning hours, while Elisima's is waning, so . . ." Rapidly she flicked to other pages and began making minute adjustments to the silver rods, sliding them into positions marked by notations that matched her book.

She was at it for the better part of an hour, making adjustments, walking them back, making other adjustments, consulting the book two or three times for every time she moved one of the rods.

Finally, Aelis was reasonably sure she had it right.

"Only one way to find out," she muttered. She drew her dagger from behind her back and centered herself, let her mind reach outward and her senses focus in. She fingered the first rune on the dagger's blade, uttered a single, twisting syllable, and drew with the point of the dagger in the air— inscribing in faintly visible trails the same rune she had fingered.

Then she aimed the tip of the blade at the orrery and released the gathered-up power. It was truly very little.

She felt the crystals and silver of the orrery absorb and store the energy. The back of her neck tingled from the release of power.

"Well," she reasoned, "it didn't explode. Nothing to do but sit and watch."

Another quarter of an hour passed, during which she seized a chair, gave it a light dusting with her sleeve, and sat. She saw the contraption of silver and crystal begin to make the slightest movements as time passed, the moons moving in relation to one another and to the center post and its tiny globe. The anchoring magic within it had, it seemed, accepted her celestial calculation.

It was a small task, and laborious, but it satisfied Aelis somehow. It was the first work of any magical significance she'd done since taking her three Tests, graduation, and the weeks-long carriage trek north.

She put her hands on her hips, let out a small sigh, and looked around for more work to do. The upper floor presented itself as the most likely place to find it.

She considered the rickety ladder leading upward, grasped it with both hands, and spoke aloud a single strong, hard syllable. Instantly, she could feel the wood strengthened by her Abjuration.

The second floor of the old mage's tower—her tower now—was twice the mess of the first. She saw two bird's nests in the upper rafters and the crusted whiteness of their shit along the walls. There were broken bits of crockery scattered about the place, a wooden table that sagged dangerously in the middle, two windows with thick but unfortunately broken glass panes, and a layer of dust that was already tickling her nose.

However, amid the rubble, Aelis spied something—a square corner of heavy ceramic.

"Let that not be broken," she murmured, as she carefully shuffled forward. The rafters the flooring sat on seemed quite sturdy, so the only danger was the missing or splintered floorboards that were easily avoided.

Carefully, she bent down over the heavy bit of earthenware, and as soon as she set her hands on it she knew it was whole and knew it was going to be too heavy to move.

"A genuine calcination oven," she muttered, running her hands over the cool, smooth sides. She tried, briefly, to see if she could stand it up.

The floor beneath it creaked menacingly and she stopped immediately. "Why, by all the moons, would it have been dragged to the second floor in the first place?" she wondered aloud. "And *how?*"

Regardless of its provenance, Aelis could see that she wasn't moving it, much less bringing it upright and into any kind of useful position on her own. She glanced around and saw no workable way to vent its emissions on this floor.

Most of what else she could see was garbage. Some water-damaged books that hosted thriving mold colonies caught her eye. She knew in her heart those were likely a total loss, but she wasn't going to let them go without a thorough investigation.

Her instinct was to pick them up gingerly with two fingers, one at a time, but she was practical enough to admit that wouldn't do. She untucked her blouse to make a kind of apron and began putting the books in it, feeling their sagging weight and the moisture in them beginning to wick into the dark silk.

"I am deeply sorry, Drewic," she muttered, an apology to her tailor. With the books in a pile, she made for the ladder.

And since she'd dismissed the ward holding it together, the first step crumbled under the weight of her boot.

As first instincts went, *save the books* was not unusual or unexpected, but she was also rational enough to know that she had to save herself to do that. Her only hope was a cushioning ward laid just above the stone floor below her, and lasting only long enough to safely slow her descent. It was a Second Order Abjuration *at least* and one she was going to have to perform without her focus.

She flexed and bent the fingers of her left hand and spoke the two syllables necessary; one to summon the ward and the other to place it low against the floor.

She hit something semisolid, wavered for just a moment, and then hit the floor hard enough to knock the wind out of her lungs. She lay there gasping, feeling the damp from the books leaking onto her skin, embarrassed but whole. One by one, she set the ruined books aside and then stood.

"First things first," she said. "Time for a new blouse."

She selected one similar to the first, set the wet one outside on the stone railing of the walkway, as she had no better idea what to do, and made space on a table to lay out the books.

Then it was back to cleaning, dusting, and airing out what had been left behind for her.

3

THE WELCOME

The sudden loud rumble of her stomach finally drove Aelis out of the deep work fugue she'd fallen into. The books were laid out, the bottom floor at least was clear of dust, all her belongings were as squared away as she could make them, and she had cleaned and polished her sword, her dagger, and her wand for good measure. She walked outside to check the sun and squinted as its low-lying glints reached to stab at her eyes. "Damn. Later than I thought."

She considered her clothes, and threw her formal black robes on. "If they're going to be frightened of me, I might as well embrace it." Briefly, she thought of her Introductory Abjuration instructor, a burly dwarf, Professor Vosghez, with a beard so long he tucked it into his belt in three braids as thick as her wrist. He'd been a terrifying presence in the lecture hall, with a thunderous voice and a fist that, legend held, had broken straight through more than one hard oaken lectern while enumerating a student's inadequacies. Students came to his classes in abject fear. Thus, they did exactly what Vosghez asked, and found it within themselves to overcome the limitations they thought they had. Perhaps a healthy fear could be turned to her advantage.

Sword and dagger belted on, and wand secured up the left sleeve of her robe, she set off for the village and the inn. It was a more pleasant walk this time, with a soft breeze rustling the trees. Aelis took a deep breath, then suddenly gagged.

It seemed that in the country, the summer breezes so often romanticized by the minstrels could carry a heavy scent of sheep shit.

At the Lyceum and at her family's hotel in Antraval, and even in the more distant keeps and holdings throughout Tirraval, efficient and often magically enhanced drainage and sewer arrangements kept those odors distant at the worst of times. In the countryside, though, the stench seemed oppressively, suddenly present.

She assumed there was some recently performed chore or other that explained the smell. Aelis had been born in the city and preferred it to all other places. Lone Pine, she suspected, was going to hold many fragrant mysteries for her.

"Which reminds me," she muttered, "I ought to see if I can get hold of a good map of the place." She was already sketching one in her head; the crossroads, with the king's road running north–south and a local road she'd no name for running east–west. The inn, then a cluster of homes and workshops. In the southeast corner of the crossroads, an open and well-kept sward that she assumed was used as the grounds for fair or market days. Opposite it, to the northwest, a minuscule chapel, though no presence lamps burned in the windows and no priest seemed to be in residence.

"How many people live here? Do they have a . . . a list? A roster? I should know them all, shouldn't I?" Aelis kept nagging herself with questions of this sort as she walked to the inn, till she wished she'd brought a scrap of paper and a stick of charcoal to make notes with.

Soon enough, though, she stopped just outside the inn, listening to the convivial murmur inside, the clatter of crockery. No one was singing, which she supposed was a good sign. Nor could she, by listening closely, detect any denouncements or anyone stirring up any fervor for the burning of necromancers.

Boldly, she walked to the door, pushed it open, and crossed the threshold. She tried, very diligently, not to pause and acknowledge the stares she knew were coming. She was ready for them.

She wasn't ready for the wave of silence that greeted her, a silence so sudden she could hear the crackling of the small fire laid on, the sloshing of beer in a jar one man had paused in mid-lift, and, she thought, even her own breathing.

She moved quickly inside and while conversation and the eating and drinking resumed, they were kept hushed. Scanning about for an empty table, she saw none. Rather than allow herself to awkwardly walk the room, or linger by the counter until someone left, she slipped into the nearest seat at an otherwise nearly full table.

Aelis didn't need the shrewd instincts of a merchant to read the body language of the people she sat with. Some were tucking into their supper, and couldn't well leave in the middle. They might be afraid, but food was food, and not to be wasted under any but the direst of circumstances. Even those who were only drinking weren't going to abandon ship mid-pint. But they pulled back from her, cast their eyes down into their plates or mugs. Hands slipped under the table and were, she was sure, making superstitious and ineffectual warding signs.

"Good eve," she said in her brightest voice. "I'm Aelis." She focused on the man sitting on the bench across from her, a broad, stubbled farmer a number of years older than her. "And you are . . . ?"

"Otto, m'lady," he muttered, refusing to meet her eyes or acknowledge her beyond responding to the direct question.

She flicked her eyes to the man next to him, who looked like an older brother, a suspicion she doubled down on when he muttered, "Elmo." She decided not to press the point as she felt a presence arrive behind her and then a mug was set down before her, followed by a basket of bread and a small bowl of butter. She turned around to glance at Rus, who was already retreating, but not without an encouraging smile.

"You forgot the m'lady," a child sitting next to Elmo said, poking him in the arm.

"Oh, there's no titles needed now, laa . . . child," Aelis said, unable to land decisively on either "lad" or "lass." She soldiered on, regardless. "My name is Aelis."

"Have you ever raised the dead?" Of the half dozen at her table, the child was the only one who looked closely at her, and so far, the only one to actually make eye contact when addressing her.

"Of course I haven't," Aelis said. "Though in fact the very question is misguided. What a necromancer *can* do, but shouldn't, is bind energy into the remains of a human or other animal—though human is easiest—in order to *animate* it as a servant or soldier. But *actually* raising the dead, returning a dead person to the living, body and soul, would be a miracle and well beyond the scope of our . . ."

All around her people were shuffling away. The one woman sharing the bench she'd sat on scooted as far down as she could, till she was practically crowding on to the already full second bench. The child alone was listening, rapt.

Stop. Talking. She wasn't sure if the voice she heard was her own or Urizen's or some combination, but she grabbed one of the loaves of bread Rus had set down in the basket, tore off a hunk, and dragged it through the butter.

"Well, have you ever done that . . . bind energy thing?"

Aelis stuffed the bread in her mouth as soon as she'd grasped the child's question, so she'd have a moment to formulate an answer. Of course she *had*, as one didn't pass a Necromancer's Test in the Lyceum with Highest Honors without having done it. *Under strictly controlled laboratory conditions*, she thought as she chewed—slowly, though the bread was good and she was once again starving.

"Of course I haven't," she finally answered. "Such things are an abhorrent misuse of my knowledge and power—"

"A what?"

"It would be bad, and wrong of me to have done it. So I haven't."

The child looked disappointed. Elmo looked relieved; he and Otto had rushed through what remained of their meals and their beer and now stood, gathered the child, and ran for the door without a goodbye. The child, though, tried waving to Aelis as Otto and Elmo hustled out.

The other folks at her table seized the opportunity to follow them, gulping down their last bits of food and drink and scurrying away.

She sighed and took up her beer as Rus set down a platter. "Stuffed cabbage leaves," he said. "Save room."

There were four slightly greasy white-green leaves wrapped around what, exactly, she couldn't tell. She took up the two-tined fork and the knife that had been set on the platter and cautiously lifted one to her mouth.

It was hot, but not too hot to chew and swallow. Inside was finely minced meat—goat, she thought—that was far more heavily spiced than she'd been expecting, all of it held together in a slightly sweet, piquant red sauce.

She'd eaten all four by the time Rus returned with two other bowls; one with roasted beets and the other with potato and turnip mashed together.

"Skipped anything at midday, didn't you?"

"I had work to do," Aelis admitted, with slight embarrassment. Anyone too close to her had left or moved to the farthest end of the big common room they could find.

"Well, I'll pass the compliments to Martin," he said as he swung onto a seat across from her. "If I were you, I might avoid talking about necromancy," he added in a whisper.

"Hard to do, when it's my primary School," Aelis said. "But," she added, raising a hand, "your point is taken. My enthusiasm for the subject is leading me into trouble." She busied herself with the beets while Rus seemed to enjoy being off his feet.

"Elmo and Otto," he said, keeping his voice low, "are good men. Brothers, as I'm sure you've guessed. Pips—Phillipa—is their third brother's daughter. All three of them went for soldiers, and the eldest, Oscar, never came back. Never talked about who her mother was, and now they've got the raising of her. Frankly, they probably need all the help they can get—but the girl warmed up to you. Where she goes, they'll follow, mark me."

Aelis stirred her spoon through the turnip and potato mash, never her favorite dish, though Martin had clearly not skimped on the butter. "If everyone is going to go scurrying off at every word I say, how'll I get to know them? More importantly, how will I know when they need help?"

"Just have to trust to your luck and your intuition, I suppose. And failing that—" Rus stood and shrugged casually—"if orc raiders come screaming out of the trees, I don't expect you'll need much warning from the locals."

"Don't even suggest it," she said, though he was already gone. Just as quickly he returned, bearing a tray that held a small plate with two sweet-smelling cakes, a teapot, and a dainty cup.

He set these down and said, "We don't get much supply of tea up this way. And what we do get, we have to supplement to stretch it out. So don't expect *real* tea so much as tea mixed with some local flowers and herbs." He paused for a moment, then added, "I'll see about getting food brought to you if you prefer that. It won't be Martin's best *every* night, but there's plenty of farm families who know how to set a good table."

"Until I can get them to look me in the eye, perhaps it's best if I eat in the tower most nights," Aelis said, after swallowing a delicious mouthful followed by a sip of tea. She was delighted to find it strongly flavored with mint, and sat up a bit straighter in surprise.

Rus took notice and smiled. "I'm glad you like the tea."

Aelis kept her preference for coffee—and merely thinking the word was enough to twist her throat with a wave of intense longing—to herself. "Thank you, Rus. You're being far too generous. I've not even done anything yet."

"That's not true," Rus said as he rose. Aelis helped herself to the second cake, sticky with honey and smelling of roasted nuts. "We called, and you came. That counts for something. Good eve, Warden. May the moons find you well back to your home."

Aelis finished the cakes and tea while Rus moved about, collecting the plates and mugs left behind by the folk who'd abandoned the place. She could hear Martin muttering and fussing in his kitchen in the back. She savored the tea till it was nearly cold in the cup, and finished the cake morsel by morsel.

THE HEDGE WIZARD

It was as close as it was going to get to true darkness as Aelis began the walk back to her tower. Only the green and red moons hung in the sky, the former shedding little light and the latter obscured by clouds. She strolled leisurely, largely content but for a nagging wish for a snifter of decent brandy to finish a better meal than she'd expected.

She was well beyond the welcoming lights and hearthsmoke of the village center when she felt the hair on the back of her neck stand up, her stomach tighten, and all her instincts yell at her to throw herself to the ground.

Aelis ignored all that and drew her sword. When her fingers wrapped around the hilt, she could feel, instantly, the power gathering in the world around her.

Two syllables, and the night was briefly illuminated with the faint shimmer of her ward, radiating from the crosspiece of her sword, enveloping her.

A small ball of purple light came hurtling toward her.

Second Order Evocation at most, she thought. *Might be in for a tingle.*

She braced herself for the jarring clash of power against power, but there was none. The ball disintegrated as soon as it touched her ward. With spots dancing in her eyes, she traced the path of its flight by the faint shimmer it had left in the air. A shadowy outline, tall and thin, with a long staff in one hand, stood a few yards away.

Her mouth set in a hard line, Aelis shifted the sword to her right hand alone. Another ball of light formed out of the air and sped at her. She swept the sword in the air before her, pouring through the hilt the briefest of First Order Abjurations. The purple ball was swept away like so much dust before a broom.

The shadowed figure resolved into a man of later middle years, with a wild and tangled beard and a fringe of gray hair, wearing filthy brown robes. He called up another ball of light, but another sweep of Aelis's sword dispelled it before it even left his hand.

By the time she'd closed to five yards, she flexed her left wrist and caught her wand as it fell into her hand. She raised it and spoke a syllable while tracing the tip of the wand through the air. For the briefest of moments, the glyph she'd traced hung there, bright green, a delicate latticework. It dissipated as the power in it fled toward the ragged-looking man.

He tumbled over backward, his staff falling from nerveless fingers as he hit the ground, dead asleep. Aelis ran forward and kicked it away from him. She was half certain it was just a length of wood, but there was no harm in being sure.

Then, sticking the wand through her belt and sliding the sword back into its sheath, she bent over, placed her hands on her knees, and tried to get her racing heart under control. For a moment, she felt like she might spew the spicy stuffed cabbage, roasted beets, turnips and potatoes, honeynut cakes, and mint herbal tea all over the grass.

For the second time that day, she called to mind the presence of Professor Vosghez.

The racing heart, the sweating hand, the panting breath—they are all signs of weakness. They are caused by fear. Fear is a response to danger. The Abjurer does not know danger. The properly prepared and ever-vigilant Abjurer is the antithesis of danger. Thus, she cannot fear. Thus, her heart does not race. Her breath does not pant. Her palms do not sweat.

Slowly, as she focused not only on those words but on the techniques he'd later taught her—to control the breathing by inhaling through her mouth and exhaling through her nose, holding the breath in her throat for a moment, straightening her back—her breath came back under control and her heart rate settled to its normal pace.

That took only a few moments. The man she'd laid low with a Somnolence was snoring and twitching on the grass. She bent over to have a look at him. He was as thin and gnarled as driftwood, but tall enough that there was a lot of him. Aelis didn't fancy carrying him back to the tower, and no one else was about, so she decided to engage him right there on the grassy verge of the road leading out of town.

She loosened her sword in its sheath, pulled her wand free from her belt, drew in the air with it again, then tapped it against the man's forehead.

He woke with a start and would've surged to his feet, if he hadn't, almost immediately, seen the green glowing point of her wand hovering before his face, heard the whisk of her sword drawn.

"Good evening," she murmured, her voice just this side of sweet. "I am Warden Aelis de Lenti. You are the man who foolishly attacked an Abjurer of the Lyceum using the pathetic illusions of a first-year student who is destined never to graduate. I would like to know your name, and your purpose."

The man hesitated, biting his lip. Aelis saw his eyes roll, as if he was casting about for an escape.

"I can compel your answer," she added. "But I would prefer not to. It can be an unpleasant experience."

The man blinked once, then sagged back against the grass. "I'm sorry, Warden," he said, his voice reedy and pathetic to her ears. "My name is Dalius. Please, let us go to your tower and discuss our positions. I promise I will attempt no more magic."

"I'm afraid a promise isn't going to be good enough, Dalius," Aelis said. Her wand dipped forward and flashed against his forehead as she released the Interdiction she'd called up.

He recoiled, tried crabwalking backward on his elbows. "What did you do, what did you . . ."

"I verified that you'd be performing no more magic for the next hour. Now, come," she said, "and don't try running. I don't want to have to chase you."

＋   ＋   ＋

Seated in her tower under the light of her alchemy lamp, Dalius was a pathetic figure indeed. Tall, spindly, with a mud-stained peasant's robe tattered at its hem and cuffs and his scraggly gray-and-brown beard, he looked like an aged beggar.

Do not allow yourself sympathy for this man. He attacked you, with magic. By law, you can put him to death.

"I'm sorry, Warden," he was saying, for the sixth, or perhaps the seventh, time. "I don't know . . . I just, I took it on myself t'watch over these folk, and I heard the word *Necromancer*, and I thought . . ."

"Did you hear the word *Warden*, hedge wizard? What did you think to accomplish by attacking me?"

Dalius sniffed and looked at her with brown eyes wide and liquid beneath wild brows. "I don't know. I didn't know, didn't think women could be wardens."

"By the Worldsoul, man, women have been wardens as long as there have *been* wardens. That's ignorant nonsense." The snap in her voice brought a low whine out of him, and he raised the heel of one hand to his forehead, rubbing hard.

"I'm sorry. I'm sorry. I thought the folk here were in danger."

"From what? And who are you to appoint yourself their guardian, at any rate?"

"I'm a . . . a practitioner, lady Warden, a fellow dabbler in the great arts, and I took it upon myself to look kindly over this village and its folk. We are comrades, of a sort. I'm sorry I didn't realize that—"

"We are not fellows, hedge wizard, for I am no dabbler. And my appropriate title is Warden. *Just.* Warden," Aelis said. She had been about to sit, but something in his whining tone, coupled with his appeal to their supposed comradeship, ignited new anger in her. She drew herself up to her full height—which was perhaps a bit above average, but not tall compared to a beanpole like Dalius. Thankfully he had shrunk down into the chair, and she loomed over him.

"I am a fully accorded Warden of the Lyceum. I am a graduate of three of its Colleges, Abjurer, Enchanter, and Necromancer in one, and we are no more colleagues than a gnat is colleague to an eagle simply because they both have wings." She wasn't shouting, but she felt her voice rising. "Luckily for you, you posed about as much danger to me as a gnat would to an eagle. What exactly were you trying to accomplish?"

"To . . . drive you away. The people are frightened of you, so if you left, perhaps I could occupy the tower, then. Be their guardian? Have a bit of respect."

Dalius appeared on the verge of tears. Aelis snorted and whirled away from him.

"Drive me off with what, exactly? A construction of light and air that even a first-year student of Illusion would die of shame to have cast?" Dalius quailed in his seat.

Aelis let her hand fall to the hilt of her sword. "You know," she said, "that by law, for having assaulted me, I've every right to kill you."

That seemed to break him. Dalius began to weep, huge tears rolling down his cheeks, choking sobs pulled from his thin chest, globs of snot forming in the wide, hairy caverns of his nostrils.

Aelis took a half-step away, her anger leaking out of her like wine from a punctured skin. "I'm not going to kill you, hedge wizard. I'm not even going to hurt you. But I will warn you: never, ever cross me like that again."

"Then what . . . what do you intend to do with me?" Dalius lifted his eyes hopefully, wiping the tears away with a gnarled hand.

The pathetic sight of a man older than her father looking at her like a kicked puppy nearly weakened Aelis's resolve. But she kept her face as implacable as she could manage.

"I'm going to make *use* of you," Aelis said. She held up a hand to stop whatever babble he'd been about to launch into. "No. Not magical use. If you think you've any objects of power, I want to look over them. But what I really want out of you, Dalius, is your knowledge of the people and places. What, in the area of Lone Pine, do I need to know about? And whom?"

◆   ◆   ◆

Maybe I should've killed him, Aelis found herself thinking two hours later. She sat, pen in hand, writing desk on her lap, taking less and less meticulous notes as Dalius spun the local folklore and the exhaustive genealogies of all of Lone Pine's leading families. The lines of drying ink began in her confident and controlled hand before gradually sloping down the page. Eventually one or two even became barely more than crooked scribbles.

"Now Agatha, y'see, I mean old Agatha, she's the great-grandmother of the goodwoman Agatha of the village today, word is that her third daughter, that'd be our Agatha's aunt Eugenia, she might not be her father's daughter, if you take my meaning. Vicious gossip, that, but then where'd that red hair come from, eh? Not from old Lars, no madam, it didn't indeed . . ."

"Dalius," Aelis said, finishing a hasty doodle of one figure in robes stabbing a second, taller figure. "I think we can stop there for the night." *Shouldn't have wasted the ink*, she thought as she stood and set the desk down, then quickly slipped the parchments she'd made notes on inside it.

"Well, I've got lots of other good information, m'lady Warden. Old Dalius has lived here and watched this village for decades."

"Then you knew my predecessor?"

"Barely. He wasn't here long till the frontier claimed him. Dangerous place, m'lady. Dangerous indeed."

"What about before him? The wartime Warden?"

That brought Dalius up short. "He was a hard man."

"Did you know him at all? What were his talents, his—"

"I don't like to talk about him," Dalius snapped. "He was cruel, and the people feared him."

"Fine, I'll not ask any longer. I would like to know—tomorrow, not tonight—about any local landmarks, folktales, traditions, that sort of thing."

"Ah, Dalius is yer man then, m'lady Warden . . ."

"Just Warden, Dalius. Or Aelis."

The hedge wizard looked rather longingly at the walls of her tower and the chair he'd been sitting in.

"Off you go," Aelis said, merciless. "Be well this night. If you wish to come speak with me again tomorrow, or the next night, come two hours after dinner."

"I don't eat dinner most nights," Dalius said, pitifully. "The village folk, they used to trade me bread for charms, cheese for reading the weather, milk for keeping their sheep healthy, but now they've all forgotten about me."

"If you come back tomorrow, when the moons are high and you see a light in this tower, I will have some bread to share. It might not be much, and it may just be bread. But it will be yours. I'll get cheese if you tell me anything useful."

That lit a fire in his eyes. "I'll have the choicest bits of lore for you tomorrow, m'lady Warden Aelis," he said, and fairly skipped down the short hall and out the door, his stick clacking loudly on the stone path all the way.

Aelis wished for a bottle of good wine. Better yet, a bottle of brandy or port. For Humphrey's arms. For Miralla's fingers twining into her hair. For wide, bustling streets and magic lamps floating above the crowd like tiny copies of Stregon's blue moon. She'd always thought the light of the lamps made everyone it touched more beautiful, as if through the force of will and the application of art wizards had conquered night itself.

She looked up through the holes in the floor above her and the holes in the roof beyond, and was so overwhelmed by the curtain of stars that she felt like the smallest ember of a fire flickering distantly from the hearth, trying to will itself into burning on.

Then she realized that this metaphor extended into her burning Lone Pine down, and decided to give it up and go to bed. It was later than she'd expected; Dalius must've gone on even longer than she'd imagined.

5

THE WORK

Aelis woke early that morning, a character failing that the last year in the Lyceum had done a great deal to drub out of her. *The folk I'm responsible for are early risers*, she thought, then, only just repressing a shudder, added, *I suppose that means I should be as well.*

"Besides," she muttered aloud as she stretched the kinks out of her back, "it's not like there's anything to do at night in this place anyway."

Resolving to get something in the nature of bedding squared away later that day, Aelis changed into her work clothes, gathered and released a quick First Order Necromantic Pulse into her orrery, and went to seek work.

It was only once she was out the door that Aelis realized just how early it was; the two visible moons were still dominating the sky, with the sun only just beginning to compete.

She wandered down to the crossroads, twice passing flocks being led out to pasture. *I assume it's to pasture. I can't really say for sure. Where else does one lead a flock?* She shook the thoughts away and walked on, enjoying the slight briskness of the early morning air. The day's heat would see to it, and the dew, soon enough.

When she neared the inn she was surprised to see a large figure bending down just in front of the back door, setting down what looked like a freshly killed and cleaned deer.

Only when she got closer, she realized it wasn't a deer carcass; it was an elk, and the figure that straightened up after placing it on the ground was *enormous*. In fact, his size—she assumed it was a man, though she couldn't see past a tangle of braided hair spilling out the sides of a hooded jerkin—had simply made the cow elk look, for a moment, like a deer carried by a normal-sized man.

The figure's shrouded face turned toward her, as if he sensed he was being watched. Then he bent down and picked up a bulging sack with one hand and trotted away with long, ground-eating strides. In a few moments, he was up the hill and melting into the treeline.

He disappeared so completely and so quickly that Aelis halted in place, wondering if she'd just seen an apparition. Then the back door of the inn creaked open and Rus stuck his head outside.

"You took my words about early rising to heart, Warden," he called out. In Aelis's estimation, he was far too full of good cheer for the dark of the morning, but she resolved to let it rub off on her, and offered a nod as she drew closer.

"I thought I might as well see if there was work I could do," she said. She looked back up at the treeline behind the inn, hesitated over the question she wanted to ask.

"You saw our Tun, eh?" Rus gestured to the elk that lay before him. "I'm going to have a job of butchering this. You must've scared him off."

"Me? Scared him off?" Aelis snorted. "I'd sooner imagine I could scare off a mountain."

"He's a bit skittish. Traps, hunts, helps keep the village in meat and hides. We trade him bread, wine, the occasional tool. Come fair days, Martin and I sell furs for him and convert the coin into things he can use."

"He trusts you to do that?" By now Aelis had come forward and the pungent animal smell of the enormous carcass rang in her nose.

"Says the silver is of no use to him," Rus replied, with a shrug. "And what merchants come to Lone Pine don't tend to bring gold, nor would he have aught to spend it on. We try to do right by him, because he does right by us." Then he looked down at the elk. "Anything you could do to help with this?"

"There might be," Aelis said. She squatted down, eyeing it for a moment. "If we could lever it up, I could get a ward under it and hold it in place. I might be able to walk it somewhere, but . . . I'm not too sure of that." Then she straightened up. "If you're prepared to help guide in the cutting of it a little, I can break it down awfully quickly."

"Right here? In the back yard?"

"I can cut it into quarters," Aelis said, "and I can do it fast." She pursed her lips. "I might be able to get its spine out, too. Planning anything for the head?"

"Warden," Rus said, his cheeks a bit pale, "I mean no disrespect, but I don't know if I want . . . if I need to see . . . whatever sort of ritual you're planning."

Aelis sighed and drew the dagger from its place at her back. "It's not a ritual, Rus, I assure you. It's knowledge, and an Anatomist's blade. That's all." She turned the dagger around in her hand. It was plain enough; a straight blade a bit over half a foot long, double edged, no quillons. But in the light, Aelis knew Rus would see that while the blade seemed to be simple steel, the edge and the point gleamed a dark black.

Rus didn't look at it long. He shouldered open the swinging back door and yelled, "Martin! Bring out the biggest platter!"

Aelis rolled up her sleeves, bent down and seized one of the elk's legs, pulled it taut, felt out the edges of the joint with her fingers, then traced around it with the tip of her knife, exerting only the slightest pressure.

The knife slid in with no resistance.

She drew it in a tight circle, then pulled.

The leg came away in her hand and she laid it carefully on the ground. The other three limbs joined it. Some blood leaked out here and there, but by and large the carcass had clearly been drained by the enormous hunter who had brought it.

She looked up at Rus, the knife in her hand unstained by blood or gore. His eyes were wide as he stared at it.

"What is the secret of that blade?" He looked sheepish asking.

"No secret. I told you. It's an Anatomist's blade. It's a focus for my Necromantic casting . . . and it has certain properties."

"Can it cut anything like that?"

"Only dead flesh," Aelis answered. *Though I'm damn well not supposed to be using it on venison*, she thought. With Rus's help, she flipped the carcass over, and began slicing away the hide. It came away easily.

"Why would you need a magic weapon that only cuts dead flesh?"

"Well," Aelis started to answer, before biting off the words as she cut. "Sometimes you need to cut up a body. Find out what killed it, and how, and for the very best Anatomists, even when." And all of that was true, if only a part of the truth.

"Seen enough bodies in my day. Never felt the need to cut on them any more than they already were."

Aelis's hands were quickly reddened to the wrist, but the butchering was done, the animal reduced to pieces she or Rus could move. A few minutes in Martin ventured outside carrying a large wooden platter. He took one look at what they were doing and gasped, dropped the platter, and ran back inside.

"He's not got much of a stomach for butchery these days," Rus said, though he stuck his head into the doorway and yelled for Martin to bring them a bucket of hot water, soap, cloths, and a brush. Then he piled up as much as would fit on the platter and stood, shouldering the door open.

It took him several trips, but in the end the work was done, some bones were in a stockpot, some were handed off to the village dogs, some of the meat was hanging in the cold room, and Martin was busy deciding what to do with the rest of it. She watched him for a moment as she took the bucket back inside. Now that the bloodiest work was done he didn't seem to mind dealing with the pieces. She watched as he reached for a large-bladed knife. Then his hand paused in midair, fingers trembling. She was about to approach him when Rus came to her with a tray and gestured back outside with his chin.

There was an old, weather-beaten wooden table behind the back of the inn and he directed her to it. The tray held bread, butter, a jug of small beer, two plates and two cups.

They sat, ate for a while in silence.

"So, is Tun local? A village lad who decided he just liked the life of a woods bachelor?"

"Don't know," Rus said. "I doubt it. He started coming into town about a year after Martin and I took over here. Refugee, maybe, or a veteran, scarred by what he had done, what he had seen. Some of the folk who come back from a war don't want to spend too much time among other people. I don't ask. Don't expect he'd answer if I did."

"And some come back with their wages saved and buy a crossroads inn in a remote village, hmm?" Aelis raised an eyebrow over the edge of her cup.

"Missed the bit about not asking and not answering, eh?" Rus smiled to take the sting out of his reproach. "Some of it was wages, yes. We didn't come straight here after our term. Spent some time back home. It . . ." He paused. "Didn't work."

Some pieces fell into place in Aelis's mind. A warden was constantly developing the information they got, after all, making facts fit with other facts. *Martin's war-haunted*, she thought. All available evidence pointed to it; his skittishness, problems with blood, his shaking hand as he reached for the knife.

"What did you and Martin do in the war?"

"The same thing most everyone else did, Warden," Rus said.

Aelis sensed that she'd overstepped, for Rus lapsed back into silence and quickly finished his breakfast.

"We'll do better by you at supper," he said, and stood.

"Before you go," Aelis said quickly, brushing past the instinct that told her to apologize, reasoning it might make her look weak, "is there other work around the village I might be able to help with today?" She had something in mind, but it didn't seem quite the time or place to suggest it.

"Someone, somewhere, is always trying to repair a fence," Rus said. "Walk around and look for the gaps."

"What can I do to help repair a fence?"

"Extra hands are always welcome," Rus said as he disappeared into the back door of the inn.

Aelis sighed, and went looking for work.

✦ ✦ ✦

She found it about a quarter-mile walk from the crossroads and the inn, where outside a farmhouse a boy was working overtime to keep sheep penned up while his father and mother worked at repairing a fence, just like Rus had said she'd find. The fence was made of rough branches lashed together, barely seasoned and smoothed, not the finely planed planks she'd expected. The woman was holding one end of a long branch against the sturdier posts, while the man held it with one hand and tried to lash it in place with the other. She swallowed her hesitation and tried to seem naturally interested as she walked close.

"Could you use some help?"

The boy's attention turned to her and he lost track of the sheep he was trying to turn back into what remained of their enclosure. His mouth fell open as he stared at her sword. The woman, startled, nearly dropped her end of the post. The crude sign she made, bending her middle fingers and thumb into the palm of her hand, didn't help her resettle it.

Aelis tried not to let her disappointment show.

"It's nothin' to concern yourself with, Warden," the man said, fighting the urge, she thought, to knuckle his forehead as he did. "We're doin' just fine on our own." He turned to glance over his shoulder at the son, who was still gawping at Aelis.

The sheep, a small herd of only a dozen or so, were starting to edge away toward the boy, nosing at the sparse grass, which got thicker and greener near the large gap the farm folk were trying to repair.

"Abel," the man barked, "mind your work!" His tone jolted the boy out of staring at Aelis but also startled the sheep.

She didn't think, she just did; Aelis grasped the hilt of her sword with her left hand and raised her right, her fingers bending and moving in ways that made her knuckles ache and would've blurred the vision of anyone looking too closely.

The ward she drew was simple, low to the ground, but larger than usual. Extending in a semicircle from one part of the complete fence to another, it wasn't built to absorb energy or any force stronger than a running sheep. Which it promptly did, as more than one of the startled animals ran headlong into it. Aelis felt the impacts in her hand and in her head as gentle throbs, though they weren't painful.

Yet.

"They'll not pass this barrier so long as I hold it," she said slowly, carefully. "Though any of you could step over it just by lifting your leg a little higher than your lower cross-posts there." She gestured to the complete parts of the fence to either side of the gap. "It'll be no trouble to keep this up while you get a workable fence in place, goodman . . ."

"Bruce," the man said, "and this is my wife, Ada." He gaped at the sheep milling in front of what appeared to him to be empty space. When Aelis looked, she could see the shimmering band of her ward, little more than a foot off the ground. Had she expended the power, she could've made it visible to the others, but there was simply no reason to do that.

"I'm Aelis, Bruce," she said. "And I can do this for some time, but . . . perhaps it's best if we get on with fixing the fence, hmm?"

Bruce and Ada nodded quickly, and Bruce waved a hand for Abel to join them. The boy scurried over and helped to keep the branches stable while his parents tied them off.

It hadn't been a hard ward when she cast it, but five minutes in, as the family got a second branch in place, then a third, she was sweating. In ten minutes, she was as grateful to drop that ward as she would've been to set down that calcination oven in her tower, assuming she could've lifted it in the first place. Hoping that she hadn't visibly sweated through her shirt, she gratefully unwrapped one hand from the hilt of her sword and let the other fall limp to her side before it could cramp up.

"Stregon's Knuckles, Warden, do you think you could just cast those sorta spells around our pens all the time? I'd no idea your sort had such useful magics," Bruce said, coming to the edge of the newly fixed fence. He appeared to have forgotten his earlier reluctance.

"Not that would stand for much longer than I just did, goodman," Aelis answered. "As for my sort . . ." She smiled, though she knew it was weak, and she saw the smiles on the family starting to disappear. Quickly, she hitched at her belt, patting the leaf-bladed sword in its leather scabbard. "This marks me as an Abjurer. What I did was the basis of our work; we call it a ward."

"But that dagger means you're a Necromancer, don't it?" Abel had crept up behind his father till his nose was pressed just over the second branch of the fence. "All raisin' the dead and suchlike."

Bruce and Ada both turned glares that promised punishment on the boy, but he was too rapt, staring at Aelis, to pay them much attention.

"It does mark me as having studied Necromancy, Abel, that is true," Aelis answered. She wasn't bound never to lie, exactly, but had often heard that it was bad policy, so she decided to give the boy as honest an answer as she could without frightening him. "But what you say is not what the College of Necromancy of the Lyceum does. We do not raise the dead, as you say—we study how to destroy that kind of creature in all its guises, and those who would create them." She saw the boy's eyes widen and she allowed herself a smile. "If you know what the dagger means, Abel, then what of the sword?"

The boy frowned. "Abjurer?" He was slow and careful around the sylla-bles of the word but got there in the end.

"Which means I protect people, with wards and other spells."

"And your sword?" Abel was suddenly very excited, his eyes wide and focused on the hilt.

"Only if I have to."

Abel seemed about to say more before his father's hand descended upon the back of his neck. "Well, there'll be no call for that around Lone Pine," Bruce insisted.

"Of course not, goodman. Of course not. But in the unlikely event that there is . . . I'll be here," Aelis said with a faint smile. Then, with a slight nod toward both Bruce and Ada and a wave at Abel, she set off back around the village.

In the hours she spent walking about the green and the nearby farms, she saw no one else who appeared to need her help at any task she could conceivably help them tackle. She offered greetings and made small talk about the weather—which the locals seemed to take far more interest in than Aelis ever had—and the coming change of seasons.

She ignored the superstitious and inefficacious signs she saw half a dozen people make behind their backs as she passed.

"What more do you need to know about it than how to dress for it? Why would anyone think I could *read clouds?* What in Seven Hells does that even mean?" She'd kept those thoughts to herself as long as she was in the village proper, but once she left it she couldn't help but marvel, and to take the first deep breath she'd allowed herself since the sun had started bringing out the headier notes of wool and shit.

As she neared her tower, Aelis turned her mind to the puzzle of the calcination oven and how she might get it into a usable position, what she might be able to do with it. Something else nagged at the back of her mind, some task she'd meant to do, but she couldn't quite recall what it was.

Then she saw that the door to her tower was hanging open, with its lower hinges twisted away. She ripped her sword from its sheath, shook her wand down into her left hand, and began to advance cautiously up the low-rising stone walkway.

She paused and listened at the door. The only sound she could hear was the incredibly faint metallic whirring of the orrery's minute movements. Lessons from her swordmistress flashed in her mind. Stance wide, weight shifting, sword held loosely enough to move but tightly enough that it couldn't be snatched away. Breathe deeply through the nose, exhale lightly through the mouth. Lavanalla, at six feet tall and with three feet of curved sword in her hand, had always made it look easy and sound ridiculous.

Balance and pain, Aelis thought. *Always balance and pain. She had a knack for the cryptic. Never met an elf who didn't.* It wasn't always cryptic, though, as she remembered the elven abjurer hurling small, sharp stones with uncanny accuracy and bruising force while her students stood on a plank balanced on a short log. Deflecting the missiles with a ward was the right answer; trying to do it with a blade led to more rocks and more bruises.

Aelis dismissed the reminiscence from her mind and quashed her hesitation. Sword and wand in hand, she barged through the door, relying on power on the basis that stealth would give her no advantage. She'd already gathered and sharpened her will, pushing it toward wand and sword both, ready to call up a ward or unleash some manner of charm.

There was a blur of motion in front of her. She called up a Second

Order ward, the two syllables and her concentration on drawing and then expending the power through her sword. The air changed around her and the hair on her neck stood up as her power solidified in the air.

With no idea what to expect, she'd called her ward to protect against physical and magical force; it radiated out from her like a shield clutched in the hand that held her sword, and she crouched low to make herself small behind it.

And when the goat that had been loitering inside the tower bounced off of it and then let out an aggrieved scream, she very nearly aimed a cut of her sword at its neck instead.

Aelis expelled her ward and felt it pop like a soap bubble, sending a tingle over her skin and spine. Then she sheathed her sword and busied herself chasing the goat out of her bottom floor.

With the goat yelling and clattering its way down the stone walkway, Aelis's first instinct was to check her orrery, which seemed untouched. She watched it for long enough to see the subtle movement of the tiny crystal moons around the slightly larger blue earth, then placed a hand over it and found the trace of her own power humming within.

Then, with a mounting terror, she thought of her books and dashed to the other room, separated by the curtains she'd hung to divide the bottom floor of the tower in half.

With relief that drained most, if not all, of her lust for the blood of that goat, she saw nothing out of order. Aldayim was sitting atop her writing desk. The books were arranged in their alcove.

She went to sit down, picking the Aldayim and the desk up, when something drew her eye back to the books.

They were not in the order she'd placed them.

Falling to one knee in front of the shelf, Aelis walked her fingers along the spines. She kept her books arranged by subject and then alphabetically by author. Necromancy was mixing with Abjuration at the very head of the shelf.

"Oh gods," she muttered. "Where's Dwergoch?" Quickly, she sorted through the books on both the shelves in the alcove, then looked around the base, then rifled through the books again. With rising panic, she searched the entire floor, top to bottom, lifting and moving anything—a cloak, a jacket, her robes, every book, her lap desk—that could conceivably have hidden the book. She looked under the chairs, under the wardrobe, under the tables in the front room where she'd set her alchemy equipment.

She spent at least an hour scouring the entire bottom floor of the tower before she finally admitted defeat.

It was gone. Her copy of Dwergoch's definitive *Wards and Combat Abjurations for Sword or Axe*. Creamy, heavy-weight paper, silk-stitched into oak boards covered with leather dyed a blue that matched the College of Abjuration's official color. The margins were filled with her meticulous notes on sword forms and the way various hilt and blade styles functioned as foci for her Abjurations. Her time with that book had ultimately led to the design of the sword she carried on her hip, with its leaf-shaped blade and twisting quillons.

The notes were in a cipher, and there was little a layman could do with the book. But its loss cut her in ways she didn't want to think too deeply about.

Dalius snapped into her mind, and she recalled his pretensions of being her equal.

"If he has broken into my tower and stolen that book, I *will* kill him," she said aloud, though she knew even as she said it that her judgment, should it become official, would stop short of death.

She considered her options. "I can't simply go down into the village making accusations," she said as she sat down and took up her writing desk. From within, she took out paper and a charcoal stick and began to write out a list.

1. *Ask Rus about Dalius.*
2. *Find out who in Lone Pine is lettered.*
3. *Keep an eye out if merchants come to town.*
4. *Prepare draft statement warning merchants if anyone tries to sell books to them.*
5. *Get the fucking door fixed.*
6. *Make goat stew.*

She read over the list she'd written out, thinking which items she could act on immediately. She lingered over the first point. Did she trust Rus and Martin enough to go involving them in something potentially serious?

"Have to trust somebody," she muttered, writing *casually, not openly* in tiny print beneath her first item. Two, three, and four would be longer-term goals.

Five was something she could and would begin to deal with right that very moment.

She stood up, gathered her formal robes from the wardrobe—thankfully it didn't seem to have been disturbed by her intruder—and as she left, considered what to do about the door.

Aelis placed her hand against the warped wood and drew her wand. What she had in mind was complex, perhaps devious, but not dangerous. She took a few steadying breaths, but in truth, anger had always sharpened her Charms.

With the fingers of her right hand tracing a sign upon the door, a ward that would require dispelling before anyone entered, she pressed the tip of her wand into the center of it with her left, spoke two syllables, and stepped back, nodding with satisfaction.

Anyone opening the door until she'd carefully taken down the ward would be in for a surprising few hours.

6

THE THORNS

Aelis was shocked to find the village a sudden flurry of activity, as if every shepherd, goatherd, and farmer had come running back to its very center in the short time she'd been gone.

The children, boys and girls alike, seemed to be running about to no real purpose. She spied Pips and Abel among a group of children who'd all taken up sticks and were slicing them through the air like swords.

Many of the adults had gathered into clusters, speaking closely to one another. They drew back when she approached, made signs, whispered superstitious charms invoking the Worldsoul, Stregon, and Anaerion. More tellingly, she saw more than one stout farmer holding a thick wooden walking stick or a woodaxe at his side. They tried to look casual, like they'd just been caught splitting wood or were going out for a hike in the surrounding hills. But she saw the way they nervously settled and resettled their fingers, the way their eyes shifted to other men and women standing nearby, similarly armed.

She ignored it, then caught the eye of Pips and waved the girl over, squatting down to look her in the eye—a decision she regretted almost instantly as Pips's stick-sword whipped viciously through the air just inches from her nose.

"Pips," she said, "what's going on? What's got everyone so excited?"

"Warden Aelis," Pips said, bubbly and excited. "It's adventurers comin'! Bois n' his brother Juval took their family's herd up right up to the pass. Not much more than two hours after breakfast said they saw 'em come trundling down in their wagon, a big war wagon . . ."

"Adventurers? Prospectors or pioneers, you mean?"

"No, I mean adventurers, s'what my uncles call them," Pips insisted.

"Very well then. What do you know about them?" From the corner of one eye, she saw Elmo and Otto trying to thread their way gracefully through the crowd toward her and Pips. Thankfully their idea of "threading gracefully" seemed similar to a bull getting caught in a fence and then trying to drag the fence with it. She had some time.

"I know there's a dwarf among 'em," Pips proclaimed, "a real dwarf with a long beard and an axe and everything, and the wagon had a big bow on it . . ."

For a moment, just a moment, Aelis pictured an armored wagon with a huge ribbon tied around it, and then felt so ridiculous she blushed in embarrassment as she realized the girl was talking about some kind of weapon mounted on the thing. Thankfully Pips didn't seem to notice her shame, so Aelis gave the girl a pat on the shoulder and stood. "Go with your uncles, Phillipa," she said as Elmo and Otto finally came free of the crowd to drag the girl away.

She scanned the crowd, wishing for a moment for a few more inches of height, and found Rus and Martin lingering outside their inn. Rus was trying to calm people down enough to listen to him.

Aelis set off determinedly in their direction, her boots thumping into the dirt track that circled the green until she was close to them. "Screen me for a moment," she muttered. They stared at her blankly and she said, "Screen me. Stand between me and the crowd. Do it."

She must have summoned enough of an air of command, for the two stepped in front of her as she slipped her wand into her left hand. The Charm she formed in her mind and then released with a stab at the air and an uttered syllable was quite simple, but took a good deal of concentration to spread out over as wide an area as the few dozen people before her were occupying, especially in open space without walls to give her boundaries.

All she did, really, was float the mental suggestion that they should turn and listen to her, quietly, with an open mind. Not a compulsion or a command, not even close. She saw enough of the crowd turn that as she slipped her wand away she was already raising her voice.

"Listen to me, good people of Lone Pine. If it's true that a band of frontier explorers and salvagers are coming our way, we've nothing at all to fear. Like as not they'll have gold to spend and will be looking for beds, food, and drink, perhaps more than goodmen Rus and Martin alone can provide. Their horses will need shoeing, their clothes and tools mending and sharpening, and they'll want food and other necessities for their long trip south. And more than coin, they'll bring stories to trade, perhaps a bit of music."

"We've had rough sorts here before, end of summer before last," said one farmer, holding a quarterstaff as if ready to choke the life out of it. "Busted up some of our homes, stole horses n' livestock, put ideas in our children's heads, and worse."

As the man spoke, Aelis flicked her eyes toward Rus, who gave her a tiny affirming nod. Aelis cleared her throat and the man stopped speaking, surprised.

"Tell me, goodman. Did Lone Pine have a Warden that day?"

There was a general shaking of heads in the crowd.

"Then this day will be different."

Something about Aelis's attitude mollified them, and in short order most of the crowd melted away from the green, back to their daily tasks—even if in many cases those tasks seemed much closer to the green than they had been before. The children kept running about, slashing their sticks in the air, clattering them into one another, declaring themselves to be this or that war hero. Aelis fixed her gaze on the western horizon, where any band in a so-called war wagon would be approaching from if they'd come down out of the mountains that morning. She was briefly distracted when she heard Pips boldly declare that she wasn't some war hero, but rather a Warden come to defend the town with her sword and staff.

For once, Aelis found herself envying the Invokers their staves. She could lean on it, or hold it forthrightly before her in some kind of wizardly pose.

She settled for turning to Rus as he walked slowly to her side. "If it should be a group of ruffians," she said, "how many veterans in the village besides you and Martin?"

Rus snorted faintly. "What happened to the confidence? 'This time will be different'?"

"I can defend myself. I can manage a band of ruffians, if it comes to it. I can probably do both at the same time. I probably can't do those two things *and* defend a dozen villagers."

"You've no lack of confidence, Warden—"

"Please answer my question, Rus," Aelis said, her words coming out rather more curt than she'd meant.

"Me and Martin, but I won't ask him to fight anyone and neither will you. Elmo and Otto, but don't look to them for subtlety. Emilie, blond woman who lives just on the outskirts, is a devil of a hand with a bow, but I've not seen her on the green today. A few others were wound-dressers, grooms, runners, servants, and the like."

"Thank you," Aelis remembered to say, and nodded. "I don't think we've really a need to go posting an archer. What's the worst these adventuring sorts can get up to?"

"The worst? Murder, theft, ra . . ."

"It was a rhetorical question," Aelis said, cutting Rus off. "Is it common they go bad like that?"

"It didn't quite come to blood with the crew Ewig was talking about from the other summer. But it was damn near. As it was, they made off with a good deal more than they'd paid for. There was a lot of anger, hurt feelings. No one was hurt in a permanent way, but around here, horses and sheep are the most wealth anyone's got. You steal them, you're stealing a livelihood."

"No one's stealing anything, horses nor sheep nor a scrap of food, on my watch."

"There's that confidence again," Rus said, his tone slightly puzzled. "If they are ruffians, I hope they're similarly impressed."

Aelis didn't answer, for the sun suddenly glinted off metal at the crest of the hill in the west. She leaned forward, squinting. A pair of horses were leading the "war wagon," if indeed it was such a thing, straight toward Lone Pine. It started out large and kept getting bigger. A murmur ran through the crowd as it neared, and even Aelis was taken by just how large it got.

War wagon proved to be a more apt description than Aelis could've imagined.

Only once it was passing the edge of houses near the green could she estimate its size; thirty feet in length and ten or a bit more wide, and on its back was indeed something like a huge arbalest—the bolts must've been half again as long as most longbow arrows—mounted on a rotating platform. The horses pulling it, she realized, were some of the biggest draft animals she'd ever seen, a soft brown with dark cream feathering on their fetlocks. A ram was mounted on the front, a heavy blunt wedge of iron, along with a winch.

The wagon itself didn't seem to have a central structure, just canvas strung across poles and lashed to either side. Two dwarves sat side by side on the driver's bench, their beards flowing over their laps as the wagon pulled onto the green. She saw at least two taller folk, humans, she thought, crawl atop it, checking the ropes holding various barrels, chests, and crates in place.

Two more tall folk rode animals of a piece with the draft horses that were hitched to the wagon, and each led another horse behind.

The amount of baggage and equipment strapped to the wagon was astounding. Up close, she judged that each one of the horses was eighteen
hands at a minimum, broad and heavy to boot, and that all that sweating
horseflesh carried a powerful scent.

The dwarves wore hard studded leather jerkins and matching gloves
that went to the elbows, leaving their arms bare but for thick iron bands
fitted closely around their biceps. One of them now rose, keeping one foot
on the runner and one on the board. His beard was twisted into thick
braids, mostly red with streaks of light, nearly blond brown mixed in, and
his head was bare.

"Greetings from Timmuk Dobrusz and his company," the dwarf
roared, posing for a moment with hands on hips, before going on. "Lately
returned to civilization—such as it is—from the frontier wilds beyond
the Durndill Pass. We've stories to trade and treasures, too, from the ruins and the delvings and the holdings lost to the wilds those many years
ago. What say you, folk of . . ." He looked down at the other dwarf, muttered something in their own harsh tongue that Aelis didn't catch, then
back at the two humans—one man, one woman—who had walked to the
front of the flatbed. Similarly attired in leather, armed with an ironmongery's worth of short swords and knives between them, they both offered
eloquent shrugs.

Aelis stepped forward. "Lone Pine is where you find yourselves, Timmuk Dobrusz and company. And I am its warden, Aelis de Lenti."

"I wouldn't have thought Lone Pine rated a warden." That comment
came from one of the riders, who threw a dark green hood back off her
face as she spoke.

Aelis had had enough social schooling in her life as a count's daughter, added to Lyceum training, to keep from gasping. But deep down she
wanted to, because the revealed face was not quite elvish and not quite
human, but a mix of the two, and stunningly, arrestingly beautiful. Aelis
found herself flushing slightly at the auburn hair, cut short along the sharp
line of her chin, the ice-blue eyes, and the high, fine cheekbones.

"I've only recently arrived," Aelis said, keeping her voice smooth and her
face composed, she was reasonably sure. "But I am its warden nonetheless.
As such, Timmuk Dobrusz, I assume you've your paperwork and charter
in order?"

"Of course!" The dwarf smacked one of his gloved hands against his
thigh, sending a cloud of dust into the air. "Of course we do. Darent!" he

shouted, turning to the leather-clad man standing on the wagon behind him. "Fetch the paperwork!"

It was a short wait while Darent clambered beneath the canvas tent erected on the wagon. The rest of the party—the two dwarves, the half-elven woman, the human woman on the wagon, and the other rider, whose hood was still up, obscuring their features—stared down at Aelis. She felt the weight of that collective stare—and she ignored it.

What do they think I am? Some country margrave's daughter gone to her first ball? Never had someone stare at her before?

On the wagon she heard the sound of locks being turned and something opened. She saw faces appear in windows of the houses around the crossroads as people were drawn back to the scene.

Finally, Darent came hustling out of the back of the wagon, holding a cylindrical leather case. He handed it to Timmuk, who hopped down off the wagon and strolled up to Aelis, holding it out to her.

"You'll find it all in good order," Timmuk said as Aelis took the case and popped the cap, sliding out a thick roll of parchment bound with red ribbons. She handed the case back to Timmuk and unknotted the thong that held the roll of papers closed.

Aelis was still conscious of the eyes on her as she unrolled and began to read. Though in truth she wanted to read every word, she didn't think she could keep everyone waiting for too long. She'd gotten past the official rhetoric at the top, explaining that this charter was issued by the Crowned Heads of the Three Nations and Ratified by the Power of the Estates House.

The bearers of this document are entitled to salvage and treasure beyond the northern borders of Ystain, she read, just as the half-elf on the spare draft horse cleared her throat.

"Tell me, Warden. Are we going to be here all day as you read?"

Well, now you damn well are, Aelis thought, even as she smiled. "I think you could perhaps dismount and see if our fine innkeepers will provide you refreshment. While you stay outside."

Timmuk grumbled something under his breath and Aelis pretended not to notice as she leaned her back against one of the pillars holding up the inn's front porch. She heard a child-sized someone trying to clamber up onto the railing to look over her shoulder, and glanced back to find Pips balancing there.

With her eyes bright, she extended a finger and pointed to the top. "What's that say?"

"Can you not read, girl?"

Phillipa half shrugged, half shook her head. "I can make my name and I know a few other marks, that's all. My uncles aren't too learned."

Aelis tsked. "We'll have to work on that. For the moment, though, I need to focus on this." She turned back to the page, trying to ignore the girl balancing on the railing behind her.

> *Entitled to salvage and treasure beyond the northern borders of Ystain in all former holdings and properties of Ystain, Her Allies and Colonies for a period of two years extending from the date of issuance. The bearers must pay a tax totaling . . .*

Aelis let her eyes skip down the page, as it detailed the complicated percentages of fees the company would have to pay to the Crowns and the Estates House, in the unlikely event that agents of the various exchequers could track them down. In most cases, Aelis knew, the companies paid a flat fee to be issued a charter and did pay something to various officials, and theoretically to the crown, upon their return.

> *The members of this company, known as the Thorns of the Counting House, are herein named and undersigned, agreeing to abide by all clauses, codicils, and addenda to this agreement . . .*

> > *Timmuk Dobrusz, dwarf of no fixed residence*
> > *Andresh Dobrusz, dwarf of no fixed residence*
> > *Darent Lash, human of Lascenise*
> > *Dashia Lash, human of Lascenise*
> > *Maurenia Angra, of Lascenise*
> > *Luth, human of Lascenise*

Aelis didn't have long to puzzle over why there was no race listed next to the name of Maurenia Angra, but she felt certain that was the woman on horseback. Aelis sneaked a glance at her over the top of the document, and realized the entire company was staring at her. *Studded leather and lethal steel seems to be the uniform,* Aelis reflected. Maurenia was dressed much the same as the Dobruszes and the Lashes, though she made the leather *stylish*, somehow. Instead of steel, her jerkin appeared to be studded with bronze, and her gloves were thin, supple leather. The sword at her left hip was a foot longer and a good deal slimmer than Aelis's leaf-bladed Abjurer's sword. She had a long basket-hilted dagger balancing it on the other side of her belt, inlaid with silver. Luth, the remaining member of the company, was still hooded, and Aelis couldn't take the time to study him, but she was reasonably sure she saw a pair of throwing axes tucked into the front of his belt before she flicked her eyes back to the parchment.

She briefly checked many of the remaining clauses, carefully reading those regarding the acquisition and possession of magical items or equipment, all of which became the legal property of the Crowns and the Estates House as soon as it entered the country. She lightly skimmed the penalties for nonpayment of tax, crossing borders legally agreed upon with *Foreign Heads of State*, and had a chuckle that the Crowns were forced to acknowledge the orcish chieftains as heads of state. She could imagine them choking on it. Each member of the company had entered wills and arrangements for disposition of assets in the event they did not return. The documents also indemnified the crowns, the estates, and their agents from all injuries and losses the company might suffer, while generously offering to create a small trust for personal burial or cremation, with the deposited money nonrefundable in the event that a body was not recovered and heirs did not specifically request a symbolic burial.

"They really cover every contingency, don't they," Aelis said as she flipped to the last page to check the seals. The largest, in red, was the outline of the dozen columns outside the Estates House. Slightly smaller, in purple wax, the three crowns of Ystain, Imraval, and Tyridice in a tilted triangle. None of the crowns had any identifying marks; all were simple icons with three points.

"Well," Timmuk said, "there's no hard limit on the weight or volume of phoenix feathers one can harvest." Aelis laughed faintly at the joke. While she read, more village folk had crept back toward the crossroads and the green, whispering curiously about the company.

"I do have one question," Aelis said as she began to roll the parchment back up, then using it to point to the oversized arbalest on the back of the wagon. "I didn't see any particular license for that . . ."

"No licenses are required beyond the borders," Maurenia put in, quick and curt.

"Well, you're no longer beyond the borders," Aelis answered smoothly, feeling that she'd somehow scored a point. "I am going to ask that you disable it while you're in Lone Pine."

Maurenia seemed about to speak up, but Timmuk raised a hand. "Not a problem, Warden. You'll have no trouble from us. See to it, Renia," the dwarf said, fixing a look on the elfling that didn't seem to brook disagreement.

With a there-and-gone frown, Maurenia hopped up onto the wagon in one stride and carefully picked her way past all the lashed baggage to begin fiddling with the arbalest.

"Our Renia is a tinkerer and a designer of lethal tools," the dwarf said conversationally as he turned back to Aelis. "That arbalest, its mounting post, and the platform it stands upon are all of her design. She's got it working just the way she wants it, and we'll have no end of fuss from her when she has to fit it back together."

"I do apologize. But something that size, and with the kind of power it must have . . . I'd just prefer it inoperable while you're here. I'm sure you understand," Aelis said as she handed the documents back to Timmuk, who slipped them into the case and capped it with the heel of his other hand.

"Of course, Warden, of course. Now, are there any other rules or local customs you'd like to instruct us about?"

"Well," Aelis said, "I'm not about to ask that you surrender your weapons, and I've got no wire to make peace bonds. But if you could show some discretion about how much steel you wear at any one time, I'd be grateful."

"You'd leave us to the mercy of our enemies, Warden?" Timmuk was grinning behind his great beard, but Aelis didn't join in with a smile.

"You're not likely to have any enemies here, Timmuk," Aelis said. "All I ask is a little consideration for village folk who are heartily sick of war and its implements."

"You get to carry a sword."

The voice that spoke those words was low and throaty, scratched, it seemed to Aelis, from little use.

"Luth," Timmuk began, "there's no call to—"

"Carry a dagger, too. Who're you to tell me what I can't carry?"

Luth, who'd so far been the only member of the company Aelis hadn't gotten a good look at, threw back his hood.

Aelis wished he hadn't.

Half of his face and head were smooth and hairless, the skin white and livid—burned, Aelis knew, and likely by magical fire. It wasn't easy to look at, with his lips burned away and half a rictus grin exposed. The other half of his face was that of a man who lived rough and outdoors, heavily lined, thick brown and gray stubble on his scalp and chin. His eyes, dark brown, focused on her with an intensity that answered too easily to the word *feverish*.

"Who I am," Aelis said, trying to focus on the unmarred side of his face, "is the Warden of Lone Pine. And I haven't *told* you to do anything. I've merely asked."

Luth shrugged his cloak over his shoulders, then reached up and unclasped it with one hand, letting the dark green garment pool at his feet. He wore the same leathers as the rest, only up to his chin, his armor buckled just beneath it in a series of iron-banded collars. He wore a sleeve and a glove on only one arm—the same side as his burns, the left. His right arm was free from the shoulder down, scarred and inked with designs Aelis didn't have time to study.

There were axes on his belt; she was right on that first guess. But beneath the cloak there had also been hidden a long, slim sword with a lovingly worn hilt wrapped in shagreen. While it had a foot of length on hers, she was just now realizing that he was so tall—he towered over her by close to a foot—that it didn't show beneath the hem of his cloak.

"Luth, the Warden is makin' an easy and sensible request," Timmuk began. "I'll not have you endangering—"

"I agreed to take your orders out in the wilds, dwarf. We're no longer in the wilds. And it seems they make children into wardens now."

"I don't know what's gotten into you," Timmuk said. "Trying to pick fights all the way back. What is . . ." On the back of the wagon, Darent and Dashia had frozen in place like frightened game. Maurenia looked as though she wanted to hastily reassemble the arbalest. Andresh muttered something to Timmuk in Dwarfish.

Luth dropped his hand to the hilt of his sword. Aelis kept herself relaxed, her hands loose at her sides, though her palms were moist. Breath was held.

"You can have my sword if you can take it away," Luth said, slowly curling his fingers around the hilt.

"A fair bargain," Aelis said, then she twitched her wrist. Her wand fell into her left hand and as she brought it up she was already speaking the two words of the Second Order Enchantment she'd called to her mind and repeated, silently, over and over while things had started to turn sour. By holding the spell in her head, ready to gather power and project her will through the wand, she'd honed it till it was like a blade that could've cut silk. Had it been a blade, and had it been meant to hurt, that is.

What it was meant to do, which it did, was manifest as a green flash that only briefly seared the eyes of anyone standing in front of her wand—and made them forget, for a moment, their aggression.

What it did, solely to Luth, was reach out to his mind and instantly flood him with weariness by suggesting that he'd not slept in some time.

His sword slid back into its sheath with a loud click and he stumbled forward onto the dirt like a felled tree, stirring up some dust about a foot from Aelis's boot. She stepped carefully to his side, bent down, unhooked his sword's scabbard from the frog on his belt, and stepped away.

She had a moment before the rest of Timmuk's company would remember what was happening, so she seized it, strolling over to their dwarf leader and holding Luth's sheathed weapon out to him. Timmuk took it uncertainly, blinking away his daze.

"Timmuk Dobrusz and the . . . the Thorns of the Counting House," she said, trying to keep the disbelief out of her voice. "Collect your man. While you are in Lone Pine he will *not* be armed, and you will keep his weapons under lock and key. Had his blade cleared its sheath, he would have committed a crime of serious consequence. As it is, I will leave him in your parole, and this entire incident will be labeled a misunderstanding. Am I understood?"

As she spoke, Aelis kept her voice level and calm, her wand raised, and her free hand on her sword's hilt. Maurenia recovered the fastest, no surprise there, and Aelis believed she read something new in the elfling's features; respect, perhaps fear, but none of the earlier disdain.

The dwarves and the humans came around at the same time, and Timmuk was nodding at her suggestion as though it were eminently sensible. He rattled some quick Dwarfish to Andresh, and he and Dashia hopped off the wagon. The former began stripping Luth's other weapons away. Dashia gathered his hands and slipped some cordage from her belt, began tying them together at the wrist.

Meanwhile, Luth snored like a man in a deep and guiltless sleep.

Aelis uncurled her hand from her sword hilt, grateful no one could see the sweat her palm had left behind on the leather.

✦   ✦   ✦

A few minutes later, Aelis was relaxing in the inn with a mug of small beer. Rus had set it down in front of her and leaned close. "You've never drawn that sword when it mattered, have you," he'd said, his knowing glance making it more a statement than a question.

"Depends on what 'mattered' means," Aelis had mumbled in response.

Instantly her mind flashed back to her Abjurer's test.

Lavanalla, that long two-handed monstrosity of a sword in her hand, battering at Aelis's wards with her own. Desperately parrying that curve of bronze—Lavanalla had always said that she couldn't stand the touch of steel—constantly giving ground, letting her weight fall too much onto her back foot.

"You can't always run, girl!" the elf shouted at her, as she bore down on Aelis's sword, pushing her toward the ground. More than just the clash of blades, there was the clash of magical power. Before the duel had even started—seconds that felt like hours ago—Aelis had been instructed to call up her strongest ward. She managed one of the Third Order, she had thought; it should have been proof against blades, missiles, and Lower Order Evocations. It projected from the hilt of her sword and she made herself a low target behind it.

Lavanalla had bowed, drawn her sword with one hand—Aelis wasn't sure she could've lifted it like that—called up a ward with the other, and attacked her with both.

She'd known that wards could cut down other wards. They had practiced it, tested it, smashed their own shield-sized wards against one another in their practicums. She'd hardly been the brightest would-be Abjurer in the College, but she'd always held her own in that contest of will, focus, and intellect.

Lavanalla's ward ground through hers, smashed it to tatters like an axe would an overripe apple. Startled, with tingling hands, it had been all she could do to knock aside the flashing bronze blade that had cut at her neck.

"Poor form. Slow hands. Weak wards. You are no Abjurer." Lavanalla had pressed her attack; every time Aelis bought herself enough time to call another ward—each one a little weaker—the elven Archmagistress simply battered it away.

"What will you do when it is not one attacker, but many?" Lavanalla had swept at her legs, forcing Aelis to awkwardly hop the blade. Some distant part of her told her that the hop wasn't awkward if she landed back on her feet without losing one of them or her balance.

"What will you do when there are monsters, and your wards are all that stands between them and the folk you want to guard? What will you do when your magic must hold a murderer to account? What will you do, Aelis de Lenti un Tirraval?"

Aelis had gritted her teeth, not answering, not having the breath to answer. The circle of light around them seemed to be growing smaller; the darkness beyond the twenty feet allotted for their duel was so complete it could only have been provided by a skilled Illusionist.

"You cannot hurl your money at them," Lavanalla taunted. "They'll kill you and take it anyway." Aelis brought up another ward, bashing it forward as though it were a shield clutched in her left hand, leaving only her right on the hilt of her sword.

She was startled when the elf's own ward was knocked away. Not destroyed, no—but Aelis had pushed back for the first time in their fight. Lavanalla's almond eyes widened a touch.

"Your name will be meaningless to the nightmares of the frontier, or the orc band that's refused the treaties, or the company of robbers intent on plunder!" The elf brought every point home with a swing of her sword. Aelis's arms ached with the effort of being lifted, much less parrying, but she did, though each blow grew sloppier.

She pressed forward with her ward again, though she felt now as if the shimmering disc of air was no bigger than a duelist's buckler. Still, she pressed forward with it, grinding it into the ward extending from Lavanalla's left hand, caught the glittering bronze sword in the upward twist of her hilt's crosspiece.

For the first time in their fight, Aelis took a step forward. Her teeth ground together. Sweat blurred her vision, but she didn't dare blink it away.

At closer quarters, the elf's longer arms and longer blade became a liability. Aelis had it locked up. She pressed forward, her shorter stature and denser arms suddenly giving her an advantage.

She dimly remembered the rules of the duel—that it was to involve the blade and Abjurations only.

That memory was all that kept her from smashing her forehead into Lavanalla's chin.

From above them, a voice yelled, "Time!"

Instantly, the elf flowed away from Aelis's press. There was the orange-gold glitter of bronze as Lavanalla sheathed her weapon.

"What will you do, Aelis de Lenti un Tirraval, if any of those things come to pass?"

With a deep breath, sheathing her own weapon slowly and carefully, Aelis said, "Stand my ground, with my blade and my ward and whatever else I have to hand."

"That you will," the elf said. Then she paused, and slowly added, "Abjurer."

Aelis was pulled from the memory by the loud squeal of Pips from the seat next to her.

"That was AMAZIN'!" the girl yelled, holding out with a stiff arm the same stick she'd been swishing in the air outside, then saying, "That's a fair bargain."

The only thing that stopped the flattery from going straight to Aelis's head was the nasal quality in the imitation of her voice. "Now now, Phillipa," she muttered, "there's no call to go boasting." She had an eye for the stairs to the upper floors, which Maurenia and Timmuk were even now descending. They made an odd pair, with the elfling's slender grace and the dwarf's barrel-chested swagger, but they shared some quiet words Aelis didn't catch, and both of them laughed.

The dwarf went to Rus at the long counter that served as a bar and to separate the kitchen from the common room, while Maurenia came toward Aelis's table, ducking her head to indicate a bench and ask to sit. Aelis nodded even as she saw Timmuk lay a heavy purse upon the bar and tip out a piece of gold so bright it seemed to grasp at all the light in the room, from the open windows to the small fire in the hearth.

Aelis had never lived a life short of coin and was no stranger to the sight of gold, but she'd a hard time tearing her eyes away from the glint of that open bag, the heft of it.

Until she traded it for a view of Maurenia, anyway. The half-elf had pushed her hair behind her ears, leaving her high cheeks and strong chin unframed and somehow even more intriguing.

"I'm sorry for how Luth acted," Maurenia said, which apology Aelis took with cool disinterest. After a moment of silence, Maurenia added, "He's always been . . . unpredictable."

"I'd think a company like yours wouldn't want someone who answers to that description," Aelis noted.

Maurenia pulled free the studded gloves she wore and set them on the table with a sigh. Her hands had long, delicate fingers, but thick wrists, and Aelis would've bet the palms were thickly callused. "You can count on him in a tight spot. He did every bit of the work we needed done in the frontier; did the same last season. But we never can tell how he'll act in the clean light of day."

"And what kind of work did you do?"

Maurenia shrugged. "The usual. Tried to dig up old hoards, dodge any orc bands—"

"Did you?"

"The former, yes. The latter, largely, and what orcs we did see were as happy to barter, swap stories, and trade news as they were anything else. We shed no blood there." A beat. "No orc blood."

Aelis raised an eyebrow, something she could only accomplish with her left brow while simultaneously lowering her right. But it got the job done.

"Remnants of some of the mercenary companies gone marauding. Rabid now. They tend to run if you show them a fight, and they don't like to hear my arbalest sing a second time. We saw a horror or two, as well . . ."

"Now now, Renia," Timmuk rumbled, having strolled up behind her with a stealth that was uncanny for a dwarf, Aelis thought. "Don't go telling tales out of turn."

It was only on reflection that Aelis supposed that a giant dragging a tree-trunk club could sneak up on anyone staring at Maurenia from across a table. In the moment, she was entirely surprised by the dwarf's sudden intrusion.

Maurenia turned around to face him with a sigh, and the dwarf invited himself to a seat at the table. Aelis felt Pips clutch her shoulder and half hide behind it; when she looked down the girl had leaned over and only the top of her head and her eyes, glued to the adventurers, were visible.

"We'll have tales to tell, of course," the dwarf said, "of harpies and gigants, of desperate men and cunning monsters. But not for such a small crowd, y'see? Never tell a story twice in the same place, I say."

He set down mugs, larger but likely with the same small beer Aelis was sipping, for himself and Maurenia. The elf sniffed at it lightly and shoved it away, while the dwarf half drained his at a toss.

"I have to know," Aelis asked, "why *The Thorns of the Counting House?*"

"Ah," Timmuk said, wiping at the foam that had caught in his prodigious beard when he drank. "Well, you see, Andresh and I . . . we come from a family of moneylenders and traders down in Tyridice, with the sea to our east and the long Desert Road to Usir to our west. Plenty of ways for a man to get rich there, what with all that coin flowing both ways—"

"With all due respect, Timmuk, I do not need lessons in basic economy and geography."

The dwarf harrumphed, but the sound turned to laughter quickly enough. "A woman with things to do, I see."

"A Warden," Aelis corrected. "Who always has things to do." She saw Maurenia smile and the dwarf color a bit beneath his dark tan.

"Very well; our eldest brother had inherited control of the concern. Darent and Dashia were employees. Luth was a . . . contractor," the dwarf said, after taking a moment to choose a word. "Our brother Lavosh had some plans. Extended nearly everything we had to fund a massive caravan and to hire ships to carry gemstones, books, and alchemical instruments that came to us from Usir up here to Ystain and Imraval, and bring furs back."

"Allow me to guess. Neither paid out."

"I was the best caravan master the firm had. But with our father gone, and Lavosh childless, he wouldn't let me or Andresh take the field. We were confined solely to local collection. They never did come back, not even one. Even so, we'd have been able to cover the losses if one ship hadn't fallen foul of pirates . . . so Lavosh did the honorable thing and had to pay ransom just to get the crew back. A king's ransom," he added with a theatrical sigh. "Between that, the losses of the caravan, and worse prices than we'd expected—" He shrugged. "There was no longer enough money to lend or invest. Lavosh sold the counting house to the Urdimonte for a new branch and took a job with them. I'd been working with Renia here to design wagons to try to sell to the army, mobile siege platforms, that sort of thing. We couldn't keep simply hanging around, thorns in my brother's side . . . so we quit counting houses and ledger books forever."

"Except in keeping count of shares, of course," Maurenia said.

"Except that," Timmuk agreed. "Luckily Andresh is a deft hand at sums and tables. Never much for them myself—I was more a hands-on type. At any rate, when little brother and I left the family counting house knowing that Luth and the Lashes were at loose ends, and that Renia wanted to field test our designs . . ." He waved a hand vaguely.

"I see," Aelis said, only she didn't. As the dwarf had been talking, she'd glanced at his forearms and thought it highly improbable that the corded layers of muscle showing beneath the coarse dark hair were developed in any counting house.

Neither are the scars all over them. Knives, mostly, she noted.

"And what brings you to Lone Pine, Warden Aelis?" That was Maurenia, leaning forward as she asked, her hand toying idly with the rim of her mug.

"Assigned by the Lyceum," she replied, "as we all are." She stood suddenly, taken by an impulse to get away, to seem less accessible. "If you'll pardon me, Maurenia and Timmuk." She looked down at Pips, who'd slid off the bench and was clutching her leg. "Oh . . . do allow me to introduce you to Phillipa here—though she is more often called Pips. I daresay she will be a font of questions and a dedicated listener."

Phillipa leaned out and waved at the half-elf and the dwarf, with the latter smiling a great face-crinkling smile at her. Maurenia tried to smile, but it was halfway between "grimace" and "trying to swallow bad wine," Aelis thought.

"Can I see that big crossbow up close?" Pips blurted out before Aelis was out of earshot.

"Well, I'm sure Maurenia can be persuaded once we've let her have a bite to eat and a drink or two."

"Or three or four," the half-elf said, just loud enough for Aelis to hear as she retreated, and she found herself trying not to laugh.

She tried to catch Rus's eye at the bar, but by then the Lashes—with the chance to study them, she realized their features were so similar that they must be brother and sister at least, and possibly twins—had come down and were taking his attention.

Well, she reasoned, *they're paying customers, and I'm not. Best I just get out of the way for now.*

She headed outside to find things on the green and at the crossroads returning to normal. The ridiculous wagon the adventurers had come to town on was too large for any barn or stable, so it stood like a great sleeping dog along the long wall of the inn, with most of the gear that had been strapped to it carted away and the tent in its middle laid flat.

As she walked, she took stock. Flocks were being tended. People were doing whatever they did in gardens and fields. She was headed to her tower, thinking on the report she needed to write.

How am I even going to send it, she wondered, *with no birds? The orrery is for emergencies, and this hardly counts. I suppose I simply write them up and put them on the next post carriage, as if a place like this is likely to see two in a year.*

Aelis squared her shoulders and dismissed the thought. She was the Warden of Lone Pine, and she'd proven it today, and being Warden meant writing reports.

"Feel sorry for yourself another day," she half muttered, half spat as she marched resolutely on.

7

THE BEAR

Aelis was halfway through her report, with one entire closely written page already set aside. Instead of taking the desk onto her lap in a chair, she'd used a table, for benefit of a flat surface to create the tiny, ciphered lettering the Lyceum required in a Warden's official correspondence.

She'd hoped to get the report onto one page, but as she'd formulated it in her mind first, she knew it was going to require a second. So instead of simply relating what had happened with the adventurers and her first official use of power directly against another person, she also described the conditions generally.

Aelis felt as though she was missing details and paused several times to rack her brain for anything she needed to add, coming up empty each time.

She struggled over whether to mention the theft of the book, and twice nearly set the nib of the pen to the paper to include it. In the end, she decided that since she hadn't formulated her official response and begun an investigation, it wouldn't be proper to include it in an official report.

She had a hard time swallowing her own decision, but by the time she'd finished the report, dug wax and a seal from inside her desk, folded the letter and sealed it, stuck it in an envelope and sealed that, it had slipped from her mind.

After all, she reasoned, as she set the report down under a candelabra, *the book may simply have been misplaced.*

As she sat, she massaged her writing hand; making those precise, tiny ciphers had taken months of learning.

She recalled Professor Corbin, who kept his white robes as clean as a saint's conscience and his Diviner's diadem mirror-bright every single day she saw him, leaning over her shoulder and peering close at her first attempt at them.

He'd snorted, snatched up the paper, and held it aloft as an example to the room full of students.

"Were I an Invoker—and I thank the blind god every day that I wield a less clumsy art—I would combust this bit of scrap, because fuel is all it would ever be good for. Each time you form a letter it must be *uniform* in size, do you understand? Each instance of a character must look as precisely like every other instance of a character as is possible *and then some*." Here, Corbin had turned his monocled eye on Aelis's paper and sniffed. His lips were pinched, his cheeks thin to the point of gauntness, as was the rest of him. She'd often thought he was the kind of man who begrudged the world every breath he had to take, every morsel of food he had to eat.

"So far as I can tell, this paper would likely be interpreted as a battle to the death with a vicious flock of chickens, in which forty civilians, give or take, died due to the Warden's actions. Is that what you were assigned to write, Miss de Lenti?"

She sat up straighter, focused her eyes on a far wall, and said, "No, Magister."

"No. Since you are incapable of writing a coherent message, Miss de Lenti, you will go back to practicing characters. Fill a sheet with rows of the first five." It was a humiliating assignment, a first-year student's work, and this had been her third.

Eventually she'd learned that those sorts of humiliations were doled out by small-minded men like Corbin, and Archmagister Ressus Duvhalin, who saw something in her power and her intelligence that made them need to visit their petty miseries on her.

But she never, ever got *used* to it.

Aelis was well on her way to completely forgetting what she'd told herself on her way back to her tower when she heard the sound of a fist pounding hard on the door.

She snatched up her sword and rushed to the door, threw it open.

Outside was one of the village shepherd lads, breathing hard.

"Rus . . . said to come get you, quick," he said, panting. "One o' the lads came stumbling in all bloody, said a bear attacked his flock. Rus says bring a needle n' thread . . ."

Given a task to focus on, Aelis snapped instantly from her self-pity. She buckled on her swordbelt and slipped the dagger onto it, then snatched up her heavy calfskin-and-brass case and hurried out the door, pausing only to throw a simple ward upon it. The boy had not run all the way there as she'd feared; two stout horses were tied at the end of her walkway.

She quickly outpaced the boy to the horses but he caught up as she paused to figure out what to do with her case so she could gain the saddle. Without time to tie it on, and nowhere to affix a rope anyway, she held it out to the boy, who took it, surprised. Once she climbed into the saddle, she took the case back from him.

The boy leapt quickly onto his own horse, clicked his tongue, and it exploded into a long stride and then a gallop. Aelis's mount bolted after it. Only the breathing of the horses and the pounding hoofbeats marked time as the landscape slewed past them, fields turning into gardens and then houses. She saw people gathered outside the inn, including a couple of the armored Thorns, standing in the rough circle crowds always formed.

She slid out of the saddle and almost thumped face-first to the ground as her boots skidded, but she kept her feet and rushed forward, clutching her case to her chest.

"Out of the way," she huffed, "out of the way." The circle parted, and her first impression of what was inside it was blood, far too much blood for the source of it to still be alive. Rus was kneeling at the side of a young boy who was crying hysterically, with his hands flailing away at Rus's arms.

She took the boy's keening wail as a good sign. *A dying body'd not have the energy to scream*, she thought.

She slid to her knees at the boy's other side, across from Rus, who was holding a rag tight against the boy's scalp. "Let me see, let me see," she hissed at him, waving his hands away with one hand while snapping open her case with the other.

There was blood all over the boy's face, obscuring his eyes, and a flap of skin loose along his forehead—the only obvious wound. From her case she snatched a small dark cake, the size of a small bar of soap, smelling strongly of resin and wax. She rubbed the thumb of her left hand along the top of it; wherever her finger touched it, it softened. She snatched the bloody rag from Rus's hand and made a swipe at the blood, then began wiping the waxy, pine-smelling stuff across the wound.

She glanced up, made eye contact with an unfamiliar face. "You," she said firmly, "go fetch clean rags. Freshly laundered. Now!"

The boy was still thrashing and crying. She searched for and found a First Order Charm, a spell of calm and quiet, not as powerful as the overwhelming fatigue she'd laid upon Luth's mind earlier. It was hard to grasp, slippery like an oil-slick stone, without the focus of her wand, but she found it and laid it through her left hand. Instantly, the boy's thrashing ceased and his crying diminished to a weak sob.

"What's your name, lad?" Her voice was as calm and smooth as she could make it.

"Burt," the boy, whom she put at about thirteen, whimpered.

"Well, Burt," she said, "I know this hurts, but if you give it time, it will diminish." She looked back into her case, then back at the wound in his scalp. "That's the only wound I can see; is it the only one you've got?"

"I think so," the boy said.

"Then where's the rest of the blood from?"

"From my flock," the lad muttered as she grabbed a jar from her case with her fingertips and held it toward Rus, miming opening it.

"And it was a bear?"

"Aye. Bear slaughtered some of the sheep . . ."

"Is that how you got hurt?"

"I ran into a tree branch . . ."

Around the circle there was a titter of laughter. Aelis lifted her head and glared; by then, Rus had the jar open, and a pungent stench emanated from it. She dabbed a finger into it and took the minutest bit, then said, "I'm sorry, Burt," and plunged that finger directly into his wound, spreading it around as quickly as she could.

Despite her charm, the boy squirmed and screamed, but then her finger was free and he calmed down almost instantly.

Aelis nodded at the jar and Rus closed it back up, setting it down. The farm lad she'd ordered to get rags returned and set down a pile of clean, fresh smelling cloths, and she took one and began to carefully dab at the blood that had obscured the boy's features.

"Scalp wounds bleed freely, Burt, because the vessels that carry your blood there are quite close to the surface," she said as she worked, and she felt the boy nod under her hand. "So I understand why this frightened you. But they aren't too dangerous, really. You'll come out of this well. Perhaps with a little scar, but what man doesn't feel better about himself with a scar or two?"

Around her she heard the crowd laugh again, but it was a laugh she could live with.

"If someone would fetch us some warm water, and this boy some fresh clothes, I think we can move him indoors," Aelis said as she gently wiped blood away from his eyes. One of his eyelids was nearly crusted shut; with careful strokes of her hand she coaxed it open. The boy's eyes were blue, his gaze faraway.

She nodded to Rus and the two of them helped him stand on unsteady feet. "Water'll get hot fastest in our kitchen," the innkeeper said.

"You walk him in," Aelis said. "I'll be right along." She stood, keeping her bloody hands away from her already likely ruined clothing, and gestured toward the boy. "Please, get my case and that jar."

Then, only just realizing how hard and fast her heart was pounding, she followed Rus and Burt into the inn.

+ + +

By the time she was seated in the inn, with a needle threaded and a pain-dulling infusion working its way through Burt's system, Aelis was calm once more, with only the memory of sweat on her palms. With hot water and rags she had cleared the last of the blood from Burt's head and face and washed her own hands, and now she set to the task of sewing the flap of skin that had been torn free back into place.

"You might be young enough yet not to scar today," she murmured as she worked. The boy's eyes turned toward her, slow to focus. "Even with the tea I've given you, this will sting. I'll count to three and then begin."

Then, without counting a single number, she slipped the needle through the loose edges of skin and drew the wound tightly closed. She leaned close and sniffed; she could still smell the faint tang of the compound she'd rubbed into it earlier.

She made the stitches minute, concentrating on the task with the tip of her tongue held between her front teeth. She felt people crowding around, watching her work, but it was easy to shut them out.

This kind of work, the nonmagical—or only mildly magical—work of an Anatomist, had always come easy to her. It had driven Duvhalin to distraction when she had consistently outperformed all the other students in the basics of suturing, surgery, and dissection.

Her long fingers were nimble, and tasks that relied on their fine use, no matter how complex, had always been a joy. She had outstripped her music tutor at the flute and the whistles by the time she was seven years old, and she could draw, sketch, and paint well enough that her father had brought in a succession of artists as tutors.

The memories, most of them pleasant, had absented her mind and let her fingers attend to their task unencumbered. Before she knew it, the wound was tightly closed and she was snipping the silken thread off.

"If it does scar, you can always let your hair grow long over it," she said, standing up to straighten her neck and back, before bending right back down to peer into the boy's eyes. "Or just wear it boldly. Scars tell a story."

"The story of one who isn't smart enough or fast enough," someone muttered. She glanced over her shoulder as she straightened her back, to find Maurenia, Dashia, and Timmuk, all having settled on the bench across the table from where she sat.

"He's a child," she voiced, barely audibly, back at the half-elf who'd made the remark. Maurenia shrugged.

"Who can tell, with humans?"

Aelis rolled her eyes and looked back to Burt, whose blue eyes were slowly drifting shut. "I think we need to let this one get some rest. Have his parents been fetched?"

Slowly it dawned on Aelis that a bigger crowd than she'd anticipated— perhaps a dozen villagers—had crowded the room. When she said "parents" a thin-faced, compact woman rushed forward and grabbed the boy in her arms, with a wider, slower-moving man rolling along behind her.

"What'd you do with the flock?" the man rumbled, his arms crossed over his chest. Burt feebly stammered an answer while his mother leaned close to stare at the stitches, lifting a finger toward them hesitantly.

Aelis didn't hesitate; her hand shot out and she stopped the woman's grimy hand before she touched her son.

"Pardon, good miss," Aelis said, lowering the woman's hand firmly with her own. "You're going to want to leave those alone. I'll look at them in a week, and then again, and pull them out when I'm ready. In the meantime, don't touch them. Don't allow him to pull at them, or scratch them; cover his hands with mittens if you have to, or just trust that he's a good lad who'll do as he's told."

The man advanced on her, trying to loom over her; he succeeded mostly in watering her eyes with the stink of his body and his breath.

"He still hasn't answered for what he did with the flock," the man insisted, trying to look over her shoulder at the boy. Aelis realized that the village man clearly wanted nothing to do with getting close to her for his own superstitious reasons.

She stepped forward, forcing him to take a step back, his eyes rolling. But it put him out of arm's reach of Burt, which seemed important to her at the moment.

"He did nothing with the flock. Bravely, your boy ran to the village to warn folk of a bear attack upon them. And now you are going to take him home, feed him, put him to bed, and not bother him with any further questions about the sheep. Do you understand?"

"Yes, Warden," the man muttered, turning on his heel and beating a hasty path for the door. Half carrying Burt, the woman went slowly after him, but not before almost apologetically turning to Aelis.

"Thank you, Warden," she mumbled, her darkened cheeks coloring more, "for looking after my son." The crowd melted away behind Burt's parents, leaving just Aelis, the Thorns, and Rus.

"Suppose I have to go bear-hunting now," Aelis said, to no one in particular.

"You know," Maurenia said, casually, slowly, as if savoring the words, "if you're going to go hunt a killer bear—or worse, a mad bear—it sure would help if there was a large, mobile, powerful, accurate arbalest you could use. A *functional* one."

"That would be the case," Rus said from the bar, which he was wiping unnecessarily with a rag, "if people in these parts didn't have a long and deeply held proscription about killing bears."

Aelis felt her heart sink as Rus's words settled over them. She set her needle down carefully, took one of the rags the innkeepers had provided to wipe her hands, and walked over to the bar, gritting her teeth so hard her jaw trembled.

"Please explain," she said slowly and quietly, "what is meant in this case by 'proscription.' Because it seems to me like you meant to say superstition."

"I suppose you could equate the two if you like, Warden," Rus said with a shrug. "But the fact is, if you go killing a bear—even one that's a danger to Lone Pine—the people here'll not go thanking you for it."

"I hear it gets cold here and bear fur is good for that," Aelis replied. "What exactly *would* they do that I should stop dreaming of a bear hide over my bed?"

"You'll not make any friends. People are afraid to touch you now, but you come back with a dead bear, they'll be afraid to cross your shadow, they'll ward themselves with signs every time they see you. None will go near your tower, and none will offer you food, fuel, or house-room should it come to it."

"They're obligated to do those things under the charter . . ."

"...that none of them can read, and most of them know only vague, secondhand rumors about. I am telling you, Warden, if you kill this bear, you'll make life here impossible for yourself."

"I am not even sure if any of the magic I can call upon will *work* on a bear," Aelis said, fighting the urge to throw up her hands and walk away. "Unless we can arrange for someone to kill it, then raise its unquiet spirit or its rotting corpse. Then I'd do just fine."

"Warden," Rus warned, nodding toward the door, where a few people were filtering back inside. "People are listening."

Aelis took another deep breath, closing her eyes and looking for a store of patience she didn't have. "Not being an expert on bears, folks, I could use some advice. It has apparently just eaten well. Is it, like a man would, likely to sleep?"

She heard only a buzzing of low-pitched voices. *Do not let them see frustration. Do not let them see anger. Not now. It is not the time.*

She forced her eyes open and looked at Rus, who shrugged. She looked back at the people and picked out one—the tallest man of the bunch, a wiry, hardy-looking fellow with a big farmer's knife stuck through his belt. "You. What's your name?"

"Con," the man half squeaked.

"Con, what do you know about bears? Have I some time, or do I have to go deal with it immediately?"

The man shrugged. "I don't know. When we've had trouble with a bear in the past, we just started givin' it, ya know . . . the odd sheep, ewes that were past their lambing or an old ram . . ."

"Is this the same bear?"

The man shrugged.

Aelis sighed. *I may need to consult my books before I try to enchant a bear. Surely someone else has tried it.* A moment later a second, more impassioned thought. *You don't have time to do research when lives are at stake.* "Very well. Can someone direct me to where Burt took his sheep to pasture?"

She'd no sooner said the words than Phillipa had materialized at her side, tugging at her sleeve. "I can show you, I know the pastures he uses."

Aelis looked down and carefully plucked her robe from the girl's excited grasp. "I'm not taking you anywhere dangerous." She looked up to the villagers only to find them, to a woman and man, melting out the doors as quickly as they were able without running.

"Looks like the girl is taking you," Maurenia said. "Timmuk and I can come along and provide moral support, if you like. And," the half-elf added as she sauntered toward the bar counter where Aelis stood, "we can make sure no harm befalls the girl if things go badly."

"Aye," Timmuk said, stumping up on his short legs, "and I'm sure you've all heard the joke about only needing to be faster than the dwarf. But," he added, hooking his thumbs in his belt, "should it come to that, local superstition be damned. I'll go down that bear's craw the same way I came into the world; kicking, screaming, and covered in blood."

The loudest, hardest laugh at that came from Pips.

After a quick rush of preparations, but before Aelis knew it, she was heading outside.

"A dwarf, an elfling, a girl, and a wizard walk out of a bar," Maurenia said as they stepped outside. "That seems like the beginning of a joke."

"More like a tragedy," Aelis said. "Wizards don't leave a bar until there's only water left to drink. And not even then if they're a deft enough hand at Conjuring."

"Dwarves wouldn't stop there," Timmuk said. "We'd tear the place down, rebuild it into siege towers, and invest the nearest brewery with them."

"Maybe hundreds of years ago, dwarves would've done that," Maurenia shot back. "Nowadays they'd be more likely to try and buy the lease out from under the publican and raise the rents till the poor bastard had to give the whole concern over, lock, stock, and barrel."

Timmuk sniffed. "They are both kinds of siege warfare, but only one results in hundreds or thousands of dead bodies, all the attendant diseases and horrors . . ."

Aelis tuned them out as she kept a close eye on Pips, who skipped ahead lightly, with no thought of the dangers they might be walking toward. She took stock of their weapons; she had her sword, dagger, and wand, not that either blade was going to help her with a bear. Maurenia had retrieved her bow and wore her sword, while Timmuk had a heavy mace on his belt and walked with an axe clutched in his hand like a walking stick.

She also had time to reflect on the mistake she'd tried to make, one that Urizen had warned her about as both her adviser and as a professor of Enchantments.

"Enchantment is an art, an instinct," the gnome had said in a tutoring session. "And you've got an analytical and bookish mind. Your impulse is going to be to run back to your books and check over the Orders and

Forms, and make certain that you have the right idea. And in a tense moment, when a Charm or a Somnolence or a Dazzlement is going to serve
you best, you've not got the time for that sort of nonsense. You've got to
take wand in hand and *act*."

"I don't think they tell Invokers that," Aelis had muttered. Urizen had
snorted and taken off his spectacles to polish while his clear blue eyes
stared daggers at her from atop his desk.

"Of course they don't. Any fool with a muscle in his head can start a
fight with a handful of fire. A proper Enchanter can stop a fight before it
begins, and harm no one in the bargain. Don't go running to your books
when action will save you or the people you're responsible for!"

That was my first instinct, she told herself. *Well, that's not true. When
Luth wanted to draw down on you, you took care of him, and you did exactly
what Urizen said to do. Took wand in hand, acted.*

But, she countered, *as soon as I heard of a nearby threat and knew I'd have
to deal with it, I wanted to run for the books. And I still don't know if any of my
enchantments will work on a bear.*

Aelis was so lost in her thoughts she lagged a few steps behind, causing
Maurenia to stop, turn, and stare at her. When she met the half-elf's eyes
with her own she felt heat rise in her cheeks and briefly she cursed the
indoor life that had kept her skin paler than it might otherwise have been.

"Maurenia," she said quietly, sidling closer, "if it comes to it, can you
drop a bear with that?" She gestured to the short, tightly curved bow she
carried.

"Depends," Maurenia said, fingering the string.

"On?"

"Black bear, or brown? Boar or sow? If the latter, are there cubs about?
Has it gone Foaming Mad? If you want to be sure of it, let's get the wagon
and reassemble my arbalest."

Aelis shook her head. "Too obvious. The people'll know. If it comes to
it, we'll . . . improvise."

"What'll you do? Conjure another bear?"

"I'm no Conjurer. Even if I were, to Conjure a living animal of that
size . . . it'd be well beyond the grasp of any Conjurer who ever lived outside of a story, surely."

"Trick it with some kind of illusion, then? What scares off a bear?"

Timmuk and Pips had drawn several yards ahead, and the dwarf appeared to be entertaining the girl by making coins appear from behind her ears.

Aelis shifted her eyes back to Maurenia and shook her head. "I'm no Illusionist, either."

"Well, you're an Enchanter. I've seen that much. What else . . . ?"

Aelis cleared her throat and lifted one black-clad arm. "I don't wear this color because of what it does for my complexion."

Maurenia chuckled lightly. "Well, it doesn't hurt. Black suits you. I don't suppose you dabble in fire or lightning?"

"Abjuration."

"Hold a bear off with a ward?"

"Depends on the bear, I suppose."

"Well, that could come in handy. Come on," Maurenia said then, jerking her chin toward where Timmuk and Pips stopped and waited. "They'll start gossiping if we spend any more time whispering."

Aelis laughed, perhaps a bit uncomfortably, at Maurenia's jest, but laughter soon drained out of her as Pips began leading them more intently toward this pasture. They were heading east of the village, putting the afternoon sun behind them and their shadows onto the grass before them.

"It's not too far," Pips called back, her voice light and carefree, as if this was nothing more than an afternoon walk. Aelis felt herself wishing they'd brought the entire company of the Thorns, but then reasoned that two, at least, were likely watching over Luth, leaving only one to safeguard the company's goods.

Be an odd story for adventurers to be robbed blind by farmers, she thought, holding back a laugh. *Imagine the poor dears, limping back to the big city, bereft of coin and goods, weaponless, being consoled after trusting the big bad villagers.*

Aelis amused herself with the fantasy for the next few minutes, but soon enough they'd crested a hill and broken tree cover, with the thin dirt track they were on branching.

And even she could smell the blood on the air.

Pips stood on the edge of the grass, her jaw dropped till her chin neared her chest. Maurenia and Timmuk both brought weapons to hand, instinct taking over. Aelis found her own hand wrapping about the hilt of her sword, for all the good two feet of steel would do against a bear.

The meadow itself was a scene of gore, with parts of at least a half dozen sheep strewn about the grass, which was itself slicked with blood and viscera. The coppery tang of blood and the scent of sheep shit mingled into something nearly overpowering. For a moment, Aelis felt her gorge rising.

No, she told herself. *You are an Anatomist and a Necromancer of the Lyceum, and there is nothing here you have not seen or smelled before.*

And that was true, as far as it went, but the scale of the carnage and the waste of it tugged at her nonetheless. She doubted any family in Lone Pine, much less Burt's, could afford the loss of so much of a flock. Even if only six had been killed, surely the rest were scattered.

"Where is it?" Aelis said aloud. "Moved on? Can we track it? Is it hiding behind those rocks?"

While they were standing there, Pips had casually, slowly drifted back, step by step, till she was hiding behind Aelis's robes.

"Warden," Maurenia said, her voice a pinched whisper, "those aren't rocks."

"Oh," Aelis responded. Then, as she took in the size of the thing, "Fuck."

It was curled up on its side, apparently sleeping off its feast. Brown, with gray here and there, she guessed that the thing would near ten feet if it stood.

"It's got to be over a thousand pounds, and it's not got winter fat on it," Timmuk breathed. "I know many a nobleman'd pay well for that hide in his chambers . . ."

"We're not killing it unless we've no other choice," Aelis said. She settled her sword back in its sheath and stepped forward, shrugging her wand into her hand.

She nearly dropped it, so slick with sweat was the skin of her palm. But she held on and walked forward, reaching for a confidence she didn't feel.

"Elisima," she breathed, "please let this work. And if it doesn't, don't let me die a coward." *Why couldn't the green moon be in a propitious phase?*

She was forty yards from the bear when it sat up, unfolding itself, and snuffled audibly at the air, its great muzzle moving up and down with slight, jerking motions of its neck.

Suddenly the beast scrambled to its feet and turned to face her, moving faster and more nimbly than something that damned big ought to have been able to.

Raising her wand, her mind scrambling for the right Enchantment, she wrapped her right hand around her sword's hilt. *Can't hurt to have a ward ready,* she reasoned.

The bear sniffed at the air some more, dug one of its forepaws into the churned mix of blood and mud beneath it.

Aelis breathed. She tried to recall Urizen's advice, to empty her mind and act.

She lifted her wand. A few plans suggested themselves; putting it to sleep, blinding it, trying to trigger its fears.

A bear doesn't fear anything, she suddenly thought, *except maybe men.*

Her thoughts were almost too scattered to grasp and form into a coherent Order.

Over a half ton of bear casually slouching its way toward her sharpened her focus.

Ultimately what she seized was the simplest and most direct of Enchantments; a Command.

GO HOME, she shouted, silently, with every fiber of her being, wand extended toward the bear. Green flashed in her eyes, like the afterimage from staring at a flame and then turning away from it quickly.

The bear stopped, drew its head back, and snuffled at the air again. It seemed no longer interested in advancing on her, but she didn't know how to read its intentions, even if she could've made out the eyes hidden deep beneath the thick brow ridge and the deep brown fur.

She took a deep breath and lifted her wand, curling her fingers around it till they crossed and overlapped around the rune-carved wood, and poured all of herself into the Command, the single elusive syllable she spoke aloud.

HOME, her power shrieked, like a blast of wind from a hurricane that lasted but a second, with a flash like a strike of green lightning.

The bear regarded her a moment more. Its shoulders rippled and shifted, and for a moment she feared it meant to leap, or at least to stand and show its full height.

Then, casually, it turned and walked away, its enormous clawed feet tearing the dirt, leaving behind prints Aelis could've planted both boots in with room on all sides. In the stillness after it departed, shambling over a rise, the smells and sights of the pasture returned, the stink of death, of coppery blood, and the strong animal scent of the bear itself threading through all of it.

"That was damned brave." Timmuk was first among them to find his voice. "Didn't know a bear could *be* enchanted."

"What you know about magic wouldn't fill up a thimble," Maurenia said, and Aelis only just stopped herself from pointing out how true that was about everyone but a wizard.

It helped that she was nearly bowled over by Pips, who ran to cling to her leg and side, hitting her with the force of something twice her size.

"Of course it can! Our Warden can enchant anyone and anythin', your man Luth or a bear or a monster or a dragon if she wants!"

Aelis wasn't quite sure how to respond to the young girl's exuberance. She settled on an awkward arm draped around her thin shoulders and took a careful step.

"No need for boasting, Pips," she said, flattered. She was about to take her arm off the girl's shoulder when she was struck with a sudden dizziness; she had to press down in order to keep herself upright.

"Are you well, Warden?" Aelis didn't think the concern in Maurenia's voice was so much for her own well-being as for the possible inconvenience if she passed out. Regardless, the dizziness passed and she waved a hand to stop the advancing half-elf in her tracks. She pulled herself upright and nodded in confirmation.

"Fine. Just . . . spent a lot of my power today, on Luth, now the bear. Four Orders' worth of Enchantment at least; not regularly taxed that way. I'll be fine. Need some sleep tonight."

"Ah, but then tonight you'll miss our tale," Timmuk said as he turned back toward the setting sun, once again swinging his axe before him like a walking stick. "A tale of dread monsters faced down, of grave danger overcome . . ."

She let the dwarf's voice fall into a background drone that made the walk back to the village pass in a haze.

8

THE BED

"How much for a bed?"

Rus blinked. "If you just need a place to fall in for a few hours and get some rest, we'd charge you nothing, Warden. Let me get a key to one of the empty rooms."

"No," Aelis said. "I mean how much for a bed, an entire bed, the best one you can spare, carted up to my tower. Permanently."

"You want to buy one of our beds?"

"Have I been unclear? I'm tired of sleeping in a folding camp chair. All I've got otherwise are stone tables and those'll be no better."

As Rus hesitated, she sighed. "Rus, please. Name your price. Make it fair. I will pay it on delivery and I'll do it today. In hard coin."

"Wasn't cheap to ship the bedding up here."

"I won't need blankets, pillows, or quilts. Just the mattress and the frame."

Rus licked his bottom lip. Aelis took it as the universal sign of the man calculating his claim.

"A gold tri-crown."

"Make it happen in the next two hours and I'll pay two and tip the men who cart it up in silver."

Rus frowned, raised a finger as if to protest. Aelis cut him off by raising her own hand. "Don't mistrust your luck, man. Just do it."

"That's a lot of money, Warden . . ."

To you, she almost said, but checked herself at the last moment. "I am not without my own private resources," she said, deciding in the end it sounded better than saying *My father is the Count de Lenti and I could draw enough money from the Urdimonte bank on that fact alone to purchase your inn for twice its real value.*

Rus finally decided to take her at her word and stuck out his hand. They shook. The swordsman's callus on his hand was unmistakable, as was the strength of his grip.

Aelis set off on the long, winding walk home.

She was halfway there before, in a haze, she realized that she'd thought of the rickety tower as "home," but she lacked the energy to think much on what that signified. By the time the tower swam into her sight she was trudging, one foot in front of the other.

"Overextending yourself in Orders in too little time is dangerous," she remembered one lecturer saying. A man, not much older than she was now, though this had been her first year at the Lyceum. He was making his first attempt at a proper wizard's beard but what he'd managed was barely a wisp along his chin and jaw and but small patches on his cheeks.

She hadn't found him terribly credible, but she'd be forced to admit that there might have been something to what he had to say in this particular moment, as her limbs turned leaden and her mind filled with clouds.

"Onoma's cold tits, I haven't even been drinking," she muttered. She tried to recall more of the lecture as she plodded on.

"For example, an average wizard should attempt no more than eight Orders' worth of magics in their primary school in one day until their reflexes and the spiritual pathways they rely on are built up over the years to withstand more. And certainly in a secondary or the rare tertiary school, no more than three to five Orders in any one day . . ."

"Well," Aelis said aloud, to her own memory of the teaching assistant whose name was lost to her, "good thing I'm no ordinary fucking wizard then, eh?" She gave her head a shake and walked the rest of the way to the tower without being waylaid by either her own weariness or her memory.

When she got there, she dispelled the ward she'd left on the door; it had weakened to the point where it would have done little more than annoy anyone who tried to brush past it. Still, no one had.

"Progress," she said as she shut and barred the door behind her, frowning at the way it hung crooked in the frame. "Well, I'm no carpenter," she said, once more to no one in particular, and strode away, busying herself with making space for a bed.

Once done, she scanned the horizon, but there was no sign of a wagon or a cart or any conveyance that could haul a bed up to her tower. Her feet throbbed, her head was beginning to ache, and her limbs were still heavy, so she guided herself to the chair she'd been sleeping in and sat down.

It seemed just minutes later that she was jolted out of sleep by a heavy pounding on her door, but given the dark inside the tower it must've been some time. She cursed and sprang to her feet, running for the door.

She opened it and was startled to find Maurenia's slim, cloaked figure standing in the falling dark. The jingle of harness drew her eyes down the walkway to where one of the company's draft horses was hitched to a small cart, into which was loaded a disassembled bed.

"Didn't take you for a carter," was all Aelis could think to say before placing her fist in front of her mouth to block an enormous yawn.

"Well, your man Rus wasted an hour trying to find someone who'd take your coin," Maurenia said. "Soon as he explained the particulars, that they'd have to actually come into the tower and deal with you personally, volunteers dried up faster than a Grave Maiden."

Aelis chuckled, but something in the half-elf's words stung. "I patched up one of their own lads and drove off a bear that, apparently, would've been allowed to slaughter them wholesale and they still won't come to my door." The words came out in a rush, and Aelis felt embarrassed by them.

Maurenia shrugged. "At least none of them made warding signs with their first and littlest fingers. Progress?"

"Well, I've only been here a week. At this rate, they'll speak to me without calling in a priest or clutching charms in, what . . . a year?"

Maurenia snorted and waved a hand. "Come on. Let's get this inside."

"Just a moment. Give me a chance to make some light."

Aelis didn't bother with candles, lighting only her alchemy lamp, with as wide and bright a setting as she could coax out of it, and setting it near the front door. Elisima's moon was a sliver in the sky, its phase almost ended, with Anaerion's dominating the clear night and casting a faint ruddy glow over the landscape.

Maurenia had thrown back her hood, and the moonlight seemed to bring the red in her hair to the fore, giving it the color of an Invoker's robe. Aelis took a deep breath and followed her to the wagon.

Quickly and capably they carried all the pieces up. It was a simple thing, made of thinly stained wood; four pieces held together by old, splintery pegs and three slats that went across the middle of it. It sat only half a foot off the floor on thick, unadorned posts.

Carrying the mattress up the walkway proved a little more difficult.

"It occurs to me," Aelis said, halfway up the walk, as they both struggled to keep the thing aloft, "that it would've been easier to un-stuff the ticking, carry it in, then restuff and sew it shut."

"I'm no seamstress," Maurenia said contemptuously. "Are you?"

That seemed to provide the spark they needed to wrestle the straw-stuffed thing into the room and toss it onto the frame. It hadn't much of its shape left, but Aelis reasoned that could be dealt with later.

She turned from looking at the results of their labor to find Maurenia standing with her hand extended.

"Well," the half-elf said, "you weren't going to try and stiff me on the promised payment, were you? Two tri-crowns for the innkeep and an unspecified amount of silver for the 'men' who carted it up here."

Aelis reached for the purse that hung at her belt, prying it open with two fingers and pulling free a handful of coins. Gold gleamed brightly in her palm, and she pulled three coins—round, thin, larger than the silver that surrounded them and stamped with three crowns on one side and the columns of the Estates House on the other—and handed them over.

"Do what you will with the difference between the silver and the gold," she said. "I'm too tired of sleeping on a chair to care."

"Three tri-crowns is a princely sum for a worn-out bed, even including the delivery. Where does a Warden—those notoriously spartan wizard-justices—learn to be so free with coin?"

Aelis shrugged and sat down heavily on the mattress. It shifted under her weight, with air blowing through the ticking and straw threatening to poke its way clear. *Still an improvement over a chair*, she told herself, only to be surprised as Maurenia sat down next to her.

"If I were to guess, I'd say it's because your father is the Count of Tirraval. You *did* say your name was Aelis de Lenti, yes?"

"I did say that," Aelis replied, drawing the syllables out slowly, surprised that the half-elf had picked up on it. *No reason to make yourself a liar.* "And your guess would be correct. Stay abreast of your lineages and holdings, do you?"

"Well, you didn't use the final honorific in your name, so it was just a guess," Maurenia said, turning toward Aelis and grinning. The slight upward curve of her lips changed the symmetry of her features, just slightly. It highlighted her cheekbones and shifted the sharp line of her hair against her jawline.

Aelis found it took an effort to pay attention to Maurenia's words.

"But keeping track of the families with Imravalan holdings is something of a hobby of mine, I suppose. I didn't know Count Guillame had a daughter gone to the Lyceum."

"Well, it's hardly gossip of the top drawer now that five years have passed. Besides, it's not as if it were a scandal. As the youngest of four, I am distant enough from succession for it to be of little worry, and having chosen the Lyceum, I will not cost my father a dowry."

"But you didn't just choose the Lyceum," Maurenia pressed. "You chose the *Wardens*. You could have become a researcher, a teacher, immediately become some margrave's Court Wizard. Why?"

Aelis smiled faintly. "I don't believe in half measures. Real wizards become Wardens, and Wardens are the real wizards, aye?" Then she shrugged. "I could've done those things. And then I would've wondered if I truly had it in me."

"Had what?"

Aelis struggled to come up with an answer. "*It*," she said. "The quality, whatever it is, that makes a Warden, as opposed to some timid associate professor of something who never moves beyond teaching introductory classes, or a Diviner who spends her life reading cards for noblewomen in the salon, or with her hands buried in birds' entrails, trying to augur a good match for a knight's bucktoothed, walleyed son."

Maurenia laughed, lightly, musically. "So it's about testing yourself, then? Adventure? Learning your own qualities? I would've thought that noble obligation might factor into it."

Aelis thought of her shock and horror on the day that the Warden postings were announced, at how she'd scrambled for explanations, for a way out of her assignment. At just how much she dreaded her daily walks to the village and the reek of sheep shit and the drudgery of what little work she'd found to do.

"No," she answered flatly, "it doesn't."

"You should've just taken your degrees and joined some pioneers, then."

"To do what? Fight monsters, dig for trinkets in the ruins of once-great holdings? Steal gold and silver out from under the noses of the orcs?" Even as she spoke the words, she regretted them. Maurenia turned away, but behind the neatly cut curtain of auburn hair, Aelis could read the hurt in the set of her jaw.

"Is that all you think we do? Sure, we risk our health and our minds for riches . . . but we are blazing the trail to Ystain to grow again. Settlers will follow the paths we're laying, when the time comes. And besides . . ." The half-elf turned back toward her and Aelis found herself caught in the bright optimism of her green eyes. "If you want to test yourself, there's no better place. The frontier doesn't even *try* to kill you; it doesn't need to; it just will. If you're weak, if you're slow, if you're dumb, it'll just happen."

"I like my bed and my hearth at night," Aelis said. "I like walls and streets and people . . ."

". . . but not cow-paths and muddy cart tracks, not crumbling stone towers and simple farmer folk, am I right?" Maurenia poked Aelis's arm with one finger. "You're a city girl. I can tell. And you're at a loss out here."

Aelis rocked to one side from the sharp poke, then rubbed at the spot on her arm. "That's true. I hoped for a post to Antraval, Tirraval . . . any place with good cellars and streetlights, really."

"Why didn't you get it?" Perhaps as an apology, Maurenia briefly rubbed her fingertips over the spot she'd poked as she turned to face Aelis directly. Though it was only a moment, warmth spread from the half-elf's fingers and up Aelis's arm and shoulder to her neck.

"I don't know," Aelis said, picturing Archmagister Ressus's smug, satisfied face.

"Perhaps there's something in the landscape your schools are suited to?" Maurenia's voice took an encouraging tone, and she leaned a bit closer.

"I'm a Necromancer first, an Enchanter and Abjurer second and third, in whatever order you like. Have you *seen* a musty old crypt full of the unquiet dead? If so, please do point it out to me."

"I've not," Maurenia said. "But Timmuk way well have. He was a map collector before his family fortunes changed. Like as not there's plenty he could tell you about the surrounding area."

"My warrants don't extend to the frontier unless the pursuit of my duties takes me there," Aelis answered.

"It's a shame. Many a company could use an Anatomist, especially one that stitches as well as you, not to mention an Abjurer. Timmuk has even spoken of trying to fit the wagon with a laboratory in order to attract an alchemist, but I suppose that's just talk."

"You wouldn't want to run a calcination oven on a wooden wagon anyway," Aelis said. "The temperatures it reaches could make the wood combust."

"Set it on a steel plate and keep buckets of sand handy," Maurenia countered. "Everything can be accounted for with the right planning."

Everything except where I am and what I'm feeling, Aelis thought, but once again, didn't say. They lapsed into silence for a moment. Aelis's awareness of the woman sitting next to her grew, the smell of her body—leather, metal, wind, sun, and soap all mingled together—and its heat, her weight on the mattress.

Then Maurenia stood, and Aelis as well, clumsily. For a moment they bumped against each other, nearly face to face, or face to chin, as the half-elf stood a couple of inches taller than Aelis. They quickly stepped apart, but Aelis knew that she was flushed, and she thought, for a moment, that Maurenia was as well.

"Will you come down to the inn? There'll be tales—Timmuk loves an audience. And Dashia and Darent have lovely voices, if they can be coaxed into singing. I've no doubt there are a number of musicians among the folk here . . ."

Aelis shook her head before she even knew what she was answering. "I'm for bed. Been a long day . . ."

". . . and you can't mingle with the people you're set to protect, and, need be, to judge. Understandable. Good night then, Warden Aelis. Will you be down in the village tomorrow?" Aelis thought that Maurenia's eyes, the set of her mouth, were showing a guarded hope of some kind, one that she'd only just stopped herself from voicing.

"If no one delivers any breakfast, I expect so. Be walking about, looking for places to stick my hand in and do some work."

"Well then, perhaps I'll see you. I imagine we'll stay a handful of days . . . Timmuk likes to spread coin around in every village, make sure everyone sees us."

"Perhaps," Aelis said. "Good night. A safe drive under Anaerion's moon."

Maurenia nodded and strode toward the door. She gave a backward glance, her eyes hidden in the dark and by the fall of her hair.

With the door shut and latched, Aelis busied herself in digging out bedding and smoothing out the worst lumps on the hay-stuffed mattress. Then she took her alchemy lamp and Aldayim to bed, and wondered why exactly it was that a half-elf adventurer flustered her so.

9

THE SWORD

Aelis woke up sweating, with the blanket tangled around her legs. She had dreamed of Humphrey, of the hard muscles of his arms and chest under her hands, of his reticence and her enthusiasm when their tryst had initially begun, of how quickly he had learned.

There'd been an element of competition; Miralla had once remarked to her how attractive she found Humphrey when they were all first-year novices. That, as much as Humphrey's own sterling qualities, had been impetus enough for Aelis to bed him first.

In her dream, though, whenever she'd finally peeled his robes off and been about to have him, he'd changed to Maurenia, clad in her studded leather and watching her with one immaculate eyebrow raised, her lips in a fine and kissable grimace.

"Well, I could lie here and try to catch that dream again," she said, pulling up the blanket haphazardly and then flinging off her nightshirt and wishing for a cool breeze, "or I could dress and see to some of my sword exercises. Wouldn't do to have my arms getting weak. Lavanalla would thrash me if she even suspected it."

For a moment, she pondered her elven swordmistress. Certainly, by any standard, she was beautiful, with her high cheekbones, golden hair, and fine features. She was perhaps the only elf Aelis had known to any personal degree, but something about her power, her position, her gravitas, had put paid to anyone's notion of trying it on with her.

She missed the understanding that had developed between her, Miralla, and Humphrey. They'd never really done more than pretend that what they had was meant to pass the time at school as pleasantly as could be managed. There were awkward goodbyes and promises to write between them, but Aelis thought if she was ever going to exchange letters with either of her former lovers it would be Miralla, whose mind had been more of a match to her own.

She made use of her washstand and basin, then dressed and took up sword and dagger before going to her door in hopes of food.

Aelis threw open the door and startled the goat that was standing just outside. He bleated at her before clattering down the walk. She was sure it was always the same one; it had the same gray coat, the same whiskers, the same curled horns.

"Stregon as my witness, if I were an Invoker you'd be a dead gods-damned goat," she yelled after it, raising her fist and half drawing her sword. Then she looked down and saw what had attracted the goat; a bas-ket, enticing her nose with the scent of fresh bread.

"If that goat ate my breakfast, I am going to kill it, and then I am going to reach into Aldayim's forbidden lore, bind and raise it, and spend the next week killing it *again*," she swore. She bent down and twitched the nibbled cloth aside.

Everything in the basket—two round brown loaves, a stone bowl of butter and a smaller one of cheese—seemed untouched. Her stomach lurched and she had a loaf halfway to her mouth before she thought of Lavanalla's cold-eyed stare.

"After exercise," she said, carrying the basket inside and setting it down on a table.

The sun had dispelled most of the night but the red moon still flanked it. The green was no longer visible even as the waning sliver it had been, and, as she glanced at her orrery, she expected Onoma's moon to rise.

She walked over to the table where that contraption of silver, brass, and crystal glided in its silent song and cast a simple, unfocused First Order necromantic spell into it. She felt the buffer inside it give and then absorb most—but not all—of the power.

"Hmm. Could probably let it go a couple of days at this point."

Then she seized up her swordbelt and the heaviest leather vest she owned and went outside in search of a suitably flat and secluded spot, warding the door shut behind her.

Aelis spent a good hour working up a sweat. She began by simply roll-ing her shoulders and swinging her arms, jogging in place to get her blood moving. Then, hoping that no one was watching, she brought out her sword and began her exercises. First, guards, moving from low to high, right and left hands both. Then, still switching hands every five or so rep-etitions, she practiced her first steps, short and great, back, forward, to either side.

Forget the sagas. Forget the courtly entertainments. A fight is won and lost on first steps. Speed and determination.

Speed and determination had been the elven Archmagister's watchwords. Well, Aelis reflected, *that, and telling me my first step had gotten me killed.*

She practiced each first step a dozen times, then a dozen times again. It wasn't until she already felt sweat plastering strands of hair to her forehead that she even began practicing cuts. Her weapon, with its willow-leaf blade, was not made for thrusts, but she practiced those too. She moved from short cuts to longer sweeps and back, stepping into each attack and feeling her muscles move in ways they'd become unaccustomed to on the long ride to Lone Pine. The movements came back to her, her feet and hips and arms moving in concert with the blade, sweeping it fast enough to cut the air.

Got to get out here every morning, she chided herself.

Ideally, she would've been making wards, either with her free hand or the hand that held the blade, and working in concert with them. But after yesterday's exertions, she didn't want to push herself too far again today, though Abjurations, in general, required less power than an Enchantment.

To make magic interfere with the natural order of the world—to create a Ward or Summon Fire or Throw Lightning—one must only convince the inert stuff of that natural order to be other than it is. To enchant the mind of a living thing, a wizard must do considerably more.

Aelis easily recalled Urizen's first lecture on Elathan Tilarus's *Enchanting,* the standard text for the first two years of instruction at the College. A densely written and weighty tome, Tilarus had seemed, to Aelis's undergraduate certainty, entirely too concerned with proving the difficulty of Enchantment as opposed to other College disciplines.

Someone had Abjurer envy, she remembered joking with Miralla and Humphrey over wine more than once. But after yesterday's exertions, the most complicated Enchantments she'd ever cast in such a short time were weighing on her. There'd been the exertions of the previous days to consider as well. She'd been free with her wards and pouring a First Order Necromantic charge into her orrery each day since she'd set it up.

Aelis dismissed her reminiscence and chided herself for weakness. She prescribed another dozen of every guard, step, attack, and parry.

By the time she was done she was well soaked, and the moons were invisible behind the sun's brightness and the hard distant blue of the sky.

She sheathed her sword, kept a wary eye for goats, and devoured the meal that had been left for her. With that done, her "rooms" as tidy as they were likely to get, and the upper floor still too much of a challenge and a hazard, she wasn't sure what to do with herself.

She went to her writing case and dug out the list of items she'd made.

1. *Ask Rus about Dalius.*
2. *Find out who in Lone Pine is lettered.*
3. *Keep an eye out if merchants come to town.*
4. *Prepare draft statement warning merchants if anyone tries to sell books to them.*
5. *Get the fucking door fixed.*
6. *Make goat stew.*

Biting her lip and frowning at the paper produced no tangible results. She smoothed the wrinkled sheet out atop the writing case's inclined leather blotter. "I can do one and two in the same go if I wander down to the village," she muttered. "Should've done them yesterday." Something about doing that stung wrong, though. Obviously someone in Lone Pine was warming to her; the bread, butter, and cheese she'd just eaten were proof enough of that. But going down to the village, milling around, looking for work to do like a day laborer?

Or, said a little voice, *are you just avoiding Maurenia?*

She shook her head, sighed heavily, and decided that item four was immediately actionable. She took out ink, pen, and parchment, and set about drawing up something suitably circumspect.

Attention Traders and Merchants: If in the village of Lone Pine and its surroundings, anyone attempts to pawn or sell a copy of Wards and Combat Abjurations for Sword and Axe, *I must insist on being informed immediately. It is not a rare nor a Controlled text, but its appearance in this region would be irregular. I am prepared to reimburse any outlay made for a genuine copy that you acquired in recent days, and moreso for one of particular description.*
—Aelis de Lenti, Warden of Lone Pine

It felt odd to leave the last honorific of her name out of her signature, and to regard herself as something other than Aelis de Lenti un Tirraval, the count's daughter, the student at the Lyceum.

Aelis regarded her copy and frowned. It didn't immediately reveal the theft, which would be a sign of weakness. A suitably alert peddler or trader would almost certainly see through the ruse and deduce what had happened, but she was counting on the promise of remuneration to override suspicion.

She set about making multiple copies, careful with each one. The monotony of the work set her mind temporarily at ease. She stopped thinking about the village, about Dalius, about Luth's aggression, the Thorns in general and Maurenia in particular, about the oddness of her encounter with the bear, of everything except the task of scratching the letters into the sheets of parchment with her pen. When she'd half a dozen copies sanded to let the ink dry, she got out her wax and seal. She was entitled to use the Lyceum seal in black, green, or blue.

"Blue," she said aloud as she held it over a candle to warm and positioned her seal. "Blue is the one they're likely to respond to best, even if unconsciously. I'll save black for when I want to terrify someone."

Given that black was the dominant theme of the clothing hanging in her wardrobe, she wasn't sure she hadn't already made that choice.

"Well, the merchants don't need to know that." She didn't, of course, know of any merchants in the region, or what they sold. "Surely there are some, though. Peddlers, at least, that kind of thing." She looked to her writing case and the pile of notes she'd taken from her one interview with Dalius.

"The book going missing coupled with him never turning up again . . . I mistrust it," she said. "And I don't trust a word he said to me of the gossip and the misshapen family trees, and wouldn't know what to make of it if I did," she added.

When each letter was folded and sealed, she set them on the table near her orrery. "I'll have to take them down to Rus eventually," she muttered. She decided to put on her formal robes and had just seized the letters, intending to head out to do just that, when she opened the door to find a startled Pips about to knock.

The girl was carrying a leather sack slung over one shoulder and a heavy sloshing skin in one hand.

"Warden," she squeaked, startled at Aelis's sudden appearance. "I've brought you a midday meal. Bread, cheese, and beer. Oh, n' Rus said to tell me if you wanted to come down for dinner or have it brought up."

Aelis took the sack and skin from the girl and carried them inside. She looked back to see Pips standing on the threshold, wringing her hands.

She waved a hand and the girl took one hesitant step forward, then practically danced into the ground floor of the tower. She watched as Phillipa's eyes bugged out as she tried to take in everything she saw all at once: Aelis's sword and dagger on the table by the letters; the orrery and other implements on the other table; the piles of books; even the incongruous bed set up in the middle of the left side of the tower.

"Haven't you any chores to attend to?"

"This one," Pips answered with a shrug, gesturing vaguely toward the bag Aelis held and then letting her eyes roam again. She couldn't stop her hand from reaching out toward the sword; Aelis set the sack and skin down and hurried over to cover it with her own hand.

"You don't want to touch an Abjurer's sword if you are not one yourself," Aelis said. "You never know what wards lie in wait."

"Wards? Would it turn me to a frog? Or cook me with lightning? Or just blow me up like a corked bottle dropped in a fire? Or . . ."

Aelis raised a hand to forestall the line of, she had little doubt, increasingly gruesome fates Pips had in mind, and the girl quieted instantly. "No. None of that," Aelis said. "To do any of those, I'd have to be a Conjurer or an Invoker, and I'd have to put so much of my power into a ward that I could scarce cast anything else the rest of the day."

"Oh." The girl was clearly disappointed, her features falling and her eyes drifting toward the toes of Aelis's boots. She perked right back up, though, with another question as she lifted her eyes. "What *could* you do with a ward?"

"I could scramble your mind, make you forget yourself and what you meant to do, put you to sleep . . ." *Strip years from your life, rip your essence from your body, and turn you into my undead servant,* Aelis thought. *But I wouldn't.* Some part of her wanted to impress the girl with her power, but any further explanation of what a Necromancer could do was more likely to just frighten her.

"More importantly," Aelis said, "I can make it so that the sword can't be drawn from the sheath by anyone else."

That seemed to get the girl's attention, as her mouth opened slightly. "Could you show me that? Or . . . or anything?"

"You saw me perform two complicated Enchantments yesterday, you know," Aelis said.

"I know, but it just . . ." She waved her hands as if trying to demonstrate the impossibility of saying exactly what "it" was. "It's so boring. Almost nothin' happens here. There's just sheep and goats and diggin' carrots in the dirt and I can't damn well stand it . . ."

"Phillipa! Watch your language!" Aelis was taken aback at how quickly and easily the reproach came, and instantly regretted it when she saw the girl's expression fall and her cheeks color.

She turned and started to slump toward the door. "Pips," Aelis said, trying not to sound sheepish, "I'm . . . sorry I yelled." *Be direct, be honest, don't talk down to her. She'll know.* Aelis only had to reach back to her own childhood to remember how awful it had been when adults had clearly lied to her. "I've no right to scold you or correct you. That is for your uncles."

"Well," Pips said, a mischievous smile suddenly curling the corners of her lips upward, "they don't give a shit what I say."

Aelis couldn't help herself; she burst out laughing and the girl joined her, then suddenly Pips ran forward and hugged her around the waist. The impulse to wrap her arm around the girl's shoulder took her by surprise, but she gave in to it, and together they laughed for a moment longer. "Why don't you come and have lunch with me," Aelis said.

"I already had my midday bread, but all right," Pips said. Aelis took up the food that had been brought and quickly cleared space on a table. On the way to it, though, Phillipa's eyes wandered again, this time caught by the orrery, which made a soft sound as the moons subtly shifted positions.

"What is that?" The girl lifted a hand and pointed.

"An orrery."

"What's it for?"

Aelis walked to the side of the table where she could stand over it. She lifted a hand. "Here is the earth, the orb we live upon . . ."

"How d'we live on somethin' round without that we fall off?"

"Magic," Aelis answered quickly. She had only ever been an indifferent student of astronomy and had no desire to try explaining it to anyone, much less a largely unlettered child. "It shows the movement of our world in relation to the six moons . . ." Here her finger moved from hovering over the faceted blue crystal to each of the smaller, differently colored moons, naming each one in turn.

"And why d'you need t'know that?"

"It bears on the casting of spells and the potency of magic," Aelis said. "Magic gets stronger or weaker depending on the phases of the moon it corresponds to, and sometimes with the phases of opposing moons."

"So your spells get weaker n' stronger with the moons? Is that why the songs and tales of wizards and wardens always mention them?"

"I suppose it could be," Aelis said. *I need to apologize to my astronomy and my literature professors*, she thought, remembering the too-few hours spent laboring over the books on those subjects, certain they'd never come up once she was a Warden.

"Does it run like this forever?"

"Nothing," Aelis said, "can run forever. That is one of the first rules we learn. Nothing, whether made by the skill of a person's hands or by the craft of their magic, can run indefinitely. Everything has only the amount of power we give it."

"Well, couldn't someone just give a spell enough power to last forever?"

Aelis shook her head. "No. And even if we could, why would we want to? Things can't last forever, Pips. Nothing does, for good reason."

"Well, doesn't a water mill keep turnin' as long as the river flows? Or a windmill, if there's always wind?"

"But there isn't always wind, and there isn't always water, and sometimes there's too much, and wind and water mills both can be destroyed that way. And even if the wind and the water stayed constant, eventually, just by working nonstop, the wood and the metal and the cloth and the rope holding such things together would fall apart," Aelis said.

"But what if you used magic to hold it all together?"

"If one were to employ wards to hold the parts together—and renewed them every day—then I suppose a machine like that could last a while longer, but nothing like forever."

All her talk seemed to have confounded the girl, who looked back to the orrery. "How does this run, then?"

"I power it, a little bit each day, with a small spell. Slowly, the magic builds up inside and keeps it running along with the phases of the moons, so long as it is properly set when activated."

"But it would eventually stop runnin'?"

"Aye," Aelis answered. "As will all things."

"How long could you keep it runnin'? Like, say you were to pour in as big a spell as it could handle . . ."

"A wizard's orrery is designed to only accept so much magic at a time. Enough to run it for a week, perhaps, and no more," Aelis said.

"Why?"

She shook her head, pulling free one of the two round loaves in the sack, and holding half of it out to the girl. "Too much to explain." She brought two stools over to the stone table, on the farthest end from the orrery, and sat down, while Pips climbed onto the second and took the offered bread.

"Why's it too much to explain?"

"Because it involves a lot of complicated magical theory that I don't know if you could understand . . ."

At this the girl's face fell again. Aelis was astonished at how expressive the girl's features were; the merest hint of a slight or of a disappointing answer and the girl's eyes would fall to the ground, her mouth descend into a frown, her entire posture slump. Growing up the child of a nobleman had made Aelis conscious of constant observation, and the necessity of steady composure had been impressed upon her from a young age.

"And because it involves a Warden's secrets . . . and those I *cannot* tell you," Aelis added, leaning forward and dropping her voice into a conspiratorial whisper.

At this, Pips brightened considerably, sitting up straighter and lifting her eyes as she tore at the bread with her teeth. They ate in silence for a few moments before Aelis remembered the day before.

"So, Pips; do you want to learn to read?"

The girl shrugged. "Uncle Elmo says it's devilish hard—he had to learn when he was in the army, says he had to not only learn letters n' sums but also ciphers."

"Oh? Was he a quartermaster?"

The girl shook her head, stuffing a wad of bread into one cheek with her tongue to clear up space to answer. "Scout. Said he had to report orc strength and learn how t'send and leave messages in cipher. Said he never wants to look at another book the rest of his life, nor a pen and ink or a charcoal stick."

"Well, regardless of what Uncle Elmo says, do *you* want to learn?"

"Why should I?"

"You said nothing happens here. Sheep and goats and carrots, right?" Aelis shrugged. "Learn your letters, and books make the world that much bigger."

"There's naught but two books in the entire village, and Rus owns them both. I saw him readin' one and he snapped it shut and told me it wouldn't do for children."

Aelis frowned. "Is there no priest in town?"

"We get a circuit rider now 'n then. Priest of Stregon. I expect he'll make it here sometime next year."

"Well," Aelis said, eating a last bit of a dry, crumbly cheese that she suspected was past its best date, "there are considerably more than two books in the village now." She stood up and beckoned the girl after her, toward the nooks in which she'd stored her library.

The girl wandered over, still nibbling a crust. Her eyes widened, but only faintly. "How many's that?"

"Two dozen," Aelis answered.

"Are they books of spells? Grimmaws?"

"Six of them are grimoires, yes," Aelis said, gently correcting the girl's pronunciation, thinking that in truth, there was one fewer than two dozen and only five grimoires. "Three are histories—one of each of the kingdoms—and two are collections of all that is certain about the orcs, their ways, alliances, chieftains, and the islands they came from, and the lost territories. There's the official history of the Wardens, and two books on the lives of famous Wardens—"

"You mean there are stories about wizards?" Once more Aelis was startled by the expressiveness of the girl's face, the wide, hopeful eyes and the mouth ready to break into a smile. "Could you read them to me?"

"I could," Aelis said, "or I could teach you to read—and that would serve you better."

The girl's face scrunched up in trepidation. "Do I have to? Couldn't you just read them . . ."

"Phillipa, if I agreed just to read them to you, you would hear the stories and perhaps remember some of them, but if I were gone, or I had no time, or my duties called me away, they'd just be so much ink and parchment to you," Aelis said. "If I taught you to read them, you could read them at any time, you could take them into you in a way so that no one could ever take them away. The stories would be yours to remember and to read again—as would every story that's ever been written down. You could write your own stories, if the mood took you."

"How many stories is that?" The girl's face screwed up in severe calculation.

Aelis shrugged. "More than I could name. More than anyone could read in a life, probably."

Pips sighed heavily, a martyr heading to her doom. "Fine. I'll try . . . but would you read me a story for each day we work?"

"I'll read you *part* of a story," Aelis said as she bent down to her bookshelves, scanning the spines with eyes and fingers both. She lingered over *The Fighting Wardens*, thinking of the grisly battle scenes described within. *The woodcuts of Daevar impaling his foes upon his conjured animated spears might be a bit much for the child*, she thought, before selecting *Lives of the Wardens: The Good, the Great, and the Grim*, and pulled it free.

"Let's start by learning of Dahja the Gray, shall we?" *If you'd wanted to be a teacher, why did you become a Warden*, Aelis asked herself silently.

Oh, she answered, dismissing the worry, *how hard can it be?*

✦ ✦ ✦

"It is so fucking hard," Aelis breathed as she shut the door behind Pips an hour or two or twenty, she wasn't entirely sure, later. "How does anyone stand a roomful of them at a grammar school? How does anyone stand *two* of them in a nursery?"

She leaned her back against the door, taking a deep, resigned breath. After endless frustration at trying to get Pips to read words and sentences, Aelis had ultimately settled on basic letter shaping and sounding, using their own two names as a basis. By the end, the girl had been able to scratch out something resembling both of their names, and identify each letter in them. Aelis had sent her home with her third-best pen, a tiny stick of ink, and two sheets of her roughest parchment, with instructions to practice forming letters.

As a consequence, Aelis had been obliged to read aloud the story of Widraw the Invoker from *Lives of the Wardens*, putting up with both her own indignation at the ridiculous depiction of magic—the Invoker calling down columns of fire the size of a siege tower, wiping away entire enemy formations with sweeps of lightning—and Phillipa's constant questions.

The most prevalent one was, of course, "Could you do that?" almost always immediately followed up with "Why not?" Aelis had only just avoided repeating some of her early introductory lectures before students chose—or were chosen by—their Colleges. Finally, she'd had to set the book down and explain.

"No wizard, and no warden—for all wardens are wizards, though the obverse is far from true—can cast spells from every school. The most any one person has demonstrated any competence in, verifiably, was five—and that was an elven Archmagister who could only just manage Second Order

Divinations on top of what was an impressive assortment of Conjuring, Enchanting, Illusion, and Abjuration."

"Why's it matter that he was an elf?"

"Because elves once lived a good deal longer than humans."

"Do they not anymore?"

"Yes, somewhat. But not hundreds and hundreds of years as they once did."

"Why not?"

"I don't know, and if they do, they aren't telling such as me."

"Did you know any very old elves?"

"One of my Abjuration teachers—my swordmistress—was reputed to have taught at the university for eighty years."

Pips had sat up in her chair then, eyes wide. "Tell me . . ."

"Her name was Lavanalla Elysse Ymiris Cael Na Tenyll, and if you ask me one more question I am going to make you learn to spell it by writing it five hundred times."

That clammed the girl up and allowed her to finish the story.

Now, in the quiet and solitude of her tower, Aelis couldn't decide if she missed the life and the noise the girl brought with her.

Then she remembered the two precious crates she had stowed under a table, and the bottles of wine carefully packed in straw within, and she knew exactly how she'd pass the rest of the afternoon.

"Be better if Humphrey and Miralla were here to drink it with," she said as she prized the lid carefully off the crate and selected a bottle. *Or Maurenia.* She dismissed that thought as she lifted a heavy bottle, running her fingers over the vintner's mark stamped into the glass and scattering hay over her worktable in the process.

With an air of a woman on a mission, Aelis hefted the bottle in her left hand, seized her sword in her right, and drew it from the scabbard. In one motion, with no hesitation, she cut upward and swept the cork and the neck above the ring clean off.

"Lavanalla would have my hide for that," she said, "blunting the edge of an Abjurer's blade. Still, it's not as though I have a fire and tongs and ice or really any other proper way of doing it aside from smashing it against a table and hoping for the best."

She set the bottle down and began searching for a suitable vessel to drink from, eventually settling on a clean bronze flask. "No sense in bringing silver without someone to polish it . . . I wonder if Pips could be taught to polish . . ."

Aelis colored in shame at her own thoughts of exploiting the girl that way. She decided the best method of recovery was to have a first drink as fast as possible, so she poured. After the first sip she amended her plan to *enjoy* a drink at a moderate pace, as the warmth of the wine, its forward spice and fruit, had her relaxing almost instantly. She examined the bottle; no older than her, being one of the only postwar Tirravalan bottlings that had really come into its maturity already.

Aelis took bottle and flask to a chair along with the book she'd been reading to Pips from, and settled in.

10

THE GOLD

Aelis woke with a start to a sound like sword banging against shield. She realized, groggily, that she'd been dreaming of her sword training under Lavanalla, of the constant advance of the tall elf's three feet of curved bronze, like a scythe she could only ever just stay ahead of. In parts of the dream, Lavanalla had become Maurenia, and the practice duel had become both less and more real; more because she thought perhaps she stood a chance, and less because she knew nothing of how Maurenia would fight.

She was blinking all of this away as she stumbled toward the door, kicking over both the empty bottle and the empty alchemy flask she'd been drinking out of. The door seemed farther away than it ought to be, and she was forced to throw an arm out to steady herself against the table as she passed it.

Whoever was knocking at the door rattled it with a startling blow. Reasoning it must be her dinner, Aelis called out, "Just leave the basket and I'll get it, thanks. I'm not decent . . ."

"I'm not here to bring your dinner, Aelis," a voice beyond the door called out. "I'm here to fetch you to town. Hurry up about it. And bring your case. I hope you're ready to ride!"

Slowly, it dawned on Aelis that the person speaking was Maurenia. The seriousness of her words was like a slap across the face. She threw open the door and saw the half-elf standing windblown on her doorstep in the dusk giving way to the light of the moons, and two horses step-hitched on the grass beyond the walkway.

"Good goddess, woman, you smell like wine," Maurenia snapped. "Are you in any condition to—"

"Yes," Aelis shot back, seizing control of her wandering mind. "While I gather my things, you will tell me what is going on."

"A brawl has broken out in the village."

Aelis's head shot up as her hands, suddenly steady, buckled her sword-belt on. She absently checked both dagger and sword sheaths to make sure they were secure. "A brawl? Who started it?"

"Impossible to say—but it wasn't any of the Thorns. We've been keeping Luth out of sight. I was upstairs when I heard the commotion start—the only one of us among it was Timmuk, and I've never known a dwarf less inclined to his fists when drinking. I only saw him acting to keep the peace, but that'll change if Andresh gets involved. You don't want to see the two of them go back to back against a roomful of farmers."

"Damn it. What's gotten into them?"

"I don't know, but Rus seemed reluctant to wade in. He saw me at the top of the stairs and yelled to fetch you."

She took a look at her orrery and almost reached for it, but pulled her hand back and turned to Maurenia. "Let's ride."

She wasn't the rider Maurenia was—the half-elf had simply jumped onto the horse's bare back and seemed to will it to run—but Aelis, mounted on the company's other riding horse, nearly kept pace. Mercifully, hers was saddled, so it was only moments before she was swinging down and running for the door of the inn, sweeping her sword clear and shoving the door open with her left shoulder.

Inside was a scene of chaos, of flying fists and broken crockery. Soon enough someone would break a chair for a cudgel, and then all the furniture would become so much firewood.

Holding her sword behind her hip and lifting her left hand toward the nearest pair of combatants—burly farmers with skinned knuckles and red faces whose names she didn't know—she thrust a paper-thin ward between them, sending them reeling apart. This she repeated twice more, separating brawling pairs and drawing their ire to her.

Then she gathered as much power as she could and slipped her wand into her hand. Her fingers flexed and bent into channels for the forms she was calling on, and her arms rose into the air.

One of the first pair of fighters she'd separated came toward her, raising his fist, as she pointed the tip of her wand at the floor and bent down, stopping just short of smashing the thin reed of wood into the plank floor and releasing her gathered strength in one command. The word she spoke she couldn't have pronounced without the aid of her gathered will, nor could she have written it out exactly, and none who heard it could've said exactly what it sounded like—each would've given it a slightly different sound.

The effect was the same; some inexorable force convinced them to be *calm.*

The fighting ceased. Farmers and tradesmen gave their heads disbelieving shakes and stared at their clenched, bruised fists in astonishment.

"NOW," Aelis snapped in the silence her spell had won, "EVERYONE will sit down, and ONE person," and here she pointed at the man who'd been about to try to hit her, "will tell me what happened."

They began to act, Aelis reflected, rather like the sheep they tended; milling about, waiting for someone to tell them what to do, their eyes firmly on the floorboards and the toes of their boots.

"What," she said to the man she'd pointed at, "is your name?"

She sidestepped to one of the tables, and steadied herself by resting a hand on it. She seemed to have shaken most of the wine off, but coupled with the power she'd expended, her knees were suddenly a bit wobbly. *Wouldn't do at all to let them see that,* she thought, resisting the urge to sit and willing her legs to still themselves.

"Yohan," the man murmured, speaking thickly over bruised lips and a cheek that would soon swell. He reached two fingers between his lips to pluck at a tooth; she reached up and snatched his hand, tugging it away.

"Stop that. If you've a loose tooth, give it a chance to heal and it might. Pluck at it and you'll lose it for certain. Now. Tell me what came over you."

"What d'ya mean?"

"Why were you fighting that other man?" She extended a hand and one finger to point to the fellow he'd been swinging great looping blows at when she walked in. He was more compact than Yohan, with a thicker trunk and arms, and looked none the worse for their exchange of blows.

"Me 'n Cab just sorta get to blows every now and then. We're neighbors n' old friends, it happens."

"It doesn't usually happen to the entire village all at once, does it?"

At that, Yohan could only muster a shrug. "Some nights it just gets into a body to do a bit of riot, ya know?"

"I am certain I do not," Aelis replied. She looked out over the crowd and saw lips curling and fists clenching, muscles flexing along arms. Violence hung thickly in the air for reasons she couldn't begin to fathom. Impulsively, she stood up straight and cleared her throat. While the faces of the crowd turned toward her, she gathered a trickle of power with her wand and tilted it upward, directing the stream into her voice.

"The inn is closed for the evening. Everyone is to return home for the night and not to leave it except under the conditions of direst emergency; that means it is *life* or *death*, and if you leave your house, you come seeking me. Do you understand?"

The tiny stream of power that she let out with her words acted as a mild suggestive, barely even a First Order Enchantment, and one dispersed to multiple targets, at that. She wouldn't have liked to try anything stronger at the moment.

To a mild astonishment that she worked hard to keep from her features, it seemed to work. Alone, in some cases in pairs, they drifted wordlessly out of the inn, till the only people left standing in the common room were Aelis, Maurenia, Timmuk, and Rus.

She looked past the bar to the kitchen and saw Martin, his face pale, looking hesitantly out from above the counter. There was a creak on the stairs and she whirled about, lifting her wand to point and her sword to a guard position. Andresh stood on the second step from the top landing, his hands slowly lifting into the air, one bushy brow raised. He rattled off some words in Dwarfish, of which she'd none, so she looked to Timmuk.

"Wants to know if all the fun is over," the dwarf relayed. Aelis was prepared to roll her eyes until Rus hissed at her from behind the bar.

"What do you think you're doing?"

"I think I already did it," Aelis answered, sheathing her sword and slipping the wand back into her sleeve. "I spared you a good deal of time repairing your furniture in addition to the coin you'll spend on new crockery, and I stopped blood from being shed."

"But ordering folk about like that, confining them to their homes, it's . . ."

"Well within my rights and authority, and what's more, it is an accomplished fact, so I'll take no whining over it," Aelis said. "I can order folk confined to their homes for up to three days pending an inquest, indefinitely if I suspect them of a more severe crime."

Leaving Rus gaping, she wheeled on Timmuk. "Dobrusz, does trouble follow your company? In the days since you've arrived, we've had a bear slaughter half a herd of sheep and the entire village lose its mind in a bar brawl the likes of which I'd wager Lone Pine has never seen."

"Now, Warden Aelis," Timmuk said calmly, spreading his hands, "you can't go blaming us for ill luck and clouded judgment. And you doubtless studied enough logic at the Lyceum to know that our arrival preceding the events you've named does *not* mean our arrival has caused them."

"I'm well aware of the fallacy you've alluded to, Master Dobrusz," Aelis said, her voice cold, her mouth twisting sourly as she thought of her torturous logic classes. "But I do not greatly believe in coincidence. The past two days have been *troubled*."

"That they have, and the Thorns of the Counting House stand ready to assist you in whatever capacity you require," Timmuk said smoothly. "But we have come here intending only to trade tales and gold."

When the dwarf said "gold," something clicked in Aelis's mind: the glimpse she'd had of the bag of glittering coin the dwarf had paid Rus with when they took rooms, how it had seemed to grab her eyes and refused to let them go, how the bright orange glitter of it had drunk the light from the room.

"Timmuk, Maurenia, I have two questions: Where in the frontier did you find the gold you've been trading with these past two days, and whom have you paid with it?"

✦   ✦   ✦

"A Warden is *always* observing. A Warden is *always* recording facts," Bardun Jacques yelled, pounding the floor of the lecture hall with his steel-tipped Invoker's staff. In truth, what the old Warden carried was rather more a cross between club and walking stick than it was a proper staff, with a thick knot curling around a dark red crystal at the head. It came only to his waist, and he leaned on it, right hand clenched white-knuckled around it, left leg never quite bending properly. "Every fact is part of a larger whole, and you will never know how they fit together unless you are constantly recording them, assessing them. These," he suddenly shouted, lifting two fingers to point to his eyes, "and these," the fingers stabbed toward his ears—one of which was a smooth hole in the side of his head—"are your best tools. Not your staff. Not your sword, not your diadem, not your mirror, not your dagger, not your wand, not your orb, not any piece of thaumaturgical mayhem you cling to in order to call upon your all-too-pathetic power."

As he lectured, he limped back and forth across the front of the room. Bardun Jacques—though the Lyceum's Aldayim Chair in Magical Praxis, he refused the titles of Professor, Magister, or Archmagister, despite being well entitled to them all—taught without notes, without a lectern, and without standing still for more than a few moments at a time.

"Many of you think you'll be able to record your facts just with your eyes and ears. Almost all of you are wrong," he shouted, his voice more suited to a parade ground, Aelis had thought, than a lecture hall. "But we're not going to talk about boring minutiae like proper note-taking. Let the fourth and fifth years teach you that. We're going to talk about *hunches*."

He wheeled on them then, showing his bald, puckered face, with his gray eyes still as sharp and bright as any in the room. "Well, *I'm* going to talk, and you're going to listen. A hunch, an intuition, a guess, a gut feeling—whatever you like to call it—they are the most helpful and the most dangerous thing you'll deal with as Wardens, if indeed any of you are ever worthy of that august and esteemed title."

He leaned both hands on his stick for a moment, pulling himself up to his full height, or as near to it as he could.

"Sometimes, a hunch will seem to take you from the clear sky, and it will seem as pure and bright and visible as Peyron's moon. And some of those times, it'll even be right," he added, once more tapping his way across the front of the hall.

"Other times—most times, in your early days—it'll be dead wrong. And the thing you have to do then is learn that a hunch is not something to cling to; you'll have to discard it like broken glass. At best, its remnants can be melted down and reused." He cleared his throat with a harrumph and muttered, "Metaphor gettin' away from me." There was a titter of laughter from the front of the hall and he whirled, his staff suddenly flying into his hands.

"I've killed men for less than laughing at me," Bardun Jacques shouted, and Aelis thought in that moment, with the knot on the end of his staff already glowing red, that the old Invoker was not lying.

The crowd got deathly quiet and he lowered his staff with a faint sneer on his wrinkled, gray-whiskered face.

"But every time you get a hunch—every time that feeling crawls up from your stomach into your mind and your tingling hands, you'll run it down. Every time. Because the one time in ten, or twenty, or a hundred, depending on how thick you are, that the hunch is right, it'll save lives."

✦ ✦ ✦

Rus carefully set the purse, with its drawstrings pulled tightly shut, down on the table in front of Aelis, while she carefully watched Maurenia and Timmuk.

"It looked," the dwarf was saying, "for all the world, like an orc hoard . . ."

"Orcs don't bury hoards of coin. They prefer practical objects and wearable wealth, and silver into the bargain," Aelis said. "They'll trade gold, but they disdain it because of how soft it is, or so it is said. So why would orcs have a hoard of gold?"

"It wasn't any hoard," Maurenia put in. "It was just two chests of it in an otherwise unremarkable ruin."

"How big were the chests?"

"Still got 'em on the wagon," Timmuk said. "Do you want—"

"Yes," Aelis said before he even finished asking. The dwarf slid off the bench and went to the stairs, calling out in his guttural language. Soon, Andresh came stumping down and the two disappeared into the falling dark outside.

Maurenia watched them go before turning her startling eyes back to Aelis, who had to resist shivering. "What do you think the boxes might tell you?"

"More than they tell someone who is not Lyceum-trained," Aelis replied coldly. While they waited, she carefully picked open the knots in the drawstring of the coin purse before her and drew the bag open.

A single orange-tinted gold coin slipped out onto the table, and Aelis bent down, studying it.

"Coins like this haven't been struck in my lifetime," she said. "It's got Old Ystain marks."

"Well, that makes sense," the half-elf said, "as we found it in Old Ystain."

"And yet it looks as bright and clean as though it were fresh from the mint and untouched by anyone," Aelis said. "Does that not strike you as odd?"

"On the frontier, you don't stand about asking questions about found treasure."

Aelis looked up from the coin. "Out there it may be all well and good to say that gold has no provenance. Down here, where folk live . . ." She trailed off and looked back to the strangely orange gold. It was bright and the edges of the design it bore were sharp; a crowned helm with a fox standing over it, and tiny script beneath it, illegible without a glass to magnify it. She knew what it said, though: *Astride the Mountains*, the motto of Old Ystain. Hesitantly, she flipped it over with one fingertip. It was cold to the touch, and her skin tingled from the contact in a way that could only mean one thing.

"There is magic in this gold, of a kind," Aelis said.

"How do you know?"

"Felt it with a touch." Aelis sat up straight and pushed back the sleeve of her robe.

"Can't you tell what kind?"

She shook her head. "I'm no Diviner. If I were, I'd delve it—push my awareness into the magical existence of the thing, and see the space it occupies and how much of it." She flicked her eyes from the coin on the table to Maurenia and said, "If I start to do anything untoward, knock it out of my hand."

Then she snatched the coin off the table with one sweep of her hand. When her fingers closed around it she felt the slight tingle of magic in the coin clashing with the power contained in her own flesh. As a wizard, she had a natural resistance to magical objects, even benign amulets and potions.

As a Warden, she also had an acquired resistance, learned through years of mental and physical training at the Lyceum. She'd often heard it said that Abjurers were particularly resistant to the magic of devices, but she'd never seen real evidence of it.

The training she had was dual-purpose; to resist and to allow. She took a deep breath and slowed her breathing, spreading her hand so that the coin rested on her palm. Then she slowly, deliberately gathered up her power and pulled it deeply within herself. She had an immediate physical reaction; the heat of the fire beside her was suddenly stronger, the coin heavier, its weight comforting and reassuring.

In fact, the weight of the coin was a wondrous thing. It was gold, heavy and pure, and it was hers. Why shouldn't it be? She'd done a good deal of work for these people in the scant few days she'd been in town, and with nothing to show for it but a drafty tower full of bird shit, a goat that wouldn't leave her alone, and a pestering child.

Yes, this gold was hers by right, as was the rest of the bag. She had half a mind to dip her hand into it and let the heavy warmth of the coins seep into her skin, to heft them and feel their weight. Slowly, her hand closed around the coin and she began to reach for the bag with her other hand.

Suddenly her hand stung and the coin went flying away. Aelis looked up in startled anger, and her hand was on the hilt of her sword and drawing it out before she even looked from her now empty palm to the half-elf across from her.

Maurenia's eyes were open wide, and Aelis saw fear in their blue ice, in the slightly open O of her mouth. Then the power she'd withdrawn into herself rolled back into her body, out to the very tips of her fingers and beyond. She shook with the shiver of it, the kind one might get from a metal washstand on a cold winter morning, and snapped back to her senses.

"This gold is dangerous. Unbelievably so," Aelis said, carefully lowering both hands to the table, her palms flat. "I am sorry, Maurenia, but I have to confiscate it. And I need to question the Thorns."

"I'll be damned if you're confiscating our legally won property," Timmuk said from the door, which had just opened. He and Andresh had long, narrow brass-bound cedar chests resting easily on their muscled shoulders. "Or questioning my company as if we were common criminals."

"Maliciously enchanted objects are *illegal* by their very nature," Aelis said, standing and turning on the dwarf. "I am afraid, Master Dobrusz, I am not going to give you a choice. If you attempt to resist me on this matter, you *will* be criminals."

Every figure in the room was suddenly tense. Aelis was ready to drop her wand into her hand or draw her sword or both. Behind the counter, Rus watched like a hawk, a rag held inches above the surface in one hand. Leather creaked as Andresh flexed his free hand into a fist and then straightened the fingers out. Timmuk stared hard at her, his jaw bunching.

From behind she heard a soft rustle as Maurenia stood up and took a deliberate, slow step back.

"Warden," the half-elf said, her voice still and soft, "I promise you we did not knowingly bring enchanted gold to Lone Pine. But please understand that this represents the vast majority of our realized profit from an expensive expedition."

"As to the first, I can determine that easily enough," Aelis said, still unwilling to break her eye contact with Timmuk. "Subject yourselves to a simple First Order Enchantment, a compulsion to speak truth, and that is settled. As to the latter . . ."

Maurenia walked around to stand halfway between Aelis and the Dobrusz brothers. "Could you not . . . dissolve the magic you've found? Release the enchantment?"

"It's possible," Aelis said. "But the process of researching that could take weeks, and we all know you can't stay in Lone Pine that long. It's possible I could work out compensation with the Lyceum."

"Fuck *that* for an idiot's game," Timmuk spat. "I used to be a banker and a moneylender, Warden. I know exactly how likely an institution like the Lyceum is to give up gold once it has got it in its hands . . . and I know how badly they need it to train up a new generation of wizards and Wardens. Not a fucking chance."

"The wheels of the Lyceum's bureaucracy grind slowly," Aelis said, "but if you were to petition—"

"The petitioners would have to appear in person at the Lyceum's whim or it would all be forfeit. *No.* And I'll thank you not to go rooting around in my or my company's heads after you've stolen our gold to the bargain," Timmuk snarled.

Andresh's fist flexed again. Aelis heard movement on the stairs, a creak of wood that almost matched the leather for menace, someone in soft-heeled boots treading carefully and quietly and up to no good.

"What if," Aelis said, "I wrote you a letter of credit for an agreed-upon sum to offset the loss of the gold?"

Timmuk raised his chin. "Does the Warden of Lone Pine get paid in aught more than bread and mutton and butter?"

"For the purposes of this letter, I would not be writing it as the Warden of Lone Pine, but as Lady Aelis Cairistiona de Lenti un Tirraval," she said, even as she was thinking, *Please, Father. Forgive me.*

"De Lenti un Tirraval . . ." Timmuk said the words slowly, as if tasting them. Maurenia's eyes widened, but only briefly, before the half-elf resumed her typically imperturbable mask.

"My father is Guillame Robert de Lenti un Tirraval," Aelis said. "More properly styled *Count* un Tirraval. I assure you, a letter of credit in my *full* name will more than repair your losses."

The footfall on the stairs stopped. Maurenia regarded her carefully, lifting her chin and tossing her auburn hair lightly. Timmuk and Andresh lowered their burdens.

"I think," Timmuk said, "there's an accord to be made," and he strode forward, thrusting out a gloved hand.

"Later," Aelis said, drawing a deep breath of relief at the change in the dwarf's posture. "First, I need to know who took gold from you, and how much. Because I have to go get all of it back." She glanced over her shoulder to find Dashia halfway down the stairs, one hand resting prominently on a hilt.

"Right," Timmuk said, clapping his hands. "Dashia, go get your brother. We've a list to make."

✦ ✦ ✦

Aelis was up the night through, knocking on doors. Before she'd gone, she'd taken up a collection—from Rus, the Thorns, and her own purse—to come up with enough silver to cover the cost of all the gold she was setting out to confiscate.

While the Thorns worked up a list, she went over the details in her mind. *The coin wanted me to keep it. And it would've made me do violence to hold it and keep more of it if Maurenia hadn't knocked it away.*

Timmuk had been busy, making accords for the purchase of supplies for their trek hundreds of miles south to their homes in Lascenise; mutton, salt, cheese, beer, wood to make repairs for the wagon, fodder for their horses. All in all, he'd stimulated the economy of Lone Pine to an extent that was going to drain much of Aelis's ready silver, and she noted the hungry-eyed looks Rus and the adventurers gave her as she ventured out of the inn clutching a heavy purse.

She was a half dozen or more long steps out into the growing darkness before she heard the door open and then shut behind her. Aelis turned to see the long, lean form of Maurenia following after her.

"This is Warden business," she began.

"There's naught in your warrants about working alone at all times, I'm sure," the half-elf said, cutting her off. "Besides, I saw the light that single piece of gold put into your eyes. Imagine what a handful of three will do to an ordinary peasant."

"Probably rather less," Aelis said, as they fell into step together. "Wizards are made, not born—but one of the ingredients is an increased sensitivity to the magic that circles the world with the moons. We're drawn to it, and it is drawn to us. As we're taught to manage that, we learn to harness that sensitivity into a shield. But in order to determine the nature of the magic in that coin, I had to drop my defenses."

"So it seized hold of you faster than it might a farmer?"

"Almost certainly."

"Well," Maurenia said, "that's brightened our prospects considerably. Speaking of bright, couldn't you use some light? My eyes do well enough with starlight, but . . ."

Aelis cleared her throat. "Onoma's moon is rising. It provides light . . . of a kind."

Maurenia stopped in her tracks. "Explain."

Aelis sighed. In truth, this was a far more delicate subject than the natural sensitivity of wizards to magic.

"I can't, really. I've always been able to pinpoint the position of Onoma's moon."

"Well, that's simply a matter of algebra. Surely you mighty wizards study that."

"We do, but I could do only enough of it to pass the basics. Advanced math, horology, and astronomy are beyond me." *Or too boring to concentrate on*, she thought. "I just *know*. I have since I was eleven. And the more Necromancy I learned, the better I became at knowing it. And then it started to light the sky for me."

"How?"

Aelis shrugged. "Hells if I know. It simply does. As long as Onoma's moon is in the sky—even a sliver—the night is not dark for me."

They'd been talking as they walked and had now come upon some of the houses they needed to visit. Maurenia bowed coquettishly and smiled. "After you, Dread Necromancer." Aelis grumbled and walked on, raising her hand to the door of the nearest house.

She knew that before they were done they'd be dragging people out of their beds. There were too many houses on the list Rus and Martin had drawn up in concert with Timmuk for it to be any other way, and Aelis had no intention of waiting for the morning.

Now she realized it was the house of the shepherd family whose fence she'd helped mend with a ward when she'd first arrived.

She knocked as gently as she could and as loud as she dared, and called out softly, "Warden here. Please come speak to me." It was a few moments before the door opened, and even then, Bruce had a long-bladed farmer's knife in his hand.

The only light cast from inside the house was that of a banked fire, and the man wore a simple long nightshirt; the whites of his eyes were bright, wide open with unease, if not fear.

"Bruce," Aelis began, giving him no chance to ask questions, "I need you to listen to me. Earlier tonight, a dwarf of the adventuring company purchased supplies from you—sheepskins, I'm told. He paid in gold. I need you to get the gold coin or coins he gave you, and bring it to me. I will exchange it for an equivalent amount of silver."

His eyes narrowed and his brow furrowed as she spoke, until, when she finished, they were clouded, just this side of angry. "Here now," he began, "what right have you to—"

"Every right," Aelis said, trying to make her voice snap the way Bardun Jacques's had when he lectured. "Questioning my motives is going to waste time that I do not have. Fetch the gold. You are losing nothing in this exchange. For each gold coin you bring me, I'm going to give you three silver."

His nose wrinkled. "Four."

"*Did* I give the impression this was a negotiation?" Aelis reached to the purse on her belt, prized it open, took three coins out, and held them on her palm. "Go now. Do not make me wait a moment longer."

With a sigh and a longing look at the silver—and the heavy purse it had come from—Bruce turned and walked back into his cottage, setting down the knife he held on a sideboard.

He was gone only a few moments, and Aelis—resolutely standing outside his threshold but filling the frame of the door to make it impossible to close—could hear him murmuring to other occupants of the house.

Bruce came back clutching a single gold coin in his callused hand. His eyes were fixed upon its glow in the darkness of his doorway. Before he could say a word, Aelis snatched it from his hand and scooped it into a second purse on her belt, this one hanging empty. She pulled the drawstrings tight and dropped the silver coins into his palm before he even blinked.

"Thank you for your cooperation, goodman. Sleep well," Aelis said as she stepped back, leaving him gawking in his doorway. Then, when Aelis and Maurenia were a few steps away, the door was shut and the heavy bar was thrown over it.

"This is going to be a long night if you have to talk them all into it. Can't you just enchant them to it?"

"Not one at a time like this. With the power I'd have to expend, you'd have to carry me home before we were half done."

Maurenia chuckled. Aelis turned toward her and saw the half-elf woman's mouth open as if she were about to speak, then her lips clamped shut. She thought for a moment. "Gather them all together, then?"

"And deal with dozens of folk at a time being told to trade in their gold for silver in an exchange they may not think is fair? I don't think 'Dear Magisters, I incited a riot, town in flames, locked in tower, please advise' is the kind of message I want to be sending to my superiors."

Maurenia laughed. "Discretion is all well and good, but do you really think these folk might revolt openly?"

"I think that the magic of the coins could drive them to it. And I suspect that putting all the coins together into one place in front of people who've already been worked at by the enchantment laid upon them could be disastrous."

"Then how is it you want to carry them all by yourself?"

"I don't *want* to. I want to toss them all into a fire and then bury the result six feet beneath my best wards inscribed on silver bands. But I need to get to the bottom of what's enchanted them, how, and probably who. And no one else in the vicinity of Lone Pine is more qualified to resist the effects than I am."

"The Dobruszes carried in chests full of them and seemed none the worse for wear."

"Did they touch the actual gold, or just the chests? It's possible they may be naturally resistant, but unless there's something I don't know about them, neither has passed the test and earned a stripe from the College of Enchantment at the Lyceum, which still leaves them behind me in qualifications."

Maurenia had no chance to answer for Aelis was already knocking at another door. This interaction went much like the first, with Aelis's commands smoother and more certain and the business concluded quickly. They lapsed into silence as they moved from house to house, with Maurenia drifting away from the little light each doorway shed.

Two hours passed, with Onoma's black moon a tiny sliver high above them. Clouds shrouded the other moons in darkness but Aelis had enough light to see and a bulging pouch of gold coin that dangled heavily on her belt. She passed her fingertips lightly over the rough hide of the pouch and felt the tingle of the magic within. She stopped in her tracks, frowning.

"Where did you say you found these, Maurenia?"

"Rather unremarkable ruin. An old fort. The kind that were hastily thrown together all over Ystain when the orc emigration started. Made of barely worked rocks and wood and never really used, except to turn into a strongpoint for the bands to rally around after they'd taken them."

"And there were just the two chests, naught else?"

Maurenia shrugged. "Might've been some broken tools, weapons. Nothing of consequence that I can recall."

A long walk to the next house gave Aelis time to ponder the problem. "None of this makes any sense," she said. "This gold is freshly minted; orcs would not have done that, and certainly not with Old Ystain marks. Gold doesn't hold onto magic very long. These coins can't have been sitting in some hoard, cursed and enchanted, just waiting for someone to trip over them, since the time a warband overran some Ystainen fort. There's something I'm missing."

"If you've only read about orcs, then you aren't acquainted with the reality," Maurenia said. Aelis hadn't time to interrogate that statement, for they'd come to Otto and Elmo's ramshackle cottage. While the fences were all in good enough repair to keep the sheep in, the thatch was spotty at best, the door hung crookedly, and holes pocked the thin hides nailed over the windows. The stone walls wanted the attention of a mason if they were meant to stand for another year.

Aelis hesitated in front of the door, afraid a loud knock would send it tumbling out of the frame, then rapped her knuckles against it as sharply as she dared.

They waited so long in front of the darkened house that Aelis thought of turning away, when the door swung open without warning.

Had she not been able to see by the light of the black moon, the axe handle Elmo swung might have struck the crown of her head.

As it was, instinct and training had her flinging a ward up with her left hand, while her right drew her sword. The axe handle crashed into the ward once, twice, with real menace in the swings. Behind her, she heard steel clear leather as Maurenia armed herself. She could step back and draw the half-elf into what certainly looked like a fight; that much was clear. There was help to be had.

She gritted her teeth against accepting it and stepped forward, swinging the pommel of her sword into Elmo's midsection. She didn't put the full force she could have into the blow, but she drove the steel of the pommel straight into the cluster of nerves above his navel. He wore only a thin, stained nightshirt that offered no protection from her blow, pulled though it was.

Elmo immediately doubled over, retching on the dirt floor of the cottage, with Otto running forward from the second room—there were only two—sputtering.

"Sorry, folk, sorry, Elmo doesn't know what he's doin' when he's woke like this," the elder brother said, immediately snatching up an iron and stirring the coals in their sad little hearth, which threw little light and less heat into the room. By the time he'd gotten a stinking, smoking lamp lit with a piece of straw, Aelis was bending over Elmo's supine form, having kicked his axe handle away. Maurenia had melted into the shadows just outside the door.

When Otto saw who knelt over Elmo's form, her hands checking his breathing, the beat of his heart at his neck, and his eyes, he went pale and sputtered unintelligibly for a few seconds.

"I'm sorry, Warden, I'm sorry," he finally stammered. "Elmo's impossible to manage sometimes, but he means no harm, just . . . still thinks he's in the war, sometimes. Nights, he just loses himself. I won't keep blades in the house but he finds weapons all the same."

"It's all right, Otto. No one is hurt, except, I'm afraid, your brother." His pulse was fine, if quick, and his breathing was slowly returning to normal, but his eyes were rolling in his head and his hands were clenched, his arms gripping their opposite across his chest. "You say this happens often?"

Meekly, Otto nodded. "In a bad week it could happen near every night."

Aelis cast her eyes around the two mean rooms, barely furnished with one rickety table and three wobbling stools, with simple shelves and pegs holding the meager clothing and tools they owned, and struggled to keep a frown away. "Where's Phillipa?"

Otto cleared his throat and rubbed his foot against the dirt floor. "When it looks like Elmo's going to have one of his moments, I try t'find somewhere else for her to sleep. Sometimes Rus'll take her in exchange for a bit of work on his patch. Tonight, Emilie took her. She's always happy to go."

"I see." Elmo had by now uncurled himself and sat up. Aelis could see his face grow red. He snatched up his axe handle and stiffly walked out the front door, heedless of the fact that he was barely dressed.

Aelis couldn't have been sure, but she would've bet whatever silver she'd have left tomorrow that Elmo didn't see Maurenia as he passed within five feet of her.

"I'm sorry to have disturbed your rest, and his, Otto," Aelis said. "But I need to ask if you transacted any business with the Dobrusz company today."

"The dwarf? Aye. Agreed to do some work on their wagon and to provide some fodder for their horses for the journey."

"Did he pay in gold?"

"Elmo brought gold home, so I assume he did."

Aelis turned her face away from the guttering light of the lamp. "I'm afraid I have to buy that gold from you. Willing to pay you three pieces of good silver per gold coin. I'll attest to the equivalence in value."

"Nothin' good comes of gold in the house," Otto said, with a half sigh, half laugh. "Our mother used to say that. Never knew what she meant. I'll go fetch the coin box." With a slight hitch in his walk, Otto stumped off to the second room, a ragged blanket that fluttered behind him serving as a door.

Maurenia ghosted into the doorway as soon as Otto disappeared. "Your man ran off into the woods muttering to himself," she whispered. "Should I follow him?"

Aelis gave a quick nod and Maurenia disappeared into the shadows again as Otto came walking out, rubbing the two gold pieces together in his hand. His steps slowed and he stared at them.

Aelis hurried to his side and swept the coins away from him. He looked up, startled, but calmed as she pressed six pieces of silver into his hand. She took a quick gauge of how much silver remained in her purse and weighed it against the ramshackle conditions of the cottage, and quickly plucked a seventh piece and pressed it into Otto's big, callused hand.

"Is this all of it? This is very important, Otto."

"You think we have so much gold in our box I'd lose track of it, Warden? Elmo handles our coin, mostly, but this is all that was there."

Aelis nodded. "Elmo been like this since the war?" she asked quietly as she dropped the gold into her other pouch as quickly as she could.

"Aye," Otto said. "Comes on him over the course of the day. Just see him change. He keeps lookin' at the horizon. Won't crest a hill. Reaches to his side for a weapon's not there. Good days, he'd not hurt a fly. Bad?" The big man rolled his shoulders.

"Thinks he's still there sometimes? Especially at night?"

Otto nodded; Aelis could read the sorrow peeking out from behind the cracks in his detached facade. "Worst is times he wakes up with a scream," the farmer murmured.

Aelis wanted to set her hand on his shoulder, reassure him somehow, but Bardun Jacques's voice came back to her once again.

You're not their friend, you're not their confidant, you're not their barman, and you certainly aren't their gods-damned lover, the old Warden had said, wheeling stiffly in front of the lecture hall. *You're their* Warden. *You're among them, not of them. The day may come where you have to judge them, carry out a sentence. Harder to do that clearheaded to people you've supped with, drunk with, laughed with. For some of you it'll be impossible.*

"The next time you think he might be having a moment," Aelis said, "send for me. There might be something I can do for him."

"You mean . . . reach into 'is mind? With a spell?"

Aelis tried not to frown and nearly succeeded, but she took comfort that Otto couldn't see in tonight's dark nearly as well as her. "That's precisely what I mean, Otto. It could calm him, help him get past these moments."

Otto took a deep breath. "If I can tell the next time it's comin', I will," he said. Then, trying to hide it behind one big swollen-knuckled hand, he yawned.

"We'll let you get back to your sleep," Aelis said. "We've got more houses to visit this night."

"Would you check in on Emilie and Pips?" he asked sleepily. "I don't think Elmo'd go there, but . . ."

"I will," Aelis said as she headed out and shut the door behind her, fore-stalling further conversation. Emilie's house was not on her list, a fact she was reminded of as Maurenia slipped out of the uneven shadows of the house.

"Don't recall hearing the name Emilie come up," she murmured.

"It didn't, but he asked."

"And are you to do everything they ask of you, or what is most important to protect them?"

"When the two go together, I can do both. We don't know what direction Elmo hared off in."

"He went haring across the open field to the north at a skirmisher's trot. Stand of trees beyond there. Be my guess that was where he was headed."

"Skirmisher's trot?"

"You didn't fight in the war, did you?"

"I was fourteen when it ended," Aelis said, sourly. "How would I have done?"

Maurenia tsked. "So young, then. Younger than I would have guessed."

"This is not answering the question."

"A skirmisher's trot is two running steps followed by a shorter, slower one. Conserves energy to travel a long distance at a high speed and still be ready to fight when you get there."

"I'd thought Elmo was a scout."

"Scout, skirmisher, it all depends on the army, the officer, the day."

"So that's what you did, then?"

"Briefly," Maurenia said. "But I had too good a head for geometry and too many good ideas to waste in the infantry, or so I eventually convinced them. Spent most of my time as an engineer, cobbling siege equipment together."

"I thought orcs didn't build fortifications."

"Didn't stop them from inhabiting what they'd already rolled over when they saw it was to their benefit."

Their feet crunched on the small rocks and dry grass as they wound their way farther from the village center, to Emilie's house. Of a similar size and construction to Elmo and Otto's, it looked like a more reputable and well-heeled sibling. It had square corners, whole walls, doors that fit their frames, shutters over the windows, and a chimney that didn't seem to be in danger of filling the house with smoke. Aelis imagined Pips's uncles' cottage looked like this twenty years ago.

As she raised her hand to the door, it swung open as if on its own. Maurenia was at least as surprised as Aelis, as knives appeared in her hands, and she'd no time to melt into the darkness beside the door as she'd done at every other house. There were no lights on inside, which didn't hinder the Warden or the half-elf much, and apparently not the occupant either. Aelis saw a woman taller than Maurenia and as broad as many a man, with blond hair cut near to the scalp on the sides and gathered into a warrior's queue along the back of her neck, holding a long, antler-handled knife in one hand. She didn't wear a typical nightshirt, but instead woolen leggings that were wound around her legs with leather thongs and a dark blue shirt that reached halfway to her knees.

"Strangers come to my door past the turn of the night with steel in their hands means no good, I am sure," she said slowly. "What is it you want, Warden?"

Setting aside the various questions that occurred to her—how did Emilie know they were coming, how could she see and identify them in the dark, to name two—Aelis said, "We've recently come from Elmo and Otto's place." She hesitated briefly. "They wanted us to check on Pips."

"You mean Otto wanted you to check on Phillipa while Elmo runs wild and howls his rage at a moon he cannot see and plays at being a wounded man. Very well," Emilie said, slipping the knife into a sheath at her back.

Without a weapon in hand, she stood oddly, her right shoulder cocked upward, her elbow slightly bent. "Phillipa is asleep and well and her uncle would not come near this place even were he able to cope with what he has seen and what he knows. I do not intend to wake her up, nor to invite you in. Good night, Warden."

The door shut and was bolted with a severe-sounding finality. Aelis had one hand half lifted and her mouth open to speak.

"That," Maurenia said, sounding shaken for the first time Aelis could remember, "was odd."

"One gods-damned mystery at a time," Aelis said aloud, even while adding it to the list she needed to ask Rus, and other friendly locals, about: *My missing book. Her. The bear. Was the bear a mystery, or just a bear? Something else. Something I'm forgetting.* She worried at her bottom lip with her teeth.

She was going to need time alone in her tower with pen and ink to sort these thoughts and questions out and decide how to approach, but for the moment there seemed nothing more to do but collect the coins and move on.

"Come on then," Aelis said. "We've a couple more hours of walking. Time to head even farther out of the village."

✦　✦　✦

Onoma's moon had nearly set, the encroaching sun lightening the sky to gray by the time Maurenia and Aelis were taking their last weary steps to the doors of the inn. Too tired to talk, or to do much more than put one foot before the other, they trudged into an empty common room.

And to a clatter and shouts on the second floor, thumps on the ceiling over their heads, and voices raised in anger.

Maurenia beat her to the stairs, Aelis comforting herself with the thought that the half-elf's stride was simply so much longer that she couldn't compete; she'd reacted just as fast and gained the landing only the shortest moment later.

A door just to their left was open and the sounds of fighting emerged from within. Aelis heard dwarfish cursing—Andresh, she was sure—and a deep voice she suspected was Timmuk's yelling, "For fuck's sake, Darent, get his legs!"

They looked to each other, filled their hands with steel, and ran in side by side. Maurenia tried to slip in first, but Aelis slipped her shoulder under the half-elf's arm and nudged her out of the way with a hip-check.

And the fact that she was able to bring a ward up in time to deflect the clay pitcher that was thrown at them, sending it crashing into dozens of pieces on the floor, proved the wisdom of her decision.

In the far corner of the room, Luth stood, making use of what furniture the room had to keep Darent, Andresh, and Timmuk at bay. The basin the pitcher matched was already shattered and the washstand they'd been kept on had been broken into so much kindling, two long spear-like pieces of which Luth was jabbing at Darent and Andresh as they feinted toward him. The bed already looked ruined, with one of its posts broken and the blankets nowhere to be seen.

Luth's expression was madness personified, beyond even his burned rictus. He was wearing only drawers, and Aelis saw that whatever had given him the burn on his face had indeed burned that entire side of his body, starting at his neck and moving down his shoulder, leaving his entire arm twisted with livid white scar tissue—except for two patches that glistened a raw, wet red that Aelis couldn't look at without feeling queasy.

Luth was holding the others off easily, and it wasn't hard to tell why; he was armed and ready to do violence, and they weren't. Darent seemed the closest, one hand drifting to a long knife at his belt. Andresh came forward and tried to seize one of the broken lengths of wood as Luth swung it at him. He managed it, but the second clouted him hard enough to send him reeling away. What was more, Luth's position between the bed and the wall made it hard for most of them to approach him.

Maurenia looked to a cringing Timmuk for orders or ideas.

Full of confidence, Aelis just went for the same Enchantment that had laid him low days before.

When she released it, wand extended gracefully from one hand, she expected him to slump to the floor, his erstwhile weapons clattering harmlessly to the ground.

She did *not* expect him to turn toward her with a nightmare of a grimace, vault the bed, and raise his clubs.

She threw up a ward and knocked his blows aside without feeling them. Her first instinct was to draw her Abjurer's sword and bury it in his stomach, and she would've been well within her rights.

Aelis did draw her sword, to focus her wards through it. Luth's attacks had no subtlety and no plan; he was hammering away at the ward that shimmered in front of her as though it were a shield on an enemy's arm.

Convincing him that he hadn't slept was not going to work on the heels of having slept all day. She could hold the ward he battered for some time, but not indefinitely. Like a man crazed, he didn't even bother to shift his attacks, wildly swinging his broken chair legs at her nearly invisible shield. His eyes were wide and shot with red, and the sides of his mouth were flecked with foam.

Aelis glanced at his smooth, burned skin, and a new Enchantment occurred to her. She called it to her mind as she withstood a few more blows. It was a Second Order Enchantment, and she couldn't hold the ward and cast it at the same time. She bent low beneath her ward, drove the pommel of her sword into his stomach—aiming for that same handy cluster of nerves that had laid Elmo low—and stepped away as he clutched and gasped for breath.

Then she released her spell, and Luth screamed in a kind of liquid agony. He dropped his clubs and began flailing his arms, dropped to the floor, and rolled back and forth upon it.

"I'm sorry," she muttered, as she stepped forward and brought her pommel down on his forehead. Mercifully, he stopped screaming and lay still on the wooden floor, though his breath wheezed and whistled in his chest and he let out a soft moan.

Timmuk and Maurenia were a babble of questions, as was Andresh, though she couldn't understand a word he rumbled.

She held up a hand to silence them and immediately bent to Luth's side. She felt for his pulse, which was fast, but not dangerously so. Then her hands moved to the waistband of the short trousers that were all the clothing he wore, and she felt carefully along it, fingers moving slowly and questioningly along his waist.

"What did you do to him?" Maurenia finally asked through clenched teeth.

"And what do you think you're doing now?" Timmuk grated.

"Embarran's Memento," Aelis answered. "I recalled to his mind an experience he'd had."

"His burns," Maurenia said. "You made him relive them. The agony of it."

Aelis was a bit stunned at the speed at which the half-elf had guessed, but not at the anger in her voice. She wanted to jump up and explain. *It did him no lasting harm, and it was brief, and it was the best way I could think of to stop him without killing him, which I didn't much want to do,* but she'd already found what she was looking for.

Luth, it appeared, had worn a coin belt under his trousers, just against his skin. It was a simple length of cloth, really, twisted and then knotted to keep coins securely and secretly upon one's person. She cut it free with the edge of her sword and lifted it out, yanked a bit of shiny orange gold from one of the pockets formed by the twisted knots.

"Here's the answer," Aelis said, holding it aloft. "There must be ten, twelve pieces of gold folded into this." By now, Aelis realized, Rus, Martin, and Dashia had all gathered outside the door, and likely had seen most of what had happened. She dumped the gold onto the only table the room had remaining. All the gold was of a kind with those she'd been collecting. She began sweeping it into her pouch. "And he'd been wearing it against his skin for days on end." She turned her head to Timmuk. "Had he been acting strangely?"

"Luth was always a strange one," the dwarf answered, and Aelis could read the evasion in his side-shifting eyes and twisting mouth. "But . . ." He sighed. "He was faster to pick a quarrel, for sure."

"When he challenged you in front of the entire village that'd turned out to see us," Darent said, his voice a hoarse croak, "that wasn't much like him. He's an odd one, with a prickly kind of honor. Not much of a braggart."

Dashia came to Luth's side and knelt by him, taking his scarred arm in her own. She looked to Andresh and murmured something in Dwarfish. Darent and the dwarf both rushed to help her pick him up—no easy feat—and slide him onto the bed.

"I don't know if I'd say he wasn't a braggart," Maurenia put in. "But he's the kind would be more likely to want to impress a village full of peasants. Not frighten them."

"Check his boots," Aelis said, "and his pockets, and all his gear. If he's got more of this gold secreted around himself, I need it." Briefly, she let her eyes close, and a wave of weariness hit her. One way or another she was going to get some sleep. Soon.

"Rus," she said, "have you a spare room? I . . ." She stopped as she almost said *I can't make it back to the tower just now* but didn't want to admit that kind of weakness. "I ought to stay *in* the village, close to hand, if I could."

"We do," Rus said, cracking a yawn. "But it's the one you just bought the bed out of. It'll have to be blankets on the floor."

"It'll do," Aelis said. She forced her eyes open, blinked encroaching sleep away, and made for the door. She felt eyes on her as she moved away, following a sleepy Rus and Martin to another room down the hall.

Inside there was a great empty spot where a bed would've been, a clean grate across a fireplace with no fire behind it, a small table, and two stools. She fell heavily onto a stool, setting her still naked sword on the table and following it with the bag of gold.

While she waited for the innkeepers to gather spare blankets from the linen cupboard, she considered the gold.

"Who made you?" she muttered. "And why? To what end? And why did you have to come here to this village?"

"Should I be worried, you talking to a bag of gold? A bag of *that* gold? Am I going to have to duel you to take it away?" Maurenia, her footsteps all but silent even on the wooden floor of the inn, came into the room and took the other stool.

Aelis unbuckled her swordbelt and slipped her blade into its scabbard. Maurenia leaned forward, smiling very oddly.

"Not answering my question, but taking your belt off; it's clear you don't want to talk to me, but just what *do* you want to do, Aelis?" The half-elf had leaned forward across the table until her face was only a scant few inches away, a lock of hair falling over one eye.

Rus had lit candles from the stick he'd carried when he came running to her confrontation with Luth. Between that and the dawn that was breaking outside, it was well lit. Too well lit for Aelis to hide the flush that immediately hit her cheeks or the way her breath caught when she looked up and found Maurenia's face so close to her own.

"I wasn't talking to the gold so much as . . . whatever malevolence it represents," she muttered in answer.

"And what about my second question?"

Aelis was unable to summon an answer to that. Maurenia's lips opened faintly and she brushed her hair back behind her slender, slightly pointed ears. The skin of Aelis's cheeks burned. She was suddenly aware of how close their hands were upon the table.

Rus coughed politely at the door, and Aelis popped up as though she were a child caught at mischief. Maurenia chuckled throatily and stood, but slowly, languidly almost. Rus and Martin, silent, began building a pile of blankets on the floor. They'd found a spare mattress ticking that had some hay filling it—though not enough to make it a proper bed—and laid it flat upon the floorboards. With blankets piled about it, it still looked as depressing a bed as Aelis had ever occupied.

Nevertheless, she was ready to fall in it the moment they filed silently out. Almost.

She turned back to Maurenia, who looked at the bedding and sighed. "I'd point out that with Dashia attending to Luth, I have a room to myself for the next few hours. But I won't, because I think you don't know how you want to answer that invitation." She held up a slender, graceful hand. "You do not need to try. But . . . should you come to any understanding before we depart Lone Pine . . ." Maurenia shrugged and smiled, and Aelis remained rooted to the spot, the burn on her skin moving down her neck to her chest and radiating down her arms and back.

"Good night, Warden," the half-elf said, then turned and left. Her steps were slow and deliberate, but confident.

Aelis had her boots off and fell into the bedding, letting out a small, frustrated sound, only moments after Maurenia had closed the door.

Almost immediately, she drifted off to sleep.

11

THE KNIFE

Aelis's dreams were a muddle of flashing orange-tinted gold, of Maurenia's mouth and eyes and hair, of a shadowy figure flinging orbs of spidery lightning at her. They landed with fiery impact and buffeted her about as she strove to recall the name of the tall and spindly shadow that hurled them.

She dreamed of a trio of menacing figures in robes and the gold lying on a stone table before them.

When she woke, she was sweating, slanting light filtered through the shutters on the window, and her back was as stiff as the floorboards that she felt all too keenly beneath the inadequate mattress.

Doesn't seem to be anything for it but to get up, she told herself. *Rather lie here and revisit some of those dreams,* she thought in reply, but she rolled to her knees and palms and pushed herself up with a groan. She went for her swordbelt and the purse on the table and settled them both about her waist again, and tried to sort out her feelings about Maurenia.

"That," she muttered, "is not something I'm going to figure out without breakfast. Or wine." She dragged her fingers through her knotted hair and wished for a washstand, combs, and a change of clothes.

When none of those appeared, she threw open the door and headed downstairs. The entire company of the Thorns were assembled and occupying a table to themselves; a few village folk sat at others. The smells of woodsmoke and baking bread were omnipresent, and her stomach rumbled.

The adventurers seemed to be keeping their own counsel. All of them looked to her as she appeared at the top of the stairs, though Luth immediately looked away. Maurenia's gaze lingered, and Aelis met it for only a moment before seeking out breakfast.

Rus had a tray ready for her: bread, butter, goat cheese, a mug of small beer. He set it down as she settled at the counter.

"Otto was already in to look for you," he said, standing back while she immediately tucked into the bread.

"How'd he know I was here?"

"Well, he came here first to ask how he ought to ask at your tower. He didn't say it was any kind of emergency."

Aelis eschewed the knife that was set on her tray, preferring instead to drag chunks of bread through the warm butter and the soft cheese, speckling them with crumbs as she did.

"What did he want?"

"Elmo hadn't come back. Said he was wondering if there was aught you could do to help find him."

Aelis sighed. "I'm neither a tracker nor a Diviner. There's not much I can do for him till someone else finds him." Motion from the table where the Thorns sat caught her eye. She saw Maurenia beginning to stand up from the bench, only to hear Timmuk mutter something she couldn't catch—that she suspected were words in Dwarfish she'd not have understood in any case—and the half-elf sat back down without argument.

She took a moment to study the adventurers; they wore their black leathers, their weapons. Rus, still standing behind the counter, saw the direction of her glance.

"They've already fed and saddled their horses, rolled the wagon out, and greased its wheels. I think you'll find them gone before too long."

"I'm sure Lone Pine won't be sad to see them gone," Aelis muttered in reply, before hastily gulping down the rest of her breakfast. Rus went back to his work in the back with a shrug.

The last thing Aelis wanted to do was trudge out to that depressing shack the brothers shared and try and squeeze more information out of Otto. What she wanted was to have a talk with Maurenia, contrive some kind of bath, go back to her tower, change her clothes, and spend some time sorting out all of her many confusions with pen, ink, and paper. This seemed to her the best possible way for the day to unfold.

She thought for a moment on what Bardun Jacques would have to say to a Warden who was more concerned with their comforts than the needs of the people under their charge. She sighed, finished her bread and cheese, had a long look at the sour, cloudy beer and left it sitting in the mug as she stood.

Aelis was nearly at the door when she heard Timmuk clear his throat.

"Warden," he began, swinging his legs over the edge of the bench, "if you'd be so kind as to clear up the matter of—"

"I have no time to draw up any documents or read any that you've already done, Timmuk," she answered, a little more curtly than she'd meant to.

"Now, it's not a matter that can be left hanging." The dwarf edged a few steps closer to her. None of the other Thorns, save Maurenia, looked up from the surface of the table. "We're to be moving on."

"If you want to leave before I return, then you'll do it without any letters to any bankers in my name," Aelis snapped. "I've got people to attend to." The combination of poor sleep, simple food, and bad drink was doing her nerves no good, Aelis knew. The best course of action would be to absent herself from the conversation, so she pushed open the door.

"That really won't do, Warden," Timmuk called after her, his tone incongruously obsequious. "Promises were made. I'm going to have to insist."

Aelis whirled back into the room, her hand falling to the hilt of her sword, her eyes flashing. "The only one of us with any right to *insist* on any gods-damned thing, Timmuk Dobrusz, is me. Your payment is neither my priority nor my problem. The assault a member of your company has twice made upon me *will become both* if you say another fucking word. I will begin by arresting you and seizing your property in order to pay back damages to the people of the village, and that's *before* I decide if I put you to an inquest for multiple crimes."

Whether he was merely surprised or genuinely frightened, Aelis wasn't sure. But the dwarf at least took a half step away from her before raising a hand and opening his mouth.

"Do not doubt me, dwarf," Aelis said, drawing the words out slowly, carefully, like a blade slipped from a sheath.

In the resulting silence, she made her exit and walked hastily toward Otto and Elmo's cottage, blinking at the morning sun. Her anger at the dwarf's impertinence was such that she ate up the ground, ignored her surroundings, and didn't once look back to see if anyone was following her.

By the time she reached the brothers' rickety farmstead, a light breeze had kicked up, and the door was banging against the frame. Aelis sighed as she considered the life they and Pips must lead. *How does it even keep the weather out,* she wondered as she watched the door slam against the wall. *In the winter they must bring their animals inside—do peasants actually* do *that or is that some silly assumption? It must reek, if so,* she thought, lost in her rumination, imagining the strong scent of goat or sheep in close quarters, the place filling up with woodsmoke, the scent of blood.

She stopped in midthought as she realized that she'd thought of the scent of blood because she *smelled* it, brought by that gusting wind through that banging door. It was a scent all Necromancers came to know.

Aelis was through the door before she even knew what she was doing. Otto lay on the dirt floor on his back, the hilt of a knife jutting up from his stomach, blood turning his shirt to a ruin. She resisted the urge to kneel at his side and immediately see to the wound, instead quickly glancing around, her sword half out of her sheath. There weren't many places in the mean little hut for anyone to hide, so she quickly knelt, putting her hands to Otto's neck. He was breathing; that much she could hear, the little pained wheezes forcing themselves out of his slack mouth like a bellows in need of replacing.

Blood didn't flow freely from the wound, but he'd lost enough to worry her, and she could feel it hot and thick on her hands as she put them to the wound. She measured the hilt with her eyes, trying to gauge the length of the knife blade given what she could see.

"Not more than six inches, surely," she told herself with a confidence she didn't feel. "Otto!" She put some snap into her voice when she said his name, trying to draw his attention. His eyelids fluttered, and perhaps he moaned a bit louder, but no words came.

Aelis was already scanning the room for what she could use to treat the wound. *Pressure. Binding. Delving.*

With a grimace, she reached with her right hand to her left shoulder, where her sleeve met the shoulder of her robe. She dug in her nails and tore, ripping the stitches out a few at a time, shaking her Enchanter's wand free and letting it clatter to the floor as her left sleeve came loose. Then she did the same to her other sleeve.

With her left hand, she drew her Anatomist's Dagger from the back of her belt, and placed the right hand, palm down and fingers flat and extended, on Otto's blood-smeared stomach.

She focused her senses on the dagger, and then through it, toward Otto's body. In her mind's eye it was a heavy prism in her hand through which the body of the wounded man before her was reflected and refracted into a panoply of colors and textures. A pulsing dark red that seemed to weaken and wane as moments passed indicated not merely the flow of his blood but the vital force of life that sustained him. Blues, yellows, greens that she hadn't time to sort through and look upon individually indicated specific organs. His mind, his consciousness, his brain was merely a dull gray. And worst of all was the seepage of black into other parts of the prism.

The blade was longer than she'd feared, it had pierced his innards, and devastating consequences would follow soon; infection, rot, disease in his organs, a slow death as his body poisoned itself.

There was nothing she could do for the loss of blood except to try and stanch it to a trickle. She pressed one of the sleeves against the edges of the wound, folding it haphazardly with one hand. The other she quickly cut into a longer strip so that she could bind it around his stomach. Otto was a sizable man, but the short rations and hard life of a farmer had kept the fat from gathering around his middle, and for that she was thankful. She made as tight and fast a knot as she could, tying the whole around the knife that was stuck in him. That, she wasn't pulling out till she had her case of instruments and bags of herbs and medicaments to hand.

And getting it was going to prove a problem. She was already running through her options; she hadn't the strength of an Enchanter to reach to anyone's mind from a long distance, nor had she the Illusion or Conjury to call forth a bird—real or otherwise—to act as a messenger. All she truly had in the moment were her lungs.

Aelis ran for the door of the cottage and was there in two steps, having snatched up her wand in one blood-smeared hand. Her uncertain mind called up feeble arguments. *A Warden can't be seen to panic,* it said. *Spreading fear is to be avoided at all costs.*

"A Warden also can't leave a man to fucking die because she's afraid to look frightened," she told herself.

"Help!" she screamed, her voice as loud as she could muster the wind to make it. "Murder! HELP!"

She heard her voice carry across the village, echoing back at her, and almost immediately she could hear the pounding of feet, the yell being taken up and passed on.

The first to arrive was some young, fleet-footed lad, sweaty from his early-morning labors but barely breathing hard as he came toward the door of the brothers' cottage at an easy lope. She didn't know the boy's name, but guessed that he was perhaps a year or so younger than herself.

Aelis brought her wand up and, before he could brace himself to offer any resistance, released a Second Order Enchantment upon him; Holbein's

Compulsion. Green flashed from the tip of her wand and his eyes went wide, his face slack.

"Run to my tower! If you see a horse along the way, take it and do not spare the beast. Inside there is a large leather case with two handles and brass fittings. It will be heavy. You are to bring it back here, immediately, as fast as you can, with no thought of anything else! GO!"

Having paused only long enough to absorb her orders, the boy took off at a sprint that made his earlier run look like a casual stroll.

He'll pay for that later, she told herself. *You'll have other wounds to treat. Strained muscles and ligaments.*

Yes, she answered, *but Otto might live.*

As other villagers arrived, she spared them the brunt of her Enchantments and simply issued garden variety orders; to one, the cleanest cloths he could produce. To another, boiling water. A third she set to fetching wood to build up the fire.

And as she waited, agonizingly, for the boy to return with her case, she knew Otto's life was slipping away and that she'd but one chance—and it was an experience neither of them would find pleasant.

Aelis splayed her hand out around the handle of her dagger so that she could touch Otto's skin with both her blade and her fingers, and then she reached for the words to one of the most complex Second Order Necromantic Bindings she knew: Aldayim's Refinement.

For almost as long as magic had been practiced, Necromancers had been feared and reviled for that most basic of functions ascribed to the working of Onoma's magic; raising the dead. In truth, they did not raise the dead, but rather animated dead flesh, sometimes with their own spirits, more often with whatever free-floating spirit or magical energy was available to the caster.

Aldayim, the greatest of Necromancers and among the handful of the greatest wizards of the past few centuries, had been the first to realize the lifesaving potential of that very magic.

Running the words through in her head half a dozen times before speaking them aloud, Aelis felt the power coalescing in her, gathering from the power inherent in the world, focused by the enchantments bound into her dagger. The silver runes engraved upon it began to glow faintly.

And with this small change to the basic spell to animate a corpse, Aelis bound Otto's spirit, his soul, his life-force—so much ink had been spilled over what, exactly, to call that spark without which flesh was so much meat—into his own dying body and held it there for the near quarter of an hour it took the boy to return.

When the farmboy came pounding on the door of the shack, her case in his hands, he was practically stumbling. She took the leather handles from him, still holding the words of the Refinement in her head—and keeping a tight metaphysical grip on Otto's spirit. The farmboy collapsed into a panting heap, his arms and legs twitching.

"Someone fetch him water, get him sitting up and stretching his legs out. Don't let him drink too much, but don't let him fall asleep," she yelled to the crowd that had assembled outside the door.

Once Otto's soul had been held, protesting, it seemed to her, in place, she no longer had to stand still and keep herself and her knife in contact with his skin. In fact, had she done so, Aelis was not entirely certain she would've remained conscious. By holding the spell as one small hard point of brightness in her mind, she could move and perform other basic tasks without losing herself to the demands the magic was making of her. She hadn't been idle.

She'd gotten the fire built up and irons wedged deep into it, elevated Otto's head and legs, and located a bottle of vile-smelling hooch that one or both of the brothers had kept hidden inside the thatch of their roof; it was mostly clear, it smelled strong enough to strip paint from wood, and she had splashed half of it into a cauldron she'd plopped right into the fire, there being no hook or spit set over their mean hearth.

Otto was still alive, thanks to the Refinement, but the blade rising and falling in his guts with his breath was doing him no good. Her barked orders—and her blood-smeared hands and heavy, rune-written black dagger—had cleared out the crowd, or at least kept them from pushing inside the cottage. She heard shrieking and crying, but pushed it away, thankful for the amount of light the loose thatch and uncovered windows let in.

With her case of instruments open beside her on the floor, her hands splashed with the most powerful astringent she had, strips of cloth, and three needles of varying sizes threaded and stuck against one of the cloths wound around the upper part of her forearm, Aelis finally paused for a deep breath.

"I'm sorry, Otto," she muttered, then seized the handle of the knife and pulled it free in one smooth motion, while the big farmer moaned and wheezed and blood burbled from behind the long—and, Aelis realized with a thud in her stomach—serrated blade.

◆　◆　◆

Aelis spent the next hour with her fingers buried in Otto's steaming innards, making the minutest of movements, pausing to take a reading through her Anatomist's Dagger, it seemed to her, every half a minute.

She should've been performing this surgery in a room of stone and marble that an Invoker had swept clean with controlled fire just before her entry. The instruments should've been silver and steel and meticulously cleaned by Conjured servants. If she were truly lucky, an Illusionist would've been on hand to create images in a large mirrored surface of exactly what she was doing.

That was all, of course, little more than a dream. Perhaps if one of the Crowns or a leading member of the Estates House were to require the ministrations of one of the best Anatomists of the Lyceum, and they spared no expense, such luxuries would've been possible.

Otto could've used any or all of them, though. Instead, she had her dagger, her case of instruments, and her own two hands.

Which are as good as those of any Anatomist currently living, she told herself. Still, trying to tie knots with the smallest movements of the tiniest scissors and tweezers she owned, with her own hands slippery with blood and gore, was proving more than slightly difficult. She'd never performed surgery of this complexity before, and there was a significant chance that she was going to have to fix one or more mistakes she was making at that very moment at a later date.

When Otto's healthier and has had the time to replace the blood he's lost and recover his strength, she told herself. *When*, she repeated firmly, as if to ward off the *if*—and it was indeed a large and lurking *if*—that her mind wanted to supply.

There were limits to what Otto's body and spirit could stand, and to her own endurance, physical and mental, and they were all drawing close, if not already passed. When she made the last knot that closed the ugly wound in his stomach, Aelis wanted to collapse right there on the dirt floor and sleep.

Caring for the wounded immediately after performing surgery is likely to be just as important as the operation itself, she remembered, words from some textbook or lecture she didn't, at the moment, want to recall too closely. "And there is no one else here to do it," she muttered.

Finally, as her senses came back to her, she was conscious that a crowd—the entire village, give or take—had gathered outside the cottage. Bruce, Rus, and a few other men had kept the curious villagers back from the door. She made a mental note to thank them all later, but for now, it seemed likely that more imperious action was called for.

Wearily, she pushed herself to her feet and went outside. Emilie, tall and fierce-looking in the front rank of the crowd, was holding a crying and terrified Pips at her side, but could keep her back no more. The girl took off like a quarrel loosed from an arbalest's string, slipped past the knot of men blocking the entrance to her home, and nearly bowled Aelis over in her rush. She tried to grab at the girl's sleeve but she made it into the doorway and saw the spectacle of her uncle lying on the floor, blood drying over his entire torso, Aelis's dirty instruments, the bright red line of the wound. Phillipa let loose a scream of anger and frustration.

Aelis moved to the girl's side, intending to comfort her, when Phillipa whirled on her, her jaw fiercely clenched, eyes narrowed.

"Who did this? You're going to find who did it and punish 'em, aren't you? That's your job, isn't it, Warden?"

The entire village could not have failed to hear what the girl shouted in that tiny room, and so she was bound by the moment, and Aelis knew it.

"Yes, Phillipa," she answered, trying to steady her voice with what remained of her energy. "It is my job, as you've said. And I mean to do it," she added, pitching her voice louder for everyone to hear. "But first I must see to Otto's health." She extended one hand to Pips, and the girl moved to take it before seeing the blood and gore still smeared on it and recoiling away.

Aelis sighed and waved her out the door, following with commands in her voice. "I'm going to need the strongest, steadiest men of the village to carry a litter," she began. And, to her surprise, the people of Lone Pine snapped right to every task she set without so much as a complaint.

12

THE TRACKER

When Otto was settled in one of the ground-floor rooms of the inn and she had washed her hands with water as scalding as she could stand, Aelis finally lowered her chin to her chest. For a moment, just one, she allowed herself to feel all the fear and panic she'd kept at bay while dealing with Otto's injury. The residue of the emotions was too dim and distant to do her any real harm, and as the immediate threat was past, she could allow herself these few seconds.

A ripple of fear and a shiver passed down her arms, which she only just seemed to realize were bare. She felt the trailing threads where she'd ripped the sleeves off to bind Otto's wound, and suddenly remembered that she was in the kitchen of the inn, a far too public space to go to pieces, even briefly. She walled the impulse away and looked up to find Martin watching her closely.

"Are you well, Warden?" The lankier of the two innkeepers moved rather awkwardly, with his right arm oddly bent and stiff, his shoulder slightly humped. But the kitchen was his domain, and though he did appear awkward to Aelis's eyes at first, as he bustled about, looking at this or that bit of progress—rising dough, a pot on the stove, the heat and height of the fire, the woodpile—he moved with total assurance.

"As well as I'll need to be, Martin, thank you," she said, summoning as much steadiness as she could into her voice.

"I think that's true of most of us," he murmured as he reached for a ladle hanging from a peg fixed to the wall above the woodstove. "Lone Pine folk'll be shaken, except maybe those who were in the fighting. But the sheep and the goats still need tending, and the barley and the oats don't stop growing, either."

She watched him drag the ladle through whatever he had cooking in the pot and hold up a bit of it to his nose to smell. He began rummaging around in some wooden bowls he had set on a long table behind him. She could see the thousands of knife blows the wood had taken, could smell the scents of bread and meat and broth that hung perpetually in the air in the room.

"When's the last time Lone Pine had to build a scaffold?" she muttered aloud, uncertain why she said it. Martin heard her, though, and only raised an eyebrow at her.

"Can't say it's happened since we've been here, but that's only four years. Not a lot of crime done around here, you know? Not much for folks to steal, little reason to kill . . ." He frowned as he set his ladle down on a spoon rest on the table behind him. "I don't think they'll look kindly on fratricide, though."

"We don't know that's what happened," Aelis said, a quick reflex that was perhaps too quick, given the disbelieving look Martin fixed on her. "And I remind you that Otto is still alive."

"Elmo'd hardly be the first who brought the war home with him and couldn't find a way to lose it," Martin said, leaning against his table. "And I'm sure I'm not the only one thinking this. Folk had been waiting for this to happen for years."

"Please," Aelis said, "don't speak as if anything has been determined. At least, not to me. I can't control what you'll say to anyone else, and I won't try—but I have to remain as objective as I can about it, and I cannot be seen to favor anyone's theory."

Martin looked a bit stung, and sheepishly turned his eyes down to his boots. Aelis sighed and headed for the door to the taproom, patting him lightly on the shoulder as she passed. "Thank you for the use of your kitchen fire to clean myself off. And for all the help, and the food, you and Rus have provided me. Like as not I'd have starved by now if it weren't for the two of you." She gestured to the heavy iron pot she'd boiled water in to wash her hands and arms. "You're going to want to throw that water out and scour the pot well. I'll help if I can."

"You've got bigger tasks to worry you, Warden. I know," Martin said. Aelis leaned against the wall of the kitchen for a moment, letting herself feel her own weariness. She watched Martin move around the kitchen, navigating it by touch and memory, reaching for tools without looking for them, composed and in control of himself and his environment in a way she hadn't seen him before. Questions bloomed in her mind, but she pushed them away, straightened her back, and went out to the taproom. Without meeting the eyes of any of the Thorns, who were gathered in their corner still, she went straight to Otto's room. Inside she found Rus, his face fallen and grim, hands clenching and unclenching at his sides, along with Pips, who was clutching her uncle's hand, and Emilie, who was standing over him with one hand on his forehead.

"That man is *my* patient," Aelis snapped. "Keep your hands to yourself."

"He was my friend first," Emilie answered absently, "and I had medical training in my home, and in the army, I am perfectly able to . . ."

Aelis hadn't the time or the patience. Perhaps it was fortunate for the taller woman that she hadn't much power left in her either, but she had some, and she used it. With her hand wrapped around the hilt of her still-scabbarded sword, she called a ward into place around Otto's bed. Emilie's hands were thrown immediately aside and she looked to Aelis in shock.

"What did you do? What witchery is this?"

Ignoring the woman's angry words and shocked face, Aelis addressed Rus, speaking through clenched teeth.

"Get this woman out of this room, and do not allow her back in, or I will bind her for an assize," she grated.

"You'll not bind me for anything," Emilie spat, taking a half step toward Aelis before Rus interposed himself. The innkeep wasn't an imposing man—in fact Emilie was taller than him by a handsbreadth or better—but he murmured to her, carefully took her arms in his hands, and guided her toward the door.

Aelis turned to Otto—and to Pips, who was rubbing her hands and eyeing her back suspiciously.

"What'd you do that for?" the girl asked, a sniffle in her voice. "She was only trying to help."

"Phillipa," Aelis said as she put one hand onto the bedstead in order to lean on it without looking like she was leaning on it. "Until I know how your uncle is doing, I can't have anyone trying to help in any way I did not ask them to. I need to help him get better, and I hope to be able to ask him questions."

"Was Uncle Elmo that did it," Phillipa said with a sigh. "I saw the knife, it was that big saw-tooth thing, yeah? Uncle Otto always told him to get rid of it, trade it away or somethin', that it was no good for farmer's work. Elmo said he would one day. Then Otto would say 'not today, though,' and Elmo would stalk off."

The girl looked down at her uncle's prostrate form and wiped her nose with the back of her hand. "It was scary, when he got all lost in his head, but I never thought he'd—"

Putting it into words made the girl's resolve crumble and brought on a fresh wave of tears. Aelis was half tempted to turn for the door and ask Rus or Emilie to deal with her. Calming grief-stricken children was hardly in her purview.

And yet, she was one of the people of Lone Pine, and that made her Aelis's responsibility. The Warden laid one hand on the back of the girl's neck and pulled her close.

"I don't know if Elmo did it, Pips. But I'm going to find out who did, and why, and mete out fitting punishment."

"What's meat got t'do with it?" the girl asked through a muffled hiccup as she buried her face in Aelis's hip.

She sighed. "I mean I'll . . . find the right punishment for them."

"Is Uncle Otto gonna die?"

"I don't know," Aelis said, instantly regretting the truth spoken aloud. "I will do everything I can for him."

"You can't find who done it and keep him alive at the same time, can you?"

Fuck. Aelis only just stopped herself from speaking the curse aloud. *Girl just pointed out the contradiction in your obligations.*

She decided to ignore that for the moment and focused on Otto. His temperature seemed normal, his breathing even if not easy, but he was deep in sleep. *Going to need to come up with something for the pain when he wakes,* she thought. *And prepare dressings.* She realized that Pips was still clinging to her, but that the girl had stepped back and kept rubbing her hands.

Aelis looked down at her, lifting a brow. "What's the matter?"

"Stung, when you did that . . . thing. The magic whatsit that pushed me and Emilie away."

"Stung? You should have just been pushed away."

Pips flexed her hands and stepped away, looking up at Aelis. "Hands are tingly, like I sat on 'em, yeah?"

Worldsoul, bury me so deep that even Onoma couldn't find me, Aelis thought, a curse she wouldn't have dared to speak aloud.

"Pips," she said, "after I make some preparations we're . . . going to have to have a talk."

"What about?"

The fact that you shouldn't be able to feel anything from a ward, and that you did probably means you can learn to do more than feel it. But I can only deal with one gods-damned crisis at a time. "About your future," she said. "Now, go on. Otto needs rest and not to be bothered. Outside with you."

The girl led the way out but the hallway was blocked with the glowering Emilie, staring daggers at Aelis. Rus had apparently quit the field, and frankly Aelis couldn't blame him, given the way the tall woman looked ready to do immediate violence.

"Pips," Aelis said, "go out to the taproom, would you?" She gave the girl a gentle shove on the shoulder, and then let her hand rest casually on the hilt of her sword. The girl walked off, slowly, with a worried backward glance. Aelis fixed her eyes on Emilie and didn't bother to hide the weariness in her deep sigh, though she hoped it came across as casual indifference to drawing her sword and spilling blood.

"Emilie, I—"

"You did some kind of foul magic to him. I could smell it on him. The magic of death."

That stopped Aelis in her tracks, and she could only blink stupidly. "What?"

"I could smell the magic of death, of the Queen of the Void on him. It is foul."

"And it was the only thing keeping him alive while my instruments were fetched," Aelis snapped. "And what do you mean, you could smell the magic?"

Emilie lifted her chin defiantly. "I may not have been to your decadent Colleges, but—"

Aelis cut her off with the raised edge of one hand. "But you're the local cunning woman, with just enough knowledge to make my life miserable and not enough wisdom to know when you're overmatched." She took a step forward, clenching her jaw, and wrapped her fist once more around the hilt of her sword. "What you smelled or sensed or detected or however you need to believe you perceived what I did, *all* I did was keep Otto's soul, or his spirit, or the spark of life—whatever you might like to call it—within his own flesh for a little longer than it naturally would've been. It bought me the time I needed to save his life using precisely what I learned in my *decadent Colleges*, specifically the College of Necromancy in the Lyceum. The important work I did—what that same College taught me—was done with thread and needle, astringent and tincture. And if you attempt to interfere or question my work again, I will show you more of what I learned. Do you understand me?"

"I will not be ordered about by some girl ten years my junior," Emilie began, only to hush when Aelis's wand came to rest below her chin, its tip glowing a very faint green.

"You will be ordered about by the Warden of Lone Pine," Aelis hissed. "Who," she added, stepping away and lowering her wand, "would rather ask for and receive your help than order and compel. You do have medical training, yes?"

Emilie's eyes remained fixed on Aelis's wand and its glowing tip, which tiny trick of its construction Aelis dismissed. But the tall woman nodded and Aelis sighed again.

"I need someone to tend to Otto while I'm away. To clean and dress his wounds, to give him medicaments and infusions on a schedule, and to be able to brew new versions of them according to my instructions if the supplies I make don't last. As far as I can tell, you're the best person available for the task."

"Why would I help you, after you've shown me your contempt, your disregard?"

"Because you said Otto was your friend, and because I think you care for Phillipa."

"And where will you be going?"

"To find the man who stabbed him."

"It was his brother Elmo. And he is long gone."

"Then I'll find someone who can track him down," Aelis said, turning and stomping into the taproom, knowing Emilie would follow with more questions.

Her eyes immediately went to the Thorns in the far corner, or the table where they had *been*, only to find it empty. Rus was making himself scarce behind the counter. Aelis caught his eyes.

"They've left?"

He shook his head slightly. "Don't think so. Gone to make their last preparations, though. I don't think the dwarf is leaving without your bank note."

"He can damn well wait for it. Who's the best tracker in the village?"

"Elmo," Rus answered, without missing a beat.

"Who's second best, then?"

"Otto, probably," Rus replied. "And he wouldn't be good enough to find Elmo if he'd a mind to be lost."

"There's got to be someone here who can."

Rus set both his hands, palms flat, on the counter and lowered his head for a moment. "There is one person who could find him. If . . . and I stress *if* . . . he can be convinced to help."

"Silver is not much of an object for me. If I'm already annoying my father with one extravagant letter of credit, a second won't do much harm."

Rus chuckled grimly. "I'm afraid that the man I have in mind has no use for silver. You're just going to have to talk to him. And hope he's willing to listen."

Rus's words triggered something in Aelis's mind: an enormous figure covered in fringed hides, carrying an elk on his back as though it weighed no more than a bundle of sticks. A shambling mountain of a man who disappeared into the woods on the hill above the inn with less noise than a fox.

"Well. Where does one go to take a meeting with Tun, then?"

✦   ✦   ✦

Two hours later, her bare arms slick with sweat, Aelis cursed as she tripped over yet another knotted root. She was half certain the damn things were animated by some mischief-minded Conjurer and set to grabbing at her ankles and pulling her to the ground.

Based on Rus's directions, she should be getting close, if she wasn't already horrifyingly lost.

"If worse comes to worst," she muttered, "I can wait till it gets dark and Onoma's moon sheds enough light for me to find my way clear."

She thrashed around in a general westward direction for a while longer, her arms getting scratched by low-hanging tree limbs. Her sweat, and the small scratches on her skin, began to attract tiny stinging insects and she wished she still had the strength of will to summon the kind of low-intensity but long-lasting ward that would keep them clear of her skin. *Precisely the kind of waste of power Lavanalla would've chided me for,* she thought.

"Or I suppose I could start setting fires until someone comes looking for me," Aelis said out loud as she came into yet another small and unremarkable clearing and leaned against the thick trunk of a tree.

"I would prefer you didn't," said a quiet voice from just behind and above her. She whirled, her hand falling to her sword and drawing it partway out of the scabbard.

Standing between two trees that looked like mere saplings next to his bulk, Tun was only a yard or two away from her, wearing the same leather jerkin she'd seen him in before, the hood up. His masses of hair—some of it braided with small ornaments and charms, much of it hanging in loosely gathered strands—and the shadows of the trees obscured most of his face.

Aelis was immediately conscious of how enormous he was. Easily a foot taller than her, probably more, with a huge breadth of chest and shoulder, his arms strained the sleeves of his jerkin. The hands that emerged from the sleeves had enormous, swollen-looking knuckles, and she thought there was something odd about the color of his skin, but the movement of light through the trees kept her from determining just what that was.

There was also a powerful scent about him. Not an offensive body odor, and one hardly got far in the College of Necromancy with a weak stomach. Even so, Aelis couldn't help but notice it, a kind of strong animal smell.

"Well," he said. "You came all the way out here. What do you want? Need to trade for meat, furs?" His voice was surprisingly gentle, careful almost, and at odds with his wild mountain man appearance.

"No," Aelis said, finally unwrapping her hand from the hilt of her sword. She swallowed hard, not out of fear, but to buy herself time to find what to say. "I came to ask for help."

Tun didn't move, and she couldn't see his eyes aside from a deep glimmer beneath the shadow of his brow, but she had the feeling of being intensely studied. He was so still that she wouldn't have known he was breathing if she couldn't hear it.

He waited a long moment before finally breaking the silence. "Help with?"

"There's been a stabbing in the village," Aelis began.

Tun lifted a hand, his forefinger extended. She paused, nodded slightly.

"Who was stabbed? And by whom?"

"Looks like Elmo stuck his brother Otto, then ran."

Tun gave a small sigh. "Elmo. Scout?"

"The same," Aelis said. "Rus told me that the only person in the village who had a chance of tracking him *might* be Otto."

"Is Otto dead?"

"No," Aelis said. "But . . ." She shrugged, saw no reason to hide the truth. "He may yet die. The wound was bad. I've done what I could—"

"Which was what?"

"I closed the wound. Sewed up as many of the cut pieces of Otto's guts as I could as cleanly as I could. But his bowels were pierced, torn in places. Lots of ways for illness to seize him."

Tun nodded slowly, but she knew that wasn't yet an assent to her request. "Are you certain Elmo did it?"

"Their niece says it was his knife."

"Saw-edged blade?"

Aelis nodded.

Tun heaved a bigger sigh, turned his head, and spat into the dirt. She thought that she dimly heard him mutter words in a language she didn't recognize, then he turned back to her.

"Those knives are a sin. Always were. Never much liked the men who carried them." Another pause as he studied her, his features and eyes still hidden from her. "If you find Elmo, what do you plan to do with him?"

"Sort out what happened," Aelis said. "Bring him back to the village to face his brother, and an inquiry, maybe an assize. It's possible he wasn't in control of himself."

"Oh?"

"He has problems, from the war. And there's a chance that a malign enchantment was working on him when he did it."

"A malign enchantment." Tun said the words as if tasting them. "You have a way with phrases, Warden. I must ask: By assize, do you mean that you will bring him straight home to the gallows?"

"Only if the law that I am duty-bound to demands it."

"That answer abdicates your responsibility."

"If he has to die, I will take all the responsibility. I'm not going to avoid that. Allow me to rephrase; the best outcome is that *neither* of these brothers dies. The best outcome, the one I wish for, is that they both find ways to go on living, for themselves and for Pips." She paused. "An old Warden once told me that I should wish in one hand, shit in the other, and see which fills up first. I won't hold tight to wishes."

Tun tilted his head very slightly, then began to laugh. It started out as a slow, quiet rumble, and grew to a roar that seemed to shake her teeth. He slapped a massive hand against his stomach and ceased laughing but slowly a few moments later, little wheezes and chuckles rolling out of his mouth.

"I like you, Warden," he said finally, the laughter replaced with careful, almost solemn speech. Aelis suddenly wondered if he spoke around some kind of injury or impediment, his words came so slowly and cautiously. "But I do not know if I will help you."

"I would pay you. Generously."

"Silver is of no use to me."

"Gold? Jewels?"

"Can't eat them, can't make decent tools with them, won't keep me warm in the winter."

"What can I offer you, then?"

"Perhaps a favor," Tun said. "But I have decided, regardless. I will help you track down this man, and bring him back to face whatever justice is due."

"That was a quick decision."

"Not as quick as you might think." Tun paused. "I will track him for you, but I will not kill him for you."

"I wouldn't dream of asking."

He came forward, extending one huge arm toward her. "If we are to work together, we should know each other's names. Formally." He paused, hand waiting in the air before her. "Tunbridge."

"Aelis Cairistiona de Lenti un Tirraval," she replied. Her hand disappeared into his. The skin of his fingers and palms was thick with calluses, and she imagined his wrist was as thick as her biceps. As they shook, he reached up and pushed back the hood and some of the mat of hair that obscured his features.

Light hit his face. His skin had a gray-greenish cast. The ridge of his brow was more prominent than she'd imagined; not so much that it overhung his eyes completely, but they were huge, dark, cavernous.

But what Aelis truly fixated on was the source of Tun's slow and careful speech; the elongated canine teeth that peeked over the edge of his bottom lip. They were beyond teeth; they were tusks.

She was conscious that she looked too long and too directly, but she couldn't tear her eyes away till Tun released her hand and turned away.

"I will go find his trail," Tun said. Now that Aelis knew to listen for it she could hear the way his lips and tongue moved around his long teeth and extended jaw. "I will meet you behind Rus's public house before moonrise."

"We're going to set out in the dark?"

"The man we are chasing has a day's head start. He can move faster than you and knows where he's going. The hours are precious, though we will not run all night."

"Is the dark going to be a problem for you?"

"No. You?"

"Not for a few more nights, at least," Aelis said. "Behind the inn, before moonrise?"

"Yes. Pack lightly. Wear sleeves; if he goes to higher country, it will be colder. And then there is the sun."

Aelis sighed. "I had to rip my sleeves to bind Otto's wounds. I do not normally go about like this."

Tun, once more a still mass of half shadow framed by tree trunks, shrugged so faintly she hardly caught the gesture. "I make it a point not to take for granted what you people know and don't know."

"You people?"

Tun snorted in a way that might have been amused or dismissive or both. "City folk."

"How did you know I'm—"

He heaved a great, long-suffering sigh. "By the evidence of my senses. You smell of it; you've not been here long enough to wash it away. I could see it in how you walked and the noise you made and hear it in your voice. Then you told me your name; un Tirraval is rather unmistakable. What parts of that county that are *not* city are hardly untamed wilderness, hmm?"

"Don't approve of cities?"

"Cities don't approve of me."

Aelis paused, felt the moment stretch awkwardly. "Is there anything else you'd like to criticize about me or my place of origin before we work together?"

"I was not criticizing. I was observing," Tun said. "I will add this: I expected your hand to be soft, your wrist weak. They were not." One of his trunk-like arms raised, a thick finger extended toward the sword she wore. "You know how to use that."

"I do," Aelis said, feeling a measure of her confidence filling the words as she spoke them.

"You have a city dweller's confidence, too." He pushed away from the tree. "We have spent too much wind trying to impress each other. Go see to your wounded man, pack. Lightly. Best if I don't have to carry anything for you."

"I can carry what I'll need," Aelis said, though she had the sense that Tun was no longer listening to her. She watched him stride away with an easy gliding movement that seemed unlikely, at best, from someone of his size. In fewer steps than should've been possible, even in such a dense wood, he vanished from sight.

13

THE KISS

"You didn't tell me he was a half-orc," Aelis blurted in response to Rus's query of how her meeting with Tun had gone.

"You didn't ask. And I'm not sure I'd go throwing that precise term at him."

"Well, then, what term do I use?"

Rus blinked, drew out the silence. "His name?"

"You know what I mean," Aelis nearly spat.

"Listen to me. Tun is no more interested in continuing the old enmity than you are. He agreed to help you, which is a victory in itself."

"What's he going to want in exchange, is what I'd like to know," Aelis grumbled. "Muttered something about needing a favor later."

"He's not likely to ask for anything that will burden you unduly," Rus said.

"I need to get back to my tower, gather some supplies, mix some medicines, and pack," Aelis said. "Send the Thorns there if they want their letter. Tun wants to set off before moonrise."

"You can keep up with him in the dark?"

"Don't have much choice about it, do I?"

"Suppose not." Rus was helping her pack up her cleaned instruments. "You could just let him track the man down himself while you stayed here and saw to Otto."

"No," Aelis said. "Not acceptable. Otto is my responsibility, yes. So is Elmo. So is anyone else he might hurt between here and wherever he's headed. Besides, Tun only agreed to track him, not do anything else."

"Well, that alone might be enough. He's the best woodsman I've ever known."

"Better than a Ystain scout, which Elmo apparently was?"

Rus stared at her, hard, for a moment. "Why do you think the Ystain scouts came back frightened, maimed, or not at all?"

"Did Tun fight, then?"

"Look at him. Take an hour and walk around him. Do you think there's much chance he didn't?"

"Being a fighter and being a woodsman are two different things," Aelis said.

"Not for an orc, they aren't."

Aelis snapped the brass fixtures on her heavy leather case shut and hefted it off the table. "As much as I'd like to hear war stories—having never gotten my fill of them from my father, my aunt, and my uncles—I've got to be off. I'll be back soon."

With her case swinging in her hand, Aelis headed out, only to find Emilie and Pips standing just outside the inn, apparently waiting for her.

"We've got unfinished business, Warden," Emilie began.

"Yes," Aelis said, "we do." She thought, perhaps, the woman was going to reach for the long knife on her belt, so she decided to head her off with quick words. "Like what I'm going to have to pay you to watch over Otto, change his dressings, and give him the medicines I'm about to make on a set schedule."

Emilie was taken aback for a moment, clearly disarmed by Aelis's calm response. Quickly, though, fire leapt back into her eyes. "Why," she began, "should I suddenly bend to your whim, arrogant child?"

"I'm twenty-two," Aelis said wearily, "a graduate of three Colleges of the Lyceum, and a Warden." She paused. "Arrogant, I'll give you." Aelis had heard that too often in her life to simply dismiss it. "I don't really want to make this some kind of legal order, Emilie. Neither of us has the time for that. Otto surely doesn't. I don't think you want him to die any more than I do, and the best chance to make sure that doesn't happen is if we work together."

Emilie's nose flared and she turned her head, examining Aelis intently with one eye and then the other. "Why would you assume you'd have to pay me?"

"If you want to do it for free, that's also acceptable. I'm authorized, as the Warden of Lone Pine, to promise remuneration, paid by the Tri-crowns and the Estates House, to private citizens who assist in my duties. I thought perhaps some extra silver wouldn't go amiss, but—"

"It wouldn't," Emilie said. "But an apology would go further. Talk to me like a person, not a servant. You aren't the only one here who's had their hands in someone's guts to try and save their life."

Aelis bit back a sharp retort. She knew she needed Emilie's help, and if she'd lasted that long as a medic, she must've known at least a bit more than the basics.

"I'm sorry, Emilie." Aelis looked the taller woman in the eye and extended her right hand. "Help me save Otto's life, and if we have to, when I get back, we can yank each other's hair out then."

Emilie snorted, but took Aelis's hand after a moment's pause. "That's why I wear it short on the sides and tight against my neck," she said. "Makes it harder for anyone to grab in a fight."

"I never could pull off a shaved look," Aelis said as they shook hands. "Looks good on you, though." Aelis knew that flattery had always worked on her, so there was a chance it could on Emilie as well. They stood for a moment, neither sure of what to say.

Before the moment could grow too awkward, Pips—who still clung to Emilie's other arm—spoke up.

"Do you really have to leave while my uncle is still hurt?"

Aelis squatted so she could look the girl directly in the eye.

"I do, Pips," Aelis said. "But," she added, glancing up at Emilie, who nodded faintly, "Emilie is going to take good care of him while I'm gone. It won't be the first time she's kept a man alive, and she'll have the advantages of my medicines and instructions."

Emilie muttered something unintelligible and chewed at the inside of her cheek, but Aelis wasn't too troubled by whatever it might've been. Then Emilie turned and went back into Otto's room. For a moment Aelis wanted to hurry after and check on what she was doing, but there was Pips to deal with. *And besides, if I'm going to trust Otto's life to her, I might as well start now.*

"And when I get back, Phillipa . . . we're going to have a long talk. I'm going to keep teaching you reading, writing, and ciphering, and reading you stories, and teaching you about wizards. There may be a lot I can teach you, and I'm not going to avoid it. When I come back, I want to see full pages of your name, written as neatly as you can manage. And mine."

"Why does it matter?"

"It matters because when my ward touched you, it made your fingers tingle," Aelis said. *No holding back now. Careful not to get the girl's hopes up.* "You felt the magic. That means somewhere, deep within you, is the capacity to learn how to use it."

"I'm magical? I could be a wizard? I could be a Warden, like that

Lavanalla elf woman you told me about? I could call down fires and lightning and—"

It was all Aelis could do not to clamp her hand over the girl's mouth. "I don't know about any of that. I know that you have the capacity to learn *something* of magic. I don't know what or how much. I do know that it must start with becoming lettered. *Must.* There is no wizard nor warden to be made of a girl who can't read."

Aelis knew even as she said it that was something of a lie, as at least one orally transmitted magical tradition persisted on the small island nations that clung like barnacles to the triumvirate's southwestern coastline.

Phillipa bit her bottom lip and twisted it between her teeth as if judging the awful weight of literacy versus the possibility of magic. "I'll work on it every day if you make me a promise."

"What promise?"

"Don't kill my uncle Elmo. Bring him back alive."

"That's a lot to ask, Pips," Aelis said. "I may not have a choice." She could see, as soon as she spoke the words, that blunt-force honesty was the wrong approach to take, as the girl's face began to collapse and tears gathered at the corners of her eyes.

"Aren't you our Warden? Supposed to take care of us, *all* of us? If you can't take good care of one of us, then what're you for?"

Aelis sighed and felt her patience slipping. *You lie to the child, and you'll lose her. You know this.* "Pips. I will do everything I can to find out what happened, what Elmo did, and why, and I will bring him back alive unless he is going to kill me or someone else. That's the best I can offer. It'll have to do."

Pips nodded, not entirely mollified, but Aelis straightened up, gave the girl a quick hug, and strode on.

*   *   *

Within the hour, she was in fresh clothes—breeches, her best-fitting and most watertight boots, and a tailored leather jacket. All of it was black, which would do her no favors in the heat, but the jacket at least was built to accommodate her needs. It would offer a whisper of protection in a fight, though in truth she'd be better served relying on her wards. There were no fewer than three places to fix her wand. She slid it up her left sleeve, as was her practice, but there was also a slit beneath her right arm, as some preferred a cross-body draw, and a similar pocket in her right sleeve. And since this was working gear, first and foremost, she no longer bothered to hide her dagger at the small of her back, but positioned it on a frog right at the front of her belt.

Once she was dressed and armed, Aelis considered what else she'd have to pack. She shook out the canvas rucksack she'd hoped to never have to use, and quickly filled its bottom with stockings, a spare shirt, spare breeches, oil and whetstone, candles and the like. From one of her chests she hauled out a brown leather case that was a smaller cousin of her large case of instruments. She transferred the most vital things into it: herbal preparations, astringents, needles, thread, bandages. Larger implements, intended for more complex surgeries, she left aside.

Aelis lingered over the bone saw, then shrugged and left it in place. "I'm not going to a battlefield surgery, after all," she murmured. She snatched up a few vials of the reagents for her lamp, measuring them carefully by eye, then set them inside slots in her smaller case.

With that done, and her rucksack looking fuller than she would've liked, she took the necessary herbs, went to her alchemy table, coaxed her alchemy ring to flame, and spent an hour brewing up the medicines she intended to leave for Emilie. Once she'd started the reactions—wishing for all the moons that the calcination oven stuck in the debris above her was operable—she drew up a schedule with ink and paper. She wrote in haste, but was careful to make it simple and legible. When the flask clamped above the burning ring began to hiss, she quickly doused the flame. The medicine went into a week's worth of small vials set in a wooden rack to cool.

There was a heavy knock at her door, which sounded as though it was ready to clatter off its hinges.

"By Onoma's cold and pale ass, if that's the dwarf after his coin I will trim his beard with a dull fucking knife," Aelis said as she strode down the hall and threw open the door. It squealed, a hinge gave way, and the oak sank to the stone floor and looked for all the world as though it wasn't going to move.

"I haven't got a beard," Maurenia said, standing in the tower's doorway with one hand casually resting on the stone wall. "But my ass is fairly pale."

"Are you here for the letter? I was just about to draft it."

"For the letter and for taking leave, yes," Maurenia said calmly. "May I come in?"

Aelis stood back and swept a hand toward the entry. "It's a right fucking mess. But at least with that door off its hinges, I expect everything of value in it to be stripped by the time I get back, so that ought to take care of the clutter."

Maurenia tsked softly. "These yokels are too fearful to steal anything in a mere week or two. Give it a month and they'll be knocking through your drawers for silver. Two, they'll take the glassware and break the alchemical equipment because they don't understand it. Three, and they'll burn your books for kindling."

Aelis wanted to protest in defense of the people of Lone Pine, but all she could do was laugh dryly. Awkward and tense as she stood close to Maurenia in the hallway, she pushed a stray lock of her hair back from her eyes.

Her fingers were suddenly caught in the half-elf's, who twirled that lock of hair lightly between the first two fingers of her left hand. "If you're going out traipsing in the woods then leaving all this unbound, fetching though it may be, won't do at all."

In the closeness of the hallway there was nowhere for Aelis to turn to hide the color in her cheeks. She decided to meet Maurenia's eyes. "What do you suggest?"

"I've got a spare headband," Maurenia said. "Bit sweat-stained, I'm afraid. I can also braid it for you."

"Let's braid it, I suppose. Got to wait a while as those cool," Aelis said, pointing a finger to the vials on her table, "before I can cork and label them."

"Come on then. Sit down," Maurenia said. She took Aelis's hand by the wrist and led her to one of the chairs, standing behind it as Aelis sat down. She felt her hair being carefully lifted and tugged into strands by the half-elf's strong fingers. "Any idea where it is you're going?"

"Wherever Tun says we're going."

"Tun's the tracker?"

Aelis started to nod, then winced as she was quickly reminded of the hold Maurenia had on her hair. The half-elf was expertly twisting the strands she'd separated into two long braids; Aelis found that the first was forming rather more quickly than she'd have liked it to.

"More like the local . . . mountain man, I suppose. Trapper, hunter, that kind of thing."

Maurenia made a noncommittal sound. Aelis felt her second braid already taking shape.

Speaking slowly, with her words bitten off as if she was speaking around something clenched in her teeth, Maurenia said, "I could probably track this Elmo for you." A pause. Aelis felt her stomach lurch slightly. "But," Maurenia added, "I have a contract with Timmuk and Andresh, and if I don't see it out . . . if I do not walk back into Lascenise with them, I lose the money I signed on for, I lose the rights to my arbalest design, I lose—"

"You don't owe me an explanation, Maurenia," Aelis interrupted. "I don't expect you to drop everything to run off and help me to my appointed task for no pay even if you hadn't those obligations against you."

Maurenia went silent as she wound the two braids together on the back of Aelis's head, then pinned them into place using the pins she had in fact clenched between her lips.

"It's not about that. I just . . ." Maurenia sighed, adjusted the pin on the last braid. "Have you a glass or a bit of polished steel or something so you can tell me if it's to your liking?"

"I do," Aelis said. She fetched a glass from a drawer and held it up. There were no real surprises; Maurenia had twisted the braids into a crown that lay close against the back of her head. Close enough and tight to keep her hair from troubling her, but not the kind of severe, painfully tight that would end in headaches and a loss of concentration.

Maurenia appeared in the small glass behind her. "If you were going somewhere to be seen, of course, I'd leave a strand down your neck, or framing an eye," she said, demonstrating what she meant by lightly trailing a finger down the side of Aelis's neck. "But I'm sure you've worn much more elaborate hair at court balls . . ."

Aelis turned and caught the hand Maurenia was lowering, twining it in her own. "I only had two seasons of balls and court functions before I went to the Colleges. The fashions called for high-necked dresses and simply bound hair. Postwar austerity and all that."

Maurenia made no attempt to tug her hand out of Aelis's. "What about jewelry?"

"Well, there's some things austerity can't be expected to apply to," Aelis quipped, nervously, laughing a little too readily at her own limp joke.

Aelis looked at Maurenia's face when the half-elf gave her a small smile. The high cheekbones, with a dusting of sun-browned freckles; the slim, faintly pointed ears; the chin-length auburn hair that looked far too clean for a woman who spent her life in the dust of the road. Last, she looked at the blue eyes; alert, missing nothing, alive in a way Aelis couldn't have put into words.

They were awkward a moment, then Aelis breathed, "Oh, fuck it." She darted upward, feeling as clumsy as a boy trying to steal a garden kiss at a dance, but her lips found their target.

She sizzled. A shock as powerful as any minor Evocation that had ever been used in training ran up and down her arms, her neck and back, turned into radiant heat in her cheeks. When Aelis felt their lips parting, she stepped back. Maurenia staggered a moment, blinked.

"Why," Maurenia asked, huskily, "did you stop?"

"Because I don't know what I'm doing. Because you're leaving Lone Pine. Because I'm also leaving but coming back, if there's any luck, and isn't *that* something I never thought I'd say. Because I hardly know you, but I also know that I haven't been able to stop . . ." Aelis trailed off limply.

Maurenia smiled faintly. "Stop what?"

"Looking at you since the moment you took your hood off when you rode up outside the inn. Thinking about you."

"You think I haven't noticed? You think I haven't been looking back?"

"No. Have you? I don't know."

"What *do* you know?" Maurenia leaned close to her again. Aelis felt the tips of the half-elf's hair brush against her cheeks.

"That I want to keep kissing you," Aelis said, and then she was, and they weren't talking for a few moments. By the time Maurenia pulled away, one hand on the back of Aelis's head and one on her shoulder, Aelis found her cheeks were flushed and prickly with heat, her heart was thudding fast and loud, and her vision was filled with Maurenia's fierce eyes.

"I have to leave with the Thorns. But I'm a free woman when we make Lascenise. I can go where I will. If there's snow on the ground, well, I can't promise it'll be back here, but . . ." Maurenia shrugged, and Aelis slid a hand into her hair. *Like silk,* she thought, only that seemed too pat and simple a comparison. "But someday I could find a reason to come this direction."

"If you found a reason to come this direction again, Maurenia, I would find a reason to kiss you again, I expect."

"How about the fact that I'm leaving in an hour?"

Aelis made a show of checking the potions she'd hastily brewed. "The medicaments still need a few minutes."

Before she was finished talking, Maurenia's arm slid around her waist, their mouths met again, and the next few minutes passed heatedly.

14

THE FAREWELL

When they left the tower, no clothes were in disarray and no profound words had been spoken, but their cheeks were flushed and Aelis's hands trembled slightly on the box she carried. In her own hands, noticeably steadier, Maurenia held a map case with a letter of credit drawn on a Tirraval family account at the Urdimonte bank. Aelis had hesitated over the amount, but the pressures of time—Elmo was getting farther away with every moment—left her simply hoping for her father not to have a fit when news of the expenditure reached him. As if plucking the thought from Aelis's head, Maurenia spoke.

"Will your father have your hide for this?"

Aelis shrugged. "It's not a sum that will stretch our family's private funds. But . . . it *will* be noticed."

"You don't mind throwing your family status about as a Warden?"

"I don't mind doing it in order to help the people who have been put into my charge," Aelis said. "Though, in truth, my legal standing to do this is . . . complex."

Maurenia paused and turned to her, one arched eyebrow lifted slowly. "I've been around the Dobrusz brothers long enough to know that 'complex' and 'legal standing' can mean anything from greasing a few palms to decorating a gallows."

"It's nothing like that. It's just that, as a warden, I have fairly free latitude in using my powers, my legal authority, and force of arms. What I am not to do is use status, influence, or alliances from outside my office. It's as much a tradition as a law, but the idea is that *all* wardens are legally empowered with the same tools, and to the same degree. A warden of high birth should be no more powerful than a warden whose parents are crofters."

"Does intention count? Seems you did it for the right reasons. And in a way that hurt you, more than it helped."

Aelis shrugged. "You've never met any group who can argue about a set of rules quite like the Wardens and the Magisters."

"You've never been in the army," Maurenia said. "Nobody loves rules like an officer."

"But the soldiers in their charge can't hurl fire or manipulate minds or summon spirits."

Maurenia nodded. "And which of those can you do, just to be totally clear?"

"A bit of the second and quite a lot of the third, depending on the spirit we're talking about."

"How many kinds *are* there?"

"Hundreds. Shall I lecture you on the formal classification? It begins with whether it is Native or External, and then there is a subheading under External for—"

Maurenia held up a hand with her palm out. "I sat through the last lecture of my life some time ago, thank you. And if I find out what External means I'm not likely to sleep very well."

"It's not as bad as all that."

Maurenia sliced the side of her hand through the air and Aelis cut off with a laugh. They walked in silence for some time then, close enough for Aelis to catch some of Maurenia's scent. There was the leather of her gear, the steel of her weapons, the oil on them. Horse and saddle soap and sweat, but also the warmth of the sun in her hair, a faint hint of a floral perfume she couldn't identify, and something clean and strong. Altogether, it was a pleasant thing, not overpowering, not heady, not delirious.

Aelis was, she had to admit to herself, confused as seventeen hells.

But she wanted to smell more and feel more of what she felt when standing this close to Maurenia.

And she wasn't prepared when they finally reached the outskirts of the village, where the Thorns had drawn up their wagon and their mounts.

"Empty saddle waiting for me," Maurenia murmured, turning to Aelis and sweeping some hair behind an ear. "Time I'm away. But . . . if I can come back sometime," she said, with a shrug that even Aelis could read as *too* casual, "I will."

"Posted here for two years. Unless I fuck up or get myself killed."

"You won't do either one. Got a calm head for a crisis, and that's the most potent gift anyone walking into danger can have, more than any

magic at your command, more than a deft hand with a blade, more than
an army at your back. Do you mind a bit of advice?"

Aelis shook her head, more because it would delay Maurenia's departure than any desire for her advice.

"There's two reasons people'll follow your orders. They fear you, or
they love you. You cannot make these folk love you. But you *can* make
them fear you."

"I don't need them quailing and trembling every time I come to town,
Maurenia."

"You know I don't mean it that way," Maurenia replied.

"Well. What if it could be both," Aelis said. "Fear and love?"

Maurenia shook her head. "Impossible."

"Difficult," Aelis replied. "Not impossible."

"You don't always have to take the most difficult path, Aelis."

"You think that's the first time I've heard that?"

Maurenia laughed, and Aelis felt herself smiling at the sound of it.

She could think of little else to say. By the time she'd gathered any
thoughts she was interrupted, as one of the mounted Thorns had peeled
off from the group, leading Maurenia's riderless horse with him. As he
moved, Aelis saw the leather encasing his neck and arm and quickly realized it was Luth.

He pulled up only a few feet away, and tossed the reins to Maurenia.

"Warden," he said, his voice still that rusty creak. "I have apologies to
make." He tilted his head, aiming his eyes at the ground near Aelis's feet.

She waited. When no more was forthcoming, she said, "Apologies aren't
your strong suit, are they, Luth?"

He laughed, a dusty and mirthless sound that died almost before it was
out of his throat. "Never have been. But I . . . I know acted wrongly. If I
have to make restitution . . ."

"You don't, because I have more immediate matters to attend to," Aelis
said. "I will levy no charges against you. You were under a powerful enchantment and cannot be held totally responsible for your actions. Your
company are all bound for Lascenise now, yes?"

Luth nodded, muttering a few indistinct noises Aelis imagined were the
remnants of his planned apology. She pressed on.

"Once you're paid out, were I you, I'd take the extra day's ride and get
myself to the Lyceum, and the College of Necromancy. If anyone in this
world can do aught about what burned you, it'll be one of the Magisters

there. In particular, if you've the coin and the patience to wait, ask for Margreth Vashdoyen mi Hanrahad. I promise you no miracles. Using my name won't make it free, but it might help you get in the door."

Luth nodded, muttered another sorry, and turned his horse by sawing at the reins rather harder than he'd any need to. Aelis resisted the urge to lift a hand in goodbye to Maurenia, but the half-elf turned in her saddle and looked back, the wind pulling short locks of hair across her eyes for a moment.

There was no crowd gathered to watch the Thorns leave. The village was all quiet, broken occasionally with the sound of a sheep or a goat, the rustle of the wind through the trees. The wagon rolled away, the horsemen who had trotted in to such excitement mere days ago now seen off only by Aelis, Martin, and Rus.

Only Aelis seemed deeply interested in their departure, as Martin and Rus had already gone back into the inn. She turned and followed them, and went straight to Otto's room. Thoughts of Maurenia tormented her. How it felt to be pressed against her, her lips, of her advice at their parting and her mute response. But the plain fact of a patient supine on a bed snapped her out of it. She checked his breathing, his temperature, his heartbeat, and found them all as satisfactory as before. She sniffed at his bandages and smelled only the astringent she'd spread on them.

She was so absorbed in the task that she didn't hear Emilie until the woman was two steps inside the door.

"You're lettered, yes?"

"Of course I am. And of course you would think that no one here—"

"Emilie, I just want to know if you can read the instructions I've written, or if I needed to give the copy to someone else," Aelis snapped. Maurenia's advice flitted across her thoughts. "We both want to keep Otto alive, so let's focus on that."

She stood from the bedside and faced the taller woman with her eyes narrowed, brows beetled. "The instructions are there," she said, pointing to the hinged wooden box. "Get them out. Read them aloud to me." Aelis could barely avoid gritting her teeth before adding, "Please."

Emilie walked to the box, popped open the lid, and pulled out the small pages and read them, carefully, in an even voice that missed no details. Aelis watched, made no sound or sign of approval till the end, when she gave a light nod.

"That'll do. I hope I'll be back in a day or two, a week at most. What

I've been able to make should hold out till then. If you've heard no sign of me when you've got but two days' worth of what's left, move to half doses to stretch it out. You have your own knowledge and expertise to rely on if there are complications or I am delayed. I am trusting you to keep Otto alive till I come back. Will you do one more thing?"

"What? Check on your tower? Sweep your floor? Wash your clothes?"

Aelis felt anger rising in her but once more she forced it back down. "The boy whose sheep were slaughtered by that bear. Burt," she said, suddenly remembering the name. "Check on his stitches. Make sure they're healing and not feverish. And the boy who ran to my tower when Otto was hurt; someone may need to check on him, after the way he exerted himself."

She saw a little bit of anger and defiance drain out of the woman's frame. Emilie hadn't been expecting that, Aelis was sure. In the end, Emilie nodded shortly. *Call it a victory*, Aelis thought.

Deciding to take the answer she wanted and move on, Aelis went into the main taproom. "Rus," she called, a bit curt perhaps, but not yelling.

His head popped out from under the counter where he'd been engaged in his endless wiping or polishing or whatever it was he did.

"I'm off," Aelis said. "I'm afraid I need to ask you for one more favor before I go."

"And what's that?" Rus began wiping his hands with a rag.

"Find someone to fix Otto and Elmo's house while I'm gone. I'll pay for the materials and whatever is considered a fair wage for it. That place is going to fall down before winter without either of them there to hold it up."

Rus nodded, set his polishing cloth down. "I think the folk can come together to do that."

"Excellent," Aelis said. "And when they're done, they can start on my tower for the same terms. I'm going to need a door when I get back."

"To be fair, Warden, we don't know when that'll be, so—"

"So it'll be a good incentive for them to work swiftly, yes?"

"How many orders are you going to give, Warden?"

"As many as I have to. By all means, see to Otto and Elmo first. But let me remind you that the community a Warden serves is obligated to provide shelter, food, fuel, and other reasonable necessities. That tower hardly counts as shelter, and I'm not putting up with it for one second longer. Not one. I will pay for the work's swift completion, but it should have been done before I arrived."

"Warden, I—"

"Get the fucking door fixed," Aelis said, clenching her hands into fists to avoid reaching up to pinch the bridge of her nose. "This town wanted a Warden? It's gotten one. Now it's on the town to live up to the obligations."

Aelis turned and hastily exited. She walked around to the back of the inn before pausing for a breath. She adjusted the straps of the pack she wore, fiddled with her swordbelt, and took a second deep breath before muttering, "What have I just done?"

"Started asserting rights you believe to be yours, I think."

Aelis was so startled by the voice intruding on her thoughts that she had her sword half drawn by the time she whirled to see Tun standing a few feet away. Shadows from the nearby trees seemed to practically attach themselves to him; he stood so still that she imagined any number of people simply walking right past him.

"Onoma's ass, but nobody your size ought to be able to move that quietly."

Tun merely chuckled, or at least she thought he did. He took a half step toward her—a half step that managed to cover a great deal of ground—and held out a stick. Or at the least, it looked like a stick when wrapped in his enormous hand. When Aelis took it, she realized it was a walking staff nearly as thick as her wrist. It was a lovely pale wood, birch, she thought, carefully cut, smoothed, and lacquered to seal it using some substance Aelis couldn't identify. It had a leather loop threaded through a hole that had been augered into it near the top, and a steel cap on the bottom. There was no ornamentation, no carving, no maker's mark that Aelis could see. And yet the thing exuded craftsmanship. It may have been a simple walking stick, but the care and the time that had gone into making it were so apparent, so plainly shouted by the gleaming thing itself, that she was astonished.

"You made this," she stated, not asking. She was certain of it.

"I did," Tun said.

"It is astonishing. I have seen workers in wood and metals who would give their best teeth to have produced a piece of work as elegant and perfect as this."

"It would be a foolish trade, best teeth for a length of wood."

"For what they'd be able to charge in Antraval for it, they could have new teeth made. Gold, silver. Fucking diamond if they managed the demand just right."

"That is still a foolish trade."

Aelis lifted a brow and finally took hold of the walking stick as it was intended, with the loop around her wrist and the cap digging at the ground as if eager to be off. "I'm too stunned to have a debate about whether the entire basis of the Tri-crowns' economy is foolish."

"Bit long for you," Tun commented, ignoring her statement, as he watched her handle the staff. "If we had time I could make one to your height and hand. But we do not."

It was then that Aelis saw Tun was carrying his own walking stick, half a yard taller than the one he'd handed her and thick enough that she honestly wondered if he'd made it from the trunk of a young tree rather than the branch of an old one. He still wore his fringed long coat, and she saw bulges in the pair of enormous pockets on either side. He had a blanket roll slung over his back but it was remarkably thin and light-looking compared to her own. Other than the staff, with which, she imagined, he could club a man in the finest armor, he carried no weapons that she could see.

"I have everything I will need," he said, clearly aware that she was sizing up his gear, such as it was. "And anything I do not have the wilderness will provide."

"How far into the wilderness do you expect we will get?"

He shrugged, a tiny motion made without much energy or expression. "Wilderness is wilderness. It is all of a depth. We are likely to be in it; how far in it is immaterial."

"We could run out of food . . ."

At that, Tun smiled, his lower lip bending around his protruding canines. "Luckily for us, most of the wilderness is edible. If you are done delaying the inevitable, I have your scout's track. We can begin."

Aelis took a deep breath, and nodded. Tun turned, swung his walking stick forward with as much effort as she might have speared a bite of cheese with a polished wooden pick at a university function, and took the first, nearly soundless step.

15

THE WILDERNESS

Aelis quickly realized that she needed to take three paces to Tun's one, and that he wasn't inclined to make allowances by shortening his stride. So three paces to one it was, and after an hour she was feeling the strain.

The Worldsoul could undertake Her seven-hundred-year change before I open my mouth to complain or ask him to slow down, she told herself.

Just as she was thinking that, Tun paused, and she was embarrassed enough at how glad she was of even a moment's respite that she felt a furnace of anger, directed inward, beginning to burn in her stomach. Her guide knelt and lowered his face to a few inches above the grass while she fumed at herself.

"He passed this way. Fast, but not in haste. Soon after his brother was stabbed. He has many hours on us."

"What does that mean, and how do you know?"

Tun looked up at her. She had trouble reading his face. His protruding teeth, which she was trying not to think of as tusks, changed the entire structure of his expressions. But the way his huge eyes narrowed, she was reasonably certain he was puzzled at her questions.

"I would have thought that rhetoric is something you studied, hmm? Fast—he is moving quickly. Not in haste—he is not doing so at the expense of care."

That only stoked Aelis's anger further, but Tun went on, pointing to the ground. "As to how I know, I read the sign. He is careful, but he leaves prints, and he is not making counter-sign, not that it would matter if he did."

"Why wouldn't it—"

"Because counter-sign is all but useless when a man is traveling alone. You can disguise numbers, you can misdirect pursuit, you can make the pursuit fear ambush, or try to disguise an ambush that is coming. An array of tricks. But the point is," he said, standing up and brushing at the front of his coat, which hung so long that the fringe swayed above his knees, "counter-sign does not *erase* the signs of passage, it changes them. He is relying on his head start, and his speed. And he is right to do that."

"When it comes to sign and counter-sign and tracking and all matters of this nature, would we save time by assuming that you're right, and I have nothing to contribute?"

Tun's lips curled in what she imagined was a faint smile. "Probably."

"Then how do we catch him?"

"He began his flight with great energy. Fear makes light steps and broad strides. He will tire faster than we will. Grow hungry. Doubt will begin to form, like grains of dirt in his boots. Then grow to pebbles. We will catch him."

"But not by standing here," Aelis said.

"No. Not much in the world is done by standing." Tun tapped at the ground, at something indistinguishable to Aelis, with the unshod wooden point of his staff. "He is doing the skirmisher's run."

"Two running steps, followed by a walking pace, yes."

"Ah." Tun smiled again behind the small sound of surprise he'd made. "You did learn something, somewhere."

"I've learned a lot of things. That's probably among the most recent."

Tun grunted and set off again. That stride of his ate up ground in a way that Aelis imagined would, in a span of hours, make for a good deal more distance than many men trying to run. Maddeningly, it seemed effortless.

Keeping up with him certainly wasn't. Conversation died as Aelis kept adjusting her pace to suit Tun's. She was reasonably certain they were heading mostly to the north, and as the sun began to sink on her left-hand side, she grew sure of it. Just keeping up occupied too much of her attention to pay much mind to scenery, or note landmarks. An hour, at least, passed in silence. Then two. She began to long for the Illusionists' trick of laying a spell over their mirrors that kept track of the hours.

"Any idea where he might be headed?" she finally asked as they trudged on into the gloaming, more to break the monotony than out of genuine need.

"North."

"I mean, are there geographical features, landmarks, ruins he might be headed for?"

"No use wondering that. You think he could be headed for an old smuggler's cave in the lee of Broken Tusk, say, and your mind will take that as a goal, start bending all the sign toward it. You don't track by thinking you know where you're headed when you set out. You find the sign and follow it."

"Broken Tusk? That a mountain?"

"A little curl of mountains and foothills that spurs out beyond the pass."

"And are there smuggler's caves there?"

"I hardly think I need lecture you on the history of Old Ystain, and how the Durndill Pass was the portal through which amber, furs, walrus ivory, and other goods flowed. And that as long as goods have moved over lines on a map, crowned heads and their finger-men have sought to take a share, and the bearers of such goods have sought to evade them."

"That was a very long way to go to say yes," Aelis said.

Tun walked silently for several more steps. She thought, perhaps, that the muscles in his back had tightened, that she'd said something wrong.

"I am not used to speaking so much," he finally said. "If I am poor at it, I shall cease."

"No, no, not at all," Aelis said, desperate not to have the only diversion on this walk taken away. "It is, well . . . just, ah . . . playing against type, I suppose."

"You expect one with orc blood to speak in what, grunts? Whistles? The noises of a pig?"

Aelis winced, despite the fact that Tun's tone hadn't changed a bit. It was still the same calm, steady, surprisingly quiet rumble.

"I didn't mean that at all, Tun," Aelis said, straining to sound as earnest as she was. "I mean the mountain man type. The fringed coat, trading meat and furs, being self-sufficient. One doesn't generally expect that kind of fellow to be so . . . loquacious."

"And now you test my vocabulary?" Tun's shoulders moved again inside his giant fringed coat, but Aelis thought this time it was in a kind of laughter.

"Not a test," Aelis said. "Just saying exactly what I mean in the words that come to hand. I don't think you'll struggle with them."

"I won't."

"Good."

"There is something else you should know, before we go much further."

"Whatever it is, I'm not going to like it, am I?"

Tun shrugged. "It may not mean anything. But Elmo is not the only man to have passed this way. Recently."

"Adventurers? Pioneers?"

"I do not think so. In the past few weeks, months, I have noted a passage of men . . . singly, mostly, heading this way. They are not prepared like adventurers or pioneers would be; no animals, little baggage. I do not like to make hasty guesses . . ." Tun trailed off here and looked to Aelis.

"But if you were going to?"

"I'd say it seemed like desperate men making impulsive decisions."

"To head into Old Ystain by themselves, with minimal equipment, before the onset of winter."

"It is, as I said, a hasty guess."

The conversation died into silence, which coincided with a reasonably steep incline up a hill that took most of Aelis's concentration.

By the time they reached the summit, Onoma's moon had risen far enough that the confusion of twilight had fled and there was light enough for her to see.

Tun stopped and turned to look at her. She could make out his features more clearly now in the strange light the moon of the Silent Lady offered to her eyes, as it gave him no shadow to hide in. He looked young, she thought, given how lightly stubble lay on his cheeks. His features were an odd mix, to be sure; the human in him handsome, noble even, with an aquiline nose and high cheeks. But the overhanging brow, the larger jaw, the protruding teeth were doubly strange against that backdrop. From a distance, he could—and likely did—pass as simply an overlarge human. Up close, there was no hiding what he was.

"The darkness does not impede your vision," Tun said. "In fact, I think it improves it. How is that?"

"It has to do with the magic I studied."

He grinned. She could see it now, a crinkling in the corners of his mouth, though his tusks made it harder to read. "I could have guessed that."

"I'm a Necromancer," she said, seeing no point in dancing about it as she had when this conversation had played out with Maurenia. "I've always had an affinity for Onoma's moon. It gives me light to see. I don't know why or how."

"Convenient, then, that our chase begins with Her moon waxing," Tun said. "We should continue."

◆   ◆   ◆

And they did continue, through most of that night. They paused near dawn, with Aelis stumbling forward but refusing to ask for a break till Tun finally announced that they'd take shelter inside a small stand of pines and nap for roughly two hours. Aelis had been too tired to ask how he was going to keep track of the time or what sleep he was going to get. She'd shrugged off her pack, and had reserved only just enough willpower not to immediately collapse.

Before she knew it, Tun's hand was shaking her shoulder. The light was gray, blurring through the trees.

"That can't have been more than a quarter of an hour," she mumbled.

"It was two," Tun said quietly. "And if we are to catch your man today we must not tarry." He reached into one of his bulging pockets and picked out a small biscuit, mottled yellow and white, and nibbled on it almost delicately, before offering a second to Aelis.

She took it and sniffed, then tested her teeth against it. What had looked like delicacy now seemed more like caution, as the thing was harder than any bread she'd ever known. Instead of biting through it, she tore a hunk off by holding it still with her teeth and pulling. She settled it into a corner of her mouth to let saliva soak into it.

"The flavor's not much," Tun admitted as he broke off another piece. "But it will keep us on our feet."

Aelis could only grunt around the hunk of biscuit in her mouth, shoulder her pack, and pick up her staff to begin trudging after him. When the hunk of bread had softened so that she could break it down without fear of injury to her teeth, she managed to swallow some. In truth, it didn't taste bad; like salty cheese over toasted two-day-old bread. But eating it took some work.

"You think we can catch him today?"

Tun shrugged. "Depends on the time we make. We are fifteen, twenty miles behind him, judging from signs I found in his campsite."

"His campsite?"

"Where we slept. He slept there the prior night. He did a good job of hiding it."

"Damn straight he did," Aelis agreed, before cautiously drawing forth another bite of biscuit. "I didn't notice."

"Sign is my job. What to do when we find him is yours."

They trudged on. Bit by bit, their biscuits disappeared, the sun rose, and Aelis's thoughts settled over a cloudy haze of little sleep. It was a familiar feeling from the university. How often had she and Miralla stayed up till dawn drinking, sharing theories, then gone about their classes and labors of the day simply to prove that they could?

She was dwelling on pleasant nostalgia when she thought Tun's step suddenly faltered. He moved on, as if his foot had almost tripped him, and she threw him an odd glance but he did not look back. They were caught in an open strand of grasses between two lengths of pine woods. As it was, Lone Pine was situated in a part of Ystain where the evergreens outnumbered their seasonally dressed cousins a great deal, but this far north, pine forests positively dominated.

Hills rose before them, hills that, had she seen them a day ago, she would've thought were mountains. Now they seemed to her like mere crowd warmers for the curtain-raising mountains that rose behind them.

By the time they passed into the second length of woods, Aelis was sure that Tun's small hesitation had been something she'd imagined. But in the cover and shade of the trees, he threw an arm out and went stock-still.

"Our passage is noted."

"Noted? By whom?"

Tun turned toward her, his face once again an unreadable mask. "Orcs."

Aelis felt her spine chill, but controlled herself. She thought carefully through her next words, and finally settled on, "Is that good or bad?"

"That depends," Tun said slowly.

"On?"

"Many things. The age and composition of the band. Their affiliation. Why they are here. How they feel about breeds."

"Breeds?" Aelis echoed, hesitantly. "Do you mean . . ." She gestured vaguely in his direction.

"What else would I mean?" He took a small, quiet breath, his eyes closing for a moment. "Know this. If it comes to violence, be swift and forceful. Hold nothing back. They will not."

"Sounds like a teacher of mine. Two of them, in fact," Aelis muttered. She thought back on lessons from Lavanalla to a class of second-year Abjuration students.

"When your Abjurer's blade leaves its sheath, it should not be for show. It should not be to intimidate. It should not be merely to use the hilt or the crosspiece or the quillons or the basket as a focus for a ward; all of that can be done with a sheathed weapon. No," she went on, from her position on the floor, sitting with her legs crossed beneath her as she always did when lecturing. "It should be because you intend to blood it. The more often you draw forth a weapon without using it, the more of its potency as a threat it loses."

And Bardun Jacques, to the Warden Cadets in their third year—a much less crowded hall than he'd addressed two years prior—still moving as stiffly and as stubbornly as ever.

"Way the world is today, any one of you who is going to be a Warden, time's going to come where you need to take a life. If you doubt me, if you think you aren't capable of it, if you think that your power and your skills are meant to be turned to the ennobling of all living creatures, then go on and get out. World is filled with savagery, *and I don't mean orcs.* Oh, they'll kill you, don't get me wrong. A half-trained orc bowman'd kill half this room before one of you stopped playing with their nethers long enough to do a gods-damned thing about it—but they wouldn't do it without a reason, not that that's any comfort to the dead. But there are people right here in this fabled university city of ours who'd stab any one of you for the ring on your finger, the coin in your purse, or because they felt like seeing how it'd feel. Then there's the 'pioneers' and 'adventurers' going up into Old Ystain, sifting through what war left behind, and they're a sorry lot of greedy blackguards who'll kill you to avoid paying a few tri-crowns of custom duties. And that doesn't even get me started on all the reasons they'll kill the people you're meant to *protect.*" There the old Warden had paused for breath before launching into a longer tirade about the decline of morals generally, on the questionable lineage of both his assembled students and most of the people in the Triumvirate realms, the lamentable fact that a Warden could spend his life up to his ass in blood and warm viscera and still not make a dent in the numbers of the people who wanted quick killing.

Aelis was so lost in her thoughts that Tun had to throw a hand out to grab her shoulder and shake her into the present. He loomed over her, lifting two fingers to his eyes, and then pointed them at hers. Though unspoken, the message was clear. *Open your eyes.*

She shook away her thoughts and paid attention to the moment. They'd passed through the trees and were faced once more with a hill.

"We go up. Quickly now. If they've bows we don't want to give them high ground."

Tun sprang forward, and she saw now that his long, hip-swung strides had been him trying to make a pace she could keep easily. He was halfway up to the crown of the hill in a blur. She scrambled after him, taking four steps to his one now, she imagined. *Maybe six,* she thought as she saw him plant the edge of his walking stick in the ground and turn back to look at her. She half expected him to swing an arm out to help her up past the last scrabble of loose rock and scrub—which she would've ignored—but instead he simply stood like a statue, hands resting atop his stick.

She joined him, heaving for breath, and followed the line of his gaze to see a half dozen forms coming toward them from their right, spread out in a ragged line across ten yards or so, dust and loose rock flung out in their wake. They'd been forced to scramble down the side of a neighboring hill and then back up this one.

They were not dressed like Tun, but neither did they fit the image she'd had of wild orcs in untanned hides and wearing armor made of ivory and rough hides. Mostly they did wear hides—tough hide armor that was tanned and cured as surely as anything in the markets in Antraval, if less supple by design—that draped down over their thighs. As they drew closer she realized the hides were banded with strips of bronze and iron. Three of them carried spears, clutching a brace in their large fists and more in cases on their backs. The other three carried axes loosely in their hands, the poles nearly as long as she was tall, the wide round blades and balancing spikes sharp and deadly. Their skin was darker than Tun's, starting in shades of deep green and running darker, though the largest, one of the axemen, had deep charcoal-gray skin. They wore heavy beads of amber or carved walrus tusk at the ends of braids or on thongs around their necks. The carvings looked runic to her, but not of any language she could read. They certainly did not wear elaborately carved ivory breastplates as the stories she'd read as a child had said.

She wasn't entirely sure what the protocol would be, but Tun stood stock-still and waited for them to approach. She mirrored him, trying not to lean on her stick, keeping her free hand at her side and away from any visible weapons.

The wand in her sleeve was a comfortable weight, though, ready to slide to her left hand with a flick of the wrist. An instinct told her to call an enchantment—a call to disarm, the fatigue she'd played on Luth, or a general charm—but she also thought she'd need to focus on the coming conversation, and she could not do both at the same time, so she let the most powerful enchantments she knew float in the back of her head.

The big gray orc—he was every bit as tall as Tun, if not as broad—stopped but two feet away, and they stared hard at each other.

They began to speak. Aelis had never heard Orcish spoken by orcs themselves, and was taken aback. When she'd heard snippets of it spoken by other races, it had always taken on a distinctly guttural quality. But between Tun and the gray orc, it was positively musical. A deep, rumbling music, but it wasn't the harsh and grating tongue she'd imagined. The other five orcs studied her while their leader or spokesman conferred. The leader gestured toward her, speaking several long words. Tun responded.

She cleared her throat. "Am I going to be let in on this conversation?"

Tun raised a hand to her. Speaking had drawn the dark eyes of the leader, who gave her a frank stare.

"Am I supposed to melt away in the face of your stare, then? Quake in fear and knock my fucking knees together? You can keep staring from now until the Worldsoul turns in five hundred years or so. It won't happen."

The orc looked to Tun, who spoke, translating, she presumed. The gray orc laughed, then so did the rest of the party.

Tun turned toward her, offered a quick grin. "He liked that."

"Who are they? What are they doing here?"

"Hunting," Tun said.

"Hunters don't carry axes," she hissed, but by then her guide had turned back to his conversation.

The leader of the orc party then gestured to some of the ornaments he wore; first one in his hair, then a stick of amber clasped in iron stuck through his brow, then something worn around his neck, Aelis couldn't see what.

She also could not see what it was Tun showed in response; something he, too, wore around his neck, that he lifted clear from the inside of his fringed coat and shielded with his hand. When the party of orcs saw it, something in their attitude, their posture, changed. She couldn't have said what it was, exactly. To that point, their attitude had been respectful. Even she could tell no threats had been made. But they had been on edge, perhaps even afraid.

After Tun showed them his amulet, fear gave way to some kind of relief. One of the axemen sagged against his weapon. A spear-carrier changed her grip on her weapons, grounding the butts at her feet. Their leader talked faster now, gesturing with his hands, pointing to the north and west. Tun had raised one hand, gesturing to her. The leader spoke more rapidly, gesturing with his hands more openly. Finally, Tun seemed to acquiesce to something, both of his hands up, palms out, his staff leaning against his shoulder.

"What happened, Tun? What did we just agree to?"

He held one of his hands toward her, taking his staff back up with the other. Then he extended his free hand to the orc leader, who clasped it. The band of hunters began gathering their weapons, turning to leave, when the gray-skinned orc turned back toward her.

"I am sorry to have spoken only in a tongue unknown to you," he said. "It was rude. But . . ." He seemed to pause and search for words. His voice was sonorous, rich, if hesitant. "It would have taken long, to explain to you. Good luck, Ay-lish Becalmer, against the Demon Tree."

"Thanks," Aelis said, too slow to digest his words to ask all the questions that came to mind before the orcs bounded off. "Becalmer? Demon Tree? What the fuck is a Demon Tree? Why do I need luck against it? Tun?"

She turned to her guide, who was silent as he watched the orcs bound off the way they came.

"What did they ask of you and why do you have to do it? I have my own task, and I cannot—"

"One question at a time, please, Warden. Please." Tun's voice was even softer than it usually was. Slowly, as if bearing a great weight, he turned to her. "Umarik—that was their leader's name—he did ask a favor of me. I have agreed to do it."

"I have my own task—"

"I know. And I was hired to help you do it, and I would keep my word. What do you do when obligations collide with one another, Warden?"

"Compromise, I suppose."

"Well. I have my obligation to aid you in your task. I have an obligation— yes, an obligation—to do what Umarik has just asked of me. I cannot do both at once; I must complete one first. What he asked is of more imme-diate import."

"And he asked you to do, what? Find a Demon Tree? Find something a Demon Tree guards?" Aelis felt her patience growing short and her tem-per flaring up.

"Finding it will be no issue. He asked me to kill it."

"Oh, well." Aelis threw up her hands and only just resisted the urge to hurl her walking stick as far as she could. "Is that all? Just kill some fucking demon-possessed tree? Is that all? I'd say we could just set fire to it from afar, but if it truly *is* possessed by some external spirit, like as not it'll jump into you or me at its first opportunity."

"It is not possessed. It is not a demon, not as you understand. It is . . . an orcish creation. From the war."

"Explain. And tell me why we ought to hare off from our pursuit of Elmo."

"Because it is more dangerous than your crazed scout. Because it is, in some way, my *duty* to kill it. Because . . . there is a good chance it will have something I need. Badly."

"What?"

"Reagents. I can explain as we walk."

"Is this the favor?"

Tun was already turning around; he paused with his foot upraised to look back at her. "Ah. You mean, am I asking you this favor as payment for guiding you? I was hoping to ask something else."

"This seems like a rather large favor."

"Look at it this way. If I go to fight this thing myself, there is a good chance I will die. Then you will be alone in the wilderness with no guide. I do not doubt, Warden, that you would find a way to survive. I *do* doubt that you could track your man."

By now, Tun had set his foot down and turned to face her. "If you aid me, I live, I help you find your scout. You return to Lone Pine with him. Justice triumphs. All is well."

"Or I go with you to fight this Demon Tree, and we both die."

"That is also possible. But if it happens, then nothing that follows is our concern."

Aelis frowned and gestured in the direction Tun had been about to set off. "Fine. Tell me about this Demon Tree."

Tun smiled and began walking, swinging his stick almost gaily. "A Demon Tree is . . . well, it is neither a demon nor a tree, to start. It is an animation of the spirits inside the things of the forest."

"So, some wizard did, what, a combination of Conjuring and Illusion and made something a little too real?"

"I am no wizard. I do not understand what you mean. I know it as a weapon devised by orcs. It animates the spirits and it sets them in motion. To defend a place."

"Can't we just avoid that place?"

"Certain innovations in the weapon made it start to, how do I put this?" Tun paused and lifted one finger to his bottom lip. "Self-perpetuate?"

Aelis felt her spine grow cold for the second time in the hour, and this time the feeling did not dissipate. "Explain."

"It begins to call to other spirits. To animals. To build others like itself."

"Onoma's embrace, man! That is one hell of a weapon to just drop some-where."

"According to those hunters, this one wasn't properly dismantled. It has reconstituted itself over time. And it has begun the process I just mentioned."

"Perpetuating itself? What form does that take, exactly?"

"It attempts to make itself ambulatory. Then it begins to spread its territory. Eventually it begins animating other spirits."

"It animates other spirits?" Aelis felt her eyes go wide, her jaw drop. She snatched control of her expression back from her shock. "There are *legions* of Lyceum researchers who would kill each other to write a career-making paper about what you're describing."

"They would not survive meeting it."

I wouldn't sell wizards quite that short, Aelis thought. "At any rate, please go on explaining this horror to me."

"It will not copy itself precisely. But it will find other spirits and awaken them."

"And how," Aelis finally said, running through options in her mind, "do you kill it?"

"With great fucking difficulty," Tun said, and they lapsed into silence as he led them west.

16

THE DEMON TREE

They had walked in silence for perhaps an hour when Tun dropped to one knee and raised a fist. Aelis crouched behind him, wrapping her hand around the hilt of her sword.

Moving slowly, without raising a noise, Tun grasped his staff with both hands and cocked his arms backward. Then, as if it were a spear, he stabbed it forward. There was a small thud and a smaller crack.

Tun turned back to Aelis, a limp form dangling from his hand; a red fox. Briefly bewildered, Aelis was making ready to protest when he held it closer.

Then she saw the stitches of green—like woven grass—that covered the fox's eyes. The same stuff was layered over its ears.

"This is how it guards its outer ranges. Spreads pieces of itself to the birds and the beasts, subverts them to its purpose."

"That is gruesome," Aelis breathed. As she looked closer at the fox, she saw the strands of green buried deep into its fur; possibly beneath, into its hide, its skull. She leaned forward, raising a hand to examine it, when Tun stopped her.

"Do not touch it. I do not know what effect it might have upon you."

"Why can you touch it then?"

"I am something that a Demon Tree cannot touch in that way; it cannot have my senses."

"How did you know where the poor thing was?"

Tun set the fox down carefully, almost reverently. Then he tapped his nose with one thick finger.

"You smelled it?"

"I did. The Demon Tree has a foul stench, if your nose can find it."

"What now?"

"It is close. It will be surrounded by trees. There may be other animals under its control. Hopefully they will be small; no raptors, no wolves."

"No bears," Aelis breathed.

"That would be unlikely. None are nearby," Tun said. Aelis offered him a skeptical look, and he shrugged. "I am a trapper. Is it not a trapper's business to know where bears make their warrens, where they hunt and fish, where they are likely to be?"

"That is not an entirely comforting answer," Aelis said.

"It does not need to be. Wolves alone would be problem enough, so discomfort yourself with them. Bears will not trouble us."

"Fine. I ask again. What now?"

"We locate it. We are at the edge of its range; we will begin moving north, taking not one further step west, trying to encircle a likely point."

"And when we see it? How will we know?"

"Oh," Tun said, smiling again lightly, "we will know. And when we do, we attack, straight ahead, with as much force as we can muster, as fast as we can. The best chance against a Demon Tree is to overwhelm it with main force."

"Direct force is not precisely my specialty," Aelis said. "I am no Invoker." She licked her lips nervously, narrowed her eyes. "Are you *sure* this thing isn't animated with any kind of undead spirit? Because, gods, if it were?" She shrugged. "A light day's work."

"It is no abomination of the grave. Orcs give the bodies of their dead to the water, and presumably their spirits as well; they make no use of such in their magic as far as I know. I have told you as best I can what it is. If you cannot summon flames, what can you do?"

"I can protect the two of us as we engage it, redirect its force. If it has anything like a person's mind, I can touch it, convince it of things, put it to sleep, make it friendly."

"That's all?"

Aelis sniffed. "I think you'll be impressed the first time you see a ward in action."

"As you say," Tun replied. "Follow me and stay close."

Tun shifted his staff and stood. Shuffling carefully, moving one foot, setting it down, then lifting the other, he began to edge to his right. Aelis shadowed him, reconciling herself to the idea that when Tun had said encircle, he'd meant it. And that it would take time.

Slowly, Aelis making more noise about it than Tun, they walked. After a half hour, they'd made no more than a hundred yards, and that was probably a generous estimate. Aelis's legs burned with the squatting and shuffling.

Her guide showed no sign of strain.

After another quarter hour, Aelis's legs were trembling, and she fell forward onto one knee. Thankfully, there were no leaves to rustle—the pine needles made barely enough noise for her to notice.

Still, Tun glanced back at her, frowning. He opened his mouth as if to speak, and a roar erupted from a stand of trees thirty or forty yards ahead of them. It was not the sound of a beast. To Aelis it sounded more like a great *inrushing* of air, so forceful that its passing shattered the silence of the wood.

From the noise, Aelis expected some giant to unfold itself above the tops of the pines. Instead, they merely rustled, and the thing—the Demon Tree—came gliding out.

Borne on legs that were pine tree trunks crosshatched with the same green that had sewn the fox's eyes and ears shut, a monster strode forward. Its legs were where its resemblance to a man ended; above them roiled an amorphous mass of coruscating green and brown light. Inside it, eyes—blazing, lidless, now purple, now red, now blue—and all of them searching. Tendrils extended from it that could have been arms, if arms were boneless and looked solely like ropes of muscle that ended in sharp wooden hooks.

"Fuck, I'd call it a Demon Tree too," Aelis breathed. But Tun was not there to hear her; he had already leapt to the charge.

She'd half expected some kind of battle cry, some wild yawp from the huge guide. But he was utterly silent, gliding forward with footsteps that barely touched the ground. Tun held his staff out in front of him like a spear, the thick wood never wavering.

Aelis stopped admiring, came to her senses, whipped out her sword, and followed after him. She couldn't match his pace so she drifted to his left and tried to keep him and the monster both in view.

An Abjurer's place in battle was to defend those who could land the decisive blow, not look for the decisive blow herself. So when one of the long, ropy tendrils with its hook end shot out at Tun, before he could even lift his staff to knock it away—a dubious prospect, she thought, no matter how strong he might be—she called a ward into shimmering existence just between him and the blow.

Tun seemed to instantly know what had happened, and ducked under the almost-invisible circle of force. Aelis realized quickly that she'd made it too large, but there was no time to adjust as the Demon Tree smashed against it with incredible force.

The blow it landed dissipated her ward, but the magic had done its job, and Tun was that many steps closer to the glowing, bilious light of the Demon Tree's body. Two more of its tendrils were lashing out toward the half-orc. Aelis called two more wards, only this time she made them smaller; just big enough to intercept the hook-ends of the tendrils.

The first one stopped her cold, rocking her back on her heels with the force of its contact with her magic. The second *shattered* her ward, but she'd done enough, and Tun made his play.

When he was perhaps two lengths of his staff away from the beast, he planted the metal-shod tip in the soft ground of the forest floor and vaulted straight at the Demon Tree.

She didn't know what he meant to do, and was brought up short by that direct an approach. Feet first, he flew *straight into* the coruscating ball of energy. She was so stunned she almost missed the limb the monster threw at her. Her instincts grabbed her by the scruff of the neck and hurled her to the ground, her sword raised almost apologetically to hold the thing off. It rebounded, hard, the impact sending shocks up the blade and into her arms.

It wasn't like chopping wood. It was like trying to cut through the iron haft of a mace with the edge of her sword.

Is a little shock going to keep you on the ground, Warden? Aelis wasn't sure if the voice she imagined was her own or Lavanalla's or Bardun Jacques's, but she was damned if it was going to have the better of her. She rolled to her feet, took the hilt of her sword with both hands.

She saw Tun sailing through to the other side of the Demon Tree, his passage impeded by the energy at its core. Faint tendrils of smoke rose from his coat where some of the fringe had burned off and from the ends of his long hair, as he sailed clear and hit the ground hard. He bounced, rolled, and came to his feet, snarling.

She knocked aside two more of the thing's ropy arms with her sword, trying to measure the magical strength she had left and what to do with it.

Tun, deprived of his staff—it lay between her and the monster now— reached inside his coat and drew out two thick, wicked-looking metal bands that wrapped around his fists. She couldn't tell if they were bladed or not—couldn't spare the time to look—but the question was answered when the end of one of the thing's ropelike arms was sliced off into two sections as Tun's arms blurred around it.

"Inside it, Warden," Tun bellowed, as suddenly the monster sprouted more arms and shot them toward him. "Get inside it, there is a stone, wrapped in grass and hair, that animates it. It must be plucked o—"

This last was cut off as one of the tendrils evaded his swinging bladed fists and wrapped itself around his throat. Tun chopped at it savagely, but the ropy blend of wood and muscle had fixed itself around his neck and cut off his air.

She could not rush to his aid and handle the Demon Tree at the same time. She saw that Tun had come through the ball of roiling energy little the worse for wear, but he'd done it fast. She would have to be thorough.

Aelis had only one choice: a Third Order Abjuration she knew in theory, and had briefly cast once, under laboratory conditions; Nieran's Sheath.

At most, she could hold it for a few seconds, so she darted forward at the thing, dodging its tendrils when she could, rolling forward to maintain momentum. When she couldn't, instead of summoning a full ward to absorb the blows, she summoned just the edges of wards to deflect them, to make them miss her. It was a risky strategy, and one that called for a precise control Aelis had never felt she had.

Fine fucking time to learn just how precise I can be, she thought as she rolled to her feet and called the Sheath to her mind.

She held it, ready to cast, but had to reserve her immediate energy for deflecting the attacks the Demon Tree made as she closed in. The paper-thin wards she called did just enough to make its limbs shed their force or redirect their impact.

Her hair was ruffled by the passage of one, and she made a mental note to thank Maurenia for having braided it for her.

At last she was close enough to lunge. Her hands tightened around the hilt of her sword. As she pushed her will through it, utilizing its focus, she felt every contour of the sharkskin and wire that wrapped about it. The steel core of the blade, forged around droplets of her own blood, sharpened her will and the words she was already intoning, bringing palpable effect in the visible world.

Aelis felt her senses respond to the ward that enveloped her, starting at her head and feet and meeting in the middle. Air ceased to move against her skin; sound narrowed to a distant roar and then vanished. The coruscating energy before her dimmed.

She only just remembered to take a deep gulp of air before it sealed her in. Her movements were suddenly faster, as if being cut off from the world by a ward shed some of its weight.

Aelis lunged, her sword extended to the length of her arm. She was no great distance-fencer, and her sword was not made for the lunge—it was a swinging weapon, made to maximize force, not reach—but the ward flowing around it allowed it to pierce straight through the magic that animated the spirit, or the weapon, or the Demon.

Soon after that followed her arm, and then her head and shoulders.

Aelis was disoriented. Inside the beast, space was distorted—there was more of it than there should have been. A latticework of grass and wooden pieces like tree roots formed a kind of crude skeleton. Nothing like any body she'd ever dissected. The Anatomist in her wanted to stop and study it, take its measurements, draw it.

The Anatomist in her also reminded her that she needed air to breathe and regulate her blood, so she shook off that impulse.

In the center of the beast, on its own power, spun a small, dully glinting sphere, surrounded by a lattice of the woven grass that seemed a hallmark of the thing. She swiped at it, almost casually.

It spun out of her reach. She swiped again, and again it dodged.

She flexed her knees and jumped up into the thing entirely, sweating inside her airtight ward.

It was, to date, the moment of purest concentration and deepest terror Aelis had ever lived, but she managed to wrap her entire warded body around the stone. The thing vibrated madly, and with her ward keeping her from covering it tightly, she couldn't actually grab it.

Aelis dropped the ward. The stone thunked into her chest, driving the breath from her lungs. The world went dark, energy tingled against her skin, and the last thing she felt was the pain of hitting the ground.

17

THE AFTERMATH

Aelis's eyes snapped open on flickering flames. Immediately, she sat up.

And just as suddenly she fell back over. She was one mass of pain, beginning in the soles of her feet and spreading across every inch of her skin to her scalp in slow, exquisite waves. It made sure to linger in her joints, behind her eyes, and to make itself felt in any part of herself she tried to move.

A huge presence loomed on the other side of the fire. She decided it was probably Tun.

"Am I dead, Tun? Is this what death feels like?"

"Death feels like nothing, I expect," the huge shape answered, in Tun's voice. "Life, on the other hand, is quite painful."

"Oh good," Aelis said, slowly. Speaking hurt her jaw. Gently, she inspected her teeth with her tongue, expecting them to hurt and feeling mild surprise when they didn't. "Do come over here and kill me then, hmm?"

"That is the last thing I would consider doing, Warden," Tun said.

"That's not very charitable of you."

"What you feel is not permanent," Tun ventured after a moment's pause.

"I should fucking hope not."

"It should not even last very much longer. You will shake off this effect. And you'll do it sooner if you stand and move."

"That is quite impossible at the moment."

"Warden." She heard the movement as Tun unfolded his bulk and felt as much as heard him coming closer. Then he was leaning over her, looking somewhat ragged in the dimness as twilight fell, half of an eyebrow singed away, some of the fringe of his coat blackened. "You dismantled a Demon Tree in a way that should have killed you. You still clutch the runestone that drove it in your hand. I should say that we are beyond the impossible now."

He extended his hand and Aelis—who suddenly realized that her left hand was curled so tightly around something that her nails were digging into the heel of her hand—reached painfully up to take it with her right.

She'd have liked to say that Tun helped her to her feet, but in truth, she'd never have stood if he hadn't simply lifted her. It was agony. Seconds stretched to hours.

Once she was upright, though wobbling, he pried open her left hand and touched the fingers of his own hand to what lay within.

The pain vanished. She could practically feel it being sucked into the half-orc standing before her, who grunted, stood rather more stiffly, but didn't collapse like she might have expected.

Aelis looked down at what lay in her palm. A stone, and not a large one. Runes covered its surface, running into one another in characters she could not read.

She peered more closely and saw that each rune was filled with traces of amber, like honey poured into the crevices of a piece of toasted bread.

There was a hole drilled through the top of the stone; through it was threaded a lock of hair so fine it felt like silk. The lock appeared unbroken, somehow secured in place.

She looked back up at Tun, who plucked the stone from her hand. He wrapped his own fist around it and took a step back from her.

"Anaerion's balls, I'd hope it would at least *tingle* when you touched it."

"Do not," Tun said, with suddenly more expression in his voice than she'd heard before, "feel as though this means you are weak, Warden Aelis. Do not. I am made to hold such things as this. Those of purely human blood cannot."

"I think we should revise that to 'should not.'"

"Are you quite sure you've no orc in your history?"

Aelis's first instinct was to suppress the laughter that rose up, fearing for her ribs. Only then did she remember that the pain was truly gone, and she allowed herself a chuckle.

"If my father heard you ask that, Tun, he'd demand satisfaction. Or die of a choking fit in his anger—and he is not an angry man, or without a sense of humor."

"The point remains that orc magic needs orc blood, so far as I know."

"Well," Aelis said, "what matters is that the Demon Tree is dead."

"How? What did you do?"

"I merely used wards. Well, *a* ward. Nieran's Sheath. It covers one's entire body, cutting off all things. Blades, magic—but also air. It is not a long-term defense."

"And yet in order to grasp the stone, you must have let it go."

"I did."

"That instant must've come very near to annihilating you," Tun said.

"And yet," Aelis said dryly, "here I am. I am not among the most powerful Abjurers, but . . . that was the most powerful ward I have managed to sustain. It is no parlor trick."

"Regardless," Tun said. "I am now in your debt."

"How? We agreed to fight the thing. Together. We did."

"It was mine to kill."

"Don't be childish, Tun."

"I am being the farthest thing from that. It was not mine in the sense of a trophy, but rather as an *obligation*."

"How can you have obligations to people you do not live among?"

"It is a fact of my existence, of my very being. You do not truly live among the people of Lone Pine, but are you not bound to them?"

"That's mutual," Aelis pointed out. "They are obligated to provide food, maintain my residence, and assist me. And being a Warden is something I chose."

"If I chose to live with an orc band, it is possible that honors and riches would be mine. I do not. But that does not absolve me of the obligation to destroy a rogue Demon Tree if I come across it. I hold very little sacred, but that . . ." Here, Tun shrugged. "That is something that comes as near the word as I am willing."

Questions rose in Aelis's mind but something about Tun's tone suggested she shouldn't ask them. Instead, she pointed to the fetish he'd taken from her. "Can I study that?"

"Actually, Warden, this is where the favor I mean to ask comes in," he said, making the stone disappear into one of the pockets of his long coat. "But we can discuss that later." He turned to a pile of loose dirt that had resulted from digging the small firepit with his massive hand and began scooping the dirt onto the fire, smothering it. "It is time we get back on the trail. Dark is falling and we have distance to make up."

Aelis had used the night vision that Onoma's moon granted her for so much of her life that she hadn't even noticed that she could see clearly once again. The silent moon was closer to fullness than it had been when they'd set out. She'd slept a day at least. Perhaps unsurprisingly, she felt

energized, more capable of keeping up than before. There was a dull buzz
in her muscles that was in no way painful or debilitating. She almost felt
like running.

That'd be a first, she thought. She'd done as much running as she'd ever
wanted to, and more, during her training. Bardun Jacques, being pulled
alongside the students in a light carriage, shouting discouragement, ob-
scenities, and occasionally zapping the legs of those who lagged with a bolt
of light that arced from the crystal embedded in the top of his staff, had
forever inured her to any enjoyment to be derived from it.

"Is it too convenient that they found you?" she wondered aloud.

"They were looking for me. They'd come some distance to do it, and
tracked us fairly easily."

"So there are orc bands that . . . know you? Or of you?"

"More or less. It is not as though I have lived outside Lone Pine all my
life."

"Oh," Aelis said, somewhat taken aback. "I suppose I assumed, with the
frontier close by, and so much contact in this region . . ."

"I was born near here, it's true. But I have traveled more widely than you
expect, and seen many of the great cities you long for."

"What do you mean, long for?"

Tun stopped in his tracks and turned to face her. "Warden. I like to
think a certain trust, even camaraderie, might flourish between us based
on our experience of fighting the Demon Tree, to say nothing of spending
days in each other's company with nothing but the sky and the country
and the hardship to share. Do not endanger that by lying. To me, or to
yourself."

Tun's words stung but Aelis was never one to shy away from the bare
truth, once she'd confirmed it was the truth, and it was no labor to
know that he had sussed her out easily.

"I don't mean to lie, Tun. I just . . . supposed I wasn't that transparent."

Her guide shrugged and turned back to whatever invisible trail he followed in the darkness. "I have a sense for these things."

"Apparently," she said, springing lightly after him. "I don't like thinking
I come off as if I hate this place. I'm going to do my best here, but I don't
know how."

"Warden, I can see the issue, but do not look to me to fix it."

"Have you any advice, at least?"

"Think of a beast. A wolf or a sheep or a goat or a fox. Whatever suits.

It does not want to be standing out in the rain, but it never occurs to it to imagine that it has a right not to be wet."

Aelis sighed and let her questions subside for the time being. Above them, clouds parted and clusters of stars appeared. She spared a glance for them and supposed that if any revelation was going to come to her it would be now, beneath the awful majesty of the night sky above the foothills and the mountains looming in the near distance.

If there were any justice, she thought, *I'd have a great epiphany about nature and the struggle on the frontier and the stark beauty of it all. I'd lose my heart to this place and learn to love sheep. I'd even make peace with that goat that keeps breaking into my tower.*

Instead, all she could think was that when she was back, she'd have to take advantage of the clear nights to make sure she had her orrery correctly engaged, and that perhaps she could curry favor back at the Lyceum by making some notes on the positions of the stars and the moons from elevation.

If I had the lenses and the notation books and cared enough to do the math, she thought.

"The beasts must just be smarter than me, Tun," she murmured. "I would trade every star in the sky for the lights of Antraval, and the great crush of people, the throbbing life within its walls, the music in the taverns, the talk in the coffee shops, the calls of merchants, the quiet blue evenings in the garden mazes . . ." She trailed off.

Tun said nothing, and Aelis kept following.

18

THE CAMP

They walked on until near to dawn, and Aelis remained shocked at how much energy she still had. Deep down she suspected that she'd pay for it later, that the strength in her limbs was somehow a remnant of her sojourn inside the Demon Tree's body. She had some dim memories of it that fled from her mind like a dream every time she tried to focus on them. But, like the memories of a dream, they crept up into the corners of her thoughts, teased her, tantalized her, darted into her vision and then away again as soon as she looked.

She was determined not to let it distract her, and Tun did his part by flinging out his hand and stopping her, planting his stick in the turf at their feet. They'd climbed steadily for most of the night. She had the presence of mind to note that breath was becoming a bit harder to find and was too grateful for the momentary pause to question whatever Tun was doing.

"This is unexpected," he muttered. "I think your man has fallen in with someone."

"With someone? Not any of the same desperate men you mentioned before?"

"That is impossible to say. There are folk out here, of course. The kind of folk uncomfortable with anywhere as populated as Lone Pine."

"You mean the kind who want to be beyond the reach of the Estates House, the law, the Wardens, and the Crowns."

"Not everyone finds the reach of the law a comforting embrace, or the growth of stone walls a warm mantle against the winter."

"Anarchists and bandits and so-called pioneers who don't want to respect the terms of the treaties signed."

"Or folk who remember living in this part of Old Ystain, or whose parents did, and want somewhere to feel like their own again," Tun said. "People who worked land or practiced trades there."

Aelis felt the furnace of her anger stoked despite Tun's reasonable tone and mild objections. She tamped it down and said, "This debate isn't getting us any closer to Elmo."

"It is not," Tun agreed. "The point is, there are the tracks of more than one figure here."

"How many?"

Tun turned and squinted at the ground, pushing the tangle of his hair away from his face. "Half a dozen, perhaps? Hard to say. No mounts, or at least, none have come this way recently."

"Dammit." Aelis bounced the tip of her walking stick off the ground. "Can you learn anything more about them?"

Tun eyed her a moment, then bent down. "Well, of the six, four are human men. One perhaps a dwarf, or a fat gnome with a lame leg. They encountered our man more than twelve hours ago but not more than a day. No signs of a fight; in fact, they appear to have shared breakfast with him." He sniffed the ground. "Eggs and old ham, I suspect."

"You're fucking with me."

"I'm fucking with you," Tun said with a nod as he stood back up. "You either haven't known any woodsmen, Warden, or you've known the wrong kind. Don't expect miracles out of any tracker, no matter what tales they'll tell you. I have led you this far, and I will find Elmo, but I all I can say is that he met with other folk here and they departed together. I see no signs of a fight; no blood was shed here. But," Tun added, drawing the syllable out, "if men came upon him with loaded crossbows and marched him back to a cave to dress him out and salt him for the winter, there would not *be* any signs of a fight."

"Well, that'd solve one problem, anyway," Aelis said. "But on the whole, I'd rather not have cannibals setting up shop just a few days' walk away from Lone Pine."

"If he has fallen in with some wild band, best we approach carefully."

"A warden does not slink," Aelis said, repeating something Bardun Jacques had told her many times.

"So, your plan is to walk directly toward a numerically superior force and then . . . do what, exactly?"

"I'll figure that out when I get there and we have a look at them."

"Does a warden plan?"

"The best plan never survives contact with the enemy, the suspect, or the objectives," Aelis said. "So why bother making one?"

"So that *we* survive contact?"

"Thought you weren't here to help me fight," Aelis said.

"I agreed to help you track a possible fratricide. Combat was not on the agenda. That being said, I would rather not watch you take on a dozen men by yourself."

"And I killed the Demon Tree for you."

"I was giving it something to think about."

"Oh? What to do with your body when it was done strangling you?"

"I was distracting it."

"By getting strangled?"

Tun sniffed in a way that Aelis thought was part laughter and perhaps part genuine dudgeon. She couldn't be sure, since his expressions were still hard to read, but she thought the corners of his mouth had curved in a smile around the protruding teeth.

They walked on in silence but, Aelis thought, in something like camaraderie.

+ + +

"Can a warden skulk occasionally?" Tun's question was whispered as they pressed themselves flat against a hillside. Stumps dotted its rise, leading to a crude timber-framed gate and flanking walls that abutted a cave face in the hillside. Whether it was natural or had been dug out or was some combination of the two, they couldn't tell, but it could have housed a dozen or two dozen or more for all they knew, and there were armed men behind the rough fence.

"In the face of overwhelming odds, perhaps, a certain amount of skulking could be allowed. Purely in the interests of developing intelligence."

"I don't suppose you can make yourself invisible or blind them to your presence?"

"I could, under ideal conditions, make one or two people forget that they had seen me, but I'm afraid that isn't what you're looking for. I'm no Illusionist."

"We could wait till dark," Tun suggested.

Aelis gave her head a slight shake as she eyed the men behind the little palisade. She saw crossbows and spears and that was plenty enough to worry her. "People approaching in the dark are *definitely* enemies to this lot, I'd expect. That's a fast way to get a bolt in the chest, or a spear, or both."

"Assuming they'd see us in the dark," Tun said. "We have an advantage there."

"I can see, yes. But in the dark I'm limited in what I can do without giving us away. All my best tricks are rather visible in darkness."

"Sword isn't."

"I'm not going in there to slit throats," Aelis hissed.

"Your sword has a pommel. A short, ugly nap and a long headache is all I meant. We study the guard patterns and pick a time."

"And then all it takes is one person up for a late-night piss to raise a cry and we're up to our elbows in blood. I'd rather find out from the start if we can resolve this peacefully. You're sure Elmo was brought here?"

"His tracks join with others and lead straight here."

"Well," Aelis said. "Then there's only one thing for it."

She rose, clearly silhouetting herself against the hillside for anyone who cared to look, and began advancing up the hill. Behind her she heard Tun mutter something, words in the same language he'd spoken to the orc hunters but considerably less cordial, as he slowly stood up to follow.

She'd made half the distance to the little compound with Tun just a few steps behind before anyone noticed them. A cry went up from one of the guards who glanced in their direction, and crossbows were leveled over the rough and uneven top of the timbers. She stopped in her tracks. At only twenty or so yards from the wall, she was within easy range of any crossbow and she well knew it.

At this range, to miss with even a decent crossbow, they'd have to barely know one end of the weapon from the other. She lifted her hands up, calling wards into the back of her mind. Only the strongest Abjurers could stop a crossbow bolt from absolute point-blank range; she'd seen Lavanalla do it in demonstration from a bow that was no more than a yard from her, fixed to a post, a rope in her own hand tied to the trigger. The better strategy was to try to deflect their flight, which any Abjurer could do from a distance. This close, it was a near-run thing at best.

Ten yards is farther than one, she thought. *Am I a tenth of the Abjurer the Archmagister is? Surely I am,* she told herself with a confidence she certainly didn't feel.

"I mean no one here any harm," she called out. "There's no need for those."

"We'll decide that," called out one of the men with the bows. "Don't come any closer till the boss has come out to have a look," he added.

"I won't," Aelis yelled. "But I'm going to lower my arms."

"Don't put a hand anywhere near that sword," another man added, his voice a bit shrill. From what she could tell at this distance, he seemed younger than his watch partner, as he was beardless while the other sported full whiskers.

"I won't," Aelis said. "I'll just rest my hands on my belt. They'll not move."

"Best not," the young one yelled out again. "Currin's comin'," the lad added. "That'll sort you."

What exactly do you think I'm going to do with two feet of steel from twenty yards when you've got height, a gate, and a crossbow between us? Aelis wondered privately. If things turned sour, she wasn't trying a mad dash for the gate, though she did admit that the words *mad dash* probably did play a role in such plan as she did have. It was just in a direction *opposite* the gate.

While she held wards in her mind, ready to summon, she spared a glance for Tun. He had not lifted his arms, but he didn't look pleased, with his lips drawn tight against his teeth. He was watching the crossbowmen intently. Aelis had a sense that Tun was measuring the distance between him and the wall and that if everything went to shit, the plan was for her and Tun to go in opposite directions.

"Tun," she murmured, as low as she could and still get his attention. His eyes flicked to her but only for a moment before going back to the crossbowmen. "You're not thinking of rushing them," she breathed.

"I do not," he whispered, in a voice that came out rather too much like a growl around his teeth, "take well to weapons pointed at me."

"It's not exactly a day at the tavern for me either," Aelis said, worried about the expression in Tun's eyes, the tension in his huge frame. In the time she'd known him, he'd always seemed relaxed, controlled, composed. She was seeing something different now and she wasn't sure how to handle it. "Calm. It doesn't have to—"

Whatever words she was reaching for were cut off with the creak of roughly hewn and badly lashed wood as the gate swung open. Out came a party of four, three men and a woman. In the main, they wore sturdy woodsmen's clothing, though the leader—she had little doubt of that— wore an old breastplate strapped over his jerkin. For all that it had seen a blow or two in its day, the plain gray steel was still perfectly serviceable, and the man wore it as though used to it. He wore an axe on his belt, not a woodsman's tool, but a weapon with a heavy spike. The two other men carried spears, and the woman had slim daggers thrust through the belt that kept her oversized jerkin from swallowing her. The sleeves were clamped back and the hem fell practically to her knees, which, Aelis was surprised to note, were in the same kind of hide trousers as the rest of the men.

"So," the armor-wearing, axe-carrying leader began, instantly confirming Aelis's suspicion, "what brings you to Currin's cave, hmm?"

"You're Currin then?" Aelis asked.

"None other," the man said, his dark bearded face cracking in a wide smile.

"Well, Currin," she said, "I am Warden Aelis de Lenti of Lone Pine. Tracking a fugitive who came this way. You seen anyone recently?"

Aelis kept a close eye on reactions as she revealed her title. Currin held his surprise, but she saw the flicker as his eyes widened before he got them under control. The spearmen to his left blanched, both of them, one of them fighting not to take a step back and the other doing it no matter how it looked.

The woman simply did not react. Her eyes didn't widen, her breathing didn't change, her body language betrayed nothing but casual boredom.

Currin smiled amiably. "Warden, you say? Empowered by a Crown and all that?"

"Three of them, in point of fact," Aelis said.

"We're not much with those Crowns out here," Currin said, sticking his thumbs into his belt and rocking back on his heels. It was the act of a friendly merchant meant to set a mark at ease, Aelis thought. *Shame the effect is ruined by the armor and the axe.*

"I haven't come to debate politics," Aelis said. "I am sure there are not many travelers in this country. I'm only asking if you've seen one."

"Politics are everywhere and in everything," Currin said. "Our position is that no man's a fugitive this side of the border, where the Crowns' rules don't bother us overmuch."

"Does harboring a fratricide bother you?" Aelis said, eager to take control of the conversation. "Or aiding him, at the least? I want to be perfectly clear here. I don't care the least about your band, or what you're doing here, or what principles or accidents of fate or personal foibles led you to Old Ystain." *To land that treaties specifically said would not be resettled yet,* she thought but didn't add. "I care about one man, who committed one crime."

"I think we could invite this one in for a drink, Currin," the woman said. Her voice was rich, and the suggestion so unexpected that Aelis found it entirely reasonable.

"I suppose you're right, Nath," the burly axeman said. "Very well. Come on, then," he added, gesturing with one hand back toward the open gate.

"Welcome to our little home," he muttered, standing back and sweeping his arm as if inviting them in.

Aelis glanced back at Tun, whose face was dark beneath his hood, with his head bowed slightly forward. She could read nothing in it, so onward she went.

It was a bit disconcerting, the way the spearmen flanked her to either side. Even more was how uninterested in all of this the woman seemed.

The walk was short and the company quiet. Aelis counted men as they passed the gate—four more, in addition to the four people they were with. The wooden palisade didn't enclose a lot of open ground, only enough for a well and two small huts that Aelis would've had to stoop to get into, much less a tallish man like Currin. Tun wouldn't have fit through their doors. Given the scent pouring out of them, she guessed they were curing sheds for meat or fish, and they both had simple open holes in their thatch where smoke would escape.

The mouth of the cave dug into the hillside was covered with a big piece of an even bigger old tapestry. A rich, costly piece of work, or it had been once, Aelis reckoned. The flash of silver and gold threads caught the sunlight and pulled her up short. She studied it, finding a courtly scene with dozens of figures picked out. The center appeared to depict a great hall, with knights and wizards aplenty, the former in grand parade armor and the latter in hugely impractical robes with trailing sleeves and improbably grand hats that were themselves haloed with concentric rings of different colors.

Something about it jarred Aelis's memory and she stopped, abandoning the pretense of only glancing at it. In the center two figures faced each other on chairs of equal height, one wearing a crown of gold and handing a similar circlet of silver to the other, both of their arms extended.

"This is priceless," she suddenly blurted out. "Or it was. It's three hundred years old or more. This depicts the King of Ystain accepting the Earl Mahlgren's homage."

"Not homage," Currin pointed out somewhat stiffly. "Not really. The Earl, Donnus I—nearly as much a king in his day as old Huld III there— willingly handed his golden seals and circlet to the king and took silver back in exchange. He ruled most of what became northern Ystain, and we now call Old Ystain. Doubled the size of the kingdom and did it without war. That earl was a hero, saving thousands of lives by swallowing his pride."

"And this tapestry was part of a series hanging in Mahlhewn Keep," Aelis muttered.

"You know your art history, Warden. Of course, Mahlhewn was lost twenty years ago and shamefully ceded to the orcs when the war officially ended," Currin added. "Mostly a ruin now. Fallen walls and rotted timbers and animal dens. Its gardens overgrown and its armory pillaged." His voice took on a heated edge as he spoke, and Aelis found she did not like the sound of the words in his mouth, or the set of his eyes. "All mistakes that will have to be remedied one day."

"By . . . whom, exactly?"

"By the rightful heir of the Mahlgren earls, of course," Currin said, and the smile that spread over his broad features was unsettling. "And those who'll follow me."

19

THE EARL

✠

The new seat of Earl Mahlgren proved to be a surprisingly expansive series of caves. Aelis imagined they'd probably begun as something natural, but they showed signs of guided hands. Timbers braced the ceilings in corners, and wooden floors guarded against mud, though not as thoroughly as she might have preferred.

No one had given any thought to ventilation, though, and even a small cookfire burning in a central pit in the largest chamber filled the rest with smoke that burned the eyes and the throat. She'd had no sign of Elmo and was increasingly worried about Tun, whose hands were dug deeply into the vast pockets on the sides of his long coat, his shoulders hunching up like boulders threatening to roll over a cliff.

So far, Aelis estimated there were more than one but fewer than two dozen people inside the caves. The haze made it hard to determine if she was counting anyone twice, or if there were simply nooks hiding men she couldn't see. Most were armed, but taken individually they didn't seem threatening. She had her doubts about taking on a dozen men at once, though, even with Tun's help.

It was to that central cookfire and chamber that Currin led them. A single heavy wooden chair sat at the head of it, along with seats of canvas stretched over wood or stumps and large, roughly flat rocks that were gathered around it. The higher ceiling of the central room made the smoke more tolerable. Currin grinned as he sat down, stretched out his legs, and crossed them at the ankles before his fire.

"So, Warden. What do you think of my new seat?"

Nath had settled behind him, leaning one arm on the back of the chair and watching Aelis and Tun with her disinterested flat eyes. Aelis tried to ignore her.

"I think reclaiming your family's land is a noble cause," she said carefully.

Albeit strictly forbidden by the terms of the treaties you or your father or your mother signed, if you are who you claim to be. "I think it doesn't concern me."

"Ah yes," Currin said. "The fratricide. What did you say his name was?"

"I didn't. I merely asked if you'd seen a man, or taken one in, in the recent past."

"Even if I had," Currin said, "my retainers number . . ." Here he smiled, and waved a hand vaguely in the air. "Well, fewer than they must, if the work is to be achieved. I'd be a fool to turn aside any willing hand."

I have had just about enough of this farce, Aelis thought, as someone glided to her side with a full cup. She took it and held it unsipped while the man, the younger spearman from outside, held out another to Tun.

For all the attention her guide paid to the youth with the cup, he may as well not have existed. Tun wasn't moving except to breathe. Aelis had the sense he was gathering himself for something.

Currin took his cup and threw half of it back. "In fact, I'd be doubly the fool to turn aside willing hands as skilled as those of a Warden—and who- or whatever your companion is. It just so happens I've an opening as a Court Wizard you'll be only too happy to fill."

Court Wizard? Too happy to fill? Aelis was getting ready to shout these, and rather more pointed, objections, when some buzzing presence flitted against her mind and brought her up short.

Her training as an Enchanter told her instantly what was happening, but Currin hadn't moved. Her eyes flitted to Nath behind the chair, narrowed, and just barely made out the wand dangling against her leg, most of its length concealed by her hand and sleeve.

The time to draw her own, or to leap forward with her sword, would give Nath time to react. So she made do with what she had to hand and threw her full cup, as hard as she could.

The bottom skipped off Currin's forehead and shed some of its force, but it still surprised Nath enough to throw off her spell, startling her as much as hurting her.

The room exploded into motion.

The cupbearer flew across the room and thudded into the far wall with a crash that Aelis didn't envy, propelled by Tun's outthrust hand.

Aelis ripped her sword from her scabbard, but by the time she had, Nath had recovered and fled. As she went, she flung a hand out at the fire and spoke a word. Aelis didn't catch it, but smoke, thicker and more

acrid than what was already in the air, began to boil out of the firepit at an
alarming rate.

Currin was coming up out of his chair and reaching for his axe, but
before he could bring it into play, Tun's staff had whipped forward, the end
tapping the would-be Earl Mahlgren in the throat. His hands instantly
went to his neck and Aelis heard him gasping for air, but Tun had already
leapt forward and wrapped one arm around him. His knee intercepted
Currin's hand as it drew his axe, and the weapon clattered away.

Tun pulled his arm tightly around Currin's neck. In response to the
man's gasps, Tun rumbled, "You'll be fine so long as you don't panic. I
didn't crush your windpipe, I just hurt it. If you strain yourself, you'll fall
unconscious, and I'll have to drag you. I'd rather not."

At just the right moment, Aelis saw one of Currin's flailing arms reach
for his belt. The dagger mostly concealed in it was only just flashing when
the flat of her sword smashed against his fingers and the small blade went
skittering away.

"Think a hostage gets us out of here?" She bent down and retrieved the
knife, sticking it in her belt.

"I think it makes a better chance than otherwise." Tun's face was getting lost in the roiling smoke that was billowing out of the firepit. It was
stinging Aelis's eyes and making navigation nearly impossible.

"Grab my coat!" Tun yelled, and Aelis did as she was bid, fixing her grip
tight on the back of Tun's fringed jacket. Currin wasn't providing much resistance, and Tun unerringly knew his way out. Aelis held her sword ready
for attacking men to leap out of the murk at any moment, but before any
could, they saw sunlight and soon they were back out into the small green
space behind the wooden palisade.

Which was lined with armed men, three of them pointing loaded crossbows, the rest leveling an assortment of spears and, Aelis was sure, a few
agricultural implements.

Elmo was among them, a spear wavering in his hands. He gave Tun and
Aelis no sign of recognition.

Nath stood before the gate, brandishing a wand. Aelis, with little time
to study anything further, threw up the widest ward she could in front of
her, Tun, and their erstwhile hostage.

She grunted with the impact of holding it as a bolt, loosed from the
wall, thudded against it and fell harmlessly to the ground.

That widened some eyes, including one of the older, more sure-looking men before them, who shouted, "Hold! Hold, they have the Earl!"

"That's right, we have your fucking earl!" Tun roared. "And we are walking out of here with him. Lower your weapons!"

"And with him," Aelis said, pointing the tip of her sword toward Elmo. "He's the man we've come for, and if we don't leave with him, your earl dies." *Along with us and as many of you as we can bring down with us,* Aelis thought, amazed at how clearly she could think on the situation, with the business ends of over a dozen weapons pointed at her.

"Do as he says," barked the grizzled man on the wall. Aelis watched for Nath's reaction; the woman's eyes merely narrowed. They seemed more alert now, but her lips parted slightly, as if she was considering countermanding that order.

For his part, Currin was nodding his head and croaking what Aelis took to be an affirmative. The tap of Tun's staff and the huge arm snaked around his throat seemed to be letting him breathe and not much else.

Nath's eyes narrowed, and she raised her wand. Aelis felt the pressure against her skin, the tingle, the force behind her eyelids. Magic was being done.

"Kill them," the Enchanter said. "He is no earl. He was the son of a gardener at Mahlhewn, no more. I will make the man who kills the Warden the new earl."

The men aimed their weapons. Tun roared and shoved the hostage back toward Aelis. Currin was too stunned to resist, and Aelis was too busy erecting wards to protest.

Then Tun began to change.

She felt two more crossbow bolts thud against wards that she kept up only long enough to deflect the missiles into the ground.

Tun grew taller, broader, wider. Where he'd once been huge in an ordinary sense—the biggest man she'd ever seen, but not beyond the bounds of what she imagined a man could be—he was now something much larger still. His hair grew longer, streaming down his back in a dark wave, and it seemed as though the long coat he wore blended with it. A hump began to form and his arms grew toward the ground, and only when his mouth widened into a muzzle and his skull thickened and a roar emerged did Aelis realize what was happening.

In the time it took to draw and loose a breath, Tun had transformed into a massive bear, the largest she had ever seen. And like a tidal wave of fur and muscle he rumbled forward. In one lope he was at the wall, where the men were too stunned by what they'd seen to attack. One feebly raised a spear, but the bear reared on his hind legs—putting his mouth and great paws at the height of the men standing on the palisade—and swiped. Spears, men, crossbow, and two or three trees' worth of timber went crashing. The bear let out another deafening roar. Men fled in a panic, throwing open the gate that now hung crookedly from the damage Tun had already done to it.

There were shouts, screams, the pressure of Nath's crude enchantments on Aelis's mind. She snatched Currin by his collar and hauled him to his feet. Tun, the bear, whatever he was, smashed both his forepaws and all his considerable bulk at the section of wall before him. Timbers splintered, ropes snapped, iron hinges squealed, men broke and ran.

The bear turned his head to Aelis, roared again. She needed no encouragement to follow, rushing after him with what speed she could muster, dragging Currin, looking futilely for Elmo amid the chaos. Nath was trying to whip, cajole, or compel the remaining men into some kind of effective resistance.

None, strangely, seemed to want to deal with an enormous bear that had once been a considerably less enormous man.

Aelis ran. Currin stumbled after. The bear loped along behind her. When they were perhaps thirty yards on and heading down the hill Tun stopped and looked back, rising up onto his hind legs again and then sinking back down.

A crossbow bolt came whizzing. Aelis reached to her mind for a ready ward but knew it would be too slow. Her magic only just impacted its flight. Where it might have taken the bear somewhere in his massive skull—perhaps the eye, or the jaw, and done real damage—instead it skidded against the meat of his shoulder, leaving a red weal behind. The Tunbear roared and reared back up, challenging the men who seemed not too eager to pursue.

Aelis kicked Currin's feet out from under him and found enough courage in the midst of the confusion and terror to yell.

"Tun! If you can hear me, we need to run, rethink a plan! They have Elmo, but we have their man. Please! This is not a fight we can win, even if we kill them all."

The great bear's head swiveled and she thought, or hoped, there was a flash of recognition in his huge brown eyes. Eyes that she realized were precisely Tun's—hanging beneath a heavy brow, deeply shadowed—only writ larger.

Almost dismissively, Aelis raised another ward and deflected another crossbow bolt. They were getting bolder.

The bear made a low growl, then turned and began loping away. She turned to follow, but stopped to grab Currin's collar. He'd been crawling away, though he hadn't gotten far, and he still offered little resistance.

Tun, in this bear form, could have easily outpaced her, she knew that. He would surge ahead by a dozen yards and then turn to look at her, sniffing at the air and growling lightly. Aelis was lagging behind, largely because she had to drag Currin along. She pulled him close and kicked his legs out from under him, looming over him with her sword's point hovering over one eye.

"You're going to run now, on your own. Willingly, with us. If you try to turn back, if you try to escape us, you're going to find out whether you can outrun the bear."

As if he were listening to her, Tun stretched his neck forward toward Currin and let out a long, low growl. With one of his huge forepaws he slapped the ground, digging a heavy furrow into it with his claws.

Mute and pliable—terrified or made insensible by stress, Aelis wasn't sure which—Currin stood, and all three of them ran.

Pursuit was slow to organize, or slow of foot, or simply not eager to engage with a bear that topped ten feet when he stood on his hind legs. Whatever it was, Aelis wasn't sure, and they ran blindly and in silence for some time. Her own breathing was loud in her ears, but the bear sounded like some great machine, wheezing in and out.

"I think it's safe now, Tun," Aelis said between panting breaths, putting aside whatever foolishness she felt at addressing a bear. The huge beast growled at her, lips drawing back over teeth that were too long and too covered with slaver for comfort.

"Tun." The deepest-seated instincts in Aelis's mind—the kind that came down from before her family was a line of counts and countesses, from before there *were* noble titles, when a beast like the one before her might be the kind of thing that destroyed an entire family, a tribe, a clan—were telling her to run. To hide. To climb a tree, as futile an act as the thinking part of her brain knew that to be. Her mind wanted fire and spears and heavy rocks levered down from a cliff atop this beast's head.

But there was more to a wizard and a Warden than instinct. *A Warden may be afraid. A Warden may be pissing down the sides of their legs,* Bardun Jacques had once told them, *but a Warden makes damn sure that whatever is frightening them should be well fucking terrified in turn.*

"Tun!" Aelis snapped, and her wand slipped into her left hand. Behind her, Currin gasped and choked whatever fearful sounds he could make. "I need my guide now. I need the man I hired. If I have to use this," she said, lifting her wand and letting a tiny comet's tail of green light form behind it, "I will. But I don't want to. I don't enchant friends unless I have no other choice."

The bear glared at her, its eyes wide, the whites veined with red. He straightened his legs, shook his massive body, let out a low growl, and began to shrink.

With a long, low growl that resolved into a man's teeth-gritted agony, the bear morphed and changed, the fur receded, the arms and legs grew shorter, the buff color of Tun's fringed coat re-emerged. Then, with a gasp, Tun—her guide and, she hoped, her friend—was standing there again, breathing hard.

"Demon," Currin sputtered. "Beast! Vile, unclean orcish savage."

Aelis turned on him, with her wand raised and spells already called to mind. She released one and he slumped over into the grass, his breathing a faint snore.

"That's handy," Tun said appreciatively.

"Won't last long. Only a First Order Enchantment. Know Your Weariness, some call it; most of us simply call it the Catnap." She cleared her throat, unsure how to approach the conversation. "So."

"I am what I am."

"And what is that, exactly?"

"I have neither the time nor the inclination to explain it in detail."

"You were the bear I chased away from the village," Aelis said. She hadn't realized it until she said it, but she knew the truth of it.

"Yes," Tun said. "That is why I agreed to help you. A lesser warden would've gone for an easier solution, and simply shot me full of bolts, tried to poison me."

"You aren't in control of it."

"It? You have terms. I know that you do," Tun said. "Lycanthropy, though it is no curse."

"There were rumors, during the fighting. Orc warriors fighting alongside bears. Riding them into battle, even. I never credited them. No one much did."

"It is something that is passed through families, though not predict-ably," Tun said. "And as to your statement, no. I do not have the control of it that I should. Which is why I live as I do."

Aelis's mind was racing ahead of her tongue, offering insights she hadn't consciously considered. "Is that why you were sought out to fight the De-mon Tree? Why you agreed to do it? You said it was an obligation," she blurted, recalling the conversations suddenly, "a fact of your existence."

"Orcs do not call up a monster they have not the means to destroy," Tun said. "There are not many like me—and my human blood makes me an imperfect specimen. *That* is why my control is lacking."

Tun spoke the words "imperfect specimen" with such a studied lack of emotive force, such precise detachment, that Aelis could only guess at the depth of the wound he was plumbing. As if sensing her thought, he said, "We haven't the time to mope and drink about it. We came out of that cave with the wrong man. I don't suppose we could dress him up as Elmo."

"No," Aelis said, chuckling faintly. "I don't suppose we could."

"Plan?"

"Walk on, make camp, interrogate our hostage, reevaluate."

Tun nodded. Then he bent, lifted the still-limp Currin, slung him over a shoulder, and walked on.

20

THE GARDENER

They walked until it was well dark. Aelis's moon-tied night vision was only going to last a few days more, she guessed, so best to make use of it now, as she'd told Tun. He found them a sheltered stand of trees beneath a rocky outcropping of a hill, quiet and secluded.

Currin had woken up after only a few bounces on Tun's shoulder, but by the simple expedient of baring his teeth and growling theatrically, her guide kept the would-be earl quiet while his hands were tied. Sullen and frightened, he proved quiet and tractable until Aelis sat him down, propped up against a tree.

Tun loomed behind her as she knelt before him, peering into eyes that seemed strangely unfocused.

"Currin. Currin Mahlgren, if you're to be believed. I told you I didn't care about your great scheme. I told you it didn't concern me." She put the best edge she could muster into her voice and leaned close. "Well, now it does. And you're going to regret it."

"Mahl . . . Mahlgren? Like Mahlhewn Keep?" Currin swallowed hard, blinking stupidly. "I think I lived there once. I don't . . . where am I? Who are you?"

"Oh, Onoma's silent mercy, did he take a clout to the head we didn't see?" Carefully, Aelis reached out and took his head in her hands, probing delicately with her fingers. "I don't feel any injury. But then it could have been a shaking, not a fracture. Do you have any pain, Currin?"

"Only in my hands and my feet," he reported, answering as quickly and artlessly as a child might.

"Currin," she said, keeping her hands lightly to either side of his head and looking at him eye to eye, "do you truly not know who I am? Warden Aelis de Lenti?"

"I'm sorry," he said weakly. "Should I?"

"I didn't think we hurt him," Tun rumbled from somewhere in the darkness behind her.

"We didn't," Aelis said. "But someone has." She hit upon an idea, and slowly reached to the back of her belt. "Currin," she said, keeping her voice neutral, "do you know the name Nath?"

"Nath . . . Nathalie? Yes."

"How?"

He thought on this for a moment. "I don't know," he said hesitantly.

Slowly, she eased her Anatomist's Blade from its sheath. "Currin, I need to see if something has been done to you. I have to prick your arm with a knife, but I'm not going to hurt you any more than I have to."

Carefully, she placed one hand over his mouth and moved the tip of her dagger so it hovered just over the meat of his thigh. Without warning, she let the tip sink just barely into his skin, while simultaneously clamping her hand around his mouth.

"Shhh," she said, as if she were comforting a child, while letting the diagnostic abilities of the knife do their work. The spectrum of colors opened in her mind.

His skin was abraded in places where he'd fallen. His feet were flat, and hurt him, as he'd said. His hands were nearing numbness from his bonds and pain crept up his arms as he held them unnaturally behind him.

There was nothing—nothing that she could find, at any rate—that was wrong with his skull or his mind. Not the parts of it her knife could show her.

She drew the knife away from his skin and removed her hand from his mouth.

"What do you remember about Nathalie?" As she asked the question, she watched his face rather than listen to his words.

Currin struggled. His eyes showed familiarity and Aelis thought she could read in them the spark of thoughts, of recognition and apprehension, of anticipating how he would phrase the words to convey his experience and his sense impressions that the name Nathalie brought to the forefront of his mind.

Instead, he struggled to say anything at all, and became increasingly puzzled.

"It's all right, Currin. You don't need to answer the question. Relax for the moment."

She wiped her dagger with the edge of her cloak and slid it home, then walked a few paces away. She balled up her fist, stuck it into her mouth, and muffled the stream of expletives she badly wanted to scream aloud into her raw knuckles.

"What is it?" Tun's murmur was pitched for her ears alone.

"That Nath must be some powerful Enchanter. I think she had her hooks so deep into Currin's mind that he can barely function without her now."

"Is that a permanent condition?"

"Very possibly," Aelis said. "At the Lyceum, we're taught never to seize the mind unless there's no other way to prevent an almost certain death. Nudge it, encourage it, bring out sensations and desires that were already lurking inside it, yes. Grab and squeeze, no."

"And this Nath has squeezed?"

"Like a citron for its juice, I think." Aelis sighed. "Come to think of it, she may have been controlling some of the other men as well."

"Why do you say that?"

"They were slow to react until she gave them direct orders. The way she seemed distracted—like a part of her mind was always on something else. Because it was."

"There's two dozen men there, Warden," Tun said. "Could she be controlling them all?"

"She wouldn't have to do it all at once. A nudge here, a squeeze there, a whispered suggestion each morning." Aelis chewed at the corner of her mouth as she thought on the puzzle. She looked up suddenly and caught a glimpse of red wetness on Tun's jacket. She snapped out of her reverie.

"Dammit, you're hurt," she hissed. "Jacket off," she ordered, even as she unslung her pack and rummaged for the medical kit she'd put together.

"I heal fast—"

"The graveyards and catacombs of the world are full of people who 'heal fast' and 'don't need stitches' and have 'never had a wound fester.' I will not brook argument. I'll put you to sleep if I have to."

Tun grimaced and began sliding his jacket off. "That would leave you in a fine pickle if the earl's retainers come upon us."

Aelis paused in threading her needle. "Are they close?"

"Well, I haven't spoken to the spirits of the trees in the past thirty minutes." Tun winced as he pulled his arms clear of the jacket and set it down. The wound looked painful, in a pad of muscle at his shoulder. Though not life-threatening, the wound had bled through the wool shirt he wore beneath the coat.

"It is not considered wise to play at nonsense with one's surgeon," Aelis said, "especially not just before she's about to ply your skin with her needle."

"No animals are disturbed by their passing. I don't hear or smell anything. I doubt they are within a hundred yards of us in any direction, and if they were, something—not spirits, something my senses could detect—would tell me. Could be your Enchanter is having a devil of a time rousing them to come after the wizard and her skin-changer familiar."

Aelis snorted. "Pull the shirt down. Got to see what I'm dealing with." She set her threaded needle aside on a clean cloth she had unrolled. With a second, and a small bottle of astringent, she wiped away the blood that had begun to dry around the edges of the wound before sewing it closed.

"Onoma's mercy, your skin is like, well, not iron, but it's more like iron than any other skin I've tried to sew." She was, in fact, having trouble getting the needle through the edge of the wound.

"Got a silver needle?"

"Not with me," Aelis replied. "Only steel. Why?" She looked up at him, her face set in concentration, brow furrowed.

"Werebear," he said, pointing to himself with one thick finger. "Silver? Have you heard *none* of the right stories?"

"Thought they were nonsense." With a grunt of effort she pulled the needle through one edge and then the other.

Tun didn't even flinch as she punched the needle through his skin repeatedly. He also didn't answer, reasoning correctly that talking would just complicate her task.

For all that his skin was resistant to her needle, Aelis took pride in her suturing, and set tight, close stitches that would knit the wound clean and even. When she closed off the last stitch and began to wipe her needle clean, he spoke up again.

"Thank you, Warden. As for the stories about my kind, well . . ." Tun shrugged. "Most of it is nonsense, yes. Silver is true. Or did you think I refuse to take coin in trade because of some obscure point of honor?"

"Does a moon bring on your change?"

"Is there ever a day, an hour, when one of our six moons is not filling the sky? There may be, but we'll not find out soon. It is simply something I *must* do, periodically."

"I know some Anatomists who'd love to make a study of you."

Tun's eyes went wide and his shoulders suddenly bunched, his lips curling around his teeth. Aelis threw her hands out wide. "Not like *that*. I just mean talk to you. Observe. Record how you change and figure out a way to measure it, control it."

Tun relaxed, then raised a hand and dug out something dangling from a leather thong strung around his neck. A charm of some sort, which was plain to see, hair and a tooth fixed with carefully worked dark green amber and set into wood and iron. "This is for precisely that. But it does not work as well as it ought, because I'm—"

"Right," Aelis said, cutting him off. "The favor you wanted is to see if I can fix it, improve it?"

"You've got a quick-moving mind once it sets itself in motion, Warden."

She shrugged. "You can call me Aelis, Tun. And wardens are expected to make those sorts of leaps. Like making a painting, one of our teachers used to say, except a warden's task is to mount the canvas and fit a frame tight around it. Only then do you worry about filling in all the messy details between the borders."

"Aren't the messy details between the borders the painting?"

"It's not a perfect analogy, and besides, Bardun Jacques is a terrible painter."

Tun snorted and picked up his jacket, slung one arm into it. "The rune-stone from inside the Demon Tree. Being orc magic, it should have common threads with this," he said, tapping at the charm he wore before covering it with his fringed coat. "Should have something you could use. If you're willing."

"Why wouldn't I be?"

Tun shrugged, then pulled his coat snug and buckled it. "Not something we need to worry about now. What'll we do about the earl-gardener there?"

Currin had slumped back against the tree Aelis had propped him on, and seemed to be fighting—and losing—against sleep.

"Join him in slumber, I expect."

"The longer we wait, the more advantages we're giving away to them," Tun said. "That is, if we intend to use force or stealth. We could always try to negotiate. Our man for him," he said, gesturing toward Currin.

"I don't think that's a deal they'll care to make. You heard what Nath said: kill him, he didn't matter. She's running the outfit and she's got no use for this one."

"Then keeping him around isn't doing us any good," Tun said.

"And we can't just cut him loose. Either Nath's enchantments have damaged his mind, or he's a fine actor and has me fooled. If it's the former, turning him loose'd be just as good as slitting his throat. The latter, and it's slitting our own."

"One of those," Tun said carefully, "is a more acceptable outcome than the other."

"If it comes to it," Aelis said. "But I'd rather hang on to him till we know more, and till we can confront Nath on our terms."

"She's got the men."

"But she has to spend her strength to keep them under her power. I don't. If I can come to her fresh and on anything close to even terms, I don't fear her."

"Your confidence is commendable, but there are a score of men who make 'even terms' rather impossible."

"We'll think of something."

"I don't do strategies."

"As long as you take orders."

"Suggestions, certainly. Orders?" Tun crossed his arms over his chest and grinned around his tusks. "Not as well."

"Fine. I'll think of something and make some suggestions. In the morning."

"I still think we're giving up an advantage."

"But we're getting a bigger one," Aelis said. "In the morning, I will be able to call on the full range of my talents."

"Be nice if those included some streams of fire or a few arcs of lightning."

"There's more to wizardry than fire and lightning, Tun," Aelis said. "Now I'm going to go see to the prisoner."

She found Currin dozing, but when she nudged him awake he briefly struggled to sit upright. "I can't feel my hands," he whined.

"I'm going to fix that," Aelis said. With some of the cordage Tun had produced from his small bedroll or his voluminous pockets—she wasn't entirely sure—she bound him to the tree itself, then untied his hands.

He thanked her, and she squatted on the bed of pine needles nearby to look at him. "Currin, what can you tell me about Nath?"

"Nathalie. I don't . . ." He frowned, grimaced, chewed his bottom lip. "I know the name. I know her. She was . . . to be my court wizard . . ."

He trailed off after saying the last five words, a light sheen of sweat glistening on his forehead. "I should know more. I have known her for . . . a long time. But I don't. I can't. Can't remember."

"In the morning I will try to help you remember, Currin. I promise," Aelis said. "For now, try to sleep and stop worrying." Her words sounded painfully hollow to her own ears. Tun retreated, though given that he slipped his hand blades from his pockets before he did, she suspected he was either going to tend to them or going on watch, and either way she was safe to sleep for a few hours.

She stretched out her bedroll and lay on it. Her limbs were sore, with the bone-deep ache of too much running on top of too little rest. Aelis stared at where in the night sky Onoma's moon—blackly invisible, sometimes an outline of empty space where stars would be—would provide her night vision for another handful of days.

My orrery's in my tower, and so are my books of orbit. These silent words felt hollow to her, though, as she knew a wizard was meant to be able to derive such knowledge on a clear night regardless of what instruments they had to hand.

She drifted off with the remnants of first-year lectures on astronomy and horology filling her mind.

✦ ✦ ✦

Aelis awoke with a start. She expected to find herself at the unforgiving desk in a first-year lecture hall. Probably in History of the Lyceum: Priests, Wizards, and War, a required and notoriously boring class. Instead she looked up to find Tun just about to jostle her awake. He drew back in consternation. "Nightmares, Warden?"

She chuckled lightly. "No, just memories of school. If I have to dream about my time in university, why couldn't it be parties, the breakthroughs as I learned to truly craft spells, the lovers? Why must it be first-year history?"

"I am sure I could not answer that for you, Warden. But dreams are sometimes the mind's way of telling us something we have seen and not understood."

"And sometimes they are just random impulses and memories jostling one another for attention."

"Almost certainly."

"Any schoolboy memories yourself, Tun?"

"I think you know the answer to that, Warden."

"You can call me Aelis. And I don't. I know almost nothing about you, excepting the bit about being a werebear, which, admittedly, is a pretty significant fact. Even so—you live the life of an outcast or hermit, but you speak like an educated man."

"Do I?"

"Yes."

Tun grunted faintly. "It's time for your watch."

"I can pass it while asking you questions until you tell me something."

"Tutors," Tun said, kneeling to the ground and his unrolled blanket, as if that explained enough and he was done.

"What about them?"

"I had them," he grunted. "In grammar, among other things."

"Such as?"

"Natural philosophy. Political economy. Rhetoric. Languages. A bit of music." With his arms propping him up, he stretched his legs out, then fixed Aelis with a stare. "Now I am going to get four hours of sleep. I have answered as many questions as I intend to."

Aelis lifted a hand, picked up her swordbelt from where it lay next to her, and buckled it around her waist. The weight of it was becoming entirely familiar, though she was beginning to develop a sore patch of skin where her sword dragged the belt against her clothes and her hip.

"Why a lecture?" she murmured, remembering again the uncomfortable desk, the ink stains on her hands, the parade of boring professors. "Why couldn't it have been Humphrey or Miralla? Or both of them?"

Aelis found that Maurenia had somehow replaced both of her former lovers in her mind's eye as she strolled around their campsite, such as it was, contemplating the possibilities of lustful daydreaming.

She brought herself up short.

"You're standing in the middle of a hostile wilderness with a half-orc werebear and a man whose mind has been deeply damaged by an Enchanter, and who may or may not be the rightful Earl of Mahlgren. It's not exactly the time to be indulging your fantasies.

"Not that it's likely to matter," she continued. "Probably I'll never see Maurenia again." Even as she spoke the words she hoped they weren't true, but she pushed them from her mind and focused on listing the assets she had available.

Tun, she thought. She wasn't sure that she could depend on him transforming himself again and wasn't prepared to ask. Even so, she was willing to bet he was worth more than any three to five of the men Nathalie had.

Myself. Nath was clearly a powerful Enchanter. *So am I,* Aelis told herself, *in addition to being an Abjurer and a Necromancer.*

"Where did she learn and what else does she know?" Aelis muttered. "Is she only good for the one trick? Is she a hammer or a razor or both? Will my defenses hold against either, if she's as powerful as it seems?"

She'd had a wand; those were not easily found outside the Lyceum. Anyone could cut a switch and call it a wand, of course, but Aelis didn't imagine that was what Nath had done. Certainly, some numbers of real wands were lost as Enchanters died in the field, or were stolen. Even so, there was the possibility that this Nathalie had the same kind of Enchanter's training as Aelis did and less scruple about misuse of her power.

Aelis found herself wishing she had brought pen, ink, and paper. Writing always clarified things for her. She suddenly recalled the list of items she'd scribbled what seemed like weeks but had really only been days ago, in her tower.

"What was even on that list? Find out who was literate. Make headway on my stolen book." She sighed, as those concerns seemed too remote. On balance, she supposed, chasing a possible fratricide did indeed take precedence over a stolen text.

"And what about that babbling old hedge wizard and his balls of harmless light?" Something about what he'd done bothered her. Perhaps the fact that he'd seemed to mingle an Illusion with an Evocation, something that ought not, so far as she knew, to be possible. At least not to anyone incapable of less than Third Order magics in both disciplines, but then, what he'd done had been harmless and intangible, which weren't the hallmarks of powerful magic.

Her concern melted away as a wind stirred the pines. She tried to refocus on the current moment.

"I'll have to work on the assumption that she is powerful. And . . ." Aelis grew silent as the night pressed down on her, and slowly a plan began to form.

21

THE WAND

"You cannot," Tun said, "seriously be thinking about a frontal assault."

"Not an *assault*," Aelis said as she checked the draw of both sword and dagger, the action of her wand in her sleeve, and wished she had an Evoker up the other one.

"Not denying the frontal part."

"Wouldn't want to lie to you, Tun."

"Warden, if you're thinking that strolling in there and starting a fight will trigger something out of me . . ." Tun let out a sigh that had a bit too much of a growl underlying it. "Well, you might not be wrong. But you might not like the results."

"I wouldn't plan that way without asking. If you're willing, though, I need you to manage His Lordship here."

"So, it is to be a prisoner exchange after all?"

"Something like that."

"Warden. I will take suggestions, and I owe you my help, but I won't go into an action blind."

"I have my reasons, Tun. The situation has to be fluid, and it may legitimately be to our advantage if you *don't* know what I'm going to do." *Would help if I did, though.*

"Does this have something to do with . . ." He waved his fingers vaguely at his temple.

"Is *enchantment* the word you're looking for?"

"If that's what you mean for magic that affects the mind, then yes."

"Well, it does. That's what I know Nath can do. And powerfully, at that."

"So you're going to challenge her at her greatest strength? Are you stronger than her as an Enchanter?"

"I would say that forcing so many minds to a single goal, and keeping up the effort this long, is the work of someone capable of the power of Fifth Order Enchantments."

"And you're what, Sixth Order? Seventh?"

Aelis cleared her throat. "Third. On a good day."

"Five is more than three."

"I said capable of the power of Fifth Order. That is not quite the same thing."

"It's a fine distinction to hang several lives on, ours not least among them."

"Tun, I'm gambling. I won't lie about that. I haven't got the raw power she seems to have. But my bet is this: that's *all* she has."

"Raw power." Tun spoke the words slowly, filling them with disbelief. "Is all she has."

"Does the strongest man win every fight if he's so muscle-bound that he can't move his feet?"

"He only needs to land one blow."

"And what if I can work out exactly how to counter it? Look." Aelis pointed to where Currin slumped against the tree. His head lolled to one side, and drool soaked the shoulder and chest of his jerkin. "We're going to have to walk this man every step of the way back to their palisade reminding him who he is. She's got power, but a wizard, a true wizard, is not about power. We're about *subtlety*. *Precision*. *Control*. The least application of magical power where it can do the most good. That's the principle I was taught. If I wanted to keep a band of desperate men dancing to my tune for weeks on end, I could do most of it with mere suggestion, a fingernail on the back of their necks now and then, and a *trickle* of magic a day. I wouldn't have to reduce them to drooling hulks with hammer blows to their mind."

"So you can, what, persuade them to listen to you by flicking your hair and swinging your hips?"

"I'll save that for an emergency." Aelis's voice was flatter than the blade of a knife. "Tun, you've felt the touch of my enchantment. Do you remember it?"

Tun let out a long breath. "I can, though it's hazy, a morning fog waiting for the heat to burn it away, but it never quite does."

"Was it an overwhelming power? Did it take away all your volition? Or was it simply a gentle shove? A reminder of who you were, what you *wanted* to be doing, and how it wasn't what you *were* doing?"

Tun held up one hand, palm out. "Fine, Warden. You've convinced me. Let's wake up our earl. Our trail should be easy enough for even you to follow."

"Even me?" Aelis couldn't really work up the effort to sound offended, and Tun merely snorted. She set about cutting Currin loose, tapping his cheek to wake him up. His breathing hitched, his head lifted, but his eyes didn't even flutter. She tapped harder, harder, until finally she gave him a light slap across the cheek.

His eyes opened, but took a long time to blink into focus.

"Nath? Where's Nathalie? I . . ."

"Shhhh, Currin. Shh. My name is Aelis, remember? Warden Aelis de Lenti. Nath betrayed you. I saved you." She knelt next to him and placed her hands on his shoulders. "I saved you, but we're going to go confront Nath and rescue the rest of your men now." She slipped one hand to the back of his neck and let loose just a trickle of a spell, barely a First Order Enchantment. It was a simple thing, meant to remind him of his ambitions and plans, of his claim to the Mahlgren title.

"Are you . . . going to be my court wizard now, Warden Aelis?"

Aelis smiled. "I would have to receive permission from the Lyceum to accept such a position, Earl Mahlgren. But one thing at a time, eh? Come on. Let's go save your men."

She hooked her hands beneath his arms and stood up, giving him little choice. His legs wobbled and he leaned against the trunk of the tree for balance. But he nodded, and took a hesitant step forward rather than waiting to be led.

Aelis decided to take that as a good sign, and off they went.

✦ ✦ ✦

"Nath! Come forth and answer for your betrayal!" On their walk, which took them perhaps an hour at a much more leisurely pace than the crashing run they'd made the night before, Currin had gained strength. By the time the palisade wall came into view—with the section Tun had brought down still lying flat on the grass—he'd worked himself up into an indignant boil. That he started bellowing before even the lazy guards behind the wall had noticed their approach had Aelis scowling.

She'd spent the walk chewing the inside of her cheek and concentrating on the spell she wanted. There was no ready-made Abjuration or Enchantment for what she wanted to do.

Onoma's cold arms, why couldn't this just be some standard-issue grave robber or spirit binder? Cut through him like a good knife through soft cheese.

The first thing was the proper ward. It had to be strong enough to deflect any physical attacks the men would launch before Nath started hammering anyone with a spell. But it also needed to be porous to magic if Nath tried what she thought she might. Ogrinden's Steel Net was something like what she wanted. *But I'd need six more Abjurers and a small army to cover it with.*

No, she finally decided. *An all-purpose ward to start. Let her try her hammer blow and recoil when I shrug it off. Of course*, she immediately undercut herself, *if she tries something else, and you've hardened your ward against an Enchantment, you're dead.*

"If she had more than one trick up her sleeve she'd have tried it last night," she finally muttered, drawing a dark look from Tun.

By the time they stopped, with Currin yelling for satisfaction regarding the dishonor done to his person, the base betrayal of his most trusted adviser, and quite a lot of other nonsense, Aelis had Adaeric's Preparation called to mind. It was among the most powerful Abjurations she could call upon. She rehearsed the syllables, drew her thumb in sigils over the hilt of her sword then pulled it free as soon as men appeared.

That they bothered to unlimber and swing open the ponderous and now unbalanced gate rather than simply exit through the hole Tun had made in the palisade further confirmed what she thought about their ability to think clearly. And when she saw Nath walking in the midst of a party of six armed men, it was all she could do to keep her focus on the ward she was prepared to call, rather than lashing out with an inducement or charm of her own.

Nath had her wand to hand. Aelis drew energy into her sword and unleashed it with the syllables of her ward, just before Nath's voice washed over them.

"Put down your weapons, Warden, and your companions as well. Come in and we'll discuss all this over tea."

That was all she said, or all she seemed to say. The words themselves were so reasonable. Her voice was honey.

But underneath them was a current of power, a thrum so loud and heavy Aelis half expected the ground to shake beneath her feet. Next to her, Currin was clutching his head. Tun's hand blades were out of his pockets, but he held them with thumb and forefinger, as if he meant to lower them carefully to the ground.

And though Aelis was rocked to her core by the roar of power that Nath managed to unleash, it was like a puff of heat from a fire that had harmless smokepowder thrown on it; intense for a moment and then gone.

Instead of lowering her sword, she tightened her grip on it, and kept her ward up. Slowly, grinding her teeth with the effort, she pushed the ward outward to Currin and Tun, enveloping them in it. Tun shifted his weapons into his hands; Currin stood straighter, imperiously shouting commands Aelis didn't have time or energy to listen to.

The assault broke off. *Now try the other way*, Aelis thought. And instantly, Nathalie did exactly that. Lifting her wand, she gestured with it at the men surrounding her.

"Kill them. We don't need them."

In her mind's eye Aelis could see the strands of power Nath was throwing in six directions. They wouldn't have to be much. Simple suggestions should do for men who were as conditioned to the lash of her Enchantment as these men surely were.

But Aelis had a plan, and she grasped forward with her own spell.

In her lessons on swordsmanship and close combat, Lavanalla had always taken on all comers. For an elven woman the word *willowy* was waiting around for, invariably there was always some noble's son who decided he'd put his honor aside and show off. And no matter how thickly muscled he was or how much training he'd had, the Arch-Abjurer would throw them, twist their arms till they begged for mercy, or trip them until they retired in embarrassment. Lavanalla had given special attention, in further training, to teaching the principles of angle, misdirection, and redirection that would allow a weaker opponent to stand up to a stronger one.

Those principles could be applied to magical combat as well.

So instead of reaching with her own Enchantment spell directly to the men who would attack them, she reached out for Nath, and *her* spell. Aelis threw out her own Second Order Enchantment—a slight modification of a Lash—and wrapped it around the enchantments that were already in place in the minds of Nath's men. And then she tugged on the deeply embedded commands that had been placed there day after day, week after week, as Nath and Currin had built their following.

"Men loyal to Mahlgren! She's ordering you to murder your earl in cold blood!" Aelis yelled. "She's the traitor! Take her, but alive so we can know the source of her betrayal!"

Two of the men kept sighting down their crossbows at her, Currin, and Tun. Three blinked and lowered their weapons.

The sixth thumped the back of Nath's skull with the shaft of his spear so hard that Aelis winced when the sound reached her. The Enchanter crumpled to the ground.

Then so did Currin. Then, one by one, like candles being snuffed, so did the six guards Nath had brought with her.

Silence reigned in the morning light, Aelis and Tun standing stock-still as if afraid to disturb the scene of their victory. A bird trilled in a tree behind them. Aelis jumped.

"I," Tun said gravely, "am going to have to haul all of them up into the cavern, aren't I?"

"Well, I think I can manage Nath," Aelis said. "Let's not lose any more time."

Her shaking hands needed two tries to get her sword back into its scabbard.

✦ ✦ ✦

Inside the cavern was much the same as out; Nath and Currin's ragged band of desperate men had all fallen where they stood. It was a small miracle that none had fallen on a weapon or into a fire, but Aelis had no time to deal with them. She wrestled Nath's limp form into the cavern with the other woman's wand stuck through her belt, and set about binding her hands.

She took out the traveling case she'd packed, found a pot, filled it with water from a skin, and set it over one of the guttering cookfires.

"Bit too much work to do to be making tea, no?" Tun blotted out the light from the cave entrance, an unconscious man on each shoulder.

"Not tea. Something to keep her from casting spells." Aelis plucked a vial and carefully scraped the wax seal with her thumb. She eyed a careful two drops into the water and carefully smoothed the wax back over the edge of the vial.

Meanwhile, Tun had lowered his load to the rock-strewn ground and gone back for another pair. By the time he came back, bubbles were forming on the surface of the water, and Aelis took the pot off the fire and set it down to cool.

"If you had something to keep her from using her power, why not lead with that?" Tun's voice betrayed nothing of the effort of carrying the dead-weight of two unconscious men up a hill.

"Because it has to be ingested and it seemed unlikely I could slip it into a cup, get her to drink it, *and* cover us for the quarter of an hour it would take for potency."

"And what're you going to do during the quarter of an hour it takes now?"

Aelis decanted her mixture into a nearby clay cup and gestured with her chin toward Nath's unconscious form. Tun got the hint and knelt beside the Enchanter, then carefully pried her slack mouth open with his massive fingers.

"I'll give her a pommel strike to the head if I have to," Aelis said as she poured the mixture of water, herb, and somnolent carefully down Nath's throat. The woman choked and sputtered, but Tun held her mouth closed till she swallowed. Her eyes fluttered for a moment, then closed again.

"However," Aelis went on, packing up her kit, "if she can manage to get off an enchantment in the moments between waking up and feeling the full potency of this dose, with her hands tied, her mind fogged, and her wand on my belt, then . . ." She shrugged. "She probably deserves to win."

"What do you plan to do with her?"

"Find out just where her power came from. I've *never* felt someone with that much force, that much energy to expend, over so long a period."

"Possible she had it stored in amulets or what have you, somewhere?"

"Then I'd need to know where she got them and how they worked."

"Such things are possible then?"

"Of course they are. Just difficult to make, and access to them is tightly controlled by the Archmagisters."

Tun grunted and trotted back the way he'd come to gather the last of the prisoners.

Aelis surveyed the insensate men, wondered where they were going to get the cordage to secure them all, and said aloud, "Well. Now what the fuck do I do?" *What would Bardun Jacques do?*

She was saved from having to answer the question by the sound of a gurgle from Nath. She turned to find the Enchanter's eyes flickering as she struggled to sit upright. She flopped to her side and her hands fluttered against her chest.

Aelis watched her in silence, until she saw Nath's eyes come into focus and hone in on her, narrowed in rage. She began mumbling unintelligibly, trying, Aelis thought, to cast a spell.

"None of that," the Warden said. "If you do manage to organize your thoughts and summon even a minor order, I'll have to do something unpleasant."

"Kill you," Nath rasped, then spat into the dirt where she lay. "My men'll kill you."

"I don't think they will," Aelis said, "because I've already laid my own power over them. Riding atop yours, of course. Impressive trick, the depth and breadth of Enchantment you called on. How did you do it?"

Nath spat into the dirt again, twitched, tried to rise. "Kill you," she mumbled again.

Aelis slipped Nath's wand into her hand, and held it up. Nath's eyes widened and focused on it; Aelis tucked it away. Nath's eyes widened. "The wand is only a focus, you know. They say the best Enchanters—the Archmagisters—don't even *need* their implements. That there have even been a few who could summon a Fifth Order spell without a word or a gesture."

"I'm stronger than all of them." The side of Nath's face was covered in dirt that her own drool had turned to mud.

"And yet, here we are. You at my mercy. In truth, Nathalie—if that is your name—I only came here for one man. Elmo. He was here last night. I saw him. Where is he now?"

As she spoke, Aelis went and knelt at Nath's side. With her wand in her left hand, she laid her right on the woman's head, or tried, as Nath lunged and tried to get Aelis's wrists between her teeth. Abjurer's reflexes and Nath's dulled limbs saved her the indignity. Before she knew it, Aelis delivered a short punch straight into Nath's cheek.

The thud was loud in the stillness of the cavern. Her fist stung. Nath looked at her, glassy-eyed and unfocused, then suddenly let out a sob.

"I only want what I promised," she said as she broke out into a cascade of tears, "and what was promised me. To protect this place, Mahlgren, and to see a rightful earl."

"Nath," Aelis said, fighting hard against the urge to shake her stinging hand, "I don't care about the Earl of Mahlgren. I don't care what you promised or what was promised to you. I care about my man, Elmo. He's who I've come for. Where is he, and why did he come here?"

Nath had lowered her head, so Aelis laid her hand on the woman's shoulder. With a flick of the tip of her hazel wand, she cast a simple Enchantment, not much stronger than a textbook First Order Encouragement. It seemed to her that Nath was driven by an ambition to see some work done, some reward earned. If, Aelis reasoned, she could convince Nath that there was still a chance—appeal to her ego and her hope at once—she might be forthcoming with the information. The spell Aelis released was designed to do just that; to draw out faint hope the way one might blow on the last ember of a fire.

"Elmo is on his way to another camp carrying messages of your attack on us, and he's to wait there for a response."

"When did he leave?"

"An hour, maybe a bit more."

"How did he know to come here? Why did he join? Have you contact with Lone Pine?"

"The coins," Nath said. "The coins I made must've been found, must've made their way there."

"The *coins?*" Aelis could do little more than repeat the word in shock.

"The coins I made. They were supposed to stay hidden. The time wasn't right."

"What are the coins, Nath? What are they meant to do?"

"Stoke anger. Prey on hope. Drive them to me."

"How did you make them?" Aelis readied another spell, prepared to force Nath to tell her, but it wasn't necessary.

"He taught me how, led me to where to find the gold, and showed me how to work the magic."

"Who did?"

"Dalius."

Aelis froze. The cavern was empty and still and utterly silent. She could not even hear the sound of her own breathing, or Nath's, or feel her blood beat in her ears.

Then the name sank in and she fought down the urge to scream expletives, to give Nath a good kick, or any number of other violent and counterproductive outbursts. Instead, she stood, yelled, "TUN! We've got to move, soon as we can."

That done, she looked back to Nathalie. Her sobbing was under control, but her tears had cut streaks through the dirt on her cheeks.

"Who is Dalius, where did he find you, and what did he teach you? I need to know all of it."

"I don't have to tell you anything more."

"That, Nath, is where you're wrong," Aelis said. "You do, if you know what's good for you. I am literally the force of the law in this part of the world."

"Fine. Cart me off to a trial if you must, but—"

"I'm a warden, Nathalie. I *am* the trial. I *am* the sentence, if need be. If I make mistakes, I'll answer for it, have no doubt of that. But if I decide your crimes warrant death, the Estates and the Triumvirate of Crowns empower me to execute you."

"Then do it. Murder us all and leave our bodies to rot the way you left Mahlgren!"

Aelis tried not to put her hands on her hips as though she were about to deliver a lecture. "I was four years old when Mahlgren fell. You can't have been much older. I was fourteen when the war ended and treaties were signed and much of the land was given over to the orcs. I couldn't change that even if I wanted to. Which I don't. What's more, I *don't* want to kill you. But I do have to take steps."

"And what'll that be? Murder all my men, leave me tied up to rot?"

"No," Aelis said. Casually, she pulled Nath's wand from her belt and tossed it into the fire. Nath strained against her bonds and struggled to sit up.

"I don't need that to use my power."

"No, but it makes it easier. You've got a big hammer, Nathalie. But you don't know how to swing it, and the wand makes it easier. If it was properly made it helped collect the energy you expended and it helped you focus it into something coherent."

A puff of purplish-gray smoke erupted from the fire, briefly interrupting her. "And there I suppose it was; that was the reagent core inside the wood. It's gone, and I'm guessing you've not got a spare, nor the tools and knowledge to craft one."

"Are you done humiliating me, Warden?" The contempt Nathalie managed to put into that word was startling. "Are you done flaunting your power and your wealth and destroying what I've managed to earn for myself?"

"I don't have time to argue with you, Nathalie," Aelis said. "You've already broken laws enough for me to do as I will with you. You've run afoul of every rule laid upon Enchanters about the use of their power, you've created items of illicit magic designed to prey upon the mind, you've kidnapped, you've put other lives in danger with your recklessness. Could be that I should execute you. There are wardens who would've done it already.

"But I'm not going to."

Aelis unslung her pack. She became aware that Tun was waiting in the entrance to the cavern, though just how he'd gotten there was a mystery.

"What I am going to do is force-feed you a dose of mountain catsbane and witsend so strong that if you ever touch magic again it'll feel like rain in the desert rather than the river you were used to. The first drink I gave you was just to put you to sleep a while. This should put your power beyond your touch for a long time. Maybe forever. Tun, if you would, please."

The struggle Nath had put up before was nothing compared to what she did now, thrashing her entire body in an effort to right herself. Had there been a wall to lean against, she would've found her feet, but then Tun was lifting her up, and her kicking feet had as much effect upon him as a fly on a castle wall.

"Pry her mouth open, please." Aelis had snapped open her traveling case again and unsealed wax-closed packets of herbs. She dropped them into a small stone bowl and began muddling them together with a practiced movement of her thumb, adding distilled water from a vial to form a fragrant green paste.

When that was done, with a flat stick and Nath's mouth opened by the expedient of Tun applying inexorable pressure, Aelis shoveled the mixture of herbs into the Enchanter's mouth. Tun clamped it closed. Aelis set down her tools and pinched Nath's nose closed.

The hatred, the panic, the fear that the other woman's eyes screamed at her as she fought not to swallow were genuinely shocking. Aelis almost felt herself wilting. Then one of the nearby men Nath had deceived and enthralled stirred from the dirt, and it was a struggle not to pinch harder.

"I don't want to cause you undue pain, Nathalie," Aelis said, her voice low and sharp. "But I will *not* leave you unpunished. Swallow this or choke on it. All the same to me."

Finally, tears gathering in the corners of her eyes, Nath forced the lump of magic-dampening and mind-fogging herbs down her throat.

Tun set her down. Aelis cut her bonds free. Around them, men were rising to their feet, blinking and disoriented. Tun's hands slipped into his pockets; Aelis kept a tight grip on her hilt and cleared her throat.

"This is an illegal gathering, and a conspiracy to violate the treaty the Three Crowns and the Estates House signed with the orcs eight years past. My associate—" here she gestured to Tun with the hand that didn't hold her sword—"could represent the wronged party of such a truce if he chose.

Dismantle this camp, disperse, take this woman with you, and I will not clap any of you in irons nor drag you to the gallows. Do it *now*. I will not offer this clemency twice."

Aelis let a First Order Ward form in her mind, and gathered it through the pommel stone of her sword; she had no intention of casting it unless she needed it, but it *did* have the effect of making the pommel stone glow a soft blue. To the men around her, that clearly meant only that magic was in the offing, but it was enough to set imaginations—and legs—moving at top speed.

She gathered up her gear, nodded to Tun, and the two made their way in silence from the cave entrance.

"Nath said that Elmo left an hour ago. Headed to an outlying camp."

"To the northwest. They've got a back entrance. Already found the tracks, though I didn't know they were his. Half a dozen of them, at least. Best we pick up the pace. If we run, we can catch him today."

Tun had been managing both their walking sticks all this time through the simple expedient of tying them to the rucksack he carried. He pulled Aelis's free and tossed it to her, then grabbed his own. Then they set off.

22

THE CAPTURE

They ran for an hour. Or, rather, Tun took long walking strides occasionally punctuated with a single trot, and Aelis trotted to keep pace.

"Feel like I'm learning the skirmisher's trot into the bargain," she muttered to herself. Or so she thought, until Tun answered.

"Except a skirmisher does this managing to stay in contact with eight or ten other men, knowing that the land swarms with people and things that want to kill him, and with specific geographical objectives in mind. You're just following after someone."

"I have specific objectives." Aelis paused for a forced breath. "They're just not geographical."

Tun grunted and Aelis supposed she'd made some kind of point until his next question.

"So, what did you do to her? Take away her ability to use magic?"

"Not permanently. Few days at least, unless she's been dosed before, built immunity." Aelis was not going to stop, ask for a rest, pause for breath, or fail to hold up the conversation so long as Tun wasn't. "It doesn't interfere with innate ability. Just clouds the mind so that focus is impossible."

"Does it affect focus on other tasks?"

"Yes. It's a dangerous thing. Didn't do it lightly."

"Why'd you bring those particular herbs?"

"Catsbane can ease a little pain, return movement to joints. Witsend does what the name suggests. It won't keep you from knowing that your arm's being sawn off, but it'll keep you from dwelling on it."

Tun grunted again. Aelis understood that this indicated that he was taking in and considering new information.

"Ever saw off any arms?"

"Only cadavers and illusory simulations. But every Anatomist knows how."

"And you've got the saws?"

"In three sizes."

"Hmm."

Silence reigned for a few minutes more before Tun spoke again.

"Why not kill her? Did her crimes warrant it?"

It was Aelis's time to consider the question, and, what's more, get some breath back in her lungs. "If her misuse of magic had led to anyone's death, then they would. But so far as I know, it hasn't, and I haven't got the time to investigate fully whether that's the case or not."

"So it wasn't simply a desire to be merciful?"

"Tun, there are wardens who would've killed her already. And there are others who would've taken her into custody, and still more who would've done worse or better than I've done. Part of our training is to never apply the laws we uphold too literally, and to exercise our own judgment in enforcing them."

"What happens to a corrupt warden, one who exercises their judgment too casually or too poorly?"

"Those are three different questions. The first goes on trial, is imprisoned, maybe executed. The second and third are reprimanded, punished, perhaps given more training."

"How do you imprison someone who can immolate you?"

"There are Abjurers who train for that." Tun had quickened his pace and Aelis forced herself to keep up with him at the expense of her own wind.

"You one of them?"

"No."

"You handled Nath."

"Not an Evoker. Hate to see one with her raw force."

"What makes someone an Evoker as opposed to an Abjurer as opposed to an Enchanter?"

"Too complicated."

"Then how do you keep one imprisoned long-term?"

"Regular doses of catsbane and witsend. Guarded by the specially trained Abjurers."

"It seems like a system fraught with peril. If they refuse to take it or somehow hide it . . ."

"Force-feed if need be."

"Does no one ever build up an immunity to the dose? Does it have long-term side effects?"

Aelis waved away the questions with a grunt. She had nothing left for talking, stumbling after him across the broken ground.

"You ought to run more, Warden. It'd do you good." Tun did not seem at all troubled by the pace he'd set. Aelis thought several curses while hoarding her breath and followed after him, doggedly.

By the time he allowed them to halt, by stopping in his tracks and becoming instantly as still as any statue, Aelis wanted to collapse. She fought to stay upright but her legs buckled and she dropped to her knees, frowning as mud wicked through her robes and trousers and soaked her.

"Stay down there," Tun whispered. He bent over her, half crouching. "There are men nearby," he continued, lowering his face till it was close to hers and he barely needed to vocalize to be heard. "Act as if I'm helping you with something."

Aelis thought she grasped the outlines of the plan. She put on a grimace and clutched at an ankle, shaking her head as though she were in pain.

"Be ready," Tun whispered. He knelt at her side and probed at her ankle. Though she thought he was trying to be careful about it, his fingers were practically iron. She let her free hand hover near her sword, but not on it.

With her eyes squinted, Aelis rolled her head as she might if she was in pain, which she found easy to project because she was, in fact, in pain—her legs had a throb pulsing through them, her feet hurt, her skin was sunburned, and the braids Maurenia had put her hair in were, after three days, finally starting to bother her. But at the moment all this allowed her to take in the landscape. The terrain was uneven, the remains of tiered and rolling farmlands that hadn't been tended for most of her life. Trees sprouted haphazardly, patches of tall weeds obscured her vision, and sudden breaks and dips in the landscape made long-distance vision all but impossible.

It was, in short, brilliant country for an ambush.

She lowered her head again. "Give me a moment. I think I might have something," she barely whispered in between her panting breaths, certain only Tun and no one else would hear them.

"We could rush them. But there's a good chance of someone dying that way." Tun's words came from behind clenched lips.

"I'll avoid that if I can." Aelis centered herself, to gather her will, to pull in energy from the world around her. She let it coalesce while she sorted her options. Sleep was probably out. *Probably only worked on Luth because he was fighting against the pull of the coin so hard.*

If these men were drawn more by Nath's magic than by love of Mahlgren, their loyalty to one another might not run terribly deep.

Onoghor's Mistrust, Aelis thought. It was a complex work, of about as much Enchantment power as she could hope to command on a good day. A Third Order spell, but on the complex end of that spectrum.

Sorry, Elmo. I hope they don't kill you.

She worked the spell with the man she knew—the newcomer, the unknown quantity—as her target. Rather than turn a half dozen men against one another, she would turn them all against one and exploit the confusion.

She went over the incantation in her mind and let loose the syllables in a quick torrent under her breath.

Aelis felt the power gather in a coil and waft slowly across the distance, felt in her mind as it caught on her target and settled into him.

For a moment, there was silence. Then shouts, a thud, a general clamor from a stand of shadowed trees just a few yards ahead of them.

She and Tun charged.

Tun got there first. One man who had stood up from cover was drawing a short, single-edge sword. Had he paid attention to the charging half-orc, he might have been able to bring it into play. Tun backhanded him with a closed fist so hard that his head whipped around, his eyes rolled up, and his sword dropped from nerveless fingers. He crumpled to the ground, his arms curling up and twitching in the posture of someone suddenly and profoundly unconscious.

Aelis advanced on two men who turned to the new commotion, pulling metal-shod cudgels from their belts yet leaving their knives untouched. That, at least, was good. If they weren't trying to cut her, she wouldn't have to kill them.

As a swordswoman, Aelis didn't have great reach, so her lunge was nothing for truly competent and prepared opponents to fear. She didn't have overwhelming strength, but she was no stripling. At the same time, her teachers had impressed upon her the notion that her survival in prolonged conflict depended on understanding angles, maximizing force—hence the curved blade that had been forged for her—and being *quick*. There were faster draws in her class, and those who could deliver a strike faster, but one of Lavanalla's favorite drills involved having two students with weapons of differing length given a command to draw and strike, all at once. They could not hesitate, feint, or step backward. The first blow to land won.

Aelis had never, ever lost that particular drill except against Lavanalla herself, who had still complimented her student on having an impressive first two steps.

So when her sword suddenly came into her hand and she lunged, her shoulder held low, she slipped inside the first man's guard with ease and brought the pommel of her sword down on the inside of his wrist with perhaps more force than was necessary. There was an audible pop, and he dropped his club and fell to the ground, groaning.

Aelis was already stepping around him, using his falling body and distance to shield herself from the second attacker. She didn't spare a glance for Tun, but sounds were telling the tale. A curse, a painful *thwack* of fist against flesh, then something was hitting the ground. It had already happened twice.

Her second attacker leapfrogged the first and raised his club, bringing in down in a clumsy two-handed arc at her head. She parried with her flat, almost dismissively, and snapped a simple kick straight between his legs. His eyes crossed and he crumpled, retching.

"Might've put a little more force in that than you needed to." Aelis turned to find Tun rubbing the knuckles of one hand.

"Might have tried introducing himself before trying to brain me." Aelis resettled a suddenly sweaty and slightly twitchy hand on her hilt. Almost delicately, she kicked weapons away from the men she'd put on the ground. In the case of the one she'd gotten in the fork, she was able to take his knife and toss it away into the grass and the mud; the one with the broken wrist was curled up too tightly around his wound. "Didn't kill any of them, did we?"

"No," Tun said. He paused and sniffed at the air, then leaped forward into the stand of trees where their ambushers had lain in wait.

Aelis watched as he bent down, hauled something into his arms, then came back into the shafts of sunlight, carrying a limp form.

Elmo was dazed from the blows his erstwhile companions had delivered, blood trickling from a split lip, but his eyes fluttered and his chest rose and fell evenly.

"Found him," Tun said.

23

THE INTERROGATION

Aelis stripped the prisoners of their weapons as quickly as she could.

They hadn't enough rope to bind them all, so she decided to count on her and Tun's ability to control them. Aelis felt her nerves fraying, her thoughts straying between cutting and running with Elmo and thinking of what lasting punishment she could levy against all the men she'd encountered so far. At least until she remembered Bardun Jacques's words about achieving goals.

You go into any maneuver, any operation, with a plan and a goal. You modify the former always, but rarely the latter. You set out to solve one problem, you'll encounter half a dozen, a dozen more. You try to fix all and you fix none. Solve the problem you set out to, and move on. Come back at the others when you're fresh. You're not a gods-damned hero out of a song. Acting like you are ends up with you dead and no one defending the people you're sworn to.

She looked at the men, her eyes settling on the one whose wrist she'd broken.

Aelis walked toward him, lowered the point of her sword till it hovered in front of his eyes. "You. Answer my questions and I can do something for your wrist."

"I know what your black clothes mean, witch! I'll not take your foul magic."

"Oh, for fuck's sake." Aelis squeezed the hilt of her sword. An irrational spike of anger made her want to smack the pommel into the bald spot on the cowering man's head. "You don't know anything. I haven't got the time to lecture you on all the various facets of Necromancy, but I will tell you this." She took a step back and squatted to get to eye level with him, though she kept her sword ready. "You can answer my questions and get your wrist set and wrapped, or I can weave Ephraze's Creeping Rot upon the injury inside your arm. Slowly, inch by inch, death will crawl up your arm, and there will be no wizard in this world who could release you from it but me. Which will it be?"

The man tried to scramble away from her, kicking wildly at the ground with his heels. He got little purchase and didn't reach his feet because he wouldn't let go of his broken wrist to use his good hand to lever himself up. His flight came to an abrupt end when he butted into Tun's legs. He looked up in horror as Tun slipped one of his hand blades into his fist and theatrically settled his fingers around it.

"I'll talk, I'll talk, just keep her dark magic away from me," the man blurted sullenly. Tun lowered his fist and nodded slowly. Aelis, her sword still unsheathed, knelt to look the man in the eye. Tun wandered off to relieve more of the others of their weapons.

"What's your name?"

"E-Erlich," he stammered.

"Are you and your fellows here followers of the Earl of Mahlgren?"

He nodded, carefully cradling his broken wrist.

"Why did you ambush us?"

"Standin' orders," Erlich said. "Use our discretion, but anyone looks like an enemy is to be waylaid, taken to determine their allegiance, and either brought to the cause or disposed of."

"You were going to murder us if we weren't willing to pledge ourselves to taking back a fiefdom that hasn't truly existed in nearly twenty years?" Aelis sighed. "Don't answer that. Now, I need you to surrender to me any coins you're carrying."

"So you're a common robber in addition to a witch?"

"I'm a FUCKING WARDEN!" Aelis screamed, the frustration and tedium and fear of the past few days pouring out of her. "Duly appointed by the gods-damned Lyceum, with the power of the Three Crowns and the Estates House to arrest, assize, and punish all those who transgress against the laws. You have until I get too frustrated to care to surrender any coin you're carrying before I start sending all your friends here to Onoma's embrace."

Erlich reached under his shirt and hurriedly pulled a purse hanging by a knotted string around his neck and tossed it at her feet. She turned to face the other men, the point of her sword swinging from one to the next.

One by one, they tossed coin purses or shirts or scarves with coins sewn into them into a growing pile. One man even tossed in his boots. Last, still dazed, Elmo pulled his coin pouch, also worn around his neck, and tossed it away with a grimace.

"Tun," she said, "if you would be so kind as to dump all the coins into the dirt, and sort any gold out from silver. Don't touch any of it with your bare skin if you can."

Tun quickly opened purses, tore open stitching, and assembled a small pile of gold coins. One large, bright gold tri-crown slipped out of Elmo's pouch. When Tun upended Erlich's, however, only a small shower of silver joined the pile.

"Erlich," Aelis began, "have you one of Nath's coins?"

He shook his head. "I swore I'd take no pay for my service till Mahlgren was restored."

"Anaerion's flaming cock," she swore. "You're a true gods-damned believer, aren't you?"

"I'm a loyal Mahlgren man, born and raised like my father . . ."

Aelis slipped her wand into her hand, pressed its tip to Erlich's forehead. He stopped mid-sentence and keeled over in a snoring heap.

"Is that dangerous, for him?" Tun paused to look up at her as he delicately let a jerkin fall to the ground.

"Who can even care?" Aelis turned to the other fugitives, slipping her wand back into her sleeve.

"All of you, save Elmo, are free to go. You can take enough food and water for two days, no blade longer than your hand, and you can walk alone in any direction you choose," she told them, delivering the words in as flat and cold a voice as she could muster. "If I see you again, I will hold nothing back. If I am forced to return here, I'll do it with an entire company of Wardens, and we'll scorch what's left of Mahlgren from the earth."

Most of the men gave her a slightly confused look and then did as she asked. One protested that the border was a hard two days' walk at best.

"Then you had better hurry."

The same man gestured to Erlich. "What about him?"

"Carry him."

*　*　*

With the rest of their prisoners dispatched, Tun was all for setting off immediately, but Aelis insisted they make camp there to take advantage of the would-be rebels' supplies. Even more vitally, she wanted to examine the golden coins.

Aelis sat by their sheltered fire, with Tun stalking the perimeter and grunting every so often. She had the coins spread out on a flat rock. Between the fire and the light Onoma's moon still offered her she was making a study of them, probing them with the tip of her wand, trying to tease out the Enchantments bound into them.

She heard Tun approaching her from behind, which she knew by now meant he *wanted* her to hear him.

"This is still a bad idea. They know where we are, or at least where we were bound."

"I told you, Elmo is going to be in no condition to travel for several hours at least, and frankly neither is Nath. If she knows how to stand up and which direction the sky is in she must be tougher than she looks."

Tun grunted. "Not going to do yourself any harm studying those coins, are you?"

"Nothing lasting. I just can't put together how Nath made them. Something like this should be beyond her training, if not her raw talent."

"Said herself she had help. Mentioned a name. Dale-something."

"Dalius. Why do I know that name?"

"I don't know, but you didn't seem pleased to hear it."

Aelis had picked up one of the coins and was running her thumb along it, careful to keep her general magical aura intact as she did so. She thought about the name Dalius, and suddenly had a picture of a vaguely talented old man, firing illusory globes of purple lightning at her on one of her first nights in the village.

"I'll be gods-damned," she said. "Tun. An old man. A hedge wizard, I think. I . . ."

Tun came over and squatted on the other side of the fire. He shrugged. "Old, young . . . all you people look the same to me."

"Humans? But you're half . . ."

"Wizards," Tun replied. He waited, then coughed. "That was . . . a jest, Warden."

"One of my first nights in Lone Pine, Dalius attacked me. He could only harness some illusions, very weak stuff. I decided he was a harmless hedge—"

"Hedge wizard. So you said. I have no idea what it means."

"Ah, well . . . I guess the idea is they were, you know . . . taught in secret, by people who didn't know much, and so they don't know much themselves. As in they were . . . teaching in hedges, I suppose."

"A hedge doesn't seem a particularly conducive space to learning anything but, I suppose, the mating habits of certain animals. Perhaps topiary."

"Tun, this is serious."

"It is in my nature to make jests when I am anxious, Warden. I mean no harm."

That caught Aelis's attention, and she focused on Tun's face, searching his eyes. "First time you've been anxious in the days I've known you."

"And this seems like the first time you've been afraid. Back to business; if this Dalius attacked you, why not kill him?"

"Like I said, he seemed harmless. But then I kept forgetting to ask anyone about him. Sometime after I brought him into my tower a book went missing, and I meant to ask around the village who might've taken it. I never did that either."

"Was this book dangerous?"

"Not really. It was a simple book of Abjurers' forms. Stances, guards, sequences with sword or axe or knife, and how they work with the mind and with wards."

"Could it be you were simply too busy to remember to ask? A new place, a new life, new responsibilities . . ."

"I've been busy since I was eleven years old. I've never been forgetful before."

"His attack upon you and the book disappearing are not necessarily related."

"I'm aware of the difference between correlation and causation." Tun smiled, and she went on. "But the forgetfulness about *both* items . . . that's not me, Tun. That's not who I am or how I work. And now we hear that Dalius was ranging in this direction, teaching Nath to harness her power, and how to make these coins. That's not coincidence."

"What is it, then?"

"I don't know," Aelis said, but she felt a certainty in her gut that they were connected. "But I'm going to take the pieces we've got—Elmo, the coins—and paint them into the frame. If we find more, I'll keep painting."

"What happened to solving one problem at a time?"

"Our first job is to get Elmo back to Lone Pine. Anything else we'll deal with on the way."

"Dalius," Tun said, carefully enunciating all three syllables. "Do not forget the name again."

"Let's make an agreement on that score. Every stop we make—for meals, to rest—every time, we talk about Dalius. We remind each other." She paused a moment, then seized on thoughts that were trying to escape from her even now.

"Tun," Aelis said suddenly. "Dalius said he hung about Lone Pine. That he helped people, with their animals, with charms and . . . small things. And you don't know the name?"

Tun shook his head slowly. "I have lived outside Lone Pine for three years. You are the first wizard I have seen there."

"No one ever mentioned him to you? Not Rus or Martin? Seems like they know everyone."

"They do," Tun said. "If I have never seen him, and Rus and Martin don't know him?" He shook his great head slowly. "Then he does not exist."

"But he must. I've seen him, talked to him. So has Nath."

"Perhaps he is some kind of spirit? A ghost? One that appears only to wizards."

Aelis shook her head. "There are spirits that will do that. Etheric Haunts, Mad Echoes come to mind. The death curse of a wizard might appear to another wizard as a kind of spirit. But I know spirits. If Dalius had been a spirit, I would've felt it. Instantly."

"Are you certain?"

"As certain as I am of where Onoma's moon is in the sky."

Tun sighed deeply. "I do not know what we can do other than what we have agreed to. Every night between here and Lone Pine, we sit and talk about Dalius. Remind each other that he exists."

"It'll have to do," Aelis said. "If you would take the watch, I want to study these coins a little more closely."

Tun stood silently and went back to pacing the perimeter. This time she couldn't hear a step.

Aelis kept running her thumb around the profile of the coin. She held it up to the light of the moon. Stories around the College of Necromancy held that some of the most highly skilled Anatomists could perform operations blindfolded in the open air under Onoma's fullness. Others said it could allow them to see through the outer layers of the body to more precisely make their cuts. Even if those were true and not mere undergraduate rumor, the moonlight was doing nothing to help her see anything new about the coin.

"Why make it of gold?" she suddenly wondered. "Where would they get all of it and how would they mint it?"

On instinct, she closed her eyes and held the coin tightly in her hand, willing herself to feel the surface of it. Suddenly the feel of it against her skin changed; the heft was the same, but it was no longer smooth.

Aelis opened her hand. She wasn't holding a gold coin any longer; she was holding pitted iron, a cloak clasp or a brooch that had lost its pin.

The other coins spread out on the rock before her had changed as well. Some were similar to what she held, others were discs of flattened copper or silver.

Aelis lacked the presence of mind to curse. This was Illusion and Enchantment magic melded together on a level she didn't understand. But with the Illusion apparently dissipated, she had a much better chance of understanding how the Enchantment worked on its own. She picked up a handful of them and smiled.

+ + +

Aelis didn't expect to find herself waiting on Tun to wake up, but there she was. Her gear was packed, the old magical brooches and coins were carefully stowed. But Tun had, she suspected, done more than his share of watch on most of the nights they'd been on the hunt.

Elmo slept on while Tun roused himself. It never took long for the tracker to pack; in a matter of moments, he was clear-eyed, walking stick in hand, nibbling carefully on one of the hard biscuits he'd brought.

"Could be we'll see the men you turned loose again, haunting our trail, dogging our steps, ambushing us," he said once the biscuit was consumed.

"It could be, but I doubt it. Most of them have only the vaguest grasp of what they were doing or why."

"Then is it possible you've sentenced them to death, set them free to wander without the means to defend themselves?"

"Nath couldn't have drawn them here entirely with the coins. It had to be a matter of location and vulnerability. In other words—"

"Most were already here, and inclined to the life she offered them."

"Exactly. I can't take the time and energy to determine exactly what every man was doing here, but they are breaking treaties and laws I am bidden to uphold. I don't have the means to take all of them into custody. But I can scatter them in such a way that they are less likely to do real mischief. Now come on. Let's get our man up and make our way home."

"As you say."

Elmo was difficult to wake. *Probably the first real sleep he's gotten since this all started,* Aelis thought. *Since he stabbed his brother,* she corrected herself. *Would Otto live? Was he already dead? Onoma,* she prayed silently, *I don't want this to end with* both *brothers dead.*

Think about all that when you get back. One problem at a time. In truth, she wasn't deaf to Tun's observations that she could've turned a lot of ambushers loose on their trail, but she hadn't seen a better solution, and none were presenting themselves now.

Once they finally had Elmo on his feet and fed, Aelis considered how best to approach their biggest problem: him.

"Elmo," she began, "if I have to keep you manacled all the way back to Lone Pine, it's going to slow us all down and exacerbate any dangers we face."

"Ex-what?" The stocky former scout narrowed his eyes in distrust.

"Make worse." Aelis tried for patience, which she knew had never truly been one of her virtues. "If I don't shackle you, you can contribute to the chores of travel and camp, defend yourself if need be. But if you run, even once, I'll bind you and drag you."

"Did I kill him? Is he dead?"

"What?"

"Otto. My brother. Did I kill him?"

Aelis bit her lip. "He was alive when I came after you. Badly hurt. But I'd done what I could."

"Shoulda stayed with him, Warden. Kept him alive. Not bothered after me."

"Not your place to tell me what I should do, Elmo."

"S'pose not. Still, not worth comin' after me. No one's gonna care if I live or die if I've killed Otto."

"I can think of at least one girl who might."

"Not fair, Warden."

"Neither is openly willing Pips to live without either of the people raising her. Now what's it going to be? Shackles or no?"

"I'll come. And I'll not bother runnin' this time. Found me too easy the once. Not likely to get away from the orc there." He jerked his chin toward Tun, a barely breathing statue a few paces away.

"Fine. Fall in, behind Tun and ahead of me." She pointed with her walking stick at a rucksack she'd stuffed full of food, with waterbags lashed to either side of it. "You carry that."

"What about my knife?"

"What about it?"

"All I got left of my time in the scouts. Second of a pair we were all given."

"You left its larger match in Otto's guts," Aelis said, without pausing to think too long on why the scouts Elmo had been a part of were deliberately issued impractical weapons designed to leave such terrible wounds. "I'll leave your hands free, but I'm not giving you a weapon to fill them with. Except at need. Now come on. We've a deal of walking to do."

◆   ◆   ◆

Aelis thought to learn more of Nath and her plans for the Mahlgren men from Elmo, but he was noncommittal at best, and unable to answer most of her questions. He wasn't sure how he'd found them, only that the coin had driven him there. When he brought up the coin he went grimly silent before asking if Aelis had it.

"I do."

"Can I see it?"

"I don't think that's a good idea."

Elmo sighed. "It's just . . . not often folk like us see gold. Especially gold that pure. Didn't seem right, having to give it up on just a rich woman's say-so."

"A warden's order doesn't come from any one man or woman. It comes from the Three Crowns and the Estates House."

"Never seen any king, or anyone sits in the House. So it doesn't much feel like orders come from them."

"I do not feel like explaining the underpinnings of our legal system, so we'll skip this part. I have your coin, and you can't see it." A pause. "But it might help to know it wasn't gold."

Elmo stopped and whirled on her. "Wasn't gold?"

"No. In fact it was simple brass. Just glamoured to look like gold."

"Glamoured?"

"Magic." Aelis lifted her free hand and waggled her fingers.

"Why make brass look like gold?"

"Probably more likely to make the folk who found it hang on to it. Made it easier for the other magics bound in it to take hold of your mind."

Given the way Elmo's face darkened and his shoulders slumped, Aelis realized this was another question that could've done with a less than fully truthful answer.

✦ ✦ ✦

The ambush came as twilight gathered around them that night, but it didn't come the way Aelis expected. It wasn't the hail of crossbow bolts or spears or rocks that Aelis had prepared wards for when Tun had tipped her they were being watched.

Instead it was a hammer blow of magical force that washed over all three of them. *STOP*, it commanded, and they did.

The power had a familiar flavor that made Aelis cringe.

Then Nath and two of her men came over the rise. None had weapons larger than a shortsword, which was small comfort. The Enchanter was a few steps ahead of them, her hands free and her smile so calm and smug that Aelis burned to do it violence.

"Did you think simple herbs would stop power like mine? I am privy to secrets College-trained weaklings like you are forbidden to know the *names* of," Nathalie said. Her voice was oddly distant and her steps hesitant—residue of the witsend and catsbane, Aelis would have thought, if her magic wasn't still so potent and powerful.

"Throw down your staves, and you, half-breed, those foolish little blades in your pockets."

Aelis tossed her staff away, as did Tun. It was quickly followed by Tun's hand blades.

"Now, Warden, though a child unworthy of the name, I'll have your wand. And your sword." Nath sauntered past Tun and placed a hand possessively on Elmo's shoulder. "In fact, take your swordbelt, scabbard and all, and toss it on the ground. My man here is going to pick it up and use it to run your half-breed through." Nath took a step closer to Aelis and held out one hand. "Wand."

Aelis unbuckled her belt and tossed it to the ground, but the throw was awkward and several feet from Elmo. She lifted her eyes to Tun, who clearly struggled against the compulsion laid on him. She did as Nath said, and slipped her wand into her hand, holding it out carefully to Nath, whose fingers curled around it almost delicately.

Nath's gloating smile filled Aelis's eyes.

"Nath," Aelis said, biting down hard on every syllable, "please do not do this. I beg you. There is another way."

The woman looked at her oddly; Aelis felt like she was being watched by a snake and not another woman.

"Fool girl," Nath said. "The only way I do things is my way."

"I warned you." Aelis whispered these words, and twitched her right wrist the same way she'd done with her left to drop her wand into her hand.

Then she plunged Elmo's knife directly into the side of Nath's neck and *pulled* down toward her collarbone.

Aelis knew it severed too many important vessels for her to do anything in the moment. She knew because she was an Anatomist, and it was her business and her calling to know.

But she ran for her dagger and unslung her pack and she tried anyway. Nath's guards collapsed while Elmo and Tun fell to their knees. Aelis grabbed the first piece of cloth she found and tried to apply pressure over the horrible wound in Nath's neck, gripping her Anatomist's blade to gauge the woman's vanishing vitals. She tried grabbing at the same Binding she'd used to save Otto, but there was not enough left for her to seize and hold.

There wasn't much she could do, or much she could've done even if conditions were right. Aelis had dealt a killing blow, and she'd known it when she'd done it, known it as soon as she'd slipped the knife into her hand and aimed it at that unprotected target.

All Aelis could do was hold the bandage as blood pumped warm over her hand and light vanished from Nathalie's eyes.

Before Nath died, Aelis felt something change, a subtle shift in the other woman's spirit, her perceptions. Something passed out of her eyes before they lost the light and turned sightless, and something insubstantial passed out of her body before her last ragged, wheezing breath. Aelis felt it through her knife, and then she felt nothing, because the woman before her was dead.

Tun, of course, was the first to come around, and he was at her shoulder. It took her a few moments to realize he was standing by her, watching her with compassion in his dark eyes.

"Had to do it, Warden."

Aelis said nothing. She nodded, stood, and began wiping her hands with the clean edge of the bandage—which turned out to be her spare shirt.

"Have we a shovel?" she asked, surprised at the calm of her own voice.

"Neither that, nor time." Tun cleared his throat, and said, gently, "No grave we could dig with the tools we have would stop the wilderness from taking its course. We can't take her back with us."

"No, I suppose not." Aelis bent down and forced herself to methodically search Nath's body. She wore an old, clearly homemade dress of no particular style other than sturdy. There were no papers in her belt pouch, only oddments: a needle, some thread, a small bell, a few coins—none of them magical. There was also an old and tarnished locket with no chain. Aelis thumbed it open; inside were poorly rendered miniatures of two people, likely enough Nath's parents.

Aelis carefully wrapped it and stuck it in her pack, though she couldn't have said why.

✦   ✦   ✦

That night, at a fire where Elmo slept and Aelis felt certain she wasn't going to manage it, Tun let her sit in silence for a while.

"First person you've killed."

It wasn't a question, so Aelis merely nodded.

Tun grunted. "I'm not going to get trite and spit platitudes at you. Did what you had to do. I do have to ask; how'd you resist her spell?"

Aelis reached under her tunic and pulled out a leather thong and a small pouch that had lain against her skin. She untied it and poured out three of the old bits of metal that had been turned into golden coins.

"Once I could see through their glamour, I had a better grasp on how they worked. I'm no artificer but I could repurpose them."

"Spare me any magical details and explain in the plainest language you can, please."

"These had a powerful compulsion upon them to make the holder forgo all other cares, all other ties, all other obligations in the defense of the Earldom of Mahlgren. It's what brought the men here. Wasn't hard to simply change the target of the obligation."

"To what?"

"Lone Pine."

"And you did this because . . . ?"

"To see if I could, because I could envision scenarios where it might be necessary, and because I might need help focusing."

"So when Nath hit us with her enchantments, you resisted because of . . . a compulsion you laid on yourself?"

"Not quite. It made resisting easier."

"Did it occur to you that passing these amulets to me and to Elmo would've been advantageous?"

"Advantageous, certainly. Also very illegal without your permission."

"You would've had mine."

"If I'd fucked it up, I would've been handing you into Nath's clutches." *Or to whatever was driving her,* she thought.

"Point." Tun took a deep breath. "You knew she'd come back?"

"No. Not at all. I hoped I'd never see or hear from her again. But this business with . . . with . . ." She faltered.

"Dalius," Tun supplied.

"Dalius," Aelis nearly spat through her gritted teeth. "Dalius. Dalius. Dalius. This business with him. I decided that being on my guard in every possible way was better than the alternative."

"Next time, Warden, I ask that you share any such concerns with me. Honesty is essential to working together."

"Next time?"

Tun shrugged. "You'll repair my amulet in payment. Your term in Lone Pine is for two years. You'll need a tracker again."

"Onoma's frozen tits, I hope not. No offense, Tun. I find your company calming and you . . . erudite beyond my expectations. Honestly," she added quickly, aware of how that might have sounded.

"No offense taken, Warden. There aren't many folk in Lone Pine who'll talk to me. They don't make warding signs with their hands, pray to Anaerion or Stregon when I pass, or mutter about half-breeds and what the Crowns *should* have done in the war anymore. But few are inviting me over for beer and bread."

"Rus and Martin might."

"They would, and they do, but I don't want to hurt their custom. Besides, until my amulet is fixed and I . . . have control . . . it's best I don't mingle too much."

"Fair."

Silence reigned a few more moments, but for the crackle of the small fire. Aelis hadn't questioned when Tun had built it, though he'd largely been against it so far.

"Why'd you decide it was safe enough to build a fire tonight?"

"It seemed important to have something to gather beside and talk."

"Waiting for me to weep and fall to pieces over taking a life?"

"You don't seem the type, no. But if you were?" Tun shrugged. "I've seen it."

"I'm not naïve. I know that becoming a Warden means projecting force into the world. During my training as an Abjurer I assisted in some operations against local thieves' guilds and the like, so I'd seen a bit of a fight." Aelis paused, looking for the right words, lips pressed firmly together. "But I hadn't had to deal a mortal blow."

Tun took as deep a breath as Aelis had seen in her time with him. "I doubt this'll be the only one, Warden."

"Most people fear Necromancers, Tun. They think we'll tear out their souls or animate their dead grandfathers or rot their hands off the bones. What we really do, what we train the most to do, is save lives. I'm a physician. A surgeon. With that knife in this hand?" Aelis held up her right hand in the fire's dim light. Her fingers were long and dexterous, her wrist thick with fencer's muscles, her palm callused from the hilt. "She didn't have a chance."

"Well, she wasn't going to give us one. I wouldn't lose any sleep over it, considering our man there was a few moments from trying to dig out my liver with your sword." Tun tapped his left hip. "I like my liver where it is."

"It's on the other side," Aelis said absently.

"Hardly the point," Tun said, though his sternness melted into laughter and they shared a chuckle for a moment. A moment of silence drew itself out, the fire crackling, before Aelis spoke again.

"I'm not sure why I put that knife in my other sleeve. But once it was there I saw no other way to play it."

"Because there wasn't. You have training and you have intuition. You used both, and you saved lives doing it. If you want to get drunk when we get back to Lone Pine and get it out of your system, I'll drink with you. From where I'm sitting you did the right thing, the only thing you could do in the moment, and I'm glad to know that you had it in you."

"You're right, at least insofar as I need to save the bathos until we get back to Lone Pine." She looked over at Elmo, who slept as if he hadn't a care in the world. "Gods, I hope Otto isn't dead."

"Otto is a good man. It would be a terrible thing for Phillipa to lose the last family she has."

"It would. And Phillipa herself is yet *another* thorny question I'll have to deal with."

"Oh?"

"The child has magical talent. How much, in what direction it lies, and whether she can be taught or encouraged, I don't know. But she has it."

"Why confide this in me, Warden?"

"You see anyone else lining up to be my confidant?"

"I think that is a new role for me."

"Well, it suits you. Either that or I don't like the looks of sleep and talking is better than playing at parlor tricks like pyroscopy and capnomancy."

"You're not a diviner."

"And here I thought I could find a gap in your vocabulary."

Tun grunted, and they fell silent. Elmo shifted in his sleep. The fire crackled.

"Talk may be better than sleep, Warden. But you're going to wish you'd done the latter when dawn breaks."

"I'm only just out of university, Tun. You think I'm not used to doing on no sleep?"

"Writing exams is less strenuous than a long hike on short rations through hostile wilderness while managing a prisoner, no matter how students pride themselves on the difficulty of their lives."

"Fair," Aelis answered. "You want the first watch?"

"No. I have no wish to keep dwelling on how powerless I felt under the sway of Nathalie's power." With that, Tun unfolded himself and stretched out, crossing his legs at the ankles.

The conversation thus abruptly ended, Aelis stood up, stamped feeling back into her feet and lower legs, and began walking a small circuit.

For all that Tun's words resonated—she *had* done, in the moment, the only thing she could have—she still wondered if she could've planned for a better contingency.

Nath's face bothered her; not because she had watched the woman die, but because there had been something wrong in it.

"Dalius, Dalius, Dalius," she muttered, repeating the name like a prayer in the hopes of remembering it. She fixed his face in her mind, but it lasted only a moment. She thought again of the spell he cast; harmless, barely formed illusion.

"And yet Nath said his name. And for a woman who looked to be my age, give or take, it felt odd to be called 'child.' Or 'barely trained.'" She tried to make a list in her mind. It would read; *1. Elmo. 2. Otto. 3. Dalius. 4. Pips. 5. Investigate history of wizards and Mahlgren,* which she instantly amended to *5. Write to Lyceum to request information on said history as no copies are likely to be in Lone Pine. 6. Find my missing book. 7. Write to Maurenia? 8. Write to Father. 9. Get day-after-exams drunk.*

It was the tenth item to occur to her that surprised her. *10. Find out who Nath was.*

All I have is an old locket with a badly painted miniature portrait.

"Am I a Warden or not? I will find out who she was, and why she became what she became. I owe her that much," she said, though she didn't find the words terribly convincing.

The rest of her watch passed in relative calm. Elmo snored. Tun didn't make a sound as the hours rolled by. Finally, as if some kind of alarm spell had woken him up, or a window-knocker had come by, he sat up, stood, and beckoned Aelis back to the dying fire.

She slept rather more easily than she expected to. Her dreams were a curious mix of Nath, Dalius, a stabbing with a knife, and Maurenia.

24

THE RETURN

The long walk back to Lone Pine passed without incident. Elmo grew more talkative and yet also more grim with every step. When at last they stood on a small hill overlooking the village a few hours past midday, Tun pulled up the hood of his coat and cleared his throat.

"I think you should take him back yourself," he said. "My presence will only raise questions. And being seen bringing him back yourself will do you no harm with the villagers."

"Tomorrow, Tun," Aelis said. "Tomorrow, I will come to study your amulet and see what repairs I might make. Tonight I have . . ." *A judgment to make,* Aelis didn't say, because Elmo was standing close by, after all. She watched Tun melt into the trees, took Elmo by the arm, and started down the hill and back into Lone Pine proper.

She was practically at Rus and Martin's door before anyone noticed them. Bruce, whose sheep pen she'd helped to fix, came into view. Upon sighting her, he gave his head a shake and yelled.

"Warden!"

"Bruce. Greeting me or warning everyone else?"

"Little bit of both," he said, his cheeks coloring a bit. It was only then that he seemed to realize that she was bringing Elmo along with her, and the color faded into pale shock.

He tugged at his forelock and scurried away.

Aelis resettled her hand lightly around Elmo's arm and they walked in silence to the inn's front door.

To his credit, he's not fighting, running, or crying. She paused before the door and sighed. "You ready to go in?"

"Don't matter if I'm ready, does it?"

"Any questions?"

"If Otto's dead, are you gonna hang me?"

"Let's answer the first part of that question before we think about the second."

Aelis pushed open the door. The inside of the place was largely empty. Behind the counter along the back wall that separated kitchen from common room, Rus and Martin stood arm in arm, with the shorter, stockier innkeeper resting his head against the taller man's chest. She smiled despite herself and delicately cleared her throat.

They looked up, both having had their eyes closed. Rus smiled to see her, and Martin's eyes widened. He took a half step toward the kitchen but stopped himself short of leaving Rus's embrace.

"Warden!"

"Please, Rus. Aelis." She guided Elmo to a bench and he sat down. She resisted the urge to take a spot on the bench next to him. *Nothing for it now.* "How's my patient?"

Rus said nothing. Instead he nodded at the stairs. Aelis steeled herself and climbed, trying not to let her hands shake or her steps falter. Once she was up the stairs and in the hallway, she heard a faint voice speaking like a chant, over the unmistakable scritch of pen or writing stick on paper.

Aelis came to the slightly open door and peered in. Pips sat in a chair next to the narrow bed, bent over a flat piece of wood, scratching away with the nub of a stick of writing coal. As she wrote, she whispered.

"A. Lish. Ky. Ree. Stee. Oh. Na. Dee. Lentee. Un. Tir. Ah. Val. Phillipa. Otto. Elmo. Emilie. A. Lish."

Aelis pushed the door open and took a loud step. Otto was laid out on the bed. She saw that he was breathing, even and steady, and she wanted to cry. Pips sat up, her eyes blinking into focus from her close concentration on her writing practice.

The girl threw her work aside, flew off her chair, and tumbled so hard against Aelis's legs in a hug that the Warden was nearly bowled over.

Pips said nothing for a moment. Then she tried to say everything all at once.

"Did you find Elmo? Is he all right? Otto is alive but he doesn't get out of bed for very long. I practiced writing every day. Emilie took good care of Otto. Rus said you weren't coming back, and Martin told him he was too . . . sinkull?" Pips stopped for a breath and Aelis seized the opportunity.

"Cynical, Pips. He said he was too cynical." Aelis pronounced the word slowly, making sure to enunciate each syllable. "And I am happy to see you too. Elmo is downstairs but I'd ask you to stay here. I have to see how Otto is."

She disentangled herself from Pips, who clung to her leg anyway, and bent over Otto's bed. She grasped her dagger with one hand and laid the other over his head, which was cool to the touch.

She laid down a simple diagnostic using the magic bound into her dagger. Otto was in pain and probably would be for a long time. He might have stomach trouble in the future, and he had a touch of fever so slight her fingers alone couldn't detect it. But he was alive, and Elmo's knife was not going to kill him, and she came damned close to letting a few tears fall from her eyes before she fought the desire down.

"Pips. Stay here. I'm going to get Elmo. And a witness."

She was down the stairs and back with the girl's other uncle and Rus in tow a few moments later. Elmo, for the first time, tried to halt outside the room, but Aelis was having none of it.

She marched him to Otto's bedside, leaned down, and gently prized open one of the wounded man's eyelids.

He flickered awake, grimacing almost immediately, then started as he saw Elmo standing over him.

"Otto," Aelis began, seizing the moment, "is this the man who stabbed you?"

"Course it fuckin' is," Otto wheezed.

"Had you threatened him?"

"Only tried to take his gold away."

"Then we have an extenuating circumstance. The gold was not gold," Aelis said. After a bit of prying she pulled free one of the bronze brooches. "It was this. Glamoured to look like gold, and enchanted to make the carrier do anything to defend the Earldom of Mahlgren, such as it is. Neither you nor Elmo had any way of knowing that. Elmo, have you anything to say in your defense?"

"This an assize now?"

"No. It's an inquiry, which is why Rus is here, so he can attest that what I say happened happened. I ask again if you have anything to say in your defense."

The innkeeper remained half-in, half-out of the room, and leaned forward when he heard his name.

"I wasn't myself," Elmo said. "It's a bad excuse, but there it is. I have my moments, since the war. I wake up angry, screamin', confused. I got a coin and suddenly I had a purpose, like I was a soldier again. I had to go north. Had to."

"Did you know that stabbing your brother Otto was wrong?"

"S'pose I did. But I couldn't stop myself. He was between me and . . . and what I had to do. What I needed."

"To keep the coin and to serve Mahlgren?"

"Aye."

Aelis turned to the convalescent brother. "Otto. Do you agree to abide by any sentence I pass and to waive appeals and legal recourse?"

"I don't want you to kill my brother, Warden."

"Answer the question. Rus, make note of his answer."

"Aye, Warden."

"I don't know what the question means."

Aelis leaned down over Otto and whispered, "Just say yes. Place a little trust in me."

"Yes."

"Good. Then, Elmo, my sentence is thus for the crime of stabbing your brother. Your knives and any other weapon that is not expressly made for farm or domestic work such as you have is forbidden to you for the period of a year, at which point I will review the case. I will decide what is a weapon and what is a tool. You will also subject yourself to any meeting or intervention I ask for regarding your episodes—your moments of 'not being yourself.' Otto: as compensation for the loss of income due to your injuries and your brother's absence, the Crowns and the Estates House as represented by me, your Warden, will pay you fair market value for whatever crops or animals you lost. Fair market value to be determined by averaging what three other farmers with comparably sized herds and fields made and comparing it to what you made, and providing the difference."

Otto blinked up at her. "What's all that mean?"

"It means Elmo is free to go but is not allowed to have knives, and he has to talk to me sometimes and perhaps accept an enchantment to help him stay calm if I think he needs it. It means I'm going to pay you in silver for whatever you lost as a result of all this. It means that this inquiry is over, and will not become an assize."

Elmo and Otto and Pips continued to stare at her with wide eyes.

"It means this is all over, and Elmo's free to go."

"There was somethin' in it about coin?" Otto sat up a little, wincing and placing a hand upon his stomach. His fingers curled as if to scratch, and Aelis quickly snatched his hand and moved it away.

"Scratch that wound even once and I swear I will tie your hands to the bed!" Her voice snapped more than she had meant it to, so she took a deep breath. "As to coin, yes, if you lose value of crops or herds from being unable to work the past few days, or for the immediate future. Are there any further questions?"

Pips practically jumped. "Did y'see any orcs? What about bandits? Werewolves? Fight any battles? Any magical duels?"

Aelis wrapped one arm around the girl's shoulders and squeezed. "Much of it was boring, and all of it I have to write down, while it's fresh, for my superiors at the Lyceum. So I'm going to have to go do that. Right after I check your uncle's dressings and adjust his medicines." Otto groaned, but then he lay back and pulled down the blanket.

+ + +

Aelis hadn't been allowed to leave until Rus and Martin had fed her. Fresh bread, goat's milk cheese, and sausages fried with butter and onions had tasted a good deal better than the hard biscuit and dried meat she and Tun had been eating on their journey. She was only just beginning to feel the weariness of what she'd done, the running, the walking, the fighting. She'd had the sense—and surprisingly, the willpower—to drink no more than one cup of wine, as she'd too much writing to do.

She was almost happy to see her tower as it grew in her vision; she was less happy to see that goat milling about in front of it, chewing a patch of grass. At least she thought it was the same goat; she hadn't yet learned how to tell one from another, frankly.

Aelis was, perhaps sadly, almost ecstatic to see the newly repaired door that fit snugly against the stone frame. The hinges it opened on were neither particularly smooth nor noiseless, but the door hung true and opened to her touch.

Inside, everything was much as she left it. She swung off her pack and flung it onto a chair. She was digging in one of her chests for her lap desk, paper, and ink, when she heard the creak of her door opening.

"If that's the goat I'm throwing you straight on the fire," Aelis said, turning slowly around.

Before she could even focus, a blast of force hit her and knocked her backward into and then over a chair. She had the vague sense of a form advancing on her, tall, in ragged robes, with wild hair and unkempt beard.

"You'll throw me on nothing, child," Dalius roared, taking slow steps down her hallway.

Aelis scrambled to her feet and tore her sword free of its scabbard. Or tried; the blade only made it halfway before another blast of force hit her hand, angled so as to catch the crossguard and tear the weapon from her grasp. It went spinning away and hit the floor, and her hand was too numb to reach for it again.

"I read your little Abjurer's book, child," Dalius said. "I know everything you can do with that weapon, and none of it will be sufficient." He gestured with one arm and she was flung like a rag doll, hitting the floor with a thud. Her jaw clicked, hard, and she tasted blood. The stones of the floor swam in her vision.

"So many years I have waited; for longer than you have been alive, I have prepared. Then you come along, with your parlor tricks and your minor powers, and dash them all to ruin."

Aelis flopped over onto her back. Dalius loomed over her from the other room. He seemed in no hurry to cross the distance. Gone was the pathetic beanpole of a man she'd bested so many nights ago; he seemed taller, but more solid, more *present*. The gentle unfocused look he'd had was replaced with a singular intent that could only be called madness. It gleamed in his eyes, it quivered at the edge of the beard that spilled onto his chest, it trembled in his hands.

"Who is the eagle now, and who the gnat? Your words, Warden— though you are not worthy of the title—to an old and beaten man. You did not know then, who I was. *I* did not know who I was. But you, in your ignorance and your blundering, you helped me to remember."

An Abjurer does not know fear. An Abjurer does not know danger. Her heart does not race. Her palms do not sweat.

Aelis's litany was not helping her deal with the advancing wizard, though he seemed prone to continuing his speech. She propped herself up on one elbow and began to back slowly toward her worktable.

"Who are you, Dalius? What did I do that I didn't understand?" Aelis thought it might be helpful if her voice quavered in fear. She did not need to pretend too much; the blasts he had hit her with were surprisingly powerful, well controlled, and done without apparent focus.

"I am Dalius Enthal de Morgantis un Mahlgren," he growled, pulling himself up to his full height. He looked far less like the whining, wretched Dalius she now remembered. He walked and talked like a man accustomed to commanding everyone around him. "I was the Warden Commander of Mahlgren. And I did what I needed to do to try and save this land, to defend it from savagery and barbarism. And now it is *fallen*, and this gods-damned shepherds' village is all that remains. And barely gifted children, untrained girls, are sent to do my job."

"What do you mean? What did you do?" Aelis's arm found the edge of her worktable and she began pulling herself up, gingerly. Her legs shook.

"I used knowledge forbidden to mewling cowards like you, like the unworthies who populate the Lyceum and call themselves Archmagisters now. In so doing I lost myself, but when I found power, I attached myself to it; the orcish demon sprouted because I gave it life. The woman, Nathalie, a reject from your own precious Colleges and gone to adventure in the wilderness until I found her. And you, who had already met the sliver of my power I left for just such as you, you conveniently found and defeated both of them. You may have destroyed the core of the army I was building, but you gave me a precious gift, Warden."

By now Aelis had lifted herself to the edge of the table. Her hand scrambled for a weapon, for anything, closing on a tall glass flask set on a ringstand. She brought it up to swing. Dalius flicked his fingers and the glass exploded. It peppered her with shards; she felt several dig into her face, others tear through her shirt and into her arm. None hit her eyes, for which she was briefly thankful.

Another controlled blast hit her and she was flattened against her table. More of her instruments and implements went flying or were crushed beneath her.

"You . . . you performed a Sundering," Aelis guessed, though she knew immediately it was the right guess. She didn't know what a Sundering entailed, exactly, only that it was forbidden.

"Yes, yes, I did. I thought by stretching myself across the earldom I could save it all." He sneered down at her, his eyes glinting with madness and the spark of something inhuman. Aelis was suddenly reminded of the way Nathalie's eyes had looked as she died. "I was wrong then, but I have learned much."

Aelis flailed for something, anything. Dalius seemed unconcerned. Her fingers brushed against something large and heavy, something that had been pushed but had not fallen from the table.

"You . . . when you do that to yourself, you do not come back to your-self alone, Dalius. Things come with you. Spirits. Powers we don't under-stand." Aelis's mind was working fast now, throwing out purely theoretical guesses, but the madness burning in Dalius's eyes didn't seem natural.

"*Knowledge* came with me, child. *Power* came with me. And now you will become my next vessel, for this one grows old and too feeble to con-tinue. I have not known Necromancy for some time. It will be enlighten-ing." Dalius bent and picked up a shard of glass, a fragment of one of Aelis's shattered vessels.

Then he plunged it toward her stomach.

Aelis twisted away; her fingers closed around the cold, heavy base of her orrery.

The glass cut across her stomach, a line of fire and pain. Dalius, with a strength and speed no one his age should've possessed, twisted his wrist and slipped it between her ribs.

Aelis wrapped her hand around the wrist that pressed the shard of glass into her. She tasted blood.

Power flowed from her orrery back into her. Every Necromantic Order she had placed into it—and all that it had absorbed from the waxing of Onoma's moon—suddenly rushed into her limbs.

Her right hand, wrapped about Dalius's wrist, became a skeletal claw so dark it drank in the sunlight that streamed into the tower from above.

Dalius withered before her eyes, his cheeks puckering inward, his eyes rolling up, as Aelis poured forth dark, harsh syllables and her hand sucked the very life from him. His body vibrated as it disintegrated, his mouth opening first in a grimace, then in a soundless scream as he tried to pull away. But the void that was Aelis's hand would not be denied.

Ephraze's Withering. A Fifth Order Necromantic spell, and utterly forbidden to use against the sentient, upon pain of death.

But if Dalius was possessed, had unnaturally extended his life through Sundering, had brought something *other* back into himself, then he was no longer truly human.

Aelis maintained the spell until the only thing holding Dalius up was her darkly glittering grasp. His bones, she knew, were withering too, ground to powder by the rippling, insatiable force of her spell. Sweat broke out on her face. Her heart pounded in her ears. The Anatomist in her told her that this was doubly bad—a quickened heart rate would pump blood through her wound faster than she wanted. But she held on as her vision dimmed.

She let him go. He collapsed to the floor and practically shattered.

Aelis released the Withering and immediately pressed her hands to her ribs to inspect her wound. The glass was deep. It had missed her vitals, but she was pumping blood, had lost some already from the side of her face and her arm.

She stumbled over to her pack, with the medical kit inside it. Her right arm was numb and cold; a side effect of most of Ephraze's more powerful incantations. Her left was slick with blood. She fumbled to open her pack. Her feet seemed far away. Her hand closed on the kit and pulled it free. She slipped as she turned away, fell hard to the floor, drove the glass deeper into her side.

The stones of the floor were too cool and too soft. Aelis's vision swam down into darkness.

She thought she heard a voice calling out to her; a child's voice, distant and frightened, but she dismissed it, and the sound of feet running away, as just a vision. She wished she knew what it meant.

Then she wished for nothing, and knew less.

25

THE REMAINS

"Fuck me." Aelis was so surprised to wake up that the hoarsely mumbled curse was all she could manage.

She was lying in her bed. Candles lit on her worktables provided flickering illumination and her eyes wouldn't focus. Blinking was like dragging broken glass across her eyes, so she settled for letting them close again. She could hear feet scraping around the stone floor of the tower. "Who's there?" she ventured weakly.

"Emilie."

"Well. That's not the name I expected."

"Phillipa came for me. She insisted on bringing you dinner from the inn. She found you wounded and ran back to the village as fast as she could, then dragged me here on horseback."

"I'm glad there was someone else around with physic training."

"I've poulticed your wounds. I've got maggots in case they fester. I've also brought some silver salts." Aelis listened close for any sense of smugness, but thought the other woman only sounded professional. She couldn't decide whether to be disappointed or impressed.

"Let's hope it doesn't come to that," Aelis said, not entirely sure if she had managed to keep the disgust out of her voice, and in too much pain to care. "The body. What did you do with Dalius's body?"

"Dalius? Was that the name of the man who looked like he'd been drunk dry by a blood-lance the size of a dog?"

"Yes. His corpse. What did you do with it?"

"Gathered his bones up in his robes and hauled them to the forest after making sure you weren't going to die. The wolves and the ravens'll do for him."

Oh, Onoma's frigid milk, no. "I'm going to have to get that body back, Emilie. I need to study it, to make sure—"

"It'll be gone by the time you can walk to it."

"I'm not that weak," Aelis said. She tried to swing her legs off the bed and succeeded only in falling over onto her elbow.

"Warden, I've seen stronger die from less than the wounds you took. Wasn't much I could do but close them and hope for the best. Too much blood was gone to risk letting any to balance the humors."

"My humors are fine. I promise." *Now is not the time to lecture her,* Aelis told herself. *She probably saved my life, even if she doesn't quite know as much as I do.* "How bad was it, then?"

"Lots of blood gone. Wounds in your ribs, your arm, your face and neck. I got the glass out."

"Thank you, Emilie. Did you say there was food?"

"Cold now, but yes."

"Please, for the love of the Worldsoul, bring it to me."

Emilie retreated from the bedside. Aelis forced her eyes open and saw the platter set down. The stew was cold and congealed, the bread bowl soaked with the gravy, but she wolfed it all down regardless. The first few bites she found hard to chew, her throat and the muscles of her neck moving oddly. Emilie's poultices were sticking to her skin. They began to itch as she ate.

"Don't crack those off now . . ."

Aelis paused and held up a hand. "Emilie. I thank you more than I can say for coming and helping me. No doubt you saved my life. You did not seem fond of me before I left, so I want to ask: Why help me?"

"I may not be fond of you, Warden, but you were dying. I'm no villain."

"You must've run to get here. You were motivated. Why?"

"You helped us," Emilie said. Aelis carefully tilted her head so as not to disturb the drying poultice and eyed the tall blonde. "You drove off that bear. You are trying to give Phillipa valuable learning. And . . ." She sighed. "I thought Otto was dead. I never saw a man in my days in Ystain's army who took a blade like that into his guts recover the way he has. If I had been left to treat him alone, he'd be dead. And then you brought back his brother alive and whole and well. Maybe you saved them both. It was more than anyone could have hoped. I noticed. We all noticed."

"Well." Aelis might have felt proud had she not been concentrating on eating and generally feeling miserable. "Good. It's my job, after all."

"Well. I'm glad you're doing it. You're tougher than I would've guessed. Heavier, too. But you're not soft like I imagine wizards to be."

"Not all wizards are wardens, Emilie." Aelis felt herself growing tired as she finished the last of her cold food. "Do me one more favor before you go to your home. Bring me my orrery, please." Aelis pointed vaguely in the direction of one of her worktables. "The metal contraption with all the moons."

Emilie brought it to her, cradling it carefully in both arms. It stood stock-still, Aelis having drained every bit of its stored magic in her blow against Dalius. Knowing it was going to be off by a few degrees, if not more, she wrapped her hand around it and put a First Order Anatomist's Diagnostic into it anyway, which drove twin spikes of pain into her head.

"I'm going to sleep now," she mumbled. "Please put it back."

Whatever else Aelis tried to say was lost as she sagged against her pillows.

* * *

Aelis woke from a dreamless sleep, and truly didn't want to face the sunlight streaming down through the broken roof of her tower, but then there was hot breath on her face and a rasp against her cheek.

The goat stood atop the bed, patiently licking at one of the poultices on the side of her face. With a cry, Aelis shoved it from the bed, more gently than she'd wanted to, but only because her arm didn't cooperate. The goat gave a plaintive bleat and clattered away.

Aelis tottered out of bed, picking up the blanket as she stood. The door was off its hinges again.

"Oh, for fuck's sake," she half yelled. Then, calmer after a deep breath, she said, "If there were any justice in this benighted world, I would spend the day in bed with wine and cheese and perhaps not alone."

Too often, Bardun Jacques had once told the warden cadets, *the only justice in this benighted world is that which wardens are willing to make. And if you can't move forward when you're hurt, or tired, or hungover, or all three and worse, then the warden's life is not for you.*

Aelis dug out a robe and as soon as she was dressed, got out her case of instruments, astringent, and a mirror. Then she set to work scraping off the poultices, which the goat had gotten a good start on, and inspected the damage. The deepest wound was in her ribs; no shame there. In fact, the scar it would leave would be rather a mark of pride. For the sake of practice, she laid the mirror on a table and cleaned, debrided, and sewed that one first.

She got out a bottle of wine before she decided to attempt the wounds on her face and neck. She was rather less hopeful of proud scars there.

❖   ❖   ❖

With her face tight with tiny stitches and her skin tingling from the tinctures she'd rubbed on it, Aelis set out after Dalius's bones. The nearest treeline from the tower was to the north, so that's where she headed, leaning rather heavily on the walking stick Tun had given her.

She thrashed about in the undergrowth for several moments before she heard a heavy footfall behind her. Sparing a moment to curse herself for leaving her swordbelt in the tower, she whirled with the staff in hand anyway, to find Tun standing stock-still, just out of her swinging arc.

"How," Aelis squawked, "does someone your size move that quietly?"

"I choose my steps carefully."

She set the tip of the staff down and leaned heavily on it. "What are you doing out here?"

"Looking for you. I went into the village this morning after having a good sleep. Rus and Martin told me what had happened, so I spoke to Emilie, then came straight this way."

"How'd you know I'd be out here instead of finding me in the tower?"

"Emilie mentioned that you were worried about the corpse of your assailant, so I found the sign of her dragging it out here. Thought I would look for it for you."

"Where is it?"

Tun took a deep breath. "It is not here."

"That can't be."

"If it were, I would have found it, Warden. This is not pride. This is the truth."

"Tell me that wolves ate it. Or ravens. Meat-eating squirrels. Anything."

"I am afraid that there is no sign of such a thing. I found the place where she left it. And it is gone."

"Onoma," Aelis barely spoke the word. "I needed to know what he was."

"Not simply an old madman?"

"So much more than that," Aelis said. "He told me—he was a talker, a gloater—that he had empowered Nath. That he had given life to the Demon Tree. I think he meant the one we fought. And that as we destroyed them, he . . ." She stopped. "Let me start over. He was a Warden, I think. And a powerful one. During the war. And he did something forbidden. A

Sundering. Split pieces of himself, of his soul, off. They would've had to find new bodies or objects to inhabit, but the thinking behind such a process has always been to increase the area a wizard can influence. If the wizard is strong enough, they can practically put two or three of themselves—all weaker than the first, but only in a way that another strong wizard could exploit—out into the world so long as all the pieces remain within a certain range. The problem is, the longer you do it, the more unstable all the pieces are. And it was forbidden during the war anyway. Certainly before he did it. It was made a hanging offense. And yet he did it."

"Why was it forbidden? It sounds like a powerful tool."

"It isn't just about becoming unstable while your selves are apart. When they come back together, they don't always do it alone."

"Meaning?"

"Spirits. Demons. Malevolent aether. I'm not enough of a theorist. All I know is that Dalius was no longer human. Not in the most meaningful ways." *Gods, I hope he wasn't human*, she thought as she remembered sinking the cold and glittering claw that was her hand into him, drinking down his life like so much watered wine.

"Well, as human corpses tend not to get up and walk away—nor do elf, orc, dwarf, gnome, or any combination thereof that I'm aware of—I'm forced to agree. What do you do next?"

"Have a drink," Aelis said. "Scratch that. Next I have to write letters. I can send a quick message to a Diviner back at the Lyceum, but longer messages require artifacts I don't have, or spells I cannot cast. But I can give them the broad strokes and tell them letters are inbound."

"I do not wish to rush you, Warden, but there is the matter of my amulet."

"Could it wait till tonight?"

Tun smiled uneasily around his tusks. "It is a struggle even now, Warden. By nightfall, I doubt I will be as you see me now. I know that you should not be out of bed, and I am sorry to ask."

"I'll rest when I'm dead, Tun. Until then, I'll always have work to do. Let's get you and the pieces of the Demon Tree's heart inside my tower and see what we can do."

"I would point out that there is one piece of your earlier statement regarding Dalius that you must amend, Warden."

"Hmm?"

"Neither the Demon Tree nor Nathalie were stopped by 'us.' I failed, rather pointedly, at both tasks. *You* did not. Take the credit."

"I wouldn't have found either one without you, Tun. And please . . . call me Aelis."

Tun smiled, and they tramped back to her tower. With the sun stream-ing down and the feeling that she'd found a valuable friend, Aelis stopped worrying for at least a few hours about the missing body of the mad, sun-dered Warden Dalius.

✦   ✦   ✦

With her orrery and her books of orbit calculation to hand, as well as some paper, Aelis found adjusting Tun's amulet far easier than she expected. It was, in fact, somehow attuned to the six moons. She was no artificer, but the structure of the thing revealed itself to her easily, and the sense of solv-ing a puzzle, of being smarter than the problem, satisfied her immensely. There were seven runes on the iron of his amulet, the same seven as were on the runestone that had animated the Demon Tree. Tun confirmed that they were the six moons and the planet itself, and the seven deities, but he wouldn't expound on the Orcish names for them.

Aelis convinced him to give up a few drops of his blood, extracted with the silver needle she *hadn't* taken on the trip. She set her alchemical ring on a solid flame and put both the back of the iron and the tip of a needle into the flame until they became pliable. Working carefully, holding the amulet with a set of tongs and bending so close to it she would've feared burning her hair if she hadn't already singed ends off of it any number of times in an alchemy lab, she etched new runes into the back of it; one for each of the six moons, one for the Worldsoul in the center, with the goddesses to her left and the gods to her right. She had to stop to heat the iron and the needle again, but when the work was done she filled in each rune with Tun's blood.

"How did you know to do any of this, Aelis?" Tun sat in stern concen-tration, his hands clasped tightly upon his knees, watching her and, for the first time she had seen, sweating.

"I don't. But the theory is sound. We need to account for the human part of you as well as the orc. What better way to do that but human runes and your blood?" The iron quickly cooled and she set to wrapping the strands of hair back around it, though with surgical tweezers rather than her hands. Instinctively she tied the strands from each opposing god to the other, and a strand from the Worldsoul to the other six. When she finished, she fretted at it.

"That . . . I don't know how I knew to do this."

She handed the amulet back to him. Tun's hand shook as he took it, then he slipped it over his neck. Almost instantly, he calmed. The lines of concentration drawn taut on his face eased. His fists unclenched. He took a deep breath.

"Warden . . . it . . . I . . . I have not felt this controlled since I was very young."

"We'll keep looking at it, adjusting it. It—"

Aelis's words were driven from her as Tun stood, wrapped his arms around her, and lifted her off her feet in as surprising a display of affection as she'd ever experienced. "Tun! Tun! I have stitches in!" Immediately, just as easily as he lifted her, Tun set her down gingerly. "Sorry," he said, and for the first time there was a hint of sheepishness in his voice. "I am not usually so ebullient." He took a deep breath and a step back, his face blank once more.

"Warden, this is payment beyond the favor I had done you. If you have need of me—for anything—you call."

"Tun. My friends call me Aelis." She thought a moment, then said, "There is some work I'll need help with around the tower."

◆   ◆   ◆

That day she and Tun made more headway cleaning up her tower than she had made in all the days since she arrived in Lone Pine. Well, Tun made progress while she sat down after the first quarter hour of work, her legs still unsteady. He even carried the disconnected calcination oven down from the second floor as if it were a bucket of water propped on his shoulder. She'd need a few pieces of ironmongery to get it attached to a chimney and make it usable, but it was in place.

When late afternoon came, so did Pips with food, and Tun made himself scarce. Aelis distracted the girl with a few lessons, but sent her home before the sun began to sink in order to send her letters. She carefully adjusted and aligned her orrery so that it mirrored the exact positions of the moons as closely as she could make it. Then she jotted the following message.

Dalius Enthal de Morgantis un Mahlgren. Sundered. Mad. Attacked me, others. Destroyed. Not in possession of remains. Letters to follow.

Aelis cast another spell into her orrery, calling upon a Second Order Abjuration, for that was most likely to be recognized as the signature of a

Warden. She inserted her tiny scrawled message into a slot in the bottom of the orrery and concentrated upon it, holding open the ward she cast—transformed by the orrery's own artifice into a beacon, a call to a diviner working at a matching orrery hundreds of miles away in the Lyceum—until she felt the connection take and hold.

When she pulled her tiny scrap of paper back out, it said, *Secure remains if at all possible. Mahlgren very dangerous area. Be on guard. Letters immediately.*

Aelis sighed, got out her lap desk and pen, and began to write. It would be several hand-cramping hours before she stopped.

26
THE DELIVERY

Three weeks passed as Aelis healed enough to resume her full workload. In that time, the people of Lone Pine had done everything they could to help her bring her home up to snuff—it had a roof again, for one thing, and a functional second floor—though there was no keeping a draft out of a decades-old stone tower. She was thankful for the vair lining her robes, and she even considered inviting the goat in for the warmth and the company. When she was well enough to walk the distance, she visited Elmo and Otto's house and found it similarly knocked back into shape and the brothers a bit too embarrassed to say anything about it.

Another month passed, the air got colder, and it *still* wasn't really winter yet, according to the locals. Aelis began to imagine her entry in *Lives of the Wardens* as a footnote in the life of another warden who found her entombed in a column of ice and stone.

The knock at the door was a welcome relief from more boredom as she paged through Aldayim and other texts, wishing she'd thought to bring some works on local history—or at least military history featuring Mahlgren and surrounds—with her in the first place. She'd asked for them in the letters she'd sent south with a merchant, but was beginning to despair of an answer before the snows came.

Pips was waiting on her front step, bouncing on her feet with energy. "It's not time for our lessons yet, but I suppose there's no harm in starting early," Aelis said.

The girl thrust up a handful of letters. "A post-rider came to town. All these are addressed to Warden Aelis de Lenti un Tirraval and sealed with wax. He also said there's a post carriage coming with baggage for you."

"My gods, do I even dare dream they've sent me replacement equipment for what Dalius destroyed?" Aelis had a chance to glance only at the handwriting and the seal on one letter. The script was slick, even spidery, and the seal that of the College of Necromancy.

The old seal; a grinning skull.

Her fingers itched to pull the envelope open and devour that letter first, followed by the others, but she tossed them all aside. "Let me fetch a scarf and my effects and we'll walk down to meet the coach."

It was a brisk walk, with the wind whipping at her robes and Pips peppering her with questions as always. Soon they were in the village and just outside the inn, where folk were gathering. Word had spread about the post carriage's arrival.

The post-rider had already left, and Aelis had a letter thrust in her face as soon as someone spotted her, a man leading a winded, lathered horse by a halter.

"Warden," he said, his features twisted with anxiety, "can you make this out? I know what the man told me, but . . ."

Aelis grabbed the letter and glanced over it. "It says if the horse he left in trade for the fresh one dies, founders, or fails to provide value, this letter can be exchanged for coin at any Post House." She handed the letter back and said, "You probably ought to see to the beast, hmm?" *And if you ever accost me while I'm walking again I will feed your bones to a ghoul.* She didn't say that part, but given how quickly he moved away she wondered how much of it showed on her face.

She was sitting at the counter inside the inn, her hands wrapped around her second cup of warmed apple wine, when a carriage pulled up outside with a great clatter. Most of the villagers went scrambling out to meet it; Aelis forced herself to dignity, which meant patience. She hated being patient, but the pain along the wound in her stomach did make it a little easier.

When she did come outside she thought it seemed awfully familiar, a long, low, boxy shape she'd seen before.

And the arbalest mounted on it she *knew* she'd seen before.

Then Timmuk, a huge ivory-bowled pipe stuck in his mouth sending merry curls of smoke around his head, was waving as he pulled on the brakes, but Aelis only barely returned his gesture.

The tall, lean form that leaped to the ground from the other side of the wagon held her attention rather more tautly than the grinning dwarf.

Aelis had come to wonder if what she'd felt for Maurenia those months before had been some passing, silly fancy, a dash of danger and spice to liven up a dull rural posting.

When the half-elf pushed her hood back and her dark auburn hair fell and curled around the point of her chin, Aelis's breath caught.

Maurenia smiled. Aelis felt as though she wanted to melt, and Maurenia's smile widened—not the knowing smirk she'd seen before, but something more than that.

"The Dobrusz brothers took themselves a royal contract, Lady de Lenti," Timmuk called, and it was a chore to tear her eyes from Maurenia to pay attention to the dwarf.

Everything else that was said and done passed in a blur; the invoice for her new alchemical equipment. A hamper of wine from her father. A chest of victuals preserved by an Abjurer's seal. Aelis signed for it all. She wasn't sure if she had the ready money to pay for any of it and she didn't care.

Maurenia left the Dobrusz brothers to the hot apple wine and drove the wagon, with Aelis beside her on the board, to the tower.

"Looks better," Maurenia said, as it hove into view.

"Had a lot of help putting it right."

"Finally impressed the locals enough."

"I suppose."

"Still going mad out here on the edge of the world?"

"A little." Aelis felt like a schoolgirl around her first crush, and searched vainly for something witty to offer.

Maurenia pulled the wagon to a stop and leaned close. Her face had the same dusting of freckles over sun-coppered skin. Her eyes were the same ice-crystal blue. She smelled the same. Aelis leaned forward and their lips met, but not for long. Maurenia leaned her head to rest it against Aelis's, and they stayed like that.

"We didn't come to stay for long. I can linger a bit. A week, ten days. It would've been presumptuous to pack up and move."

"A week, ten days sounds fine. Great." Aelis found herself on the verge of stammering, so she clamped her mouth shut, but she couldn't keep it that way for long. "I don't think a day went by I didn't think about you."

"Think what about me?"

Aelis leaned forward to kiss her again, took a deep breath of her clean, herbal scent. "Mostly that."

"Maybe we'll get snowed in here," Maurenia breathed, and Aelis was a little smug when she saw the way color rose in the half-elf's cheeks and heard the way her breath caught.

"Snows early here. Snows often. Been flurries already."

"Well, that's just awful. Wagons can't roll in snow. Even flurries. Best to be cautious, really." They lingered like that a moment, inches apart, eye to eye. "We should unload the wagon."

"Right."

"And probably drive it back to the inn and see to the horses."

"After we open a bottle of wine," Aelis said.

The unpacking went quickly.

✦ ✦ ✦

True to her word and her duty as a post-carriage wagoneer, Maurenia left soon after the wagon was unpacked, but with a kiss and a promise to walk back. Aelis wanted to grab her and not let her leave, but a glass of good Tirravalan orange had steeled her nerves and she felt more ready to face her correspondence.

Instead, she picked up the letter with the old Necromancer's seal on it. While the packet was ominously heavy, it was the kind of paper it was a pleasure to touch, of a fine weight and creamy texture, begging for ink, the kind she couldn't afford to bring with her in quantity and hadn't seen in months. She peeled the seal back, and took a deep breath.

Almost immediately, her heart sank.

Warden de Lenti,

The Earldom of Mahlgren was known, during the war, to have engaged in many dubious strategies to secure its borders and hold back the orcs who had overwhelmed its neighbors. That its resident Warden—the Dalius de Morgantis you named—would engage in a Sundering is hardly a surprise. There was little Dalius would not do to save the lands he loved; the Morgantis were seigneurs under the Earls of Mahlgren for hundreds of years. But rumors and suspicion speak of even darker forces at work in Mahlgren's heart, overseen by graduates of our own college at Dalius's urging. Necromancers of conscience such as you and I could not be swayed by promises of gold or power, but not all of our brethren are made of the same stuff. Dalius was not only the Warden Commander of the Earldom, but related to the ruling family. Uncle of its last earl, I believe, which could perhaps help to explain his passion in its defense.

It is true that war may change what a man is willing to do with his gifts as well. It is perhaps not ours to judge.

But it is ours to make right their mistakes, and to do it for the good name and good work of all of us who serve Onoma.

I have enclosed with this letter such maps and documents as may aid you in this task, Warden de Lenti. Do not fail our calling.

Archmagister Ressus Duvhalin

Clearly a late addition, in a smaller hand beneath the signature, was written one more line.

Ponder Aldayim's remarks at the beginning of the final stave of his masterwork.

Aelis was reasonably certain she knew the lines that the Archmagister referred to since she knew Aldayim's *Advanced Necromancy* as well as she knew any book. But deliberately, reverently, she went to her bookshelf and lifted the volume clear.

It took her a few moments to find the right page, holding the heavy book open on her left arm and flipping with her right hand.

The greater part of the first half of this work is dedicated to the First Art as we have known it, and the second to the healing and restorative properties to which I propose we may turn it. For most of us wearing the black, the proper raising, binding, animation, and enhancement of Servitors, Corpses, Skeletons, Gestalts, Chimeras, and Exotic creatures is the work of our days. It is right and fitting that this should be systematized and organized for ease of study; the use of animated skeletons, for instance, could ease the burden of dangerous or grueling work, and better that the already dead fall in war than the young and hale.

Even so, what one Necromancer may raise, another must be able to destroy. The First Art is ripe for exploitation by those without the discipline only to use it where it is necessary, or the scruple to use it only for the betterment of the many. I foresee the need for a different servant of Onoma; one who does not reach beyond the veil of night and roll back its touch but one who uses the powers She grants to fight death on all its fronts, not merely as physician or surgeon but as a champion of the Grave Maiden, who sees to it that death is neither unduly powerful nor stripped of its mystery. It is for this, for the Necrobane, that these following few pages are meant.

"Onoma's breath," Aelis whispered. She nearly let the letter slip from her hand as the weight of this new knowledge, and the immensity of her task, settled onto her shoulders.

27

THE ARCHMAGISTER

"Of the ten of you in this seminar, I expect one, at best, to wear an Anatomist's Dagger at year's end."

Archmagister Ressus Duvhalin's ruddy cheeks glowed with sweat, even in the stinging chill of this particular classroom. Despite that, his voice was calm and even, rolling sonorously from beneath his great white beard. Aelis felt every word settle over her like thick, clinging oil. She hated the sound of it as much as she hated the sweat creeping down her forehead. *If there was any justice,* she thought, *he'd be the one gasping for breath and streaming sweat.* She had four years of training as an Abjurer and a would-be Warden, while Duvhalin had decades of soft university living, even if all there was to show for it was a slight paunch under his black robes, soft hands, and tiny purpled veins on his nose that told of a man who enjoyed his wine.

She'd be damned if she would chase her breath in front of his withering contempt. The nine other students standing in a loose semicircle had no qualms about it, though, as they heaved and puffed.

But none of them knew the weight of the Archmagister's condescending eyes quite like she did. In fact, they rested upon her now, his mouth curled in a grin that someone who didn't know him might take for an avuncular smile.

Aelis wanted to hit him with the heel of her hand, to split his lip, possibly break his nose. She wanted to drive the pommel of a sword into his stomach to see if she could find a nerve cluster.

But she didn't have a sword on her belt that morning, and one did not strike Archmagisters in the face. Not if one wanted to graduate, in just under a year's time, from the College of Necromancy, and put one's powers to use as a Warden.

So she bore the weight of his gaze until he cleared his throat and looked out over the advanced students.

"Of course, in the old ways," Duvhalin began, leaving little doubt as to whether he preferred new or old, "we would not even be meeting in person for a class this advanced. Rather, we would use Servitors."

He sniffed. Aelis felt like the world was covered in a thick haze when she had to spend time in the Archmagister's presence. He was leading up to something.

"And of course there would have been . . . other differences," he said with another sniff. His eyes theatrically rolled before landing on Aelis again.

I'm twice the Necromancer of anyone in this room except you, you bastard, Aelis thought. *And because I know that and you know that, I'll stand here and eat shit for ten months and I will* smile *when you hand me my sheepskin. Because the one thing I'll never do is abandon my power.*

"Now, to work." Duvhalin lowered himself, slowly, into an enormous chair that was set out in just the right place for him to be able to observe his charges. With one ringed hand, he gestured to a table. "Who will be the first to make that corpse get up and take a turn about the room?"

Before he'd even finished his sentence, Aelis had stepped forward and said, "I will, Archmagister." She turned a glare back on the other students. None of them had been about to volunteer, and none were going to gainsay her now.

Shit rolled downhill in all the Colleges. *Especially so in Necromancy,* Aelis thought.

But if Duvhalin was higher up the hill than her—and he was, she had no illusions there—four years of besting them at everything had taught the other Necromancy students that she was above them.

◆ ◆ ◆

"That fat son of a festering lich. I hope he dies. I hope he is raised, with his spirit bound to his own rotting flesh, and I hope somebody sticks him in a stone coffin wound with silver wires to make a Null Cage, and I hope he keeps his senses of smell and all of his pain receptors as he decays over centuries."

Aelis stared at the letter she'd opened in disbelief. She turned the envelope over and a sheaf of papers fluttered out onto her worktable. She ignored them, read the letter and the open page in the Aldayim again. She put the book down, slowly crossed the room, and fell heavily into a chair.

She scanned the letter again, then again, then once more just to be certain it said what it said. Predictably, not a word of it had changed. It was still a pot of warm shit dumped straight into her lap.

She lowered her head toward the crook of one arm, bit off a scream, and sat up.

"The worst part," she said out loud, "is not that I'm going to tramp out into the fucking snow looking for old Mahlgren forts full of undead warriors, caged spirits, or worse, instead of spending the next two weeks buried in bed with Maurenia. The worst is that he knew I would fucking do it."

No, she thought. *The worst part is that I'm looking* forward *to it.*

28

THE POST

Once she could drag herself out of the chair, Aelis dug her rucksack out of a chest and thought to begin packing it, only to turn to the papers Duvhalin had sent with his letter and try to sort through them. The most relevant appeared to be a map. She'd need other maps to compare it to and get a sense of scale, but the locations on it seemed well north of where she and Tun had ranged in their search for Elmo.

Could I ask Tun to come with me again? I could, but I shouldn't. She was certain that Duvhalin wanted this handled by her alone.

"So, I'm going into the wilderness of Old Ystain. Alone. At the onset of winter. To find the unquiet dead or other monstrosities." She paused, looked up at the second floor of her tower. "Frankly, that last part bothers me the least."

The past couple of months in Lone Pine had been boring. Dreadfully, sometimes painfully boring. Daydreaming about winter festivities around Antraval could only get her so far when the only promenade she had to look forward to was a walk over hard mud to a village that smelled like sheep shit in all seasons.

Unconsciously her hand strayed to her stomach, where Dalius had stabbed her with a shard of broken glass. She didn't feel any twinge of ghostly pain—she wouldn't allow herself that—but she thought of the scar.

"Boring is good," she reminded herself. "For a week or two."

Once she was up and on her feet and her reports had been posted, Aelis had quickly run out of meaningful work. She'd hunted a few more times for Dalius's remains, gotten her tower into shape with plenty of help, and then walked around the village and the surrounding farms looking for something to do.

True, here and there an extra hand and a ward had helped mend a fence, but that felt like so much make-work. There hadn't been even a minor injury that required her talents as an Anatomist.

Aelis did not do well with boredom. Not when she had a limited wine cellar and an even more limited library.

She wanted to get out and do something, even if she hadn't realized it. But she damn well didn't want to do it now that Maurenia had arrived.

"And what would my teachers say to that? Vosghez? Lavanalla? Not to mention Bardun Jacques. 'Being a Warden is not about what you *want.'*"

Aelis was talking to herself and moving back and forth between her unpacked rucksack and her worktable with all its papers while accomplishing nothing. She set down the empty bag and forced herself to sit down at the table and gather up the notes and maps.

"Going to have to show the maps to Tun. I just can't tell him what I need his input for. That'll go well." She stuffed the papers into the envelope the Archmagister had sent. Then she dumped them all out, carefully folded them back up, and packed them carefully back into the envelope, which she then secured in her rucksack.

Then she picked up her walking stick, cloak, scarf, and fur-lined gloves and ventured out into the cold.

They had seasons in Tirraval, where Aelis had been born and raised. Snowfall wasn't uncommon, but it rarely lasted long. What's more, cities were full of warming fires, the press of bodies, and wizards willing to do any work to create their own comforts. The count's daughter rarely had to deal with the cold. There had been romps in the snow, elaborate parties where the dance floor had been turned to ice and skates were made available, but the cold there was never *dangerous.*

Now, living through her first early winter in Old Ystain, hundreds of miles north of Tirraval, had Aelis wondering how cold had ever been a novelty. How ice had ever been an evening's entertainment.

"Stregon's blue balls, we were a great bunch of idiots," she muttered. She was two steps down the walkway from her tower's door and already pulling her scarf more tightly around her neck and wishing for thicker fur in her gloves.

She made it a third step before she considered going back inside and putting on another robe, or her heaviest cloak, but none of the people of Lone Pine had seen fit to dress in their warmest clothes yet.

Aelis wasn't going to beat them to it.

"Not just pride," she muttered as she pulled her robes tighter and forced herself step by step down the walkway. "Got to fit in with local custom."

The cold of Ystain was like nothing Aelis knew. And from how everyone acted it wasn't even properly winter yet, just late fall. Snow swirled lazily in the air and clouds as threateningly gray as anything she could recall loomed overhead. If they broke, that night they'd see Stregon's full moon in brilliant blue, and the vaguest hint of Midarra's pristine white moon.

Pondering the fullness of Stregon's moon, Aelis briefly grasped the hilt of her sword and considered pulling up a ward against the cold. Deliberately, she loosened her grip and dropped her hand to her side.

Do not trivialize your power.

Aelis heard that in half a dozen voices all at once. Every professor, every magister, every Archmagister drilled this into their students. Yes, you could use magic to make the world a more comfortable place, and where the expenditure of power could do that for enough people to make it beyond mere self-indulgence—such as when wizards cleared city streets of snow in mere hours—it was justified.

When it was a matter of making yourself warmer on a one-mile walk where the cold didn't threaten your health in any way, only your immediate comfort, magic wasn't the answer.

"It's decidedly fucking unfair," Aelis said. "But then, I suppose a relic of another age or the spirit of a dead Warden might attack me between here and there, and where would I be if I wasted my power?"

She dug her hands deeply into her gloves, adjusted her scarf to cover her face without impeding her breath, and walked as fast as she could manage.

Pushing through the door into the taproom of Rus and Martin's inn at last was a blessing. Yes, the room reeked of sweaty wool and sweaty bodies, with the gentle undercurrent of sheep shit that was everywhere in Lone Pine.

But it was, Aelis felt as she took her gloves off, blessedly warm.

Timmuk and Andresh had commandeered one of Rus's longest tables and set it in the middle of the room. Lone Pine folk queued up in rows, filling the place near to bursting. Aelis wouldn't have thought there'd be quite as much post as their wagon seemed to have brought for a village like Lone Pine. Less than a quarter of the townsfolk could read, after all. Of course, it wasn't just letters, but also seeds, supplies, various goods, and even minor luxuries for which folk had sent money south on the last wagon to come to Lone Pine.

That, Aelis realized, had been the wagon that had carried her here.

She suddenly felt, again, just how very distant from the vital life of the Three Crowns she was, and how much farther she was readying herself to move away from it. The cold and the *emptiness* of the pine forest and rolling hills outside the doors threatened to swallow the inn and the village whole.

Those feelings got shoved down fast as she heard two or three voices calling, "Warden!"

She turned her head first to her left, then her right, seeing eager villagers clutching letters. She glanced to the long bar near the back of the room, where she saw Rus quietly reading a letter to a rapt couple.

Things clicked into place in her mind. *Doesn't matter quite so much if the inhabitants can read or write, so long as someone here can.*

Most of the locals had lost their initial fear of her, but few were willing to openly approach her for a favor. But Bruce was already at her elbow with a thick envelope in hand.

"Warden, if you would be so kind. Only letter we're like to have from my brother all year . . ." In his other hand she glimpsed the dim glint of tarnished silver.

"Of course, Bruce. Let me find a seat and something to drink and I'd be happy to." Gently, she reached out toward his hand and curled his fingers over the coin he clutched eagerly, hoping her smile appeared genuine.

This is going to take my entire fucking evening, she thought, but she went to the bar, where Rus had already set a cup and a pitcher, took a seat, and reached for Bruce's letter.

A line was already forming behind him.

✦   ✦   ✦

It took all her evening and as much of the night as Rus and Martin were willing to light with their candles and oil lamps, in fact. Aelis had lost track of the births and deaths, the cousins who'd gone to sea or taken a king's coin to shoulder a spear and see the world, the elderly aunts who were not expected to live till another letter, the children who were walking or getting married or having children themselves.

Much of the news was bad, but the shepherd and farmer folk she read the letters out to bore it all as stoically as one might expect of people who'd moved to the far edge of the civilization they knew to try to rebuild it. Aelis imagined a few would go to bed that night with tears in their eyes, but they'd wake up in the morning and go back to the endless work the life they'd made demanded of them.

She admired that in them. But all the same, she was glad when the light was finally too bad and Rus showed no sign of adjusting the lamp. The inn had emptied of all but her, Rus, and the Dobrusz brothers. She could hear Martin clattering around in the back.

Rus pulled away the flagon of small beer she'd been drinking to keep her throat wet while she read, and replaced it with a heavy clay bottle that made a satisfying thunk when it hit the bar.

"Be careful or they'll be asking you to write their replies," he said. With his other hand he produced a pair of small cups.

"That, I won't have the time to do," Aelis said. She held the bottle steady while he pried the cork out.

"Planning on going somewhere?" Rus filled the cups, pushed one toward her, and took the other himself. They lifted the cups, made eye contact, touched the edges together, and drank.

Aelis was not unused to spirits, but generally more in favor of brandy than harsh grain liquor. Still, she knocked back the large tot Rus had poured with no complaints, feeling its fire warm her empty stomach.

"Probably."

"May I ask where?"

"You may, but I'm not going to answer. Where does Tun stay during the winter?"

"Same place he stays all the time." He dropped his voice low enough that she could hear the chattering of dwarfish voices, the clink of coin, the scratch of quill on parchment from where the Dobrusz brothers totaled up the day's business. "He doesn't hibernate, if that's what you're asking."

It took Aelis a moment. "You knew. You knew he was—"

"Of course I did. Why do you think I made up that nonsense about proscriptions against harming bears in these parts?"

"So you knew it was him?"

"No, but I didn't want to risk it. Tun is a good man, and a good friend to us. And to this village, even if they don't realize it."

He poured second shots for both of them. Aelis toyed with her cup. "He's a strange one. But I'm glad to have him as a friend." She watched as Rus knocked back his second shot and immediately poured another, mouth opening in a brief rictus of mingled pleasure and pain from the burn. "Didn't take you for much of a drinker."

"I make an exception on post days. It's tough, reading up on what we left behind, delivering bad news to so many hopeful people."

"The news isn't all bad," Aelis countered, weakly. She sensed that Rus was not telling her something, so she threw back her second whiskey as she wondered whether to ask. She was saved the trouble by Martin appearing from the kitchen with a heavy board in one hand. He set it down and offered her a smile, and the thick piece of cold ring sausage, the heavy wedge of hard cheese, and several slices of bread it held drew her smile in turn.

Martin slipped a hand onto Rus's back while drawing the bottle away with the other and sticking it on a shelf beneath the bar.

"I know letter day is hard," Martin muttered, "but the morning comes just as early."

Rus grunted noncommittally, but he leaned back against Martin's hand and pushed his cup away.

Meanwhile, Aelis had picked up a knife and began cutting a slice of sausage. "So where does Tun live? Surely not in that little stand of trees."

"He has a cabin not far," Rus said, picking up a piece of bread and contemplating it. "Hard to find if you don't know where it is. I can show you in the morning. Or you could wait till he comes with fresh meat. Should be sometime in the next week."

"Better go in the morning if you can spare the time," Aelis said. "What I need to ask him about shouldn't wait too long."

Rus nodded as he stuffed half the slice of bread into his mouth and chewed. She and Rus ate in silence for a moment, till the clomping of heavy boots sounded behind them.

"Glad to see you made it back from your adventure into the wilderness, Warden," Timmuk said, though he moderated his voice slightly. "Lone Pine would surely have been a duller place to come back to without you. I trust Maurenia delivered the letters you had from the Lyceum and your family."

Aelis sat up a bit straighter. "The Lyceum, yes. Family, no."

The light in the taproom was dim, but Aelis was reasonably certain that Timmuk was grinning behind his beard. "Well, she may've forgot. Should go ask. Upstairs, third room on the left."

Aelis felt her cheeks grow a little hot, but Timmuk's tone wasn't teasing her beyond what she could endure.

Deep down she slightly dreaded any letter from her father, because by now the Thorns had surely called upon the Urdimonte bank for the letter of credit she'd written them. It wasn't a ruinous sum, but it was going to raise eyebrows, and the count would want explanations. He was entitled to them.

But she shoved all that to the back of her mind as she sliced one more piece of sausage and a hunk of cheese and stood.

"If you'll excuse me. I'll see you in the morning, Rus. Might take me a while to get here from the tower, but I'll try not to keep you waiting."

"Going to rain tonight, might freeze," Martin answered her. "Stay if you wish. Plenty of beds available. No charge, of course."

Aelis glided up the stairs with clouded thoughts and a mouthful of cheese and sausage. She hurriedly chewed and swallowed, then brushed at any imaginary crumbs on her chin and her robes. She found herself in front of Maurenia's door far too quickly.

Aelis rapped at it with one bent knuckle.

"It's open." Maurenia's voice sounded slightly distant through the door. Aelis carefully swung it open, slipped inside, and closed it quickly and quietly.

"Why, Warden Aelis. Like you're sneaking into another student's room in your schoolgirl days."

Aelis could hear the gentle smirk in the half-elf's voice before she even looked across the room at her.

Maurenia sat by the hide-covered window in the room's only chair. She wore something between a robe and a dressing gown. It was loosely belted at the waist, but the hooks along the front were undone, exposing skin that was pale and luminous in the dimly candlelit room.

Aelis felt something not entirely unlike the burn of the whiskey in her chest and throat, only more pleasant, and more apt to leave her light-headed.

"Timmuk said you had a packet of letters from my family?"

Maurenia smiled and stood. The swing of the robe exposed flashes of her legs. "I do." She pointed to the small table on the far side of the room. It held two pitchers, two cups, an empty plate, and a thick envelope.

"Why'd you not deliver it with those from the Lyceum?"

"Because this gave you a reason to seek me out," Maurenia said. She came to face Aelis, and stopped barely a handbreadth away. Lightly, she took one of Aelis's hands in her own.

"I probably would've done that anyway."

"I don't like leaving things to chance." Aelis hadn't realized she was still wearing her scarf loosely gathered around her neck until Maurenia unwound it and tossed it casually away.

Aelis swallowed hard. "I am going to need those letters."

Maurenia lifted one arm and settled it around Aelis's neck, letting her fingertips—the nails short but well maintained, not at all ragged—graze

Aelis's neck through her hair. "They're right here," Maurenia murmured. "If you need them now, feel free to take them and go read them. But I very much doubt whatever is written in them is going to change in the next hour or two."

Aelis slipped one of her arms around Maurenia's waist. Her back was well muscled, Aelis could feel that even through the thick lining of the robe she wore. She felt her own heart thudding hard in her chest. They closed the distance between them.

She could feel Maurenia's heart thudding, too.

"Probably not going to change much, no." *I have to leave. In the morning. And go do dangerous things.* Aelis dismissed those thoughts, but not before adding, *All the more reason to enjoy tonight.*

Maurenia's fingers had twined into her hair. Aelis's mind filled with questions. *Did you come back here just for me? Was I a foregone conclusion? Are the Dobruszes having a good laugh at us downstairs?*

Then she looked at the sharp line of Maurenia's jaw and the dark pools of her eyes. She couldn't make out the blue in the darkness, but she knew it was there, and then Maurenia's hair was brushing her cheeks as they leaned toward each other, and she stopped thinking about anything at all but the warmth and the softness and the taste of the woman in her arms.

29

THE CABIN

Aelis woke with faint light coming in through the window. The fire had been well smoored the night before and had kept the room warm enough to sleep in, but she half expected to see her breath when she pulled her head clear of the bedding.

Beside her, Maurenia was a languid form, her warm skin soft in places, yet taut over the muscles life had built into her.

I still hardly know anything about her, Aelis thought, but decided she didn't care as she leaned her head on one hand to study the half-elf's back, the sharp planes of her shoulder blades interrupted in places by scars. She thought about reaching for them, lifted a hand, then let it drop back to the bedding. Somehow, despite having spent the night in Maurenia's bed, that kind of exploration felt presumptuous, more private than sex.

Maurenia appeared deeply asleep. A part of Aelis wanted to bed down next to her, throw an arm around, perhaps start kissing the back of her neck.

But duty called.

Carefully, she slipped out of the bed. Maurenia stirred but did not wake. Aelis put her robes back on, gathered up her boots, gloves, scarf, and packet of papers, and tiptoed quietly out the door. She closed it slowly, leaned against the wall to pull on her boots, straightened her robes as best she could, and went downstairs.

Martin was in the kitchen; she could hear the sounds of the morning's baking. Rus was standing behind the counter, cleaning mugs with a rag. In the far corner, right by the door, with a window-hide tacked up, Timmuk was smoking an enormous pipe with a carved ivory bowl.

"Do you never sleep?"

Rus only shrugged at her question, then bent to retrieve a mug he had sheltered beneath the counter, took a furtive sip. "Less than I'd like, more than I should," he finally answered, in a voice that sounded like a hinge in want of grease.

But by then she'd already drifted over to Timmuk, sliding into a seat on the bench across the table from him.

"Didn't take you for an early riser," she murmured.

"Remember, I grew up a banker." Timmuk spoke around his pipe stem, the muscles of his jaw bunching. "Money is not made while lying abed."

Aelis studied his arms, bulging bare from the studded black leather jack he wore. "I've had cause to deal with a number of bankers in my life, Timmuk Dobrusz. I have never seen one with the kind of arms you have."

"I'll take that as a compliment."

"I meant the kind of arms accustomed to ending in a fist or an axe instead of a gloved hand."

Timmuk shrugged. "Dwarfish banking can be a vigorous business."

"So, what made you decide to branch out into running a royal post wagon?"

"What drives anyone into any business, Warden? Profit."

"There's profit to be made in bringing letters and seeds and tools to Lone Pine?"

Timmuk stood, took the pipe from his mouth, and tapped it carefully against the open window ledge. The dottle cascaded out, and he held the pipe casually in his hand as he turned toward Aelis and sat back down.

"There is if you know how to negotiate." The grin that formed beneath his great beard was less like a cat in cream and more a mountain lion in a chicken coop, Aelis thought.

"I don't think I like the thought of you reaping profit off the folk of Lone Pine," Aelis began, only to have Timmuk sit up straight, his mouth crinkling.

"Come now, Warden. The people here don't have money to take. I negotiated with the post's purser. They agreed to pay by the mile."

Aelis blinked her eyes wide. "That seems a stunningly bad deal."

"What can I say? No other teamsters were eager for the route. The easy runs you've got to bid for. Going eight hundred miles from Lascenise to the tip of Ystain's remains? Nobody's too keen on that."

"So you didn't come here, or Maurenia didn't come here, just . . ." Aelis trailed off, waving a hand vaguely in the air.

Timmuk held up a hand. "Between you and her, Warden."

"So that ruse with the letters, and . . ." She sighed.

"I think I might know what you're asking. We like Renia. She likes you. That's all of a discussion needs having, right?"

Aelis shrugged. "I suppose." She looked back to Rus, who was pulling a heavy woolen coat on. She stood and bundled herself up, swallowed her feelings about Maurenia, and prepared to head out into the cold.

✦ ✦ ✦

Rus wasn't talkative as they walked. Aelis couldn't imagine he was hungover, not from just a few tots of whiskey, but he plainly didn't feel well. The morning air was sharp in the lungs, the ground was cold mud that sucked at her boots, and she was frankly no more able to make small talk than he was.

They headed up into the pine forest that abutted the inn on a small rise behind it. Aelis recognized the place where she'd met with Tun before they'd gone to track down Elmo.

Rus seemed to know the way well enough, as he didn't seem to pause to take any reference points. He stopped in a clearing, though Aelis couldn't see why. He pointed.

The cabin was so cunningly hidden, nestled in a mess of pine branches and trees of varying heights to disguise its outline, that Aelis wasn't sure she would've seen it even with her alchemy lantern, a map, and an hour to search the clearing.

"He'll likely be home and glad of the company. If he's out, I'd say don't wait inside and try to surprise him, but I don't think it's *possible* to take him unawares."

"Thank you, Rus." She turned to him. *A Warden is not meant to be priest, confessor, or counselor to the people she protects. And yet.* "I probably don't say that enough. I owe you and Martin for more than I'd like to admit since I arrived."

He shrugged. This withdrawn man was not at all like the warm, calm veteran and innkeeper she had come to know.

"What is it?" she asked finally.

"Nothing and everything, Warden. Letter days. Remind me of everything we left behind. Cities. Family. That the world moves on without us. It's nothing much. Go to your business. If I'm not back to help with breakfast, Martin will go to pieces." He made a shooing motion at her, forced a grin to his face, and at last seemed rather more like himself.

Aelis felt a dozen thoughts surface and then vanish as she knocked on Tun's door. *Why Lone Pine? Why live this close to it yet this far outside? Why've I never been to his house before? Why has he not come to my tower?*

There was a moment of silence, then Tun's careful, measured voice. "Who is it?"

"Aelis."

She strained to hear through the wood, but she caught not a sound until the door swung open and Tun's massive frame filled it.

He wasn't wearing the fringed and hooded jerkin she was used to seeing, but instead a woolen shirt that could've served nicely as a tent for a gnomish family. Even so, it strained against the muscles of his chest and arms. In the daylight, the gray-green cast of his skin was more apparent. Lying at the unbuttoned neck of his shirt was the rune-carved medallion Aelis had repaired for him.

"Warden," Tun said, grinning around his tusks. "Please come in."

He moved back out of the doorway—if he'd remained standing in it, Aelis would never have fit through—and she still had to duck past him.

She wasn't sure what she expected, but the scrupulous neatness and homeyness of the cabin was not quite it. The floor was carefully dusted stone, layered with thick woven rugs. Hides were tacked above the windows but rolled up into dangling straps to let in what sunlight the trees allowed in. The modest hearth was so clean she could've eaten off the stones, and the poker, kettle, and pot were all so scrubbed and oiled they seemed new. A table with a chair that looked hardly big enough for Tun, a bed against the far wall with only a couple of blankets, and racks full of tools along the back wall made up the furniture.

"Please, Aelis. Sit." Tun crossed the room with a step and pulled a stool out from under the table, offering it to her. She perched on it while he went to the hearth to tend the kettle.

"I was not anticipating company, or I would have prepared food."

"I'm sorry, Tun. It's not a social call." She watched him carefully as she said that and thought that perhaps his shoulders slumped, just a tad. "Or . . . not just." While Tun grabbed a poker and began raking the coals, she asked, "How's the amulet working?"

He stirred the fire, selected a log—in his hand it looked like a stick, so Aelis assumed she would've needed both of hers to pick it up—and carefully placed it atop the coals. "As well as I had hoped. Better, perhaps. The change does not come upon me unless I will it."

"Do you, ever? Or do you prefer to stay as you are?"

"As I am both the bear and the man, Aelis," Tun said slowly, deliberately, "I must occasionally choose the bear lest it overwhelm the man. And it is easier to stay in control so long as the change is my choice. I had almost forgotten what that felt like. It is a gift I will be some time repaying."

"Nonsense. No more payment is necessary than what was already made," Aelis said, even as Tun crossed past the table in two strides and pulled something out from beneath his bed and held it to her.

It was a walking stick, much like the one she had carried into the wilderness with him before. That had been plain, if made with evidently masterful craftsmanship, and a bit too long for her.

This one, she could see as she stood up and took it from his hand, would fit her perfectly. There was a soft hide wrap where her hand naturally rested, and a strap to loop around her wrist, and a sturdy metal cap at the bottom.

Just beneath the grip were carvings that drew her eye. They were small, but detailed enough to be made out. A sword with a willow leaf–shaped blade, a dagger, and a wand.

Aelis's breath caught in her throat.

"I measured your stride and height by eye while we traveled. I carefully marked where your hand rested on the staff you borrowed. It should serve you well on further walks. Perhaps as a weapon in a pinch, although it was not made for that."

Given the solidity and the weight of the wood in her hand, Aelis didn't doubt that it could be used as a weapon, and she remembered Tun whipping his own staff like a blade of grass that hit with the force of a club.

"Tun, this is . . . an astounding gift. I must make some kind of payment for it." She held it half in her hands, half back to him. He reached out and carefully closed her hands around it.

Then he reached up and tapped the amulet he wore with one thick finger. "You have already paid."

"This must've taken countless hours . . ."

He waved a hand. "I had the right length of wood ready to work. That made it easy. I am glad to see that it meets with your approval."

"It's a piece of art, Tun."

"It's a walking stick, Aelis. But it was made with care."

"There has to be something I can do."

Tun smiled gently. "I'm sure there will be."

"Tun, I hate to have to do this . . . but I came here to ask you to look at some maps."

"Maps of?"

"Old Ystain."

"What do these maps show and why must I look at them?"

"Because I need to know how to get to where they are."

Tun lowered a brow. "That only answers my second question."

"I know. Because I can't answer the first. It's . . . Warden business." That was close enough to a lie that the words felt wrong in Aelis's mouth, like rotten food or foul water. It was Warden business, her business, but the secrecy of it stank.

Duvhalin has not reported this to the Warden command. He expects he can get me to deal with this problem by myself and raise no fuss, alert no one else to it. And he may damn well be right.

Aelis wasn't sure where this sudden insight had come from, but she was certain it was right. She knew it in her bones, but she filed it away, pushed the certainty down where she'd remember it but not act on it. It was exactly the kind of leap to insight Bardun Jacques had taught would-be Wardens to embrace and be wary of at the same time.

"Warden business did not preclude my aid last time."

"No, it didn't. This is different. I've been tasked from the home office, as it were."

"Is there actually a home office?"

"Not as such. Wardens are too many and too widespread for a complex chain of command. We're loosely organized into regional Cabals, but I wouldn't know my Cabal commander from any other wizard. We also need to respond to orders from the Lyceum, depending on who sends them."

"Then how do you know whose orders you can ignore and whose you cannot?"

"A little bit of seniority, a little bit of demonstrated power. I'm rather far down the hill according to the former. When something rolls down, I can't just pass it on."

"You are telling me an awful lot of vague things without answering my questions." Tun's mouth tightened around his tusks, his eyes narrowed beneath his heavy brow. Aelis thought she read disapproval, perhaps even hurt.

"I'm sorry, Tun. I'm saying as much as I think I can."

"I assume this comes from very high up the hill."

"As high as it gets."

Tun nodded. The kettle began its low whistle, and he went to attend it. Aelis dug into her packet of papers and began pulling out the maps. By the time she had them arranged, Tun had set two mugs down on the table.

"Are you a tea drinker, Aelis?"

"I always preferred coffee if it was too early to drink wine."

Tun chuckled very quietly. A courtesy laugh, Aelis was sure. "Good. Then this will not strain your memory of tea overmuch. The real stuff is largely unattainable here. I make an herbal infusion that reminds me of the spirit of the thing, anyway."

Aelis took the mug closest to her and sniffed. It didn't exactly smell like tea, but was perhaps reminiscent. With a little time, she could probably piece together the herbs he used.

As she investigated the drink, Tun took a crock from a shelf that looked absurdly small in his hands and set it down. He opened it, took up a small wooden stick to stir the honey within. He worked a generous measure of it into his own mug and offered it to Aelis, who waved it off with a hand.

"Not much for sweet," she said, then sipped.

She was shocked at the strength of the flavor. "Gods, Tun. I think this is better than tea."

"That," he said, taking a sip of his own, the mug lost in his hand, "only proves that your opinion may be safely ignored. Now, the maps?"

Aelis scooted the sheets of parchment over to him. Immediately, Tun began rearranging them with a finger that moved far more delicately than it had any right to.

"These," he said, "are pieces of the kind of maps carried by Ystain officers in the war. They show forts, supply dumps, that kind of thing."

"Makes sense. I need to orient them in relation to Lone Pine and figure a navigable path to them."

"Must be a half dozen locations noted here. The notations are recent. Not from the war. But they match up to lines of march." Tun raised an eye toward her. "Looking for something?"

Aelis shrugged. "How do you know so much about lines of march for Ystain soldiery?"

Tun shrugged in turn, sipped his not-quite-tea. Aelis did the same.

"Tun," she said at last, in a rush, "I don't like keeping secrets from you. I wouldn't if I wasn't forced to it."

"I understand, Aelis. I do. I hope I can at least persuade you that trying to do this with winter coming on is tantamount to suicide."

"It could be worse if I wait till spring."

"That seems unlikely."

The animated dead do not feel cold. They do not know hunger, or suffer from poor morale, or worry about the boys and girls they left behind. If they're out there, they are a disaster waiting to happen. If any malevolent spirits are trapped with them, or bound to them, or commanding them, it could be so, so much worse.

Aelis wanted to say all these things, but held her tongue. "Trust me. It could be."

If they're holdovers from the war, they've waited at least eight years. They can wait a few months. Aelis dismissed the whiny, self-serving voice that said those things. They were unworthy of a Warden.

"I trust you. But I do not think you know the weather. These will take you beyond the Durndill Pass, farther north and farther west than we went after Elmo. By some distance. You could be caught and buried in snow. The wind could toss you off a high trail. A storm might turn you around, get you so lost that you never find your way back. You cannot do this on your own. You ought not to do it at all."

Aelis had to admit that Tun had a compelling argument. "That sounds . . . pretty convincing. I'll tell you what. Just help me find out how to get to the nearest location. Just the one. That may help clarify how many of these I have to visit, and how soon."

Tun frowned around his tusks, drained off the rest of his mug in one careful sip. "I will do as you ask because you are my friend. But, also because you are my friend, I am going to ask you again *not* to do even that. Not on your own."

"It's my job, Tun. I signed up. I sought it out, spent years working for it. It's not meant to be easy."

"There's difficult, and there's impossible. People who speak of doing the latter have rarely attempted the former. But," he said, holding up a hand to forestall her, "I said I would draw you your directions. And I will. It will take some time, and I will need ink, pen, parchment . . ."

"I have all of those with me," Aelis said, digging into her bag and pulling free a leather writing case, dyed Abjurer's College blue; a graduation gift from Miralla. From it, she drew out paper, pens, and ink, setting them all carefully on the table.

"I'm not going to get out of this, am I?" Tun grinned as he carefully rearranged the map fragments and shifted in his chair.

With surprising delicacy, Tun dipped a pen in ink and poised it over the paper. He set it down and ink began to soak into the fibers from the nib, forming a dark blotch. Then he stopped and looked up at Aelis.

"This is foolish. This is suicide. Some of these markings are well beyond where we ventured last time, Aelis. I cannot help you do this in good conscience."

Aelis sighed. "I lack the time to keep arguing over this. I have a duty and I will see it done. I must report faithfully that I tried."

Tun grumbled and rearranged the scraps of map and then began drawing on the fresh sheet Aelis had given him.

She found herself captivated by the quick and careful way he drew the ink across the paper. The pen was a twig in his thick, gray-green fingers, but it danced lightly. She stepped closer to the table he hunched over; not so close as to interfere with him.

His hands were bigger than the paper he worked with, but under them Aelis could recognize the features that quickly took shape, if she assumed that the first small X he made was Lone Pine. From there he filled in the path they had taken in the summer, up to the edge of the Durndill Pass and the frontier at the edge of what had once been the Earldom of Mahlgren.

"This is an old supporting fortress of Mahlhewn Keep," Tun said, quickly sketching a tower that seemed to be just north of the place he'd marked with a tiny drawing of a cave, and another close by of standing stones, further landmarks from their journey. "It is not, perhaps, the closest as the crow flies. But it is the only one with clear trails to it and back and, likely enough, the only one with any walls still standing."

"Will there be orc bands between here and there?"

"Almost certainly," Tun said. "And so long as you carry the walking stick I have made for you, you need not fear them. They will read my signature upon it."

Aelis looked at the map he'd sketched and sighed. She could just imagine the cold, the twice-a-day meals of hard bread, and sticks of dried fruit, fat, and venison, the endless walking. But she was a Warden, and that duty superseded all else.

"Thank you, Tun. Once again, I owe you the ability to carry out my duties."

"And I owe you the ability to reconcile both halves of myself," Tun said. "It is hardly a small thing."

"Then I'll see you when I return. Thank you for your help. And the tea . . . and this work of art," she added. She stood and took up the walking stick she'd leaned against the table.

She headed for the door, stopped, turned back to face Tun. "I do consider you a friend, Tunbridge. I want to be sure you know that. I have a tendency to live in my own head, to get caught up in whatever task I have in front of me. I should be a better friend. I should have come to see you. You know you are welcome at my tower anytime."

"I do not require a great deal of company," Tun said slowly. "But it would be good to occasionally share a meal and conversation with someone who is not afraid of me."

"I have books, in the tower. Not too many, a couple dozen. You're welcome to come and read them if you like."

Tun's face brightened. "That, I would enjoy very much. It has been some time since I was able to read a book."

"It's not thrilling stuff. Magical theory, histories, lives of wardens."

"It is more thrilling than talking to the pine trees, I'm sure. Now I know you have business. We have rekindled our friendship, we both understand that. There are no hard feelings. Go. Don't make me come looking for you in winter; I will be very grumpy if I have to."

30

THE VISITOR

Aelis set off for her tower. She thought wistfully of the warm interior of the inn, of hot wine and fresh bread and especially of Maurenia, but she headed straight for her tower.

The village was bustling. A few people were driving flocks to pasture—harder and harder to find as autumn really took hold—and each farm she passed was swarming with people trying to do all the work before it got too cold to do any of it.

Aelis tried rehearsing what she might say to Maurenia before she left and rejected everything she had come up with. *Thank Onoma I didn't try writing any of this down*, she thought, *or I'd have wasted half my stock of paper and ink*. She found herself thinking about her attachments at the Lyceum, her dalliances with Miralla and Humphrey, and occasionally the three of them companionably together. Those were good, enjoyable days.

Something about her time with Maurenia felt *different*, though the demands of their respective callings made it dangerous to even think of the possibilities. A recollection of what Bardun Jacques had to say about romantic attachments flitted through her mind.

"Have all the sex you want," he'd barked when one of his rambling lectures had alighted on the subject, "so long as you take the right steps. But *don't make attachments*. And by Stregon's Mighty Sack, don't fall in love. You let that kind of thinking into your mind, you or people who depend on you end up dead."

Aelis shook the memory from her head and walked on, hastening her stride, swinging her new walking stick ahead of her like she meant to make for the wilderness immediately.

When the tower came into view, though, something immediately struck her as wrong. She stopped, dropped a hand to the hilt of her sword, and focused.

She hadn't been in it since the day before, but smoke was drifting out of the chimney at the very top. *I did not leave a fire that would generate that kind of smoke*, she thought. The structure itself was in no danger.

But someone was inside it.

Immediately, Aelis's mind flashed to Dalius's attack. To the way he'd casually smacked her sword away, the equipment that had been smashed, the shard of glass that he'd driven straight into her stomach. The scar flared cold and hard, and she drew her sword.

Won't find me unprepared this time, you fucking wraith, she thought, ignoring her pedantic self that said that "wraith" was entirely the wrong term to apply to whatever Dalius had become. Sword in her right hand, stick looped against her wrist and held under her left arm, she walked boldly up to the tower. The door was unlatched, so she carefully reached out and pushed it open with the metal-shod end of her staff.

She waited, listened, took one cautious step forward, straining her senses. A ward was half summoned into the pommel of her sword. She tested the weight of her staff with her left wrist, and found it unbalanced as Tun had warned her, but probably worth the swing, given the reach it offered.

The Abjurer's litany ran across the very surface of her mind. *Fear is a response to danger. The Abjurer does not know danger. The properly prepared and ever-vigilant Abjurer is the antithesis of danger. Thus, she cannot fear.*

Expecting a horrid and twisted Dalius-like specter, she took two more slow steps down the entry hall and burst into the central round.

Only to find Maurenia sitting in one of her reading chairs, a book on her lap, a wineglass in her hand.

"You're not going to stab me with that, are you?" Maurenia turned a page without looking up from the book.

Sighing, Aelis placed the tip of her sword against the stone beneath her feet and released the power she'd been gathering. She sheathed her weapon, then sagged against her staff.

"How did you get in?" She spoke over her clasped hands on the staff, trying to dispel the surging of her blood.

"Your physical security is . . . not very good."

"Meaning?"

"The lock is a useless lump of iron. If I showed it to Timmuk, he might cry." At last, Maurenia looked up. Aelis set her stick against the wall and took a few steps into the interior.

"I didn't take you for the sneak-out-in-the-morning kind," Maurenia said, but the warmth in her voice softened the criticism.

"I'm not. But I had business."

"What kind?"

"Warden business. What other kind could I have?"

Maurenia carefully closed the book. *Lives of the Wardens*, Aelis noted, and was glad to see the care with which Maurenia treated it.

"You're thinking something else that you don't want to say. Out with it."

Aelis took a deep breath. "I'm about to leave."

"On Warden business, no doubt. Where to?"

"Into the wilderness. Again."

"Where in the wilderness?"

"I'm not entirely sure, and even if I did know, I really can't say."

"This is something to do with that letter I brought you, isn't it? The one with the death's head on it."

Aelis thought that silence was probably as good as a direct answer in the moment, but she couldn't think of anything else to do or say. In order to avoid responding, she peeled off her gloves, scarf, and cloak and tossed them onto the nearest flat surface in a heap.

Maurenia swept to her feet and immediately picked up Aelis's discarded garments. Cloak in hand, she brushed past Aelis, folded the scarf neatly, lined the gloves up, and set them down flush with the edge of the table. The cloak she hung on one peg of a board that someone had hung up by the entryway when the tower was renovated.

"Tidy sort, eh?"

"For the last thirty years I've lived out of a backpack or a trunk. Stop trying to change the subject. I knew that death's head was bad news."

"It's just an old symbol for one of the Colleges. An obsolete symbol. But someone of rank insists on using it and no one has the authority to make him cease." Aelis found her legs unexpectedly weak, so she sank into the nearest hard wooden chair in front of the worktable.

"Is it going to be dangerous?"

"Wouldn't be Warden work if it wasn't."

"Last I checked, Warden work also encompassed casting wards to hold sheep in their pen, treating ankles that twisted when their owner stepped in sheep shit . . ."

Aelis laughed lightly. "Believe me, Maurenia, the last thing I want to do is leave while you're here."

"Then don't. Give it a couple of weeks. Gather intelligence. Lines of communication are so slow that they'll never know the difference."

"To someone with enough rank in the Lyceum, communication can move a lot faster than you'd think. But it's not even about that, it's—"

"About obligation. About who you are, what you signed up for. Believe it or not, Aelis, I understand that."

She thrilled to hear her name fall from Maurenia's lips, in her rich, deep voice.

"That I understand it doesn't mean I like it. Especially not at this time of year. Surely you don't plan to go alone," Maurenia went on.

"I think I have to."

Maurenia walked up to the chair and laid one hand on Aelis's shoulder. "Why is your hand trembling?"

Aelis sighed, and sagged in her chair. "Because the last time I walked in on my tower occupied by someone else, it was Dalius, and he nearly killed me."

The scar on her stomach flared with pain, though the anatomist in her knew it had no reason to. In her mind, suddenly, Dalius loomed over her. Every breath hurt. Her hand scrambled for her orrery, found it, was sheathed in claws so black they drank the light.

Maurenia rested a hip on the chair behind her and placed both hands on Aelis's shoulder, squeezing gently. Then she reached out to the hand Aelis had flung toward her orrery and guided it away from the heavy silver base of the machine.

"I'd prefer you didn't brain me with that any more than you stabbed me, honestly," she murmured.

Aelis laughed, and the sound of laughter from her own throat brought her back to the moment, to the warmth in the tidy tower she'd come to think of as home, to the woman whose hands were on her.

"I wouldn't try to brain *anything* with that. Alchemically treated silver is worth too much, for one. And I can make much better use of the magic it stores."

"It stores magic?" Maurenia leaned over the table, suddenly all questions. "How much? What can it be used for? Is that how it works?"

"A lot, anything I want, and yes. And before you start asking about gear teeth or pinions or rods or any of that, I don't know a single thing about the internal mechanism. As long as I put magic into it regularly, it runs."

"You mean you don't know how it operates?"

"I don't need to," Aelis said. "Is asking me questions about magical equipment really why you came all the way up here in the cold?" The weakness in her legs and the trembling in her hands having subsided, she stood up and snaked an arm around Maurenia's waist.

Maurenia looked right into her eyes and Aelis felt her knees weaken again for a moment. "I came back because I wanted you. You wanted me. More than that, probably. Eight hundred miles each way on a wagon with the Dobrusz brothers is a high price just for *wanting*. Let's just not look at it too closely. Nothing will kill an affair faster than *talking* about it."

"Then let's not talk at all," Aelis said, leaning forward and aiming her lips for Maurenia's, only to find them stopped by the half-elf's finger laid across them.

"You," Maurenia said, "need to pack. I will help. Then we can *not* talk."

Aelis tried not to sigh in frustration and only half succeeded. She stepped away and thought she heard Maurenia chuckle before the half-elf spoke again.

"How long are you planning to be gone? What's the maximum length of time you think you can stay in the field alone? And what do you *need* to bring?"

Maurenia's tone was suddenly businesslike, and it snapped Aelis out of her reverie. The twinge of pain in her stomach, the memory of Dalius, were gone. She had tasks. She was a Warden, and she would see them done.

◆   ◆   ◆

With Maurenia's expert advice, it didn't take long till Aelis had a bag packed. Maurenia had vetoed many things Aelis had seen as essential—soap, more than one spare piece of any kind of clothing, a sewing kit—and had convinced her to dress in light layers she could discard or add to at need.

"I'll put together a tinderbox for you," Maurenia said, "since an alchemy lamp will do for light but not heat, not given the amount of fuel you said you'd have to carry. Dry wood ought to be plentiful enough. Too bad you're not an Invoker."

Aelis sniffed. "Invokers think with their staves and cause as many problems as they solve. I have mastered subtler and more refined magics."

"More refined magics wouldn't melt snowfall that was threatening to hem you in somewhere to die. A big gout of flame might."

"And make it just as likely to cause a chain reaction that would bury me anyway. An Abjurer—which I happen to be—can solve the problem much more easily."

"Of course," Maurenia said. She seemed to be on the verge of saying more when there was a knock at the tower door. "Expecting anyone?"

Aelis looked up and realized that what light filtered down from the upper levels of her tower had long since faded into gray.

"Probably dinner," Aelis said. It was, in fact, having been brought up from the village by a farm lad on horseback, his cheeks red and puffing in the cold. He stayed only long enough to see Aelis open the door before retreating, having left behind a large basket from which emanated appetizing smells of bread and mushroom stew.

There wasn't much cheer while they ate despite Aelis opening two bottles of the precious wine Maurenia had brought with the post. The second bottle followed them into Aelis's curtained-off bedroom, where it stood, mostly full, on the bedside table.

"You still have a chance not to do this, you know," Maurenia whispered, after time had passed, and they lay together, sweating, under Aelis's thinnest blanket.

"Not if I want to stay a warden, I don't."

Maurenia rolled onto her back. Unwilling to let go of the contact, Aelis laid her head on the half-elf's shoulder, felt the brush of silky hair against her forehead, curtaining over her eyes.

"I know. I just don't like the idea of it."

"Getting protective?"

"Maybe. That a problem?"

Aelis was silent a moment. She felt Maurenia breathing underneath her, watched the rise and fall of her skin. "It's not that I mind hearing it. But I don't *need* protecting. I *do* the protecting."

"Around here, that may be true. Down in a city, that may be true. Out in the wilderness, though? Everyone needs protecting there."

"I've been there already."

"The worst thing you can be is overconfident."

"I think I'm just going to be doing reconnaissance, if I'm being honest. Figure out what's there and what's to be done about it."

"What do you expect to find?"

Animated corpses. Probably armed and armored. Some might remember their training. But hopefully no animating intelligence behind them, which makes them a great deal easier to deal with.

"I don't know," Aelis said aloud. Then, deciding that answering further questions was likely to be dangerous, she tossed both her and Maurenia's hair back and considered the expanse of skin before her.

31

THE FORT

They both woke early, before the sun even threatened to rise. The tower was cold and Aelis did not lay a fire, for she wasn't sure when she'd return. The only step she did take was to put a Third Order Necromantic spell into her orrery, hoping to keep it powered for as long as she might be gone. She and Maurenia, their skin covered in gooseflesh, dressed in silence. Aelis belted on her sword and dagger over her heaviest coat and slung her rucksack over her shoulders.

Aelis could feel Maurenia's eyes on her as they walked to the door of the tower. She pulled it securely closed, locked it, warded it. She found Maurenia's hand, warm and callused, with her own, and squeezed. They kissed; there was passion in it, but it was restrained.

"We'll be here another week, maybe two," Maurenia murmured, her lips moving against Aelis's cheek. "I'd better see you again before we go. I'll start breaking pieces off the wagon if I have to."

"I'll try," Aelis said, and the words felt small and futile to her. Then she hitched at her rucksack, adjusted her belt, and they went their separate ways, the half-elf back to town, the Warden on a hard northerly course.

* * *

Well, Aelis thought four days later, *this is the dumbest fucking thing I've ever done.* Tun's map had marked the course well for her and she'd made good time, driven by the twin lashes of misery and loneliness.

If the map was still good—and she'd passed the cave and collapsed palisade she recognized from Nath's fallen Mahlgren encampment—she had only a few more hours of cold, hungry, boring march.

She found herself reflecting on the long marches and runs Abjurer students were put through, with Vosghez leading them all in effortless, maddening silence. It simply wasn't right that a dwarf could make five miles around the Lyceum grounds without so much as breathing hard when his stride should've put him at a disadvantage. And yet, in that second year—when theory ended and practical study began in earnest—she'd never seen anyone match him, let alone pass him.

"True, five miles along well-paved and even roads, with only light grading, don't compare to a single mile of hard-frozen fucking wilderness," Aelis muttered as she swung her stick ahead of her for purchase. She'd amused herself for the days of constant march by imagining how each of her closest professors would've managed it. Urizen would've Charmed someone into carrying him. Lavanalla would probably have floated above the grass or flitted from tree branch to tree branch. Vosghez would've lowered his head and plowed on, covering the entire distance she did in half the time.

Bardun Jacques would've reshaped the landscape around him using the sheer force of profanity, which, Aelis reasoned, might actually have been an eighth College in his hands. Duvhalin, on the other hand, would've used some of his vast personal wealth to buy a carriage and enough teams of horses to replace the inevitable losses.

"Maybe a sleigh and a string of . . . whatever animals pull sleighs. Oxen? Who can know," Aelis murmured. "Maybe a gods-damned elephant."

The joke was unworthy of her, of her office, power, task, and teacher. But she didn't feel worthy of much; she was tired, cold, hungry, and increasingly angry.

But when the crumbling wall of stone appeared in her view on a slight rise in the distance, her anger melted away.

"Finally." Here was the task, the job. "You know, if this turns out to be a pile of rotting bones, I can't decide if I'll be relieved or furious."

She was not in the mood for doing the sensible thing, or for planning. So she went straight at the nearest face of the hill, using her walking stick to pull herself up the fairly steep grade. She was halfway up before her stick dislodged a large rock.

Aelis had just enough reaction time to call up a ward—Hogarth's Aetherial Greaves—before the rock would strike her and shatter her shin. The rock hit the barrier, sending striating lines of force up the barely visible blue glow and splintering it. But the ward held, and the rock went tumbling away.

Unfortunately, though the ward deflected the rock, she'd let go of her stick in order to cast. Her arms pinwheeled as she felt her balance tilting back, back, until she was looking at the sky and rolling ass over appetite back down the hill.

Aelis decided it was best to remain prone and contemplative for several moments, despite the cold of the ground, to give time for any fractures to report in.

None did. She shook each limb, one by one, lifted her head, wriggled her toes. She was cold and mud-spattered, and would be sore, but she seemed to be intact.

"Better reconnaissance this time," she muttered as she pulled herself up. The stick still stood halfway up the hill, like a pole stripped of its flag, taunting her. "Damned if I'm going to let it go that easily."

Aelis spent the next half hour making a circuit of the spur of hill. As far as she could tell, only the northeastern corner of the old fort still stood in any meaningful way.

"Any barracks-crypt is going to be hidden," she muttered as she eyed a couple of different routes to the top. "Not at ground level." As she spoke, she began winding her way up the hill. Walking on the angle along the leeward side of the hill wasn't easy without her stick, and once or twice she had to double over and scramble up on all fours, but it was better than attempting the straight-up approach again only to take the fast route to the bottom.

By the time she'd circled back to where she'd fallen from and snatched her walking stick from the ground, Aelis felt her dignity had largely recovered. She resettled her grip on the good length of ash and muttered a smug *fuck you* to the wilderness in general and this hill in particular.

Then she went looking for a crypt.

+ + +

The grinning skull at the base of the torch sconce mocked her.

"Really, Dalius? Are we going to be *this* cliché? A skull sconce?"

A few years of exposure to wind and weather hadn't completely eroded its features, and just as Aelis thought, the teeth were keys, of a kind. She danced her fingers lightly over them, making sure not to exert enough pressure to trigger any of them.

It was, of course, the only sconce to have a skull at the base of its fixture. When people had, in the days before such things were barred, resorted to barracks-crypt full of undead soldiers, they were always hidden. Precisely how to hide them became a question of taste, style, and money spent on builders and wizards who fancied themselves clever.

"One skull sconce in an entire building might as well be a glaring beacon and a bard singing about the undead stored beneath this floor," Aelis muttered.

There was, of course, the somewhat less easily solved problem: What combination would open the door or hatch or sliding stones?

Aelis set down her rucksack, loosened her coat, and dug out her alchemy lamp. She sparked it to life, adjusted knobs on the side to narrow and tighten the beam, and brought it over to the skull for a closer examination.

"More or less anatomically correct for a human," she muttered as she looked at the arrangement of the jaw, the lines that showed the meeting of the skull plates. "Impressive, actually." It was the teeth that interested her most, though. All thirty-two possible teeth, and each one with just enough give to suggest it could be pushed.

"Well. Fuck. Thirty-two possible keys is . . ." She tried to do the math in her head on the number of potential combinations and was stopped cold. "I can't just guess. Got to approach it more carefully."

There were probably traps built into a wrong combination, she reasoned. "Most likely an alarm, summoning living guards. I don't have to worry over that. But if I give in to blind guessing I'll be here till I'm buried in a snowdrift."

She let her mind drift, stopped focusing on the problem and started thinking, loosely, of what she knew that had led her here.

Dalius. Mahlgren. Mahlhewn Keep. Old Ystain. Barracks-crypts were built for wars, but not necessarily the war, the most recent one.

By the time the war between the Three Crowns and the orcs had reached its hottest point, traditional Necromancy—animating the dead—had been officially banned. Here and there, Aelis knew, there had been calls to ease off the ban, or at least turn a blind eye, to provide troops who could fight the orcs at lower risk to themselves. Having been a privileged child growing up hundreds of miles from the nearest battle, Aelis had been only dimly aware of the debate, and by the time she was enrolled in the College of Necromancy, it had been counted among the Things One Didn't Bring Up.

Aelis pulled herself back from undergraduate reminiscences and tried to concentrate on the problem at hand without focusing on it in such a way that she wouldn't see the answer. It was a difficult thing to do, like finding the proper mindset to answer a riddle.

Bardun Jacques used to devote entire lectures to proposing impossible riddles. Occasionally someone would shout out the answer immediately, which would make the old Warden nod. Then he'd propose something even more ridiculous and sneer while students ventured haphazard guesses.

"The point of riddling," he'd say, "is to teach you to think slantways. To get your mind out of books and into the older, barer facts of the world. To teach you to trust your intuition, your gut, the part of you that knows things it can't quite put voice to."

Aelis shook her head to clear it, and shifted where she knelt on the cold stones.

"This was designed by a Necromancer. An Anatomist. I'm sure of that. The detail is too perfect. So I can number the teeth." She dug into her rucksack again, found a small sheaf of loosely bound parchment, and dug out a charcoal stick. She quickly sketched the skull with precise detail, separating it into upper and lower halves, and numbered the teeth as a surgeon would, beginning on the back left Bridegroom tooth and counting forward from one.

"If every tooth is a key, it's not a random arrangement of numbers," Aelis muttered. On another sheet of her little notebook, she started taking stock of her flitting thoughts.

What unit housed here? Could be a designation.

Date fort was built.

Date barracks-crypt was finished.

After she'd written that one she frowned. "Damn well better not be that one. Impossible to know unless a miraculous trove of records is somewhere nearby." She scanned the corner of the largely fallen-down stone building. Unfortunately for her there were no stout chests brimming with wonderfully preserved war diaries and construction records. Just broken rocks, blown leaves, pine needles, and rodents' nests.

She couldn't let go of the idea of a date, though.

"I'm still in Mahlgren, or I would be if Mahlgren still existed. Dates that are important to . . ."

Her mind flashed to Nath's cave, to the tapestries hanging there depicting the submission of the last king of Mahlgren to the king of Old Ystain. While some people would view such an event as a catastrophic end to an old order, the people of Mahlgren had come to view it as a noble sacrifice. Donnus I had saved thousands of lives from a war he couldn't have won, or so the historical narrative went. Aelis wasn't sure how much of that was true or false, as she'd never been interested enough in regional histories to really dig into the primary sources.

But dates, dates she could dredge up.

The Mahlgren surrender stuck in her head. She'd try that first. "Nine-thirty-two," she muttered, and even as her hands slid along the skull, clicking over the teeth numbered nine, three, and two, she was certain she was right.

And then there was an empty-sounding click, and nothing happened.

"You idiot," she chided herself. With newfound confidence, certainty surging in her again, she clicked over the ninth tooth—the second of the two front incisors—and then walked her fingertip down to the very back bottom molar and pressed.

She was shocked when the tooth broke open on her fingertip, grazing it with a sharp edge. There was a click of gears turning, another crack. Aelis backed slowly away from the sconce, swinging her alchemy lamp toward her hand to inspect it. There was only a minor abrasion, the skin barely nicked. She squatted close to the sconce again, brought the light to bear on the tooth that had broken off.

Buried beneath the tooth were two vials that had been crushed together by minuscule gears. Two reagents, she guessed, meant to mingle and then release a gas or a contact poison. But the reagents had long since dissipated and the trap had become inert.

As she was cursing her stupidity and rubbing her abraded skin, Aelis suddenly remembered the droning voice of her childhood history tutor explaining the different calendars and dating systems each kingdom had used prior to coming together under the Three Crowns and the Estates House.

"Old Ystain was still on its original calendar, which was . . ."

She slid her fingers back over the teeth and clicked the ones she numbered seven and twenty-five. They both felt more solid, harder to depress. But when they did, she heard a much louder, grating sound, stone against stone.

She turned around just in time to see her rucksack and walking stick sinking out of sight as the stones they rested upon gave way.

32

THE CRYPT

Aelis's fear that the stick or her rucksack might have fallen far was quickly allayed when she saw that the stones that gave way only slid back to reveal a narrow underground passage. She fiddled with the settings on her lamp, opening the shutters and increasing the diffusion of the lens, so that instead of a small, tight beam it threw softer light in a small circle around her. She clipped it to her belt and lowered her legs through the open trapdoor.

She let herself down carefully, her boots a foot or so above the drop before she let go, and landed easily. The crumbled remnants of a rope ladder lay in a pile on the uneven dirt floor. The tunnel it revealed curved away to her left and her lamplight showed roughly worked stone walls. She took a moment to lash her walking stick to the rucksack and slung it back over her shoulder.

Aelis tested her sword in its scabbard, drawing the first few inches clear to loosen it. She did the same with her dagger.

I'm either about to die or this is the beginning of my chapter in Lives of the Wardens: The Post-war Years, Aelis thought.

She wrapped her hand around the hilt of her sword again. She drew calm from the willow-leaf blade and from her Abjurer's litany.

Fear is a response to danger. The Abjurer does not know danger. The properly prepared and ever-vigilant Abjurer is the antithesis of danger. Thus, she cannot fear.

Then she trudged on.

It wasn't a long walk, and took no more than a few moments, while she did consider practical possibilities: that the tunnel may have caved in or that it could in fact cave in as she traversed its length.

And if it does, I'll call a ward, wait for it to settle, and deal with whatever comes.

The tunnel graded downward and it wasn't long till the lamp on her belt was revealing stone that was clearly more worked than the rest of the tunnel.

Aelis turned her lamp to its highest setting; it would burn through its fuel quickly, but she needed to see what she was dealing with.

She almost wished she hadn't.

Before her was a vast stone door without visible hinges, no lock, no handles, no place to wedge a pry bar or chisel, even if she had one.

The door greeted her with a grinning skull, the match of the seal on the letter that had brought her here. The match, she knew, of the ring that only one Magister of the College of Necromancy still wore, the match to the seal he carried ostentatiously on a thick chain around his neck and likely enough the pattern embroidered on his bedrobe.

Before it, on a slim pedestal, sat a simple stone bowl.

Aelis dimmed her lamp and unclipped it from her belt, lifting it up as she approached the pedestal. As she looked over it, it was clear that the bowl and the slim length of stone it sat on were of a piece; a tiny hole in the bottom of the bowl led down into the pedestal, but she hadn't the light to see any inner workings.

A few possibilities suggested themselves. She dismissed the first out of hand.

"Not even the most desperate would design a barrier that required actual human sacrifice to open," she muttered, though she didn't feel much better.

It was possible that it required only a drop of blood, and that she could provide.

"But," she brought herself up short with a whisper, "it's possible that it has a Blood Catalogue of every specific person empowered to open it linked to the mechanism, and I'm not going to be on that list."

She began ticking off the things that it could do if someone not in such a Catalogue attempted to open it. *Most likely, nothing. Second, set off an alarm. Third, some kind of mechanical trap, but linking magic to gears is rarely predictable or worth the effort and time will have taken its toll. Fourth, respond with some magical mayhem.*

There could be passwords, but those would be closely held or routinely changed or both.

"If I can't get in, doesn't that mean that anything dangerous couldn't get out?" She considered this possibility a moment, imagined running straight back to Lone Pine, convincing Maurenia to stay the winter, hopping into bed and not getting out until spring.

This vision was abruptly interrupted with one of undead soldiers clawing and digging their way out of a none-too-secure barracks-crypt and descending on Lone Pine and other settlements, mindlessly seeking battle without any directing intelligence to control them.

Given the way the fortress was collapsing, Aelis couldn't be sure that whatever was behind the death's-head door was still there, much less sealed in. And she had a duty to know for certain. It was even possible that enough degradation of the fortress could trigger orders that had been laid on any of the undead within, and that they were attempting to burrow their way out even now.

Aelis considered other ways to open the door. Gathering her will, she walked to within arm's reach, called a simple First Order Necromantic Pulse into her hand, reached out, and laid her power against the stone.

The right eye of the skull blazed with a brief blue light, and words sounded in Aelis's mind.

Prove your mastery of the First Art to open me, the long-dormant spell told her, and her heart sank. She caught herself readying a fist to smash uselessly against the stone skull. It mocked her with its grin, promising malevolence and danger, and she wanted to have Tun by her side, if only to see whether it could stand up to his strength.

But in the end, she turned and walked back to the entrance to the tunnel.

It took a strong ward to give her some lift and a moment of struggling, but she pulled herself back up onto the floor above with a strength born of anger, and felt shame at what she knew she was about to do.

+ + +

Until the gray squirrel, fat and fluffy for the winter, climbed into her lap, Aelis wasn't entirely sure she could use Enchantment to lure an animal that close to her. She had used a powerful Enchantment on a bear, but of course that bear had proven to be Tun, and she hadn't spent much time puzzling out which part of him she'd enchanted.

But with a simple Beckoning, a gray squirrel had hopped right out of the nearest tree and onto her shoulder, then into her outstretched hand as she sat down, cross-legged, and contemplated it.

With her power laid over its small and unfocused mind, the squirrel lacked all fear. It sat in her palm, twitching occasionally, its puffed tail flicking here and there, changing position, blinking up at her.

She readied herself, with an anatomist's certainty, to snap its neck in order to use it to open the crypt.

Then she imagined Tun standing over her, watching what she was doing, and she let her tiny thread of Enchantment slip. The animal darted away. Aelis stood up, swatted snow off the back of her coat, and stomped back into the fortress, seething at herself.

She swung her alchemical lamp back and forth as she went, looking for what she needed.

"I don't have to animate a corpse," she muttered. "I just have to make the spell on the door understand that I *can*."

Strictly speaking, she wasn't supposed to attempt to bend spells the way she was going to. And even were she sitting in a laboratory or writing a theoretical paper, she couldn't be sure it would work.

But out here, in the wilderness, with the cold searing her lungs with every breath and her legs throbbing and feet hurting and stomach wondering when she was going to eat something other than bread and dried fruit mixed with fat, she had no doubts at all. It would work. What was magic, after all, if not bending the rules of the world? And if the rules of magic couldn't be bent, what could?

Aelis had only cast the spell she was about to attempt once before, under tightly controlled, closely observed laboratory conditions. She hadn't had to do anything else that day, just cast that one spell and then put down the resulting animated corpse however she chose.

She had been certain from the moment she entered the laboratory that she would not forget the events.

+ + +

The corpse had been a man, and he had been dead for some time. A week at least, perhaps longer. Necromancy labs had enchantments laid into their foundation stones, their doorjambs, their tables, their instruments, that would preserve a corpse a dazzlingly long time. The lengthy incisions in the man's torso indicated that his chest had been opened and most of the major organs had been removed. The eyes and mouth had been carefully sewn shut, and his genitals had been removed and the skin sutured over. Likely enough this same corpse had provided surgical and anatomical practice to a younger set of students.

All instruments and furniture other than the surgical table on which the corpse lay had been removed. The door was locked behind Aelis when she entered. She was allowed to carry only the implements of her Colleges. For most, that had meant only the Anatomist's Dagger, perhaps a Seer's Diadem or a Conjurer's Mirror.

For Aelis it had meant her dagger, her sword, and her wand. Though she knew full well the latter would be useless, she liked the feel of it in her sleeve. And though the sword was not the custom willow-leaf blade that would be made to her hand after she passed her Abjurer's test, the weight on her hip felt right.

A disguised, disembodied voice filled the laboratory, but she felt the slithering tones of Archmagister Duvhalin behind it.

"Animate the corpse. Give it three orders. Untether it. Then dismiss it in whatever manner you see fit."

Aelis drew her dagger, and was already gathering her will through the hilt. In the stark light of the alchemy lamps overhead, the blade glittered darkly in her fist.

Animating the corpse was laughably, seductively easy. The power gathered in her like ice on a pane of glass. It chilled her, but something in it was beautiful; there was something there to stare at and marvel over.

Was *this* what was forbidden to her? To her College? This simple power, the First Art, as the original Magisters of Necromancy had called it, that weighed in her hand like a dark and glittering gem? What small minds would sever her from this beauty?

Then she crushed the "gem" in her fist and sprinkled it over the body. A black-purple glow rose out of the chalk-white skin of the corpse, and it sat up.

Aelis knew that, with its lungs removed, the corpse made no actual noise. But her mind told her there was a wheeze, a moan, all the same. She knew, in the sensible, studious part of her mind, that what she heard was simply a pocket of air being forced through the tiny stitches in its mouth by the unnatural motion.

Aelis gathered more power into her hand, shaped it into commands.

Stand.

Walk a circuit of the room.

Lie down upon the table.

The corpse stood. It looked at her, if a thing without eyes or functional sense organs could be said to look. It walked around the room, in slow, halting steps. Amplified by the silence and emptiness of the room, its foot-falls were soft, wet-sounding things that threatened Aelis with gooseflesh. She was not shy around corpses, not unused to the sights of the body, and still there was something undeniably wrong about what she was doing now that her mind was not filled with, and deceived by, its own power.

The corpse returned to the table, lifted itself up with strength, if not grace, and lay down.

Aelis severed her will from it, and took a moment to breathe.

Something, something she could not name and did not want to know, was suddenly in the room with her. Something cold and hard and un-speakably malevolent. It ignored her.

The corpse sat up.

Instinct took over. She shifted her dagger to her left hand, drew her sword with her right, summoned a ward. The corpse lunged for her. Her sword took it in the chest, just off the centerline where the heart would be, tearing its skin like paper, splintering its already once-broken breast-bone and ribs.

On it came. The broken bones and torn flesh that would be the undoing of a living attacker were no deterrent to the already dead.

Her dagger lashed out, quick, vicious slashes. It wasn't until the third one that she recalled that it wasn't a true Anatomist's blade, had not been consecrated and enchanted to her yet, and that it required her own wit and will to work any magic.

She slashed low with her sword, felt the blade crunching through the corpse's knee and sending it toppling to the floor. She lashed out with a boot, the force of her kick sending it skidding, buying her time to take a couple of quick steps backward and gather herself.

Aelis formulated the words of a Dismissal, a Second Order work of Necromancy. She stepped forward, planted her boot hard into the corpse's chest, breaking more of its ribs, its spine, and plunged her dagger down into its skull.

Harsh, irregular syllables tore themselves from her throat. An absence of light outlined her hand in darkness. The thing beneath her foot thrashed once more as the black force around her hand sank into it.

The air went cold. Breath stung in Aelis's throat. The animated corpse ceased all its twitching and she almost felt as if fingers of ice twined them-selves around her neck for a moment, and then were gone.

"What the FUCK was that?" she shouted as the door that had been locked behind her opened and three black-robed, hooded Necromancers filed in.

"That," Archmagister Duvhalin solemnly intoned as he removed the mask that concealed his condescending smile, "was very nearly your final failure in the College of Necromancy, Miss de Lenti."

Aelis swallowed her immediate impulse, which was to correct him to *Lady de Lenti*, knowing he'd just somehow humiliate her further over it.

"However," the Archmagister went on, his smile still aimed at her like a weapon, "you also have now seen the reason we no longer allow ourselves to animate the dead."

✦ ✦ ✦

Aelis grasped the hilt of her dagger. It wasn't necessary to draw it out, only to attune her senses through it and send them casting out in the world around her. Through the hilt she felt a faint pulse; the material she was looking for was nearby. She took a step forward, carefully monitoring the strength of the pulse in the dagger. It seemed to weaken, so she stepped back to where she'd been standing. Then she took another, to her left. The signal strengthened.

It took nearly a quarter of an hour, but following the pulsing of her dagger, she found what she'd been looking for in a corner, buried beneath pine needles and dirt: a knot of bone. She pulled it free and quickly dusted some of the dirt on it away with one hand. It looked like a piece of the hip joint of an immature deer. There was no telling how long it had lain there, but Aelis was sure it would suffice. Along with it, she scraped up just a handful of dirt.

"There's no reason this shouldn't work," she muttered.

Carefully she set the bone down in the center of the offering bowl, then strung out dirt to either side in thin lines.

Not every animated dead needed to be a skeleton or a walking skin. For a powerful enough Necromancer, a pile of bone could be raised into any shape the animating intelligence could control.

Ideally, of course, she'd have special training for this, and a certain amount of Conjuring was necessary, at least in theory.

"Fuck theory," Aelis muttered as she took off one of her gloves and drew the tip of her dagger across the palm of her hand. She squeezed two droplets of blood along each line of dirt. Then she took a deep breath and searched her memory for the words she'd need.

The page of Aldayim's *Advanced Necromancy* swung up before her eyes.

Necromantic Constructs made of more than one being, often called Chimeras, are dangerous and often uncontrollable . . .

Aelis found the words and spoke them despite the warning. She watched the bone rise out of the bowl atop the pillar and the little lines of dirt coalesce around her blood into limbs. They reached out like tendrils and sank into the inner curves of the little hip bone, lifting it further.

There was a sound as of a bell ringing. The hip bone and its two limbs of bloody mud stood up, wavering, on the bowl. Then there was a lance of purple-black light, and it vanished.

The skull craned forward, the jaws parted, and steps began to unfold from behind the teeth.

The doors open, Necromancer. The Barracks-Crypts of Mahlgren are at your disposal.

Aelis drew her sword and dagger and hoped she wouldn't have to use them.

33

THE SKELETONS

When Aelis stepped through the door, she was already dividing her will into two components: the wards she was gathering through her sword, and the banishments and severings she was preparing to call into her dagger.

Before any of that could matter, though, there was threat assessment. The barracks she entered was blessedly small. Barracks-crypt was a misleading name, of course, as most storage places for undead soldiers were neither. Initially, either such space might have been used to store them simply because there was room there. Later, warehouses or even tents had been used. Later still, of course, hidden chambers such as this had been built.

The commitment to style had ended with the switch and the door, Aelis thought. A plain iron chandelier hung in the center of the ceiling, held in place with chains, the candles on it long since burned or crumbled away. The room was a simple circle of damp, mossy stone.

The damp, Aelis quickly realized, was going to be her ally, because it had caused the weapons clutched by bare-boned hands to rust and rot away.

Eight skeletons stood against the wall. Eight pairs of cold dark eyes sparked to life in their skulls, which turned to her with one uniform movement.

Somewhere there lay a control rod that would allow her to expand her will to cover all of them and control them directly. With it to hand, she could order them to combat one another until they were reduced to a harmless rubble to be thoroughly dismissed at her leisure.

Without a control rod, she could dismiss the animation of two of them at any one time, perhaps, if she had no distractions and no other demands on her power. But she'd already taken on several tasks with her magic that day.

So she re-settled her hands on her weapons and went to work. The skeletons stood up. The rattling they made was unnerving, like putting a bundle of thin sticks in a leather case and shaking it lightly.

The skeletons did not seem to see her as a threat until she gave them a reason to. She went immediately to her left. With three quick slashes of her Anatomist's Dagger, one of the animated dead lost its skull and then its arms. The spine and legs stood for a moment or two before collapsing, as she had hoped; these had been designed with care and built to release when damaged beyond usefulness.

A counter in her head clicked from eight to seven. And she knew it was about to get more dangerous.

She whirled to face the room, putting the inactive undead behind her. The remaining seven pushed off the wall. Rust showered to the floor as they lifted their arms and the weapons they held crumbled. Whole pieces of their crude short swords fell to the floor; the rotted wooden hilt of one gave way when the skeleton's hand tightened around it, and the pitted blade slipped from its fingers.

Two of the skeletons were worse enough for wear that they simply fell apart as they tried to move. The joints had been wired together with strips of cured hide and tendon, and in some cases had given way.

Five.

Aelis tried hard not to think too much about exactly who or what had provided those strips. Sometimes a Necromancer worked with what they had to hand.

Even so, this construction was better for her than copper wires or hempen rope, because these were technically dead flesh.

And her knife would cut through them as if they were seafoam.

She didn't wait for them to come on. She called a ward, a simple First Order, often called the Buckler, centered around her right hand. It was an awkward stance for her, preferring as she did to wield only the one blade at a time, but she'd had rudimentary training in it.

She led with the ward as though it were a shield and knocked aside the skeleton's ruined sword. Once again, three sweeps with her dagger and an undead soldier fell apart before her.

Four.

Aelis had less taste for subtlety as two of the remaining charged at her from the same direction. She dropped the ward in her right hand and called on more of her will. A Second Order Necromantic Bane surrounded her left fist in a coruscating cloud of purple-black. She bent her knees lightly, cocked her fist, and punched straight through the rib cage and spine of the skeleton in front of her with a form that would've earned an approving nod from Lavanalla.

It was true that with the Bane called to hand, she had no need of form. It was the magic that did the work, not her fist, not the turning of her trunk and the power driven up through her legs and torso.

But competency pleased her. A thing well executed was a joy in itself, and she felt a surge of joyous anger.

Three. The one immediately following managed to raise its blade in self-defense. She battered it aside and cut savagely into the thing with the flat of her sword, sparing the edge the contact with bone. She battered in its skull, dealt it wounds that would've killed any normal attacker, and chipped the edge of her sword despite her care.

Two, you fucking idiot, and they are dumping their Animation into each other. Fuck.

The realization came in a rush as, cut down to a quarter of their number, the skeletons of this particular barracks suddenly became a lot more lively. The lights in their skulls grew larger, brighter.

Instead of coming at her one at a time, the two skeletons stopped, then began advancing at her from opposite sides.

She hadn't counted on anything that sophisticated. Speed was her ally. She rushed to the nearest one, even as she heard the shuffle of skeletal feet behind her. She led with her sword, then planted a foot wide and spun, pivoting on the toe of her planted foot. Her dagger swept at its neck on the backspin; she was lucky, hit tendon, felt the skull go slack and tumble halfway off. Behind it now, with it between her and its remaining barracks-mate, she kicked it hard and sent it straight into the other.

A clattering of bone against bone like some nightmare mummer troupe rattled in Aelis's ears. She was settling into a defensive stance when she realized that the second skeleton had gripped the one she'd kicked and smashed it into the wall. The bones lost their guiding force and fell to pieces on the floor.

Then the last remaining undead leapt at her with a speed few mortals could match, clawing for her eyes.

She felt the tips of its fingers scrape across her cheek, but she only needed to put one hand around it.

Aelis had no need to hold anything else back, squaring up against her last enemy. Aldayim's Lash was a Fourth Order Necromantic Banishment.

It snapped in her mind like a whip. Her hand, wrapped around the skeleton's arm, buzzed with tingling, cold power. She discharged it.

The skeleton disintegrated.

Suddenly unbalanced, Aelis took three fast steps backward, arms flailing, till she hit the wall. She sank down, breathing heavily, till she was sitting against the cold, dusty, bone-strewn floor.

Aelis decided to give herself a moment before springing back to her feet. She made it about one third of the way to her feet, then sat back down heavily.

"I'll just sit a moment," she wheezed to the empty crypt. "Bide my thoughts. Carve some notches on the hilt of my sword. Eight of you fuckers," she said, kicking feebly at the nearest pile of bones.

To be fair, you only really destroyed five of them in the fight, came a voice that was one part Urizen, one part Lavanalla, and one part her own critical self.

"Well, that's probably five more at once than Ressus Duvhalin has ever faced down in open combat."

Except it would never come to open combat with him, she thought. And she had to admit that was probably true. While Aelis was a Necromancer first and always, she had thought and acted as an Abjurer.

"Face first into danger, because how else are you going to get an attractive scar?" She snorted, and finally pushed herself up. She sheathed her sword and her dagger after wiping them on her coat. "How would a Necromancer have done this, which is to say, how should *I* have done it?"

Probed first, she thought, *worked out the fact that they dumped their Animating Force from one to the other. That they would become stronger, faster, and more independent as they reduced in number because of it.*

"Then the Lash, threaded onto that coupled binding. If I had put enough into it, it might have taken them all at once. At the least it would have done three or four and staggered the rest." She could hear Duvhalin's lecture on her poor approach as it was.

"Obviously the right thing to do would be to scour all the crypts and locate the control rod that all of Mahlgren's dead were bound to," she said. "If I had a hundred competent and trustworthy Necromancers to do the searching, anyway."

She walked about the room, inspecting the remains of the skeletons to see if they could tell her anything. No marks, runic or identifying, were graven into the back of the skulls, as had once been customary. No unit or county insignia anywhere. Not even a number series on the femur.

Aelis stretched her senses, calling on very nearly her last reserves of power and will to probe the bones and scattered bits of tendon, rusted iron, and wood that lay around the chamber. She felt nothing: no stirring of necromantic power.

"Probably safe to leave it behind then." She rolled her shoulders, feeling sweat slicking against her clothes, and ducked out through the open death's-head door.

That very last reserve Aelis had saved she used to probe the basin and the plinth where her animated bone-and-blood chimera had opened the door to her.

"By my mastery of the First Art, I command you to close," she murmured, trying not to feel ridiculous, and failing.

To her shock, the voice that had spoken in her mind twice before spoke again.

When the crypts of Mahlgren are opened with the First Art, they do not close without the proper tools of command.

Aelis was silent a long moment, pondering the message. Then, aloud, in disbelief and with creeping, gnawing panic, she said one word.

"Crypts?"

THE END OF BOOK I OF THE WARDEN
TO BE CONTINUED IN BOOK II: NECROBANE

ACKNOWLEDGMENTS

A book has one name on it but many people behind it, and this one is no exception. Tremendous thanks to Ren, for seeing a pitch on Twitter, taking a chance, and loving these characters as much as I do; to Paul and everyone else at J&N, for all their help; to Chris and everyone else at Tor, for making a thirty-year dream come true.

Closer to home, thanks are due to my list of beta readers: Jacob, Yeager, Josh, Jason, Stephanie, Ceejae, thanks to all of you for taking the time.

Thanks to my mom and my family, for having put up with so much weirdness for so very long; it all mattered in the end, I promise; to my in-laws, Pat and Dan, at whose house I started writing this book almost eight years ago.

Thanks also to the dutiful editor cats: Westley, who has been with me since the very start of my first novel, and who still refuses to get in the bed if I don't; Hector, who said goodbye before this book came out but was beside me for uncounted hours while I worked on it; and Rose of Sharon Cassidy, who is still learning exactly what her duties entail, but getting good instruction from her brothers.

Thanks to all the friends and readers who bought my books, to every bookstore that's ever carried them, to every person at a con or festival or fair who stopped to listen to the pitch and walked away with a copy, or bought an audiobook or an ebook when you got home.

Thanks to the folks on the Shadow Sanctum for listening to me piss and moan about this and a billion other things.

Last but never least, thanks to L; it is inadequate to utter clichés like "I couldn't have done this without you," but I couldn't. If there are words to emphasize the thousands of ways that is true, I don't know them.

P.S. If I forgot anyone, I owe you a drink.